the
Doula

the
Doula

Bridget
Boland

G

GALLERY BOOKS

New York   London   Toronto   Sydney   New Delhi

Gallery Books
A Division of Simon & Schuster, Inc.
1230 Avenue of the Americas
New York, NY 10020

First Gallery Books trade paperback edition June 2012

GALLERY BOOKS and colophon are registered trademarks of Simon & Schuster, Inc.

For information about special discounts for bulk purchases, please contact Simon & Schuster Special Sales at 1-866-506-1949 or business@simonandschuster.com.

The Simon & Schuster Speakers Bureau can bring authors to your live event. For more information or to book an event contact the Simon & Schuster Speakers Bureau at 1-866-248-3049 or visit our website at www.simonspeakers.com.

Designed by Renata Di Biase

Manufactured in the United States of America

10 9 8 7 6 5 4 3 2 1

Library of Congress Cataloging-in-Publication Data is available.

ISBN 978-1-4516-4151-6
ISBN 978-1-4516-4152-3 (ebook)

This book is for all the families I've had the honor of serving as a doula. And to my son, Liam, for the privilege of motherhood.

Acknowledgments

Like babies, books don't get birthed alone. Thanks to all the people who acted as "literary birth coaches" to help me bring *The Doula* into the world. These include my editors, Lauren McKenna, Kara Cesare, and Aja Pollock, editorial assistant Alexandra Lewis, and agent extraordinaire, Alexandra Machinist. Writing coach Jeff Davis convinced me that I could take a slice of material from my own life and discover the fiction waiting to be born from it. The Lakewood Writers Group, including Lisa Glasgow, Pat O'Connell, Max Wright, Brian Moreland, and Paul Black (especially Paul, for inviting me into the group in the first place), were beyond generous in their valuable criticisms and encouragement. The Ragdale Foundation, with its wonderful staff and residents, provided the serene environment crucial to the artistic process. And a big thanks to all the writing students I've coached through the years, for continually reminding me of the satisfaction found in seeking a deeper understanding of life through words on the page.

I'm indebted to Ana Forrest, for teaching me to hunt and stalk the truth inside myself and then to garner the courage to speak it aloud. Also to Alberto Villoldo, Linda Fitch, and Victoria Johnson of the Four Winds Society, and David Whyte, fellow mystic and writer. Barbara Graham helped me understand the importance of story. William Foley, Sara Stevenson, Mary Holmquist, Dianna Oles, Mike Biggins, Mary Beth Leisen, Colleen Millen, Annemarie Micklo, and other friends and family gave me their friendship and unwavering support. And finally, a huge thanks to Ron Falzone, who believed this book could be birthed long before I believed it myself.

The past is never dead.
It's not even past.

WILLIAM FAULKNER,
ABSALOM, ABSALOM!

the
Doula

Prologue

Other women have babies. I watch. Help. Like Saint Christopher carried the Christ child across the river, I usher mother and babe through the raging currents of labor to delivery. Observing a new life push its way into the world is a sacred act. If I could, I'd keep watch over all babies far beyond their births. But once I've shepherded them out of the womb and onto their mothers' breasts I can only say a silent blessing that the remainder of their days might pass with as much awe as that first one.

Doula is Greek for "servant." I come from a long line of funeral directors. They're doulas of a sort, shepherding people from this life into whatever comes next. Standing as witness and helper in that in-between space is the privilege of both doula and undertaker.

Whenever someone asks why I became a doula I see my own mother, miscarrying. It might appear that birth and death lie at opposite ends of a spectrum, as far apart as any two occurrences could be. But that's not true. They're mirror images. A portal opens between realms, one we call "real" because we see evidence of it around us, and another that causes endless debate since we lack confirmation of its existence.

My mother once joked that she wished someone would find a way to call from wherever they went when they died, give those of us still alive a preview of what was in store. The portal is shrouded, but I do believe there's something beyond the here and now. Every so often, if we're paying attention, we're rewarded with a glimpse—or a memory, perhaps—of that other place. The veil between where we stand now and that other, unfathomable domain grows thinnest when we're poised at the threshold, about to move between worlds.

In the midst of our lives we don't always see where provi-
dence is leading us. I might have carried on the family business,
but when I discovered that I could assist with arrivals instead
of departures, I chose to celebrate life coming in. By the time I
completed my doula training I had already learned that birth, like
death, brings us face-to-face with the profound mystery of our
insignificance and our greatness. What I didn't know was that I
was about to experience the two transitions merging in nature's
insistently cyclical pattern.

The summer my mother miscarried I made her a promise: to
keep what I'd seen to myself. But that was just the beginning of
a season of mourning. By summer's end, all the losses my mother
refused to talk about clamored inside me, drowning out the still,
small voice of my intuition. Years of holding on to all I knew
passed before I thought to question the cost of my silence. By
then I understood all too well that the price was nothing less than
my livelihood, nearly my whole life. And like a newborn moving
down the birth canal and out into the world I had to make my
way through another dark and uncertain passageway, stand trial,
deliver myself.

PART I

Gestation

One

Childhood summers had an enchanted way of lasting forever. During the school year I longed for those three months in which time seemed to magically stretch out along with the daylight. Momma's family had a cottage on Lake Michigan, far enough from our home in Chicago to make going there a vacation. Every June after my siblings and I got out of school my parents packed up the station wagon and relocated us to the lake.

The year I turned twelve I was in my room when Momma's voice slipped under my closed door. "Caro! Are you finished packing your suitcase?" she called.

I looked at the moving boxes piled around me. There was another reason I especially wanted to get to the lake this year: two days ago we had moved from our city apartment above the funeral home into a new house in the suburbs. Momma wanted more space. I had said good-bye to all my friends from our old neighborhood but I was waiting to reach the refuge of the lake to fully mourn my loss.

"Almost." I pitched a couple pairs of shorts into a roller bag printed with a picture of Mark Grace at bat. Daddy had given me the luggage for my birthday after I declared my undying loyalty to the Cubs' first baseman. Sammy Sosa and Ryne Sandberg were the players most fans cheered for but I had a huge crush on the sandy-haired infielder who batted lefty, just like me.

"Well, finish up . . . Then I need you to help Samantha with hers, please, sweetie. Don't forget you both need at least two swimsuits. And hurry, Caro," she called. "I want to be on the road by noon."

Momma sounded harried. I felt bad that I'd spent most of the morning hiding out in my room, puttering around more than helping. I was a little worried about Momma. Over the last couple months, when Samantha and Paulie and I came home from school we'd find her napping with our baby brother, Chris, instead of baking oatmeal cookies or banana bread. Momma worked nights as a nurse, and she was proud that she could be home with us after school. When we burst in through the front door and dropped our backpacks and schoolbags in the hall she never insisted we pick them up before snack time. "Life is short, chicka-dees," she'd say as she set glasses of milk before us on the table. "It's also beautiful. Where did you see beauty today?" Momma lived with her heart wide open, her arms drawing us close to the reassuring beat that set the rhythm for all of our lives. None of us ever thought to doubt the places we occupied in it or that it would remain open to us forever.

Recently it seemed to take all Momma's energy to do the laun-dry, the cooking, the mothering. Most days I had to wake her when we got home from school; even Paulie banging the door shut behind him didn't rouse her. She always got up when I jos-tled her shoulder, but I felt guilty doing so when I saw how deeply she'd been sleeping, how disoriented she was when I woke her. I'd looked for other signs that something was wrong, but except for the naps and dark circles under her eyes Momma seemed her usual self.

I tossed a sweatshirt into my suitcase then rummaged through two boxes until I finally found my Tretorns. A rush of anticipa-tion for the lake ran through me. But then came something else: the sense that my days of carefree abandon were reaching an end. Several cousins were already teenagers and I was torn between wanting to sunbathe on the pier with them and flinging myself into the water with the younger kids, who had no qualms about displaying their delight as they splashed. Maybe this was just a normal part of taking my first tentative steps across the suspen-sion bridge of adolescence. It was exciting and sad all at once. But I also felt an unnamable worry, which made me reach under my pillow for the cotton blanket I'd had since I was a baby. It had started out white but was yellowed with age, its waffle-textured center thinning from the way I rubbed it between my thumb and fingers. The satin binding was only attached at one corner now, and it hung from the blanket like a kite tail. I lifted my blankie to my nose, breathed in deep. The cloth smelled reassuring as hot cocoa. It eased even my worst worries. I slipped it into the smaller compartment on the front of my bag, alongside *Forever,* a novel I wasn't supposed to be reading because it was about kids losing their virginity.

I was bumping my suitcase down the stairs when the doorbell rang.

"I'll get it," I hollered, curious to see who was coming to visit when we'd only just moved in. I tugged open the door. The storm door was still closed. On the other side stood a woman wearing a black T-shirt over a giant belly. A package of blueberry muffins rested atop it as if it was a shelf. Next to the woman was a girl, slender like me. She wore cutoffs and a halter top, but what I noticed most was her hair: it was the whitest I'd ever seen, and curly, twining down to the small of her back. I reached a hand to my own head. Momma had helped me put my hair in braids that morning. She had said it looked like caramel. I'd been pleased at Momma's compliment but now I envied the dazzling gleam this other girl wore like a halo. You would never miss her, not even in a crowd. She didn't seem too interested in her own striking looks. She was fidgeting, kicking pebbles with the toe of her tennis shoe.

"Hi there!" The very pregnant woman's voice was deep and warm even through the glass of the storm door. I opened it, cocked one hip against it to make sure it didn't shut again.

"Hi," I replied.

"I'm Marilyn Hanover, your neighbor across the backyard." The woman motioned with her head.

"Hi," I repeated. I was too distracted by the girl to remember my manners.

Marilyn followed my stare. "And this is my daughter, Mary Grace. I'm guessing you two might be about the same age." She sounded as if she hoped I would agree with her and lessen the awkwardness growing around the three of us.

"Are your folks home?" Marilyn asked when I didn't offer my age.

Before I could answer Momma and Daddy both appeared, making a big to-do about my being rude and not inviting our neighbors in. Momma talked in the fake-cheery voice she used when she wanted to get something over with quick.

"Want to see my room?" I blurted at Mary Grace Hanover before Momma could thank them for the muffins and see them out.

Momma shot me a look that said she was about ready to kill me. But Daddy came to my rescue. He put an arm around her and I knew what he meant by the gesture: she could relax, he was right there with her. They'd get everything packed and in the car, this was just an unforeseen detour they might as well enjoy for a few minutes.

I looked back at Mary Grace. Her pale blue eyes searched mine and for a second I was afraid she was going to say no. I'd die of embarrassment if she did. But then she smiled.

"You can call me MG," she said. "All my friends do."

I grinned at the invitation, and we bounded upstairs while the grown-ups chatted in the foyer.

"Do you have any other brothers or sisters?" I asked once we were in my room. I dug around in a box, looking for a braided friendship bracelet from the stash I'd received as good-bye gifts from my friends in the old neighborhood. I wanted to give this girl something to make her like me. Suddenly I regretted that we were about to leave for the lake.

Mary Grace shook her head no. "But I'm pretty excited about this one. I can hardly wait 'til it's born. I hope it's a girl!"

I had two brothers and a sister. I didn't tell Mary Grace that sometimes brothers were more fun. Paulie liked to play baseball as much as I did. Samantha was only interested in ponies and dolls and anything pink. We had to pay her a quarter to shag balls for us when we held batting practice. But I didn't want to spoil things for Mary Grace. She admired my Nancy Drew collection, one of the few things I had unpacked. We talked about which ones were our favorites, *The Secret of the Old Clock* and *The Mystery at Lilac Inn.*

"What's that look like to you?" Mary Grace and I were on our way back downstairs when I pointed out the odd step in the center. The stairway curved where the stair had been installed, giving it a different shape from the others, which were rectangular. Paulie had said it looked like a kite, but it wasn't a kite. It was a casket. Every time I went down the stairs I had to step over it and make a wish.

MG looked closer, shivered. "A coffin."

"Exactly," I said. "Don't step on it. It's like, 'step on a crack, break your mother's back.' Only if you land on it, you're dead!"

We were standing side by side on the stair above the odd-shaped one. Then suddenly I was alone. Mary Grace had jumped. She flew over the forbidden stair and the four that followed, landing at the bottom, where she turned to face me. "Ta-da!" She curtsied with a flourish of one hand. Her cheeks flushed pink; her hair billowed around her. "Make a wish and fly!"

I wanted to, but I was too afraid. The leap looked impossibly far. Instead I stepped down to the stair below the coffin like I usually did, pretending that it really didn't matter how I got down. I wouldn't look at Mary Grace. If she thought I was a chicken, I didn't want to know. She didn't say anything, though, just grabbed my hand as we walked back to where our parents were saying good-bye.

After Mary Grace and her mother had gone, Momma looked at the store-bought muffins and sniffed. "The ABCs taught me to always bring homemade when you're playing Welcome Wagon," she said to Daddy as she slid the box into the trash can. Then she shrugged. "Maybe she's too tired to bake. She's so big already there's no way she'll make it to September." Momma's hand went to her own belly as if in sympathy.

Unlike my mother, I didn't care what kind of baked goods Mrs. Hanover had given us. She had brought something far more wonderful with her, something that might make living in the suburbs okay after all—a friend.

After the Hanovers left I followed Momma back upstairs to my parents' bedroom, where I folded my sister's frilly matching skorts and tops into a suitcase while Momma packed for Paulie and Chris. We worked alongside one another in silence. The baby busied himself on the floor with alphabet blocks. Daddy had taken Paulie and Samantha outside to keep them out of Momma's hair. I glanced at my mother. A small smile played over her features. She was frazzled about our trip, but I knew that the minute we were all in the car she'd tilt her seat back and relax. The rest of the summer stretched out for her, too, since she usually managed to finagle her work schedule down to almost no shifts while we were on break.

I heard car tires biting into the gravel drive and looked out the window. A sleek black Cadillac cruised to a stop before the front door, directly below me. I knew who it carried but was as puzzled by their arrival as I had been by the Hanovers'. What were the ABCs doing here?

The ABCs were my mother's aunts. Shortly after the turn of the twentieth century, my great-grandmother Rosina had birthed six daughters in the apartment of the family funeral home, the same apartment that I had grown up in until just a few days ago. She had named the first five of them alphabetically: Audelia, Beatrice, Constance, Daniela, Eugenia. I knew them by the collective family nickname: the ABCs.

Beatrice, who went by "B," was my grandmother. She lived next door to the funeral home, where she had raised my mother and Momma's four brothers with the help of her spinster sisters, Audelia and Constance, who lived on the other side of the funeral home. Eugenia had died in infancy and Daniela was also gone before I was born.

In the city my siblings and I had been cradled in the bosoms of Momma's "mothers." They were built-in babysitters who watched us whenever Momma was working and Daddy got a call to pick up a body. Aunts A and C cooked dinner every night in our kitchen since it was the largest, and we all ate together around the formal dining room table. The biggest shock of the last two nights wasn't eating takeout instead of a home-cooked meal; it was how quiet it seemed in our new house, how wrong not to have B reading the obituaries aloud while C stirred the gravy and A set the table with a lace cloth one of them had crocheted. But while I missed the comfort of the familiar, I had also felt a secret thrill. Life in the suburbs would be different without the vigilant family eyes watching over us.

The front door creaked in protest but the ABCs marched in as if they owned the place, not bothering to ring the doorbell or knock. I trudged downstairs to meet them, Momma on my heels. The ABCs were prim and proper, dressed in print wrap dresses. They wore matching shoes and pocketbooks. By the time I moved into the kitchen, they were in the small bedroom behind it that my father had claimed for an office, changing from their outfits into the housecoats and slippers they wore indoors for cleaning.

"The Italian bucket brigade has arrived," Daddy whispered under his breath with a wicked wink as he came in from the garage. He passed by me on his way to the refrigerator, where he pulled out a Pabst Blue Ribbon, popped off the cap and took a long swig.

"Just one," he reassured Momma, who was giving him the same kind of look she'd shot me when I'd invited MG to my room. "I'm fine to drive, Lucille, just wetting my whistle."

"Exactly what I'd expect to hear from a goddamned Irishman," my mother retorted. But there was a twinkle in her eye and a lilt to her voice that delighted me. This was how my parents flirted, with an edge to their conversation but beneath it the passion I sensed hadn't dimmed, not even after four children.

"Goddamned Irishman" was B's nickname for Daddy. I thought he must have loved Momma an awful lot to put up with all the women who came along with her. We didn't really know Daddy's family; he'd grown up an only child in St. Louis and his parents had both passed away when he was in his twenties. Daddy had married Momma and made her family his own, though as far as I could see, the ABCs didn't believe he was necessary to us. It occurred to me that maybe Daddy was glad about our move too, despite the commute he had to make to work now.

"Why would anybody want to live out in the boondocks?" My grandmother emerged from the back room and stood before the sliding glass door that opened out from the kitchen onto the backyard.

B had a point. Unlike our cozy city life, suburbia seemed an odd limbo—it was loaded with planned developments and strip malls that didn't feel real. Our new house was on over an acre of land that was not yet landscaped. I moved nearer to B and looked out too. There were no trees in our yard, not even any grass. Nothing but dirt and rocks.

Daddy sidled up alongside me. "B, it's a whole lot of nothing right now." He stared out onto the wide expanse before us. "But Big Girl here needs some room for her own Wrigley Field if she hopes to make history as the first female player for the Cubs someday, don't you think?"

Daddy jabbed me lightly in the arm. I stifled a giggle. B was a lifelong White Sox fan who thought anyone rooting for the North Side team instead of her local South Side sluggers was an idiot.

Before B could flip her lid at Daddy's antics, Momma hustled us out the door toward the car. I heard her thanking the ABCs for all their help. They were going to unpack our new house while we went to the lake.

"Tell them not to touch my room!" I leaned across my baby

brother in his car seat and hollered out the window of the station wagon. I was squished between Chris and Samantha. Paulie was in the rear, on the seat that faced backward, reading comic books. I would have joined him there, but watching things pass by in the opposite direction made me want to throw up.

My great-aunts stood on the driveway, three slender figures in their sixties and seventies, mops, buckets and brooms at the ready. With their rouged cheeks and tinted curls, they were glamorous even in their housecoats. I knew that when we returned at the end of the summer everything in our house would be put away, neat and clean. And that Momma and I would spend the first week back playing hide-and-seek with the cutlery, plates and other items concealed in whatever cabinets the ABCs had chosen. But we would see the ABCs again long before autumn. They'd follow us up to the lake in a few days, just as soon as they finished setting up Momma's new house. We all needed taking care of, Momma as well as us kids.

Two

For most of the three-and-a-half-hour drive Daddy plied us with rounds of "There Were Three Jolly Fishermen" and "John Jacob Jingleheimer Schmidt" as we sped along the Skyway, which arced around the lake. He sang off-key but we didn't care because we'd all inherited his bad ear.

"Remember why it's called the Skyway, Sammy?" he asked my little sister after announcing that we had just crossed over the Illinois state line into Indiana.

"Why, Daddy?" Samantha scrunched her nose as she waited for the answer. Her My Pretty Pony lay in her lap. She'd been brushing its mane and tail for the last half hour.

"Because if you take it past our place in Saint Joe all the way to the UP, it goes up, up, up, right off the earth and into the wild blue yonder!"

Daddy loved to make up tall tales like this for us. He also told lots of jokes. Most adults thought that undertakers had to be somber, but Daddy was the funniest man I knew. "Life isn't a dress rehearsal," he liked to say. He believed that if you couldn't find something to laugh about you'd cry yourself into an early grave, and there was no fun going on six feet under that was worth taking life too seriously.

Chris stirred from his nap, his hair matted to his forehead from the sun streaming in through the window. It was only June but already the temperature had climbed into the high eighties. Chris rubbed his eyes with his chubby fists. I had taught him a new trick and scooched sideways to see if I could get him to do it now.

"Give me a hands kiss, Monkey Boy." I pursed my lips and Chris cracked a toothless smile. The dimple in his left cheek deepened into a hollow I poked at gently with my finger. He placed a hand on either side of my face and I felt the sweet warmth of his breath, milky from the bottle he'd had before he went to sleep. Babies were so yummy, so full of pure love that they weren't afraid to show. I loved Paulie and Samantha, but my youngest brother, over ten years my junior, seemed as much my child as Momma's. I had felt cheated by missing out on watching him be born but the hospital didn't allow kids in the delivery room, not even siblings. Instead I had to wait at home with the ABCs and my other siblings, clamoring to beat them all to the phone every time it rang in case it was Daddy calling to tell us whether we had a new brother or sister. As an infant him had been like a living doll. From the day Momma and Daddy brought him home, I doted on him with an abandon I didn't feel comfortable expressing with Paulie and Samantha, who at nine and seven felt more like my peers.

Chris laid a wet smack on my waiting lips. A burp erupted before he moved back and I made a funny face. "Ewww, Monkey!" I crossed my eyes, pretending to be grossed out. Chris laughed, then he reached a hand out again and patted my cheek, as if to say he was sorry for belching in my face. I ran itsy-bitsy spiders up his arms 'til we were both laughing so hard I thought we might pee in our pants.

We followed the lake as we drove, hugging its shore for a long while. It looked so big that I doubted we'd ever make our way around. But we always did, and soon we turned off the expressway onto two-lane roads. They wound through farmland interrupted only occasionally by a small town with a post office, tavern and sometimes a gas station. Farm-stand carts dotted the countryside at the ends of farmers' driveways, offering whatever was in season on the honor system—you took the produce and put your money in the bucket provided. We stopped at one and Momma came back to the car with a flat of strawberries and a rhubarb pie, Daddy's favorite. An old hound ambled out after Momma but he was moving so slow that he only made it halfway down the drive before we were gone.

"We can make preserves with these tomorrow." Momma

handed a few plump berries over the seat to me and Samantha. My mouth watered at the thought of vanilla ice cream drenched in the sweet, tart jam.

Soon we came upon the mushroom farm, the landmark where we turned onto the road that led to the cottage. We peered hard out the windows, looking for what was different from the year before. "Howard's got two new foals in the pasture." Daddy pointed as we went by Schnell's Dairy Farm, where we bought our milk and ice cream, and Samantha oohed and aahed at the small horses grazing there.

Next we passed Ruby Lou's, the general store that carried basic groceries, dry goods, fishing bait, and the best assortment of candy a kid could hope for. We were related to Ruby. She was the ABCs' little sister, though she was so different from the rest of them I never would have guessed it had Momma not said so.

"Momma, tell us about Ruby." Suddenly I wanted to hear the story again, be reminded that our family lineage included members more fascinating than the ones we had just left in our house.

Momma sighed and I thought she was going to say she was too tired, but then she started up instead. "Well, you know she was a little bit of a surprise, coming along eight years after your great-grandma had Aunt D," she said as she warmed to the subject. "All the sisters waited in the parlor outside their parents' bedroom door and tried to guess whether your great-grandmother would give the new baby another E name or move ahead to the F's— Frances, Florence, Fiona. But Rosina fooled them. She named her Ruby Lucille."

"Why, Momma?"

Momma shrugged. "Great-grandma Rosina was superstitious. I think she thought that if she broke the naming pattern the baby would live, unlike Eugenia." Then Momma turned and smiled at me over the seat back. "Or maybe she had a hunch that Ruby would be really different from her sisters. She is, isn't she?"

That was for sure. I looked down at the denim shorts I was wearing with a red tank top. Ruby wore denim too, Uncle Stu's old jeans, held up by brittle twine cinched around her waist. No high heels for her; she walked the sawdust-covered floors of the store barefoot or in brightly beaded moccasins hand-sewn by the few remaining Potawatomi Indians in the area.

We rounded a bend and came to the post office, housed in an old barn with a distinctive silo painted red, white and blue. An eagle was painted on the dome, perched with wings wide open, poised for flight. Across the road sat a small clapboard church. It looked friendly and welcoming, with tiger lilies blooming in a riot of orange alongside it. I didn't like going to Mass at home but now I looked forward to the coming Saturday evening, when I could pick lilies of the valley from near the rickety pine fence that bordered our property and take them wrapped in tinfoil to the side altar where the Virgin Mary stood. I liked to light a candle to her and leave the flowers there as my own special offering. My parents took us to Mass Saturdays instead of making us get up for the only Sunday service, which was at eight thirty A.M. That was the Mass the ABCs attended. Then they drove to the next town over, which had a large chain grocery where they picked up doughnuts and coffee cake, along with the Sunday newspapers from the city so they wouldn't have to miss the obituaries while they were out of town.

Daddy steered the car into the drive, then stopped at the top of the hill. I shut my eyes tight then reopened them to the dazzle of the beauty around me. The land sloped downward and I drank in the lush green of the lawn, divided only by the circular gravel drive bordered by round white stones that resembled a giant pearl necklace.

An oak tree towered in the grass encircled by the curve of the driveway. Below it stood a white wooden cross. We'd conducted the funeral of our salt-and-pepper Jack Russell terrier, Sparky, there last year. I'd wanted to be the priest but Paulie insisted girls couldn't. Ruby intervened and said I could be the bishop. I "ordained" my brother in a yellow brocade bathrobe. He performed the service the same way we had seen it done at countless family

funerals, burning incense and dousing holy water over the grave.
Then we watched while Daddy buried the casket containing our
beloved sidekick with a few deft shovels of earth, tears spilling
freely down his cheeks as he tossed the dirt then reset the sod
back in place.

I blinked back tears at the memory and looked in the other
direction. Gnarled apple, peach and plum trees huddled in the
orchard behind the garage. It was white clapboard like the cottage, weathered but chipper from the fresh coat of paint Daddy
had given it last year. Then I turned my attention forward. If I
squinted I could just barely make out glimmers of the lake shimmering a hundred yards ahead in front of the cottage itself.

The new house in the suburbs seemed like a foreign land, and
our apartment above the funeral home in the city had been too
close and cramped. The cottage was the place that had always
felt like home to me. From the small pond where we caught frogs
and minnows to the old playhouse cabin that had been Momma's
before it was passed along to us, this land and water were where
I felt most alive. For the next three months, Paulie and Samantha and I would be unleashed to roam the five acres of woods
with our cousins, to perform endless shrieking cannonballs off
the pier, to live wild and bare, skin tanned to chestnut, hair sun-
streaked. Every summer we morphed from compliant children
who wore uniforms to school, did homework and obeyed their
parents most of the time into something nearer to our true nature, the creatures our grandmother sometimes accused us of
being: savages.

Before I was free to chase butterflies and play badminton or
croquet I had to help get things unpacked. I spent the afternoon
hauling suitcases into the house with Daddy, then putting clothes
away in dresser drawers musky from mothballs. Summer meant
no homework but there were still chores. Most of them I didn't
mind, like weeding the garden or shucking the corn, since I could

do them outdoors. I also enjoyed washing the dishes. Back home we loaded the dishwasher, but we did them by hand at the cottage. I liked standing at the sink with my arms submerged to the elbows in a tub of hot water, soap bubbles rising around me. B usually dried. My grandmother had a gruff demeanor but it covered a soft heart. Dish duty seemed to soften her. She was more apt to smile or even tell me a story about her own childhood at the cottage when her hands were busy swiping a dish towel over platters and gravy boats.

I was doing the season's first load of dinner dishes that night when someone came up the back porch steps. It was already dark outside and the kitchen light was on, so I couldn't make out who was out there. I heard a soft thump. Whoever it was knew the trick for unlatching the hook from the eye—a swift, sure blow of a closed fist in just the right spot and the hook flew up and out of its bed, just like that.

"Hiya, kid. You made it." Ruby stood in the doorway that separated the back porch, where we ate our meals, from the kitchen, holding a brown paper sack. It wasn't officially summer yet but her face was tan from working in the fields where she grew the beans, lettuce, carrots, and herbs she sold in the store. Her gray-streaked hair was braided in a single plait that snaked down to the faint curve of her bottom. Ruby was wearing a man's longsleeve blue and tan plaid work shirt, knotted at the belly button. Ruby had always raided her husband's closet but since Uncle Stu had passed away a few years ago, she'd stopped wearing anything remotely feminine. The ABCs clucked and groused among themselves about what they called her atrocious appearance, but we all knew that if anybody breathed a word of dislike to her it would only make Ruby more determined to dress down. Which was why, after I'd overheard their complaining, I'd run right down to her and tattled on them.

I dried my hands and let my favorite relative hug me. The ABCs were voluptuous, all womanly hollows and curves. But they didn't let us too close to their bodies, requiring instead a perfunctory kiss on parchment cheeks caked in face powder. Unlike the others, even in middle age Ruby remained tall and slender as a sapling. "I'm grown from the ground up," she was fond of declaring, and I always pictured tree roots sprouting from the soles of her feet, connecting her to her beloved land.

"What's in the bag?" I asked shyly. I didn't want to seem eager but Ruby always brought us the most fascinating gifts—snakeskins, dried flowers, relics from her collection of religious artifacts, and Mary Janes and Bit-O-Honeys from the candy jars in her store.

Ruby glided a few steps farther into the kitchen, blinking at the glare from the overhead light. "Supplies," she murmured vaguely, holding the bag up and shaking it so I could hear its contents rustle. "Gotta have a fire to celebrate the arrival of the lost boys. And girls, too, of course." Ruby grinned, the chipped bottom tooth in the front of her smile adding to her backwoods look. Then she cocked her head and looked hard at me. "How's your mother? Everything okay?"

I wanted to ask why it wouldn't be but decided against it. Ruby had a keen instinct. If she was picking up on Momma's recent fatigue she'd tell me what it meant soon enough. Right now I wanted to enjoy the fire without worry. Ruby was fond of rituals, of marking life's passages with ceremonies that combined the Catholicism she'd inherited from her devout Italian mother with bits and pieces of Native American customs picked up from Earl and Lucinda, a Potawatomi mother and son she'd been friendly with as long as I could remember. So I just nodded my head that all was fine.

"Well then, we'd better get to it before the cavalry shows up." Ruby smirked as she mentioned her sisters. "Go rustle up your brother and sister," she said, then retreated back into the shadows of the porch to wait.

I rounded up my brother and sister as instructed, grabbing sweatshirts for all of us since the air had cooled when the sun went down. Momma was on the front porch resting on the chaise but Daddy came out and shook Ruby's hand before shooing us out the back door with her. "Keep an eye on the posse, Big Girl," he reminded me, even though we both already knew I would, not just tonight but for the entire summer.

Ruby led us through the darkness. We couldn't see much as we waited for our eyes to adjust, but the backyard was alive around us. It was too cold for mosquitoes but a few hardy fireflies blinked around us.

"Keep an eye out for the forest friends," Ruby called back over her shoulder as she trotted on. "The wood nymphs, fairies and goblins like to roam after dark."

At Ruby's words, Samantha slowed her pace until I was alongside instead of behind her. Her eyes were wide. She was still young enough to believe in the possibility of such creatures, especially when Ruby talked with an air of authority about them. Crickets chirped, cicadas whirred, an owl "whoo"-ed as we passed the tree where he was roosting. Samantha grabbed for my leg at the sound and almost took me down but I didn't holler at her; the grounds were spooky at night, even with Ruby there.

We were almost back at the road before our great-aunt finally stopped off to one side of the garage, in front of a large circle of charred grass. Ashes and a few lone branches littered the barren patch of the bonfire pit.

Every autumn, we spent weekends burning the leaves and branches that just a few months earlier had provided a canopy from the blazing summer sun. Everyone old enough to hold a rake helped gather the fallen crimson and yellow castaways onto old bedsheets. The younger kids dove into the piles, scattering the leaves like full-body kamikaze pilots, then took bumpy rides as Daddy and my uncles hoisted the bundles to the bonfire.

Most years we packed up and winterized the cottage sometime in October. But last year had been special. The weather had co-operated and we'd celebrated Thanksgiving there. Daddy roasted the turkey in the smoker and after the outdoor cleanup and leaf burning we turned our ravenous appetites to the feast the ABCs had prepared. There were nearly twenty of us gathered in the cottage's small dining room—my family, the ABCs, Ruby, my uncles, aunts and cousins. Holiday gatherings were fun when you belonged to a big family. The rarely used radiators hissed moist background music for the meal. Afterward, as we ate Ruby's contribution, pumpkin pie made from pumpkins grown in her garden, Samantha and our cousin Caleb yanked the wishbone apart. I wasn't part of the contest but I had no wish to make anyway; there was nothing I wanted, other than that we might all continue to be together forever.

As Ruby crouched near the fire pit and pulled supplies from her sack, I hoped that we could have Thanksgiving there again that year. But I didn't wish it to come anytime soon. I didn't want the summer going by too fast.

"Find yourselves a stick," Ruby told us. A pile of objects sat at her feet. There was a dinky plastic statue of the Virgin Mary, a small woman carved from wood with a gold spiral painted over her heart that Ruby called the healer, a bottle of olive oil, a pile of newspapers, a box of wooden kitchen matches, four avocados and an owl feather. Ruby moved the bag behind her a few feet then rearranged the branches in the fire pit. Samantha and Paulie and I scrounged around until each of us had a stick. Paulie's was huge and he swung it around like a sword, grinning at the whooshing sound it made as it cut through the air.

Ruby glanced over at him but said nothing as she crumpled the newspapers and fit them under and between the branches. Then she grabbed up the avocados. They jingled as she handed one to each of us, keeping one for herself. Paulie, Samantha and I giggled; they weren't real fruits but plastic versions filled with rice—rattles.

"This is the ceremony to welcome the season," Ruby intoned. Her voice deepened, and we snapped to because we didn't want her to think we were goofing around. "Before we light the fire we need to open the Directions." Ruby turned to the right until she faced the street. She raised her right arm high, then looked around to make sure we all did the same.

Ruby began the ritual. "To the winds of the south," she said, shaking her rattle as an invitation for unseen forces to join us. She motioned for us to mimic her and we all shook our rattles hard. Then Ruby turned right again, calling upon the energies of the west, then the north, then the east, until she'd made a complete circle. She dropped to one knee and placed a palm down onto the pine needles blanketing the ground. As if she was touching a loved one, her face softened as she caressed the earth, asking Pachamama to root us all firmly to her belly that summer. Finally Ruby stood up again and, rattling vigorously, raised both arms skyward. "Father Sun, Grandmother Moon, all the Star Nations, bring the light of the cosmos here to be with us in our ceremony tonight!" she called out.

The spectacle might have seemed bizarre, but we were used to Ruby's eccentricities. I welcomed any invitation to be involved with what the ABCs called her "hocus-pocus." I tended to run nervous, like Momma and B. But I always felt calmer after doing something with Ruby, whether it was peeling apples in her kitchen or something more esoteric, like this fire. She always opened the Directions before doing any spiritual act, and I'd learned them by heart from her long ago.

When she was satisfied that the space was ready, Ruby lit the fire. She started chanting, words I couldn't make out, but it didn't matter. I hummed along and soon Paulie and Samantha caught on and did the same. We all gathered around the fire, holding hands and swaying a little from side to side.

Ruby doused the fire with olive oil three times, murmuring to the blaze with each pour. After a few minutes, she spoke to us. "The fire is friendly fire now," she declared. Flames leapt and licked at the night air, a pleasing blue tip dancing at the head of each orange shape springing up from the wood. "Hold on to your sticks now, kiddos, and think about what you want this summer to bring.

"What do you wish for? What do you want to learn?" Ruby's eyes shone in the firelight, and I saw a kind of certainty there that

I longed to feel but sensed came only when earned from years of paying close attention to the lessons of one's life. So I closed my eyes and blew my wish into the stick as Ruby had instructed: that this summer might take me one step nearer to becoming the woman I was meant to be. Who that was or how I'd get there I didn't know, but I prayed that I might still find my way.

I laid my stick on the pyre and watched it burn awhile, then helped my siblings put theirs on too, wondering what they had wished for. I guessed Samantha had asked for a horse, but I'd have to ask Paulie about his wish later. He was prone to thoughtfulness so he might not have gone after a new bike or a Jet Ski, but instead asked that we all be happy this summer. Affection for him surged in my heart. I was glad we were there, and I realized I'd been missing him lately without knowing it. During the school year we got busy with our friends but at the lake we spent more time together.

After Ruby deemed the "official" ceremony over and we closed the Directions in the same way we had opened them, she went over to her paper bag and brought out a chocolate bar, a bag of marshmallows and a box of honey grahams. "You'll each need another stick if you're gonna roast the 'mallows," she grinned. Samantha stared openmouthed with delight at the unexpected payoff of having attended the ritual. We gorged ourselves on the sticky, smoky treats until we were too full to eat another bite.

"I'm gonna stay here and tend the fire 'til she dies out," Ruby said eventually. "You'd all better get on back to the house now before your Momma starts wondering about you. Off you go, follow the moon, now, straight into your beds."

We hugged Ruby good-bye and took off, pretending we were the fairies and goblins she had spoken of earlier. The three of us raced wordlessly through the night toward the beckoning glow cast by the cottage, where we knew without a doubt that Momma and Daddy were waiting to hear about our exploits with our wizardly relation.

Three

The day I left childhood behind I was supposed to be mowing the lawn. Daddy drove back to the city for work early that morning. For most of the summer he would come up only on weekends. The ABCs were due any day, but for now we were on our own with Momma. She had asked Paulie and me to take turns cutting the grass with the push mower because the tractor wouldn't start. But I wanted to go down to Ruby's. Sleep hadn't come easy after the fire last night, and once I'd finally drifted off I'd had vivid, restless dreams about being back there, this time surrounded by shadowy figures. Some looked human, others like wolves, eagles and giant cats that might have been cougars or leopards. Their shining eyes gleamed knowingly as they prowled the perimeter. I hadn't felt frightened in the dreams but I wanted to ask Ruby about them before I forgot any details. So I promised Paulie that if he cut all the lawn I'd move the pearly stones bordering the circular drive out of the way *and* back into place later. This was the worst part of the job because it required thirty-two rounds of stooping over and shoving each heavy rock out of its bed 'til your back was sore and your fingernails broken. My easygoing brother was shrewd enough to agree to my offer immediately. I hustled out and moved the rocks, then stole down the road toward Ruby's, my exhilaration at seeing her quashing the sliver of guilt I felt at disobeying my mother.

My great-aunt knew things before they happened. She got what she called visions, and they were often right. This fascinated and spooked me. Once I'd told Momma about them. She'd frowned and made me promise I wouldn't pay any attention to what Ruby said. But nothing could keep me from going to her place whenever we were at the lake. I always dreaded and hoped that Ruby would whisper more things in my ear.

When I stepped into the store, Ruby was perched atop a high stool behind the counter. Usually she busied herself with stocking the shelves or tallying numbers with a pencil in a ledger she kept for bookkeeping. When I saw her sitting so still there, I knew she'd been waiting for me.

"How old are you now, kid?" she asked when I blurted out that I wanted to know about my dreams last night.

"Twelve last April," I reminded her. I leaned my elbows on the countertop, one foot tracing a circle in the sawdust to dispel some of my antsy energy while I waited to see what she'd say or ask next. Unlike with most adults, with Ruby you couldn't guess.

"Right." Ruby turned her eyes on me. I tugged at my tank top. It had slid up my midriff, away from my shorts. Ruby had the fan going on the counter and it sent a breeze across my bare skin. That and my great-aunt's scrutiny made me shiver. "You've not had your moon time yet, have you, sweet girl?"

"You're not bleeding yet," she clarified at my blank stare.

I was sorry that I'd put my hair up in a ponytail that morning; now there was nowhere for me to hide. "No, ma'am," I mumbled, feeling the heat of a blush ignite on my cheeks as I confessed. Most of my friends had already gotten their periods and as the days went by I was beginning to fear I'd never join them.

"Well, don't fret." Ruby turned away and rummaged through a drawer below the behemoth antique brass cash register. "This is your season. Sometime while you're here you'll be initiated into the power of the feminine. You'll learn that we carry the life force right inside our wombs." Ruby grabbed something from the drawer. She looked up at me again, a joyful knowing lighting up her face. No one had ever described getting your period as something powerful. Most of the girls I knew thought it a nuisance. They called it "the curse" or being "on the rag."

"Just remember, power uses *you* if you don't wield it well. And it treats you even worse if you refuse to take yours up at all." Ruby's tone had turned into a warning.

I nodded as if I understood, but the admonishment bewildered me.

"Well, then." My deception seemed to have escaped Ruby's sharp eye. "Let's ask the cards about your night journeys." She laid a tarot deck onto the counter. I wanted to ask her more about my period but she told me to shuffle the cards. Embarrassment kept me from speaking up while I drew three as she directed.

Before Ruby could decipher the cards Samantha came in, pushing Chris in a rickety old stroller. He was gnawing contentedly on a teething biscuit, crumbs and drool adorning the bib skewed rakishly around his neck.

"Mom's been hollering for you." Samantha gravitated toward the jars of penny candy lining a shelf below the counter. She ran a finger over the silver lids, biting her lower lip as if fighting the urge to thrust a hand into one of the bins. My sister had a fierce sweet tooth. Her arrival annoyed me. Samantha was only seven but she had already learned to look out for her own best interests first, a trait I both hated and envied. Our parents believed boys and girls equally capable of doing dishes and raking leaves but Samantha had them convinced that she was allergic to grass. Her only chore was dusting. Paulie and I had to split the rest of the list between us.

"Where's Paulie?" I was sure he'd spilled the beans to Momma about my whereabouts, which meant I was in for it good.

"He's still cutting the grass but you better get on home because Momma said to find you *quick*." Smarty-pants shot me a sassy look that told me all I needed to know: it was only the second day of summer vacation but it might very well be my last.

I trudged out of Ruby's store. It was nearing noon and the sun beat down, chastising me. I passed the Anchor Inn, where a lone Harley sat parked out front by the giant rusted anchor that lent the tavern its name. The field next door was empty except for Stretch, an old brown horse, who stood tied under an oak tree. His coat was mangy, and flies buzzed around him, his tail waving in a frenzy to keep them at bay. The horse had a penis so long it dragged a good several inches on the ground. Usually we all stopped to lean on the fence, gaping and gawking at Stretch's extraordinary member. But today I didn't even glance his way. Something urged me to hurry, and I made it home in less than the five minutes the walk usually took.

When I reached the cottage Paulie was guiding the push mower up another long row, his head bobbing to music playing on his Walkman headphones.

"'Eye of the Tiger'!" he yelled over the mower's roar as if he'd heard me wondering, and I rolled my eyes and stuck my tongue out in return. Survivor was his favorite band; he'd nearly worn out the cassette, he played it so much.

I plodded up the stairs feeling hot and crabby and sorry for myself over being interrupted at Ruby's. Momma lay on her bed with her back to me. It was rare for us to be alone, and I wanted to lie alongside her in the close, stale air of the bedroom without the interruption of another kid calling, "*Mommaaa!*" Instead I stood in the doorway, poked just my head into the dim room.

"Did you want me?" My words held a defensive tone I hoped might deflect the anger I anticipated from her. My voice was the only cool thing in the cottage.

"I need you." She barked a little cry of pain, drew her knees into her chest, then rolled from her side to her back several times, making that same sharp cry. It sounded like it was coming from deep inside her. I thought of a fox stuck in a trap. I didn't say anything. Just watched. After a minute I backed away from the cavelike bedroom. I had always adored my mother. But like the flames of last night's burn a flash of anger lit in me, sparked by a fear that until now I'd been too afraid to admit had been growing inside me for weeks.

"I need you." Momma forced the words out again with three quick gasps and rolled her legs off the sagging mattress. It protested as she stood up. She clutched her arms around her hips as if holding on to something to keep it from falling away. A round red spot marked the bed, jagged edges seeping across the white cotton.

I stood there, transfixed by the gaping stain. Momma staggered past me and down the hall. The cottage had been poorly designed, with the bathroom located at the farthest possible point from the three bedrooms. Momma pushed on through the dining room and past the living room fireplace with the exaggerated sway of a gorilla, one leg forward, then the other, crouched low to the ground. A dark trail dripped from between her legs, reminding me of Hansel and Gretel. When she reached the tiny bathroom she didn't bother to shut the door. I crept forward and sank down until I was slouching against the vanity cabinet directly across from where my mother had collapsed groaning into the bathtub, nightie hitched up around her thighs. The hem had gone from pink to deep maroon, blood-soaked. Panic surged in me, setting my heart beating as hard as if I'd run all the way home from Ruby's. I rebuked myself; I *should* have run, should have known something was wrong when Samantha showed up.

Momma doubled over, gasping. An involuntary yelp took us both by surprise and I jumped up, went to the side of the tub.

"Mommy?" I squeaked. I hadn't called her that in years.

"It will be okay," Momma said, trying to reassure me. "It has to come out, then it will be okay." But she didn't sound convinced, and my fear said she was lying. Nothing would ever be okay again. I couldn't say so because an invisible hand gripped me, tightening around my throat. I remembered my wish last night, that I might become a woman. And Ruby's prophecy just a little while ago, that this would be the summer I'd discover the power of the feminine. This wasn't what I'd meant, I pleaded silently.

Momma grimaced. It hurt to see her in so much pain. My hands went to the indentation between my legs, as if by pressing there I could somehow staunch the blood flowing out of my mother. The room spun and a sharp sound filled my head. I rocked back and forth, pushing against the bony shell over my privates with the heels of both hands harder and harder until the

pressure felt worse than the gruesome images playing in my mind
of Momma lying dead in a crimson pool, the victim of a bloodlet-
ting.

"Shut up." Momma looked toward the doorway as if she feared
someone might hear. She shoved the door with her foot and it
banged closed. That's when I realized it was my screams, not hers,
echoing in the small space.

"Get me my inhaler." She coughed, a wet wheeze that ratcheted
my worry higher. I was right; she was dying, if not from bleeding
to death then from an asthma attack. I stumbled backward to the
vanity, seeking out the medicine she needed to breathe. My fingers
grazed an empty pill bottle on the countertop, sent it toppling.
I wobbled as I reached out and picked it up, then fumbled for
the inhaler with my other hand. I held the inhaler out to her but
something kept me from moving nearer. Instead, I looked through
the window at the far end of the room. Lake Michigan shimmered
there, and although I hated my cowardice I wished that I could
tear out of the cottage and dive into that beckoning water, drown
out what Momma had called me to witness. She grabbed the
inhaler, shoved it in her mouth, took a drag. We were so close in
the tight room that the sweet mist of the medicine floated into my
mouth too. It burned a fiery trail down my throat, like the drunken
cherries Daddy gave me from his Manhattans, and I shut my eyes,
as if I could transport myself out of there by doing so.

Momma moaned. I flinched, reopened my eyes and forced myself to stay where I was. The harder side of me, the pragmatic part
that believed like Daddy that death was a natural part of life, told
me to quit acting like a child. I had to shut out my terror and help
my mother. Everyone always said I was so mature for my age. I
could handle this, whatever it was. Except that I hadn't the slight-
est clue what to do, couldn't come up with a single idea for how
to make things better.

Momma's moans turned to shrieks. I started crying first but
then I saw tears on her face too as the pain took hold. Ruby had
said bleeding put a woman in touch with her power. But if this

was what getting a period meant, I wanted to be a boy. I wanted to die before I bled like my mother was bleeding.

"Stop looking and do something." Momma's features contorted with pain.

"What?" I begged, eager to know how I could save the one person I loved nearly beyond reason. "What should I do? Do you need a . . ." I hesitated, the word still unfamiliar enough that I dropped my voice to a near-whisper. "A tampon?"

Her cry grew desperate. I was failing her somehow. "Go downstairs." She winced again. "Bring me a container."

I stood there, closer than I'd ever been to the mysteries of womanhood. Suddenly I was so afraid. Afraid to tell my mother I didn't understand, afraid she'd see that I wasn't old enough for whatever she needed me to do. I glanced at the window again, wishing the ABCs were there to rescue us.

"Go to the kitchen. Call your father at the funeral home and tell him to drive up here. Then bring me a Tupperware, medium sized. With a lid that fits." I didn't move. She closed her eyes when she realized she had to explain what was happening. "I have to save the parts of the baby to take to the doctor."

Suddenly I understood.

Chris wasn't even two, yet here she was, pregnant again. Then a spooky wisdom that felt much older than me brought another flash of certainty: Momma had caused what was happening now. I'm not sure what frightened me more, the understanding or the raw clarity with which I knew it to be true. My eyes fell on the pill bottle still clutched in my hand. Before I could think I blurted, "Did you take something? You did. You took something." My voice rose as I thrust the pill bottle out where she couldn't deny it. The bathtub seemed filled with blood. Rage barged in next to my fear. Momma had done something awful and now she was about to leave me.

Momma swiped at the pill bottle but I pulled my hand back. Fury flashed in her eyes. I'd never seen her so angry. "Shut your mouth. Shut it! If you're not going to help, then leave me alone!"

Part of me wanted to flee. But I couldn't, not when I feared that if I did the next time I saw her, she'd be in a coffin. Instead I took the pill bottle, tucked it away in my suitcase. Then I went to the phone and followed Momma's instructions exactly.

"She has to take the parts of the baby with her to the doctor," I parroted to my father after I told him to come because Momma was bleeding. I said nothing about the empty pill bottle.

Daddy coughed in response. "I'm leaving now, Big Girl." That was all he said before I heard the dial tone ringing in my ear. He was gone.

So was another sister or brother. Almost another one, in this family already full of them. A narrow escape. I pushed the thought away. She needed me.

I took the container to the bathroom. A brother or a sister? We'd never know. I imagined a baby's head, shriveled like a prune with wide baby eyes, floating in a red lake. All the life sucked out of it. Momma opened the bathroom door just enough to grab the Tupperware, then shut it again. I had no desire to be on the other side.

Her voice found me, though. "Don't tell the kids about this."

Despite the door between us, her words drew me to her. Muffled but distinguishable, they declared the innocence of childhood a territory that was no longer mine to wander in. Ruby had been right about this season: during it, I would grow up in ways I could never have conceived of or wanted.

Four

After her miscarriage, Momma stayed at the hospital overnight. Daddy went with her while Ruby helped me with Paulie, Samantha and Chris. I could have confided in Ruby about what I'd seen. The weird way I'd known what Momma had done reminded me of Ruby's visions, and I wondered whether hers came in the same unbidden way. I also wanted to know if she'd had any inkling beforehand about what had happened that afternoon. But my mother had sworn me to secrecy and I wasn't willing to betray her. I told no one what I had seen. I was afraid that if I started talking about Momma losing the baby I wouldn't be able to keep from telling about the pill bottle, too. And I knew that wasn't something Momma wanted me blabbing about.

Momma had her tubes tied the next morning. She returned from the hospital with postpartum depression instead of a baby and a knot bound tight around her heart, as if the rest of us didn't matter next to the one who had leaked out. She walked into the cottage, then toward her bedroom, moving so lightly I wouldn't have believed she was there if I hadn't seen her come in. But I'd looked in her eyes for a moment. Her slack face was best described by my father's expression, "The lights are on, but nobody's home."

Momma paused in the bedroom doorway before going in and I winced, feeling the pain coming off her bowed back in waves. I'd hunted in the linen closet until I found a set of sheets that were lilac instead of white, then made the bed up with them. But if Momma noticed my attempt to ease her suffering, she didn't let on. She simply floated over to the bed and dropped onto her side without pulling the quilt back. It wasn't Momma who'd returned from the hospital; it was her ghost.

* * *

I left Daddy in charge of Momma and the kids and went to the basement to wash the bedclothes. The ABCs were coming, and I didn't want them to discover evidence of the bloodshed. To get to the basement, I had to go out back. A set of stairs led below the house to a series of underground rooms that reminded me too much of the morgue at the funeral home.

The minute I stepped into the dank basement I regretted that I hadn't put on my flip-flops. The concrete was icy cold, almost slimy, against my bare soles. Gooseflesh pricked my arms and legs. It was close to ninety degrees outside but in the cellar it felt thirty degrees cooler.

I yanked on the string hanging from the naked bulb overhead. Metal pipes ran the length of the ceiling, which was so low that I had to crouch down a little to avoid banging my head. Water skis, floats and life jackets lurked along the wall to my left. Beyond them I could just barely make out a second room, with a small window carved out near the top of the wall. There was a rusted metal cot in that back room, with a saggy mattress made of horsehair that itched horribly the one time I'd tried to lie on it. B had told me that had been her father's hideout, the place he went when he needed to get away from all the women in his life.

"The poor goddamned bastard," she'd muttered. "He'd have been happier as a bachelor. Most men would." I'd thought of telling Daddy about the room's history in case he too wanted an escape, but Momma had looked at me funny when I mentioned it.

I stepped farther into the murky space, making my way past two dilapidated refrigerators, several toolboxes, a hobbled wheelbarrow missing a wheel, and innumerable pairs of gardening gloves and mud-caked boots. At the back of the main room stood an ancient washing machine, the kind with a wringer. B had warned me about touching it; she had gotten her right hand caught in it once and said she'd never in her life forget that crushing pain, could still feel it sometimes over fifty years later whenever she gripped a pen or a cup handle.

As I came upon the washing machine I tried hard not to look into the last room to my left, but I couldn't resist my morbid fascination. This room also had a small window, and dust motes drifted aimlessly in the dull light, which was just bright enough for me to make out the figures huddled throughout the ten-by-ten-foot space. It held statuary—cement angels, various animals, busts of humans and full-sized likenesses of small children. My great-grandfather had run a side business in cemetery statuary, specializing in pieces for burial plots, though he sold lawn ornaments too. He'd been dead for decades but his inventory remained in the basement.

The room reminded me of a permanent round of statue tag, a game where when you got tagged you had to stand still. It spooked me no end to look upon all those silent, frozen forms buried beneath us. Perhaps it was too clear a reminder of the way my family made its livelihood. I steered well clear of that room. When the ABCs arrived they would harangue my father into pulling up an assortment of two or three statues to adorn the grounds. They especially favored a fat cherub with gilt wings whose eyes were painted a demonic orange, and a little black jockey dressed in jodhpurs and a forest-green jacket, holding up a green tin lantern in one hand. Every summer Momma protested, saying that the statue was offensive. The ABCs just tittered at her objection, and the jockey took up his usual sentry duty near the stairs of the front porch, where he kept an eye on all of our trips to and from the water.

I had no idea how to get the wringer machine to work, so I picked the soiled sheets up from the floor where I had hurriedly tossed them yesterday, set them in the washtub basin next to the older machine and turned on the hot water full blast. Momma used Woolite to clean things by hand, and I knew that bleach was good for stains, so I added a caplet of each to the water. A handheld washboard sat propped against the wall. When I tried scrubbing the sheets against its metal grooves, the soapy fabric kept slipping away. Instead I grabbed up two handfuls of the sheets, made heavy by the weight of the water they had soaked up, and rubbed them together, watching as the reddish-brown stains lifted from the cotton fibers. I poured some bleach right onto the worst of it. It burned my cuticles, which I had been picking at relentlessly for the last twenty-four hours, but I didn't care so long as it did the job. As I worked, it occurred to me that being with Momma when she lost that baby was as close as I'd ever come to participating at a death. I'd always thought that when I grew up I might join Daddy in the business. But seeing that loss yesterday had drained some of the vitality out of me, too. As I wrung out the excess water from the sheets I swore I'd find a career that involved the happier times of life, not the heart-wrenching last moments of its passing.

I lugged the laundry basket up from the basement and out into the backyard, where I climbed the small rise of the lawn and hung the sheets on the clothesline strung between two apple trees at the top. Clothespins were strewn in the grass at my feet. Chris had dumped out the bucket yesterday after Daddy took Momma away. I'd asked Samantha to help Chris pick them up while I heated some SpaghettiOs for dinner, but apparently she hadn't thought it necessary to obey me.

I looked down the hill to where my sister was drawing with chalk on the sidewalk, thinking that I should make her help me. She had her hair up in ponytails. This morning she'd insisted that I comb it the way Momma usually did, so I'd taken the brush and swept her hair into two nearly even hunks at either side of her head in her favorite purple ponytailers. I wasn't as good as my mother and the right ponytail rode up higher than the left, but Samantha hadn't noticed.

My sister sat back over her heels, assessing her drawing. Chances were good it was a castle, with a princess waving out one window. Samantha was still Daddy's little girl. He tucked her in at night and she insisted he read her one of the fairy tales from the Grimm's book she'd gotten for her birthday. She loved "Snow White," "The Princess and the Pea" and most of all "Sleeping

Beauty." I grew wistful remembering that when we lived in the old neighborhood our life had seemed like it was straight from a storybook. But now I felt more like Cinderella than a princess. The thought was enough to make me want to go lie down on my bed. But if I did, I'd hear Momma crying through the wall.

A breeze picked up off the lake, billowing the sheet on the line around me. I grappled to unwind myself from the wet, clinging fabric. A faint stain ran down the center. I rubbed it with my thumb, uncertain whether I was trying to erase it or make it a more visible reminder of what I had seen. Relief and disappointment rose in me when I looked at the stain again. It hadn't changed at all. I bunched the upper half of the sheet close to my face, burying my nose in the middle as I closed my eyes and inhaled the balm of bleach and detergent.

"How's your mother feeling?"

I nearly jumped a mile. I hadn't noticed Aunt C approach. I lowered the fabric and bent down to pick up another clothespin, buying myself some time to think how to answer. "Okay. She says she needs a day to rest then tomorrow she'll be better." This was a lie but I hoped it would satisfy C's prying.

She clicked her tongue and I swung my head around with the most innocent expression I could muster. Then I followed her inside the cottage, where the rest of the ABCs were taking stock of our situation. I was relieved to see that Momma was up, dressed in her bathrobe and sitting on the front porch chaise.

"Thanks for doing the laundry, darling." She gave me a weak smile as I came in, looked through the doorway toward where the ABCs were all seated around the kitchen table, then beckoned for me. I stood before her and she reached up, brought my head down nearer so she could kiss it.

"They know about my procedure at the hospital but not about before, so don't tell, okay?" she whispered, her lips pressed against my ear. Then she winked, as if to say that if we both kept quiet things would soon return to how they had always been.

Five

As the summer went on, it seemed that they might. By the Fourth of July Momma seemed more her old self, with the frailty of those first days after she returned lessening. But since the miscarriage she had only picked at her food. She'd grown so thin that one day she donned a bikini she found in the middle bedroom dresser, one that she'd worn in high school. It was navy, with white daisies and yellow dots printed on the bra top and matching boy shorts. When Momma sauntered out onto the pier in it, Daddy wolf-whistled from the water where he was playing with Paulie. "Yowza, Lucy," he groaned, clutching at his tanned chest in mock distress. "How long have you been holding out on me, woman?"

Momma giggled uncertainly, her eyes holding a doubt I'd never noticed in them before. Then, as if she'd made up her mind to believe Daddy's admiring assessment, she curtsied and sat down on her towel, looking regal as she applied sunscreen. Tawny sun-splashed highlights glinted from her shoulder-length brown hair. She had tied it back with a scarf that completed the 1960s fashion-model look.

"Let me get your back. You can't reach it all yourself. I'd better help." Daddy left my brother, who was looking at Momma with the same adoring puppy-dog gaze as Daddy, and clambered out of the water. My mother melted under his deft strokes. He rubbed her shoulders far longer than necessary to get the lotion in, but Momma didn't protest. I pretended to ignore them, a book in front of my face as a shield, but in truth I was relishing my parents' antics. I guessed that Daddy didn't know about the reason for Momma's miscarriage, and in the days following it I'd feared that he might discover the truth, and what might happen to us if he did. But in the weeks since, Daddy seemed more tender toward Momma, the two of them even more playful with one another than usual. That day on the pier I decided that Momma was over the worst of it and I no longer had to worry.

My sense that we had survived was premature. Labor Day we were all at the lake for the holiday weekend: my parents, sister and brothers; the ABCs; aunts and uncles; cousins. Since it was the last weekend of the season, even the older kids who were too cool to do much more than work on their tans all summer got into the water with the rest of us. We spent most of the weekend swimming out to a raft our fathers had jimmied together out of two oil barrels, an old section of pier and a rusty anchor, where we practiced backflips and dives while the adults sunbathed.

Late Sunday afternoon, as the sun fell behind the tree line on the opposite shore, my cousins Candace and Jake, Samantha, Paulie and I played a watery version of "chicken." We took a collective deep breath and sank down to sit on the sandy bottom. Last one to come up won. It was a silly game, because there was no real danger. We'd swum in the lake since we were babies, getting bigger and stronger summer after summer like tadpoles growing into frogs. We'd even seen our fathers push each other under the same way when they grew rowdy from drinking beer in the sun.

About half an hour earlier the men had gone into the backyard to start the grill and a game of sixteen-inch softball. The ABCs had commandeered the kitchen as usual, boiling water for sweet corn and cutting up tomato and cucumber wedges. Momma and Aunt Susan were on the pier, watching us swim and talking about the latest hairstyles for fall, when Daddy came walking down the dock toward us. He'd put on a pair of madras shorts and a ratty brown shirt he called his Sunday shirt because it was so "hole-y."

Something was wrong. The forward slump of my father's shoulders, the grim line of his mouth, signaled trouble. Daddy handed Momma and Aunt Susan each a bottle of Tab, then stood at the edge of the pier, toes curled over its splintered lip as if daring it to pitch him forward into the lake. The other kids were still caught up in our game but I moved away from them, nearer to the pier.

"I just got a call." Daddy had his pager in his hand. He was looking at it like he wanted to throw it into the lake. We all knew what getting a call meant. Momma and Aunt Susan leaned back as if to buffer themselves from what was coming next, and I wondered whether it ever got any easier to hear that death had made another visit, even when it came for a stranger. Apprehension dragged down Momma and Aunt Susan's features, which had looked so carefree while they debated highlights versus frosted tips.

My father spoke in a voice so low that his words slipped through my ears like minnows escaping rotted nets. "A kid got caught in the weeds over by Sandy Pines."

I crouched lower in the shallow water and slipped under the pier, listening hard.

Through the slats I saw Daddy gesture down the shore toward the campgrounds and resort. "He and a buddy rented a rowboat and decided to have a contest to see who could stay underwater the longest."

The adults remained where they were for a few moments, their silence pierced occasionally by the shrieks of the kids splashing, blissfully unaware.

"Who lets their children out in a goddamned rowboat by themselves on a lake like this?" Gruff anger replaced Daddy's matter-of-fact manner.

Dejection filled his next words: "These are the ones I can't wrap my head around." He hung his head, looked straight down through the slats to where I was hiding beneath him, but he didn't see me. "When an old person passes away, that makes sense. It's part of the natural order of things. But times like this . . . it's a mystery to me." The awe in his tone chilled me. I wanted to believe that my father understood everything about the world.

Two boys in a boat. I couldn't get my head around it either. I slithered through the water out from under the pier trying to imagine the boys, thinking instead of a nursery rhyme, "Rub-a-dub-dub, three men in a tub." I thought of my baby brother Chris's yellow plastic tub stuffed with a butcher, a baker, a candlestick maker, remembered the way they toppled out on top of one another when we brought the toy into the water and how the sight of their falling overboard made my brother crack up laughing like an old man.

"What happens now?" I asked my father as I reached up for him to pull me out of the water by my arms. I stood between Momma and Aunt Susan, water from my hair dripping down my cheeks like tears. The three of us looked at him expectantly.

Daddy stared out across the lake, squinting into the ebbing sun. "I'm going to help drag the lake. They'll need someone to handle the body once they find it. God knows when the coroner will get here. Last I heard, he was drunk in some bar in Lilymoor." Daddy looked dazed. He glanced down at me again but he didn't seem to be talking to me. It was more like he was working something out for himself. "Hopefully we can pull the kid out before dark. Otherwise . . ." He left the word hanging, distracted as he craned his neck and looked out over the water again.

The wind picked up, blowing hard enough to charge the somber mood Daddy had brought out onto the pier with a heightened prickly unease. Momma stood up, cupping a hand over her brow to see beyond the sun's reflection on the water. She looked left, then right, then left again. Her other index finger jutted in the air as she mouthed silent numbers. "Someone's missing." She turned to Aunt Susan and Daddy, counting off on her fingers. "Candace, Caro, Chris, Samantha, Jake . . . that's only five. Who am I missing?"

Before they could answer, Momma asked, "Where's Paul?"

"I thought all the kids were out here with you." Daddy frowned, looked back toward the cottage. "He's not in the house."

"Where's your brother? Where's Paulie?" Momma turned sharp words on me.

"He said he was bored. He wanted to go play softball with the guys." It was all I knew of my brother's whereabouts. He had gotten out of the water and wandered up the pier a little while ago. I had watched him disappear around the corner of the house, then went back to playing with the others.

"You were supposed to keep an eye on the kids." Momma's rebuke struck as hard as if she'd hit me. She turned away and hastened up the pier in search of my brother. I felt naked standing there, Daddy and Aunt Susan looking at me as if they'd never seen me before.

"Shit. Where the hell's Paulie?" Daddy turned away from me and repeated Momma's question to the horizon. His voice broke in desperation, and with it my heart. Before I could move to comfort him he turned and sprinted up the pier, moving faster than I could ever recall seeing him run before.

In much the same way the notion of my mother causing her miscarriage had a couple of months ago, an unbidden image bloomed in my mind. I saw my brother underwater. His eyes were open but blank. Was it my imagination or something real?

I had accepted the information about Momma and that pill bottle without question, but I refused to believe what I was seeing now was true. "Dead" happened to other people, not us. We had to be around to take care of them, I reasoned, knowing full well that death came for everyone eventually. I stepped forward until there were no more boards under my feet, just a second's worth of empty space and then the welcoming warmth of the familiar waters that embraced me like comforting arms. I sucked in a deep breath and sank slowly beneath the water, holding on to the algae-slick leg of the pier. I went under with my eyes wide open, as if I might see my brother if he was down there somewhere. My lungs burned but I resisted the impulse to push off with my feet and resurface. Instead I let go of the pier leg and wrapped my arms around my knees, sank nearer to the floor of the lake. *This* was my childhood home.

Eventually I had to come up for air. I felt both grateful and guilty about doing so. Because I knew, in a way I couldn't explain but also couldn't refute, that despite my pleadings and promises to fate, Paulie was still down there. He'd won at chicken for good. I knew all too well what dead meant, knew that Paulie was gone forever. Yet despite the certainty growing in my gut, my mind refused to accept that my little brother wasn't going to turn up ever again.

I hoisted myself back onto the pier. In silent response to some shared instinct the rest of the kids climbed out too. Aunt Susan followed, as if fearful to let any of us out of her sight. As I passed by the stairway leading to the front porch, I glared at the little jockey with the bright eyes, holding his lantern high. I was barefoot but I kicked him over anyway, wishing I could wipe away the permanent smirk etched on his face. I left the others in the yard, where my uncles were talking about dividing into search parties and who would look for Paulie where. I changed into shorts and a T-shirt and left my wet suit on the bedroom floor, steering clear of the front porch, where Momma was sitting on the sofa, the ABCs clustered around her in a tight knot. I heard B insisting there was nothing for Momma to do right now but let the men go looking.

As I slipped away from the throng of my relatives I considered asking one of my cousins to go with me, but this felt like a journey I had to make alone. I had to go see, face my fear, or I'd never sleep again without Paulie haunting my dreams every night. We were all so familiar with death in our family, I wasn't too surprised to find it had come for one of us kids. As I crossed through the yard I avoided looking at the white cross that marked Sparky's grave. I couldn't bear to imagine the unthinkable: putting my brother in the ground in the same way.

I continued on, reaching the road, where I followed the yellow center line, daring any traffic to come around the bend and make me yield my position. I could have made the trek in my sleep. The boat ramp was down the street from Ruby's store, not far from the Sandy Pines Motor Court. For a moment I was tempted to imagine that I was sleepwalking. But I knew that pretending wouldn't erase the reality of where I was heading—beyond innocence into uncharted waters.

There was very little to see when I reached the boat ramp. I would later learn that Paulie had wandered over to Ruby's store for some candy. He'd made a new friend there—Toby, an eleven-year-old boy from Sandy Pines. The rental resort was near the mouth of the channel that connected one bay of the lake to another. Toby's family had never been to the lake before that holiday weekend so he didn't know about the undertow that coursed through the channel. We weren't allowed in the water without an adult, but Toby had talked Paul into paddling one of the resort's rowboats into the channel so they could fish. Then the boy had boasted that he could hold his breath underwater longer than Paulie. He'd dared my brother to go first while he timed him from the boat. My affable brother had agreed and jumped overboard. The undertow pulled him down, and he got tangled in the clumps of weeds hiding below the placid surface.

It was foolish for them to go into the channel but I understood the foolishness of boys, who believed themselves invincible. Despite our family's business we all did it, took our living and breathing for granted, pausing only when an ambulance raced along the road behind the cottage and the ABCs went running onto the back porch to watch it pass by, Aunt A always offering the same dire commentary: "Somebody's gettin' a ride."

At the boat ramp, a sheriff's car was parked in the lot next to Daddy's Oldsmobile. Offshore a green boat bobbed, motor silent as it drifted with the waves. Three men stood in the boat. One was Daddy. All of them wore black rubber boots up to their knees and elbow-length rubber gloves that made them look like they were at a creepy dress-up party. They were not doing much. I kept watch, eyes locked on the sight of the men in the boat, willing them to find my brother. With their long gloves and strong arms they should have been able to reach down and pull him up from the weeds' grasp, like bringing in a lethargic fish. Anger rose within me at their clumsiness. But they were not fishermen. Their movements were awkward. It took every ounce of restraint to keep myself from swimming out to the edge of their ridiculously green craft, taking their rubbery hands and guiding them below the surface to where I could see him, half-sitting, half-lying now, a puzzled look on his face, as if he could not believe that this was the way his life would go.

Then I saw why the men weren't moving and my fury exploded into horror and sadness at a sight I would have given anything to forget. The man in the front of the boat called out to another near the back. The one in back cranked a chain, hoisting something from the water. I retched at what emerged: eight huge metal rods running alongside the boat. Gleaming fishhooks, five feet long each.

That boat had no business there, no business at all, unless the catch one was after was a body. The hooks were empty except for some strands of seaweed. Daddy reached over and removed them, tossing them over the other side of the boat. I wanted so badly for him to save Paulie, to redeem all of us from the losses whose currents pulled us down into dark whirlpools of despair that summer.

"Down!" I heard the man in the front call out again. The chain man unreeled the winch and the hooks sank out of sight. They repeated the process so many times I lost count. Each time the empty silver arms, gleaming clean, taunted their efforts.

The sun dropped into the lake. In the growing dark the land merged with the water. After nighttime the lake would grow blacker than the sky, without any stars or moon to poke holes in its seamless fabric. A few reflections from the neon beer signs of the tavern down the shore might flicker on the surface but I'd been below in the dark before, had opened my eyes to the pitch of nothingness. That's where my little brother would spend the night. In a murky, moonless hole, bound by tendrils of jealous weeds winding up and around, claiming him.

The man leading the craft turned on the engine, its sudden

roar shattering the deceptive quiet of Sunday evening. But even
when the men came off the boat I didn't abandon my focus. I
gazed hard at the lake, seeking out the spot where my brother
was lying.

I almost slipped into ignoring the harsh reality before me—I
had not seen my brother's body, nor an ambulance, and not Toby,
who must have been somewhere nearby in one of the rental cottages. I hadn't even noticed any dead fish floating on the surface.
For a moment I thought I could take Momma's cue about the pill
bottle and cover up what had happened. But I had seen the one
sight it seemed I would never forget: the empty-hooked boat. Anguish rose up in me again. My brother *had* drowned. He wouldn't
be rescued.

Long past dusk the men got into their cars, muttering about
gases bloating the body and waiting overnight to see if it surfaced.
If not, they'd go out again in the morning. They'd drag on Labor
Day, a holiday meant for a picnic, or if it was chilly the first bonfire. Instead of celebrating the holiday they would scour the lake
floor for the hallowed treasure they could not leave down there.

"Want to ride back with me, Big Girl?" Daddy's voice was tight
with sorrow when he came over to where I was standing at the
shore. He'd already given up the hunt. But it felt important that
I go back by myself. I shook my head, even when he turned the
request into a demand. Finally he gave up and I walked home on
tiptoe in the middle of the road, never turning once even though
I could hear the Oldsmobile's engine idling as Daddy trailed behind me. So straight and even, that yellow line, along every curve
and turn. So easy to follow without falling off. And on either side,
blacktop. Nothing to get tangled up in.

My brother whispered to me in my sleep that night. I turned from
side to side on the front porch swing until I came fully awake and
sat up, walked out to the pier and waited. I'd needed him to come
to me, needed to know that he was safe at the bottom of the lake.

I wanted him to place a crown of seaweed on my head and tell me he was long gone to a better place, where he was feeling light and beautiful as a bubble without the weight of a body ruled by gravity and memory dragging him down.

I imagined that what the men would find the next day would be not Paulie but a shell like the clams we dug up, iridescent and perfectly whole but empty when pried open. I felt him so close by, somewhere I ached to get to but could not see. I promised him that I would remember, swirled a toe in the black water to show I wasn't afraid to be in it with him.

When his body finally washed up after three days I wasn't there to see it. Paulie never came up for air, never lifted his head and looked around wondering where his new buddy Toby had slipped off to. He never swam back in to the dock. My brother had gone to a distant shore.

Six

Two days later, Momma nearly murdered Daddy.

We were back in the suburbs. The house, typically filled with the peals of children, was now quiet as a graveyard. My brother's funeral was tomorrow. I still didn't know whether or not I was going. My parents had been arguing all morning about taking me and my siblings.

"Of course they're going, Lucille," my father boomed. "There's no surprises about death around here. It's going to happen to all of us. They need to be there for closure."

Samantha, Chris and I were in the kitchen eating lunch. My parents had moved into the den, as if we couldn't hear the battle in the next room.

"It will traumatize them to see him like that, Dan." Anguish filled Momma's words. "I think it's best that they remember their brother when he was alive."

"Would it be better yet if they forgot he ever existed?" Daddy's voice rose to a timbre I'd never heard in it before. A sob followed his words. It cut into me, lodged hard in my chest. I was used to Momma getting emotional. She laughed and cried often. Daddy's grief was so much harder to bear.

Their fight escalated like the temperature into a heated exchange of sharp words. Then came the sharp rebuke of Daddy's feet marching angrily out of the den, away from Momma in mid-rant.

"Don't you walk out on me!" Momma yelled as Daddy went upstairs.

Chris continued mashing Cheerios and raisins into a sticky glop on his high-chair tray. Samantha, seated next to him, closed her eyes and covered her ears with her hands. The three of us stayed at the kitchen table. I held my breath and waited, the knot in my chest pulling tighter. Then Momma stalked off after Daddy.

From overhead we heard the rap of her fists on their bedroom door. Daddy had locked her out with the very device he'd installed to give them some occasional privacy from noisy kids. A final beat, then nothing.

The silence was broken by Momma's steps, heavy as she descended the stairs. She strode through the kitchen to the door that led to the garage.

I thought that was the end of it.

But then Momma reappeared, looking betrayed. Her face was set, determined. She moved so stealthily that I might have missed the weapon hanging from her hand. But a ray of sunlight entered through the window above the sink, giving her away with a glint that ricocheted off the flinty head of the pickax. I blinked, then recalled the incredible sight of those gleaming empty hooks on the boat that had gone after Paulie. This was just as fantastic. As Momma climbed the stairs a second time my wild imagination shrieked that we were about to witness domestic bloodshed. I crept from the kitchen into the foyer but I couldn't make myself go any farther. I didn't want to go stairs and find a corpse father and a murderer mother. The front door was open and through the screen I saw Mr. Blackmun across the street, edging his lawn with an old-fashioned hand tool. He glanced up at me and waved. I imagined our nosy old neighbor reading about us in the next morning's headlines, a sly smile on his face as he savored our tragedy. He'd comment importantly to the media that we had seemed okay but these days, who knew what went on next door? I nodded, then shut the door against the peeks of outsiders who had no business spying.

I waited at the bottom of the stairs, dread keeping me frozen. The metal tooth of the ax bit into the wooden bedroom door with a splintering and then shattering sound. The full-length mirror on the inside of the door wept silvery shards that tinkled as they fell to the floor. They struck me as too pretty a soundtrack for the carnage being committed. Momma swung the ax again and again, taking out her sorrow and rage on the door Daddy had shut between them.

"You"—crash of ax meeting oak—"son of a bitch!"

As if I was alongside her I saw her raise the instrument high over her shoulder, readying herself for the next blow. "You will never, *never* lock me out again!" A thud, followed by a clink, echoed as the wooden handle left Momma's hands and the ax slipped to the floor. She cried softly, her anger spent.

On the other side, the bolt slid free from the doorjamb.

I imagined Daddy opening what was left of the door, kneeling at Momma's side and taking her into his arms. I yearned for a fairytale ending, my quaint version of romantic love where Daddy was the handsome prince who saved Momma, the damsel in distress.

Instead he walked out.

Daddy stepped over the crying heap of Momma in the bedroom doorway and came downstairs. "Big Girl, take care of your mother." It was all he said before he gathered the kids in the minivan and drove off, leaving me alone with Momma. I was young but that summer I had learned well how to manage my mother. I picked her up and led her to bed, burying my fury at being cheated out of my childhood deep inside until it felt like it had disappeared.

For months Daddy punished Momma by leaving the hacked door on its hinges. The gaping hole was a giant eye staring mournfully whenever I passed, reminding me of what I had seen, even if I had kept the neighbors from peeking.

Momma fell apart after Paulie died. As that summer faded into fall I often came home from school to find her gazing out the kitchen window, eyes vacant with a terror that was out of place in our quiet if messy house. When Daddy took a business trip to a morticians' convention, Momma spent an evening hanging sheets over the sliding glass doors in the kitchen and den. She was frightened that someone lurking outside would see in, so she worked in the dark, waiting to turn on the lights until after the sheets were in place. At bedtime she checked the locks on all the doors and windows, then gathered Samantha and Chris into her bed. She wanted everyone close by where she could keep an eye on us. I kept watch beside her in the dark, the kids sleeping so hard they didn't stir. When headlights shone through the drawn shades, Momma's body stiffened next to mine until the car passed.

As if I was her understudy, when Momma withdrew into shadows I took her place. A couple of weeks after she took to her bed Daddy stood at the kitchen counter mixing himself a Manhattan. I'd helped him stack the dinner dishes in the sink and pile the fried chicken take-out buckets beside the garbage can in the back hall. A deep ache rose in me as I watched him measure the whiskey in the jigger, then pour it over the ice, stirring the bourbon and vermouth with his index finger. Momma usually made Daddy a drink before supper but this was his third one that night. He'd forgotten to offer me the maraschinos from the last two. I watched as he added another couple ice cubes to the glass, waited for him to throw in another cherry. He didn't bother.

"Your mother's not well." Daddy sat down at the head of the table. Samantha and Chris were in the den, watching television. They seemed unaware that we were living like orphans with a disturbed woman upstairs. I felt stunned most of the time, terrified over how fast things could change. At the beginning of the summer my mother had been her usual self; now she couldn't even come downstairs. The jigger rested in a sticky amber pool on the counter. I reached for it and stuck my tongue against the bottom of the tinny cup. The whiskey's sear took my breath. A relief to taste so much power, even if it was a little painful.

"You're twelve, old enough to help out more, so you'll do the laundry and make dinner, won't you, Big Girl?" Daddy glanced at the jigger raised to my lips but didn't say anything. Hearing his nickname for me turned all the fear I felt to shame. I nodded, kept my head down so he wouldn't see the tears behind my sheet of long hair. That was my role—the big girl, the one who kept everything together.

I had some help: the ABCs. Soon they started coming out twice a week to cook and clean. Momma let the ABCs mother us while she sought respite from the season's losses, which proved too much for her. Suddenly I had three new mothers. But none of them was the one I needed, and relief and resentment at their taking over percolated within me in equal measure.

One day in late September I saw their car parked on the driveway when Mary Grace and I got off the school bus. Behind the familiar sleek Cadillac sat a shabby red pickup truck. The cab was dented, the rear tire on the driver's side missing a hubcap.

"I'd better go in." I shot my friend an apologetic look. I had planned to tell Momma that I was going over to Mary Grace's, but now I needed to go see what kind of mood Momma was in. She often grew irritated when the ABCs showed up. Since they had a key, they didn't call to warn us when they were coming.

Mary Grace squeezed my hand and nodded sympathetically. She was the one person I'd told about what was going on in our house, and only after I swore her to secrecy. "Call me later if you want," she said. The words were casual but we both knew how much they meant. I choked down tears. Mary Grace was always willing to listen but I wasn't sure I'd ever be able to repay her generosity, which left me feeling worse than before.

Momma was at the dinette table shuffling through the mail, looking lost in her own kitchen. I took a head count: Aunt A stirred soup on the stove. B was on her hands and knees washing the floor, and C was in the dining room polishing the silver. They were all acting as if nothing much had changed, when in fact, everything had.

Ruby was standing alongside the birdbath out on the deck, watching a sparrow take dainty sips from the shallow bowl. It was Uncle Stu's old truck parked out front, the one Ruby rarely drove anymore. Most days it sat in the yard next to her store at the lake.

Ruby's thick hair flowed down her back over a red wool cape. My eyes followed to where the fine strands swept the moon of her bottom. She was barefoot, her gnarled feet like roots planted into the wooden deck boards. Gypsylike large silver hoops dangling from her ears caught the fading afternoon sunlight, refracting it into a shimmer that bounced off the water in the fountain. But it wasn't the light or the jewelry that held me spellbound. It was Ruby herself. The sight of her sent a jolt of primal familiarity through me. This was the person I most wanted to be like. She must have sensed my watching because she turned her head and looked through the window right into me, as if she could read everything I was thinking. She nodded but made no move to come inside, leaving me free to decide whether or not to go to her.

After Paulie died she hadn't tried to ease my pain with platitudes or sweets like her sisters, but instead had presented me with a single tarot card. It was one of the three I had pulled at the beginning of the summer, the Queen of Pentacles. It depicted a woman in flowing robes and a crown seated upon a throne in a lush garden, with a large golden coin in her hands and a rabbit at her feet. Ruby had taken me aside at the reception, the only part of the funeral service I'd been allowed to attend, and led me out into the courtyard rose garden, where a small bench invited mourners to sit and remember their loved ones. "This is a very auspicious card," she had told me. "You pulled it last, so it signifies your future. Those who pull this card are warm and nurturing, very grounded and openhearted. Trust these qualities, for they grow within you." I had wrapped the card up in my blankie and put the bundle under my pillow. I was doubtful, but I hoped those things Ruby said the card held would bloom in me if I slept on it.

I turned away from the window, glanced at Momma.

"Ruby came to pray over me." Momma looked humiliated but I was relieved. I'd wanted to tell Daddy to call and ask Ruby to bring her relics. She had a collection of slivers of the cross Jesus had died on and a tattered square of the veil Veronica had used to wipe his face. I wanted to believe that God could help Momma

feel better. But I'd been praying every night and it didn't seem
to be doing us any good. Despite my faith in Ruby, I'd kept my
mouth shut. Daddy didn't believe in the power of crosses and
saints' bones, and I wavered between my great-aunt's devout belief and the logical reasoning I admired in my father.

Since Paulie's death I'd developed a keen sense of urgency, an
awareness that things could go horribly wrong at any moment. I
was so grateful to the ABCs for helping Momma, helping me. Despite their discomfort at any sort of emotional display, something in
me needed to tell them, to be sure they knew I appreciated them.
That night when they were getting ready to leave, I helped Daddy
pack up the Cadillac. We stood out on the driveway. I hopped
from side to side, nervousness making me jumpy. Finally Daddy
slammed the trunk shut. He started the engine and turned the car
around so that Aunt A wouldn't have to back out of the drive.

"There you are, A," he said. "All loaded up."

B and C hustled out in their going-out dresses, the cotton
housecoats they'd worn for working hidden away in their bags.
From the back the ABCs looked identical in their heeled shoes,
babushkas neatly wrapped around their heads. Ever the odd one
out, Ruby followed behind them, head bare, red poncho balloon-
ing around her.

Now, a voice whispered inside me. I took on Aunt A first.
"Good night, Aunt A," I chirped as I leaned over to perform the
usual perfunctory duty of pecking the air near her cheek.

"See you, Caro," she said. She shoved a tiny packet into my
hand.

"I love you," I said. I couldn't remember ever saying the words
to the ABCs before and they felt awkward as cotton in my mouth.
Aunt A turned away and slid into the driver's seat. Perhaps she
hadn't heard me. I was disappointed but not put off.

I moved toward my grandmother. "I love you, B, bye." I said
the words first so I knew she heard me. I kissed her and waited.

"Yeah, so long, kid," she replied.

It was the same with Aunt C. I held out the magic words in exchange for a stilted "Behave yourself," and "Make sure you help your mother."

With growing disappointment, I raced back to the red pickup. My beautiful gypsy aunt stuck her head out the window, then pulled her scarlet cape up and over it.

"Bye, Ruby." My whole face quivered as I struggled to keep my tears in. I didn't dare say how I felt again. If Ruby ignored it, something inside me would break for good. She settled the cape around my shoulders and whispered in my ear. Then she reached for the rosewood rosary hanging around her rearview mirror and draped the beads around my neck.

Red circles thrown by the taillights blurred through my tears as Aunt A cautiously pulled away. I was squeezing the packet she had given me so tightly that it cut into my palm. I opened my hand and unfolded a twenty-dollar bill, the same gift she gave me at the end of every visit. I worked the fringes of Ruby's cape between my fingers, pretending they were strands of my gypsy aunt's hair. A sudden sense of yet another tragedy welled up within me; that of being too young to traipse farther than my own backyard, and the even larger dread that when I was grown I might be too afraid to venture beyond the boundaries of life within my family. But there was the promise of Ruby's cape to remind me who I might become.

"I love you all," I whispered one more time in the night as the cough of the pickup's muffler faded away. I raised the crucifix on the end of Ruby's rosary to my mouth, slipped the thin metal between my lips and sucked, the sharp metallic taste close to blood filling my mouth. Then I turned and went in search of Momma, who needed me more than ever after the ABCs left.

Seven

Fall turned to winter. Momma hibernated. It seemed she might never get out of bed again. The ABCs still came several times a week. But I needed a *mother*—someone I could look up to, craft my own life by her example. So I abandoned Momma in favor of another.

I spent all the time I could at Mary Grace's house. At first this was because she was my best friend but as I got to know her mother I went for Marilyn's company as much as for MG's. I adored Marilyn. And six-month-old Jacob was so cute. Once I went running up to Momma's bedroom when I returned from across the backyards, wanting to share Jacob's latest accomplishment of rolling over. Momma pulled the covers up a little tighter over her shoulders. Her pale face blanched whiter when I told her my news. She reached for the inhaler on the nightstand, gulping from it in the same way Daddy swigged his Manhattans. Then she shooed me off the bed. Guilt pricked at me for mentioning the baby when ours had never materialized but it passed so fast I hardly noticed it.

Marilyn was gorgeous and devoted to Mary Grace's dad, a musician with a PhD in classical guitar. Dr. Hanover traveled frequently. But at four thirty on afternoons when he was in town, Marilyn disappeared into her bathroom and turned on her electric rollers. While she waited for them to heat up she curled her eyelashes and refreshed her makeup. After the kids went to sleep, Marilyn spent the rest of the night with her husband. From Marilyn, I might learn how to become a woman men wanted to be around.

I had a girl-crush on our across-the-yard neighbor. I yearned to spend all my time with the cheerful lady who got out of bed every day without difficulty. I was not yet dreaming about boys; my fantasies revolved around life with Marilyn, Mary Grace and Jacob.

I also thought about *being* Marilyn—married with kids, in a house where I could have a housekeeper instead of a slew of relatives prone to barging in and taking over.

Pretty soon I was at the Hanovers' every day, even when Mary Grace had piano lessons or soccer practice after school. Their house became my refuge. I knew where to find the silverware and odds and ends like tape, scissors and rubber bands in their drawers as easily as in my own.

One day, Mary Grace invited me to go to a movie with her and her mom on a Friday night. "Mom says she'll get a sitter to stay with Jacob so we can have a special girls' night out," she said excitedly. "If you want, you can sleep over."

I skipped home, jubilant. It was so nice of Mary Grace to include me in their special time. I wasn't sure I would have done the same. But Momma had no time for anyone these days. When I ran upstairs and told Momma, she frowned. I'd learned not to talk too much about Marilyn because it upset Momma. But in my excitement about Friday I'd forgotten to stifle my enthusiasm until she scowled. "What if your father and I want to go out that night? What if we need you to babysit? Have you already said yes?"

I hesitated. Was it better to say I'd told Mary Grace I had to ask permission, even though Momma had guessed correctly that I had already said yes? I didn't dare bring up that she and Daddy hadn't gone out in months. Momma's shoulders slumped and she crossed the bedroom, heading back to bed.

It was only four thirty in the afternoon but she was already in her nightgown. Or maybe she hadn't bothered to take it off from the night before. Remnants of the summer's tragedies still tinged my dreams but I was growing increasingly impatient with Momma. She still had most things a woman could want: a handsome husband, sweet children, even the big house in the suburbs she'd just had to have. We were all there around her, alive. But she refused to be more than a ghost.

On Friday I packed my Mark Grace bag with pajamas, a change of clothes and my tattered blankie, taking care so the tarot card didn't slip out. Momma watched me leave from the window above the kitchen sink, where she was slicing strawberries. Mary Grace was waiting for me where our two yards merged. I didn't look back as I crossed from our side onto hers.

Later, while Marilyn drove the babysitter home after our night out, Mary Grace and I went upstairs. "I'm gonna go to bed," MG murmured. She had fallen asleep in the car and now stumbled toward her room, only half-awake. "Mom fixed the guest bedroom for you. See you in the morning." She rested her head on my shoulder a moment, then floated off.

I was alone in the guest bedroom when I heard a loud bang. I froze. The house was still. I crept downstairs, heart pounding, pulled back the gauzy curtain and peeked out the window alongside the back door. The storm door was unlatched and I screamed as the wind slammed it against the frame again. Mary Grace was in the house with me and Marilyn would be back in just a few minutes, but that wasn't much comfort. I looked out the picture window in the dinette but I couldn't see our house because all the lights were off.

Then I froze again. Momma stood in front of me in her white nightgown, barefoot on the diving board of the Hanovers' pool despite the almost wintry chill in the air. She was staring up at the light I had switched on upstairs in the guest room, the glow raining down making her seem an apparition. I waited for her to discover me, feeling caught in some awful act. She lifted one foot off the board and stretched it out over the water as if she were going to step off into the empty pool.

I might have gone running out to my mother but the garage door opened and Marilyn walked in. She looked surprised to see me standing in the middle of the kitchen. "I-I got scared by the storm door slamming," I stammered as I pulled the curtain back into place. I didn't tell her about Momma, just moved away from the window hoping Marilyn wouldn't look outside. But she squinted, then pulled the curtain back as far as it would go and poked her head into the alcove. She rested a hand against the glass, looked harder. Her reflection appeared alongside Momma. A light rain had begun to fall. Marilyn dropped her head, considering. Momma continued to stare, her face shining as clear with need as the moon above her.

Marilyn turned away from the window. "Wait here." She went out the back door and stood by the pool, gesturing with her hands as she spoke to Momma. When she came back inside Marilyn pulled me tight to her and let out a deep sigh. I peeked back one more time over my shoulder but Momma had disappeared. Marilyn and I walked upstairs together, her arm still around me.

When we reached the guest bedroom she said softly, "You know, Caro, there's only one person you can be responsible for in your life." I held my breath, wishing she wouldn't talk anymore. "Do what brings you joy, no matter what anyone else wants. Always speak your truth. You can't give up yourself just to please someone else. Not your mother. Not your husband if you get married. Not even your own kids. So don't." She drew her arm down, squeezed my hand. "Do what makes you happy. Always. Promise me?"

She waited until I nodded. I watched from the doorway as she made her way down the long hall to her bedroom, stopping first at Mary Grace's room, then Jacob's, to kiss them good night.

I turned back into the guest room. I paced, resisting the urge to look out into the yard again. Finally I went to the window and looked straight down. No body floated in the water. Relief replaced my dread. I'd been expecting the worst.

In the dark the Hanovers' house felt brand-new, as if I hadn't walked the upstairs hallway to Mary Grace's room a million times. I pulled my suitcase across the guest room rug until it sat beside me under the window. I unzipped the bag to get my blankie. Out fell the pill bottle from last summer.

I wanted to go home.

I would wait until Marilyn and Mary Grace were asleep, then I would walk home across the yards and crawl into bed next to

Momma. It was just a little farther than the walk I made from my bedroom every night when nightmares of last summer woke me. I could come back for my things the next day and tell them I'd gone home because I'd felt sick. They would understand. But then I realized our doors were locked and I didn't have a key. I was stuck until morning. I looked at the queen on the tarot card for comfort, rubbed my blankie. I would watch the moon in the night sky until the sun rose. It was not the end of the world. It was just one night.

A noise at the door startled me and I jumped to my feet, tripping over my blankie. Marilyn stood in her nightgown, hair long and loose on her shoulders. "You can't sleep either, huh?" She offered me a soft smile. "MG mentioned that sometimes you like to sleep in your parents' bed."

My cheeks burned. I wasn't thrilled that MG had shared that. But Marilyn reached out and tousled my hair. "I was the same way when I was a kid." Understanding filled her words. "You can keep me company in the big bed if you want. There's plenty of room."

I followed her down the hall, carrying my blankie. The bed was identical to my parents'. I waited until Marilyn climbed in on her side. I paused at the edge, feeling I would betray my usual partner if I got in. But in the end fatigue and the need for comfort won out. I crawled beneath the warm flannel sheets, appreciating how good the thick fabric felt against my skin. I lay still on my side of the bed. I wanted to snuggle into Marilyn the way I did with Momma but I didn't dare. It felt wicked enough to be in Marilyn's bed while Momma wandered outside wraithlike, beckoning me home.

PART II

Birth

Eight

I left home at thirty-two, when I believed someone else finally needed me more than my mother. Ruby had just passed away. "Most folks die like they lived," she once said. True to her peaceful nature, a few nights ago she had simply slipped away in her sleep. She was the last of her generation to go, the one I would miss the most. Since Paulie, Momma had avoided the lake. I could count on one hand the number of times she'd gone up in the last twenty years. But Ruby's funeral was held there, and afterward my parents, siblings and I scattered her ashes as she had requested.

Everyone else went back home after the service, the air crisp with the promise of a chill after dark even though it was only September. But something drew me into staying at the cottage overnight. I couldn't recall a time I'd been there all alone before and it was a little spooky, especially after nightfall. I spent most of it reminiscing on the front porch swing, wishing that Ruby or one of the ABCs would join me, even in ghostly form. I rocked to soothe my nerves, straining to sense another's presence, but the house felt empty. Wherever they were, the dead weren't gathering for any reunion that night.

Over the twenty years following the night I spent at Marilyn's, I'd rarely left Momma's side. For a long time I was frightened she would die too, go after Paulie and that bean of a baby she'd miscarried to somewhere I couldn't follow. Most nights I startled awake, certain she had slipped away. I'd crawl in my parents' bed and mold myself to Momma's back, my arm draped over her to keep her near. I tried to tell myself catastrophe had already struck, that Momma and I had endured. But I never stopped being afraid, because Ruby told me that bad things always came in threes. So I waited to see what more might befall us and whether or not we would survive it.

As the years passed, Momma recovered enough to go back to nursing. Anyone who knew us would have described ours as a close-knit family. There were more deaths as the ABCs took their leave, but theirs were all from natural causes in old age. Samantha and then Chris went to college, rented apartments in the city, got married, had kids. A couple of years ago Samantha moved her gang back into our subdivision. That's when I first felt stranded, as if I'd somehow been left behind while my brother and sister had moved forward with their lives until they'd come eerily full circle back to where we'd started.

Mary Grace left too, for school in Milwaukee, where she now worked as a psychologist. But some vague sense of dread kept me close to Momma, as if she was my responsibility once the ABCs were no longer there for us. I lived at home and worked with my father at the funeral home, the job I vowed I'd never do that summer I was twelve. I liked working with Daddy, but death was depressing. Plus it was hell on my dating life; not many men wanted Morticia for a girlfriend. So I decided to follow in Momma's footsteps and become a nurse.

It took twenty years but the third disaster finally visited itself upon us. Soon after my thirtieth birthday I was in my second year of nursing school, thrilled to be interning at Lakeshore Memorial Hospital, where Momma worked. But I administered a wrong dosage of medication, a child died and I dropped out of school. I was free at last of the heavy weight of waiting for that third calamity, but I'd been in search of a way to redeem myself ever since.

I shifted from a sitting position to lying prone on the swing. A pontoon cruised by on the lake, its location marked only by small red and green lights moving steadily past. Other than the boat, the night was still. I shut my eyes, letting the vivid memories of that awful, empty time surface.

Ruby had been the one to nurture the hope that I might find some way to atone. I'd last seen her two years ago, when I'd sought refuge at the lake after my nursing school debacle. For weeks I had wandered corpselike around the funeral home, silent and numb. Then one day I got in my car and found myself driving east. When I pulled up in front of the store Ruby was out on her front porch in her wicker rocker. Old age had slowed her down some, and a sturdy walking stick lay at her feet. She took up the stick and stood as I made my way to her. She was thin as a sparrow in winter when I put my arms around her, yet her eyes were bright and clear despite her frailty. She was the one holding me as we hugged, and I let down into her arms with a wounded cry that held all the emotions I'd been unable to feel until then.

Ruby let me get it all out without interruption. She plucked a yellowed handkerchief from the back pocket of her overalls, held it out to me with compassion filling her eyes. Uncle Stu's clothes were bigger than ever on her. She had lost so much weight she resembled a child playing dress-up more than a woman in her eighties. Ruby had aged gracefully, her wrinkles and crow's-feet the etchings of a life well lived. She'd savored every moment for its beauty, welcoming equally the lessons of sorrow and joy.

Once I finished weeping, Ruby led me into the store. Things hadn't changed much there in twenty years. Canned fruits and vegetables still lined the shelves, along with cereal, crackers and other staples. The behemoth cash register roosted in its usual spot at the end of the counter, and the walk-in refrigerator where Ruby kept eggs, milk and cheese hummed at the back of the room. I was surprised at how small the store appeared. The space had seemed so much larger when I was a child. I'd been in there often over the intervening years, yet I still felt a shock at how cramped and drab it looked to me now.

Ruby led me to the kitchen in her apartment behind the storefront. She put a kettle of tea on and we sat at the small kitchen table, which was decorated with a tablecloth I recognized from childhood. She offered me some sugar wafers, her wink telling me she knew they were still my favorite cookies, and we nibbled while we waited for the water to boil.

"The family business isn't the only way." We hadn't exchanged a single word since I'd arrived but Ruby spoke as if we'd been in the middle of a conversation. I looked at her and waited.

"You brought the card with you?" she asked, and I started. I *had* brought the Queen of Pentacles; it was tucked in my sweatshirt pocket. I withdrew it, hoping she wasn't asking for it back, and handed it to her. I had spent countless hours staring at that card, trying as hard as I might to divine from it some sense of where my life was headed. I'd gotten nothing, other than the instinct that if I brought it to Ruby I'd finally get the reading Momma's miscarriage had interrupted.

Ruby held the card alongside my face and peered at the woman, then at me, comparing our likenesses. "Compassion, warmth, nurturing," she murmured. She shut her eyes and hummed softly, her head cocked as if she was considering something.

"There are women who need you," she declared when she opened her eyes again. I looked at her closely. Momma had said recently that she thought Ruby might be "slipping" mentally. But my great-aunt's green eyes were clear, sharp. Ruby wasn't slipping; she was entirely present.

"I've been sitting with women in their birth time," Ruby said next.

I looked at her quizzically and she flashed a pleased grin. "I've gotta do something to keep busy in the off-season here, and I'm too old to be shoveling, or even snowshoeing much, anymore." Her expression turned momentarily wistful, then the grin returned. "You remember Lucinda?"

I thought for a moment, then nodded. Ruby's Potawatomi friend.

"Years ago, she and a couple of the other midwives up here started asking me to help their women make ceremonies of their births. I did a few here and there for a while, then word got out. Now I do one a week. Sometimes more." Ruby sounded so pleased to be sharing this information. I hesitated to tell her that while I thought it was great, I had no idea what it had to do with me.

In typical Ruby fashion, before I could ask, she answered my question. "The midwives tell me that even women who give birth in hospitals want some help. Mostly those that don't want to fool around with the drugs. The nurses don't know a thing about natural birth anymore, so those that want one are bringing in help of their own. Another woman to mother them." Ruby scrounged in the pocket of her sweater, then pulled out a scrap of paper. "Lucinda says in hospitals they call them birth coaches." She scowled. "But it's got another, more exotic name . . ." She squinted as she read the word scrawled on the crumpled slip. "A *doula,* they call them. It's Greek, means 'slave.'" She flashed me another wildly pleased grin. "Sounds to me like a synonym for 'woman,' eh, kid?"

Ruby got up and shuffled to the pantry. I thought she was going for mugs, but she returned clutching a leather satchel that smelled of sage. She searched through it until she located what she was looking for. It was the small wood-carved statue I first saw at the fire ceremony that marked the beginning of that awful summer. My great-aunt traced a finger around the gold spiral painted over the statue's heart. The paint had chipped off in spots, and I guessed that Ruby had run her finger in that same path countless times over the years.

Ruby touched the woman briefly to her own heart then held it out to me. "She's called the healer, and I'm bequeathing her to you." Then my great-aunt handed me the paper scrap too, her eagle-sharp eyes trained on my own. "Compassionate, warm, nurturing, a natural mother. That's you, kid, through and through," she pronounced.

I'd left Ruby's that day with the Queen of Pentacles back in my pocket again, the statue, and a new sense of purpose. Ruby's paper had the words *Doulas of North America* on it. I registered with the national organization, took their training program to become a certified birth coach and began building a business. I might never be a nurse but I could help women in a time of great need, could participate with life in as powerful a way as my father did.

The birth coaching had been going well the last eighteen months, but the rest of my life felt stalled. Now here I was again, back at the lake. Suspended on that treacherous bridge of adolescence long past my teen years, no longer a child, not yet an adult. With a mixture of dread and anticipation I acknowledged the disturbing notion that in order to grow up I needed to move away from all that was familiar.

Around three in the morning I gave up on the pretense of sleep. A book resting on the lower shelf of the coffee table caught my eye. It was warped and yellowed with age, but the cover photo of a boy and a girl kissing was familiar. *Forever,* by Judy Blume. I'd left it up there years ago. Momma hadn't cared much what I read after that summer. Feeling restless, I wandered out to the pier in my pajamas, a comforter wrapped around my shoulders. I thought about doing a fire ceremony in Ruby's honor, but it would have made me too sad. Besides, the lake was calling to me. My cell phone screen lit enough of the pitch-black path ahead to keep me from stepping on any acorns or night crawlers. I sat down on the crossbar of the T that was the pier, pulling my knees up tight into my chest. Then I lifted my head and looked into the sky. There was so little light pollution that countless constellations blazed there. I watched a shooting star streak across the dark canvas, tears blurring its journey as I made a wish for Paulie. Were he and Ruby together somewhere now, making fire ceremonies and magic as we had when they were alive? I hoped so, hoped even if I couldn't see them they could see me, that they wanted to be nearby as much as I yearned for their presence.

My phone rang. I fumbled it, and almost dropped it into the

water. I was desperate to see who was calling at this ungodly hour, hoping it wasn't Momma or Daddy with more bad news.

"Caro, did I wake you? Sorry, but I couldn't sleep." Mary Grace sounded plaintive. "Do you have a minute?"

The polite inquiry almost made me laugh. It was the middle of the night, of course I had a minute. I was glad it wasn't my parents calling but my best friend's call still made me wary. Luckily she had good news she just couldn't wait until morning to share.

"I'm pregnant."

Those two words hold so much emotion, as if they're infused with the extra vigor pumping through an expectant mother's bloodstream. But as if it was a spell, Mary Grace's announcement conjured the image of a gray stillborn I'd glimpsed long ago, a husk of a baby curled into itself on the steel table in the mortuary. My apprehension burst into dread. *It's too bad she won't see this baby grow up.*

There are times, like when Momma miscarried and when Paulie drowned, that some sixth sense offers me information. It's not an ability to predict the future but more a perceptive knowing, an instinct that seems best followed. In childhood I had been taught to willfully conjure false innocence, to hide the truths I couldn't bear as easily as if I was playing hide-and-seek. I had learned this skill from one who was expert in it—Momma. Fearful of their power, I had pushed those inner proddings into the shadows. Back then, it felt necessary for my survival.

It had been years since I'd received a flash like those that had illuminated Momma's role in her miscarriage and the certain knowledge that my brother had drowned. Now that insistent wisdom was here again, showing me all too clearly what I didn't want to see. Maybe there was something about being up at the lake that made it happen, I mused, trying to figure the phenomenon out. I tried by sheer resolve and magical thinking to make things turn out the way I wished them to, shoving aside that unbidden first response to Mary Grace's news. Before I could trust myself to speak without betraying my alarm, though, she said, "I wanted you to be the first to know. I haven't even told Brad yet."

"Really?" It seemed odd, yet part of me was thrilled that Mary Grace had confided in me even before her husband. I appreciated the honor.

"I'll tell him in the morning but, you know, it's kind of a *Red Tent* thing. You and I have shared all the feminine initiations," Mary Grace said, rationalizing her decision. "You were the first to know when I got my period. *And* when I lost my virginity. It just felt right to tell you before anyone else."

I detected vulnerability in the words, which surprised me. The day we met, Mary Grace had leapt over the coffin stair with wild abandon. I hadn't been able to jump in that same carefree way but she hadn't teased me about my lack of courage. Instead she'd grabbed my hand and made me her friend then walked with me through everything that followed. I thought of Mary Grace as the strong one, the one who knew what she wanted and went out and got it. As much as I loved my best friend, I also envied her this ability.

Mary Grace and I hadn't seen each other since she'd been home last Christmas, but we'd talked on the phone almost daily through the tumult of the last two years. She was as much counselor and sounding board as friend, listening to all my doubts and worries about my stalled life. I had joked once that she ought to bill me like she did her clients. She had encouraged me to put my downfall in nursing school behind me and take the doula training as Ruby suggested.

She had also been prodding me to move out of my parents' house. For several months I'd been looking through the real estate ads for places to rent in Chicago. No matter how cheery and welcoming the photos, I couldn't see myself living in any of them. Now I suddenly knew why. I wasn't supposed to be in Chicago anymore.

As I sat up, understanding brought another image: I saw myself standing at a grave, weeping. I shuddered and nearly cried out, almost dropped the phone. But I swallowed the awful foreboding back down, wishing for innocence as I had that summer I was twelve. I couldn't share what I was seeing with Mary Grace. I could only pray that I was wrong. I looked up at the sky again. The full moon shone down upon the water, casting a luminous path from the edge of the pier where I sat as far as I could see across the water, as if it spanned the width of the lake all the way to the other side. That's when something else occurred to me: my visions of Momma and Paulie had come *after* the fact. Mary Grace was still in the first trimester. She'd already heard the baby's heartbeat. So far everything seemed okay. Maybe if I was there to help I could change the vision, bring about a better outcome than what I'd just seen.

"Caro?" Mary Grace's voice pulled me from my reverie. "Did you fall asleep?"

"I'm here. But this is one heck of a way for you to get me to move to Milwaukee, MG." I struggled to keep my tone light. "I guess I'd better get packing. I wouldn't miss your big day for anything." What I didn't say was that I was coming because for the first time in our lives, she was going to need me.

Nine

I'm not afraid to die. It's living that scares me. The enormity of making my way through the world sometimes overwhelms me to where I just want to stay in bed. I'm afraid I'll trip myself up in some awful way, make an error that will cost me so dearly I'll wish I was dead for the sheer relief of it. Although I made the decision to relocate in what felt like an instant, it was a choice that had been growing inside me for a while. I'd been waiting for something, some signal that it was time to leave home. Despite my fear and the disturbing images that had accompanied Mary Grace's announcement, moving to Milwaukee felt like the right thing to do. Especially if by being there I might keep her baby safe.

A couple weeks later I packed up my car, said good-bye to my parents and drove the other way around the lake, to Wisconsin. I had some money saved from all the years I'd lived at home and decided that if I bought instead of rented I'd be less likely to give up and leave if I got spooked. In the meantime, Mary Grace had invited me to stay with her and Brad.

As I turned into the subdivision where Mary Grace and Brad had bought a new home last spring I gasped at the manicured grounds studded with opulent mansions. I thought I might instinctively know which house was MG's the minute I pulled onto her street, but looking at the mammoth façades, I couldn't place my best friend in any of them.

Then there she was, standing on the drive of the grandest one of all. Modeled after an Italian villa, the house reigned at the end of its cul-de-sac on a rise that set it above its neighbors. It spanned the entire width of the lot, impressive in its vastness. My first thought was that even counting baby, the building was obscenely large for its small number of occupants.

Mary Grace looked as if she had been born into all that wealth. Her hair was dyed now and not as white-blond as it had been in childhood, but the buttery color suited her fair skin. Its layers framed her face and softened the tight features that had a tendency to appear drawn when she was stressed. I recalled her at twelve standing next to me on the stairs, the scrappy tomboy who'd rarely shown fear. Today that same girl peered out from her grown-up face, poised on the cusp of a big adventure. The mixture of hope and wary anticipation filling her eyes nearly made me cry. Motherhood was such a gargantuan and life-changing undertaking. It was a miracle any woman found the courage to enter into it.

"You planning to hatch a dozen chickies to fill this fancy roost you've got here?" I adopted a wry wit in the arresting faux-Tuscany environment as I got out of the car and walked toward Mary Grace.

MG smiled wanly, her face pallid. "I thought I'd go for something drastically different from how I grew up. Maybe I'll have a baker's dozen. We've got the room," she quipped back.

As if she too was reminded of how much we meant to one another, her expression shifted to gratitude. "You're here." The long, tight hug she gave me was reassuring. "And you're staying. I'm thrilled." So was I. She was still MG, despite the set change.

"Still feeling pukey?" It was so good to see her. I was giddy as a little kid but too embarrassed to say so.

She nodded. "C'mon inside. I'll give you the nickel tour, though we might have to detour to the bathroom if Bean here doesn't approve of my lunch choice and sends it back up." She patted her midriff, the swell there nearly imperceptible. She was fourteen weeks but she'd been so ill throughout the first trimester that she had lost instead of gained weight.

"Geez, MG, your figure hasn't changed a bit yet." I walked around her, exaggerating my admiration because I knew it would make her feel good.

"I'm so bloated! I feel like a water balloon. I can't imagine how it will be when the baby's bigger." The satisfaction lighting her face told me she was taking it all in stride.

"Thank God for stretchy waistbands," I joked.

MG hooked a finger in one belt loop of the skinny jeans she was still able to fit into and pulled the pants away from her body. She grimaced at the small amount of give in the denim. "Just promise me I won't have to wear elastic forever." Nice clothing had always been one of MG's splurges, something she considered closer to a necessity than an indulgence. Even back in high school, after her parents had divorced and she'd had to shop the thrift stores, MG had always managed to keep herself in designer labels.

We walked inside, elbows hooked together like we used to do as kids. She ushered me down a cavernous hall to the living room. The house boasted marble floors, cathedral ceilings, and a sweeping circular staircase leading to a balcony that overlooked the current home trend, the great room. MG motioned for me to have a seat on an overstuffed leather couch flanked by antique end tables replete with expensive-looking knickknacks. The couch swallowed me up. The seat was so deep my feet came off the floor, dangled midair. MG stood in front of me, bottom lip jutting as she blew a stream of breath toward some strands of hair falling past her forehead and into her eyes.

"You ever hear of women getting hot flashes during pregnancy?" She fanned at her face with one hand, then unbuttoned the sweater she had on over a turtleneck.

"Hormones." I rolled my eyes. "Aren't they great?"

MG pouted. "It seems fundamentally unfair that not only do I have to endure the humiliations of pregnancy, like tossing my cookies every two minutes, I have to put up with menopause symptoms too." She loosed the last button of her sweater, slipped her arms out, and flung the garment over a wingback chair as if it had offended her. "You should see my sheets most nights. Totally soaked."

"Well, it looks like there have also been some perks to this pregnancy." I directed my observation pointedly at MG's chest. Her breasts were twice their usual size.

MG looked down. "Actually," she said slowly, "these aren't from the baby. Not entirely. Brad gave me an augmentation for my birthday in April." Mary Grace had the decency to let a fleeting glance of guilt slip in my direction. For most of our lives we had talked every day, but she'd never even mentioned the surgery to me.

"He gave you a *boob job*? Whose birthday was it, yours or his?" I scooted forward, battling the overstuffed cushion for purchase until my feet touched the floor again.

Annoyance passed over MG's pretty features. She straightened a little taller, looked down at me. "I've wanted one for a long time." The words were defensive and I wondered which one of us she needed to convince. "I've always felt self-conscious because I was only an A-cup. We both thought I'd look better with a little more. I'm happy we did it." She was speaking about herself and Brad as one entity, which might have seemed sweet in other circumstances but felt creepy since the subject was her body.

"You never told me you didn't like your boobs." I was testing the waters. Were fluctuating hormones making her sensitive, or was it the topic itself? "You used to say you were glad you didn't have big breasts since it meant you hardly ever had to wear a bra."

"Well these days I'm enjoying all the sexy push-ups that show off my cleavage." Indignation fired in her eyes. "And my husband really appreciates them." She was still standing before me. Now she rested her hands on her hips. There was a barely cloaked insult in her words.

All the joy of our reunion evaporated. I looked around the room again, seeking something familiar to reconnect me to my friend. But like the furniture, even the photos were all new, shots of her and Brad from their wedding and honeymoon a couple years ago. I thought of Samantha, my little sister. We were very different personalities and the two of us often disagreed about things. But we were family. No matter how opposed we might have been in our views, we knew we'd forever have one another's backs. MG had always felt like something even better than a sister to me. Beyond familial devotion, we *liked* one another. We shared similar beliefs about the world. We could be ourselves with each other and feel understood, accepted. But suddenly I wasn't sure I knew the woman standing before me.

The awkwardness between MG and me was interrupted by the doorbell. Without another word she turned to answer it. When she returned, a well-built man followed. He wasn't much taller than MG but he had a presence to him that piqued my interest. He took in the room as if inspecting it, sweeping his gaze from one end to the other.

"You still happy in your dream castle, Rapunzel?" He was watching MG intently through eyes as dark as his black hair.

She rolled her eyes at him, then gestured toward a wingback chair. "Sit, Ollie," she commanded. "And behave yourself," she added.

Then she turned to me. "I promise his bark is way worse than his bite." MG shot me a smile I hoped meant the issue of her boob job was forgiven and forgotten.

The man pitched forward from his chair and thrust out a hand. "Oliver Andrews." Earlier, Mary Grace had described her college friend to me as "metrosexual," and now I knew exactly what she meant. He was dressed in a patterned dress shirt, tailored pants and Italian loafers. And he was clean-shaven, even though it was a Saturday.

"Ollie's the best Realtor in Milwaukee," Mary Grace said. "He has this incredible way of finding people the perfect house. He found this one for me and Brad." Mary Grace seemed to think this was proof positive of Oliver's skills. I was unconvinced but not about to disagree.

Oliver grimaced. "I'll try to live up to the impossible reputation that precedes me." He checked his watch, then stood up. "You guys ready to go?"

"Actually," Mary Grace said, stifling a yawn, "I've had some things come up that I need to take care of. You two will be fine on your own." It wasn't a question, and I wondered whether she was begging off because of our disagreement. I let it go. If she was mad at me, she'd tell me soon enough.

Oliver shrugged. "Fine with me. Ready then, Caro? We can take my car."

"See you for dinner." Mary Grace draped her arms around my neck, gave me a brief squeeze. I looked for some sign that staying home was her way of saying she was angry, but she seemed fine. "Brad will be back so we'll go out for something or other." She held open the front door and watched from the entryway as Oliver led me toward his Mercedes.

He took me to Steam, a local coffee shop with all the grunginess Starbucks lacked. It was sandwiched between a bookstore and a maternity clothing store quaintly called Pickles and Ice Cream.

"Do you mind if I pop in there for just a minute?" I asked Oliver as we walked through the parking lot. "I want to see if they'll let me leave some of my business cards. It would be a great way to get clients."

Oliver nodded. "Take your time. I'll go in and find us a table."

Once I joined him in the coffeehouse we discovered we both liked complicated drinks. Oliver winked sardonically when I followed up his order for a half-caf extra-wet cappuccino with my own for a triple-shot two-Splenda skinny one-pump peppermint mocha. Right then I knew we were going to be friends.

He had found us a table near the back, out of the throngs of folks spending their Saturdays behind newspapers and laptops. The fall semester was just under way and students from the U seemed intent on starting off strong. Oliver pulled out my chair for me, then went around to the other side of the small table and set down a thick blue spiral binder that he'd pulled out of his briefcase. The words "Carolyn Connors's Home" were printed across the front in huge letters, as if they were the title of a book.

I leaned forward to get a closer look but saw nothing more to explain what that declaration meant.

"I'm not sure how much Mary Grace told you about what I do," Oliver said. I shook my head, indicating that she hadn't told me much, and he continued. "I'm interested in more than just helping my clients purchase houses." Oliver tapped the binder with one finger. "I consider myself a 'holistic' Realtor."

My worry over appearing stupid for not understanding the term must have shown. But Oliver's earnest explanation was heartening.

"What that means is that I believe people need a true home, something more than just a roof over their heads or a place where they store their stuff. That's where this comes in." He leaned back in his chair, then reached out and tapped the binder again. "This is all the information I took down when we did our phone consult. You probably thought it was a little nutty, all those questions about what you like to do for fun, your birthday and your astrological sign." He shrugged, then looked at me hard, and I saw that he wanted me to know he took his business seriously. "I take all that information and I match it against the houses up for sale. In here are the ones most likely to help you feel like you're living at your best. I won't let you settle for anything less."

I nodded eagerly to show Oliver I appreciated his fervor. He was staring at me in that same intent way he had looked at Mary Grace earlier. His eyes were piercing. My cheeks flushed hot and I fought the impulse to look away, hide.

"See, Caro, to me there's just no point in living somewhere that doesn't feel beautiful to you, doesn't offer inspiration. It's about so much more than just square footage or the number of bedrooms and bathrooms. It's about living with a kind of . . . standard of excellence." Oliver frowned, shifted in his chair again, moved in nearer. I caught a whiff of cologne, something woodsy but subtle. "The place you buy ought to speak to you. It should feel like a *sanctuary* . . ." His voice trailed off and he shook his head in frustration. It seemed crucial to him that I understand the importance of his philosophy toward home buying. He needn't have worried: I hadn't given the concept any thought before he'd mentioned it but I was already in agreement with everything Oliver had said.

A very pregnant woman carrying a Pickles and Ice Cream bag passed on her way to the restroom. I laughed inwardly. Some stereotypes were true; the one about pregnant women being perpetually in need of a bathroom was one of them. She was so full of baby that I guessed this was a second child, maybe even her third or fourth. The ligaments that hold the uterus in place stretch more with consecutive pregnancies. This baby jutted out a good foot in front of its mama. The top half of the woman's body was still slender but her hips had broadened to accommodate her tenant. They swayed as she moved, not quite waddling but sashaying, reminiscent of a dance. The deep purple of her maternity dress was a beautiful backdrop to her thick, long brown hair and olive skin, but what came to mind when I first caught sight of her was an eggplant. The harried expression on her face seemed to say she knew there was nothing to be done to improve her appearance until after she delivered.

"Mary Grace mentioned you were her best friend growing up."

I turned my attention back toward Oliver as the very-soon-to-be mother turned sideways to maneuver her belly through the bathroom door. The woman reminded me of MG's news and I almost told Oliver how excited I was about it but caught myself, recalling that MG didn't plan to announce her pregnancy until after she made it safely through the first trimester. Besides, the news was hers to share, not mine.

"We met in third grade. You guys went to college together, right?"

Oliver looked around the coffeehouse. "Yep. I grew up near here, figured I'd go to the U like most of my friends. Then I dropped out and went traveling for a while."

"Why did you come back?" I was curious to hear what might convince someone to return once they'd left their hometown.

"Good question. I hoped there might be something waiting for me." I wondered what, but since he didn't offer I didn't want to pry. I could always ask MG about it later.

Oliver shrugged. "I was wrong. But then I got into real estate and it was easy here because I knew a lot of folks, so . . ." He lifted both hands in the air, palms faceup. "Here I am. Still. After all these years."

"I know what you mean. It's easy to get stuck somewhere because it's comfortable. Familiar."

"Say more." Those dark eyes fixed on me. Oliver looked genuinely interested, so I went on.

"The last couple years were so tumultuous I became kind of a recluse." It was the first time I'd talked with anyone besides MG about the trouble I'd faced. Voicing it brought jitters. "I was caught in the web of my family and at the same time lost, like I was wandering through my life instead of living it." I stopped, afraid I had said too much. There was something about Oliver's demeanor, the quiet way he listened and let a few seconds pass before answering, that felt like the kind of refuge he had described when talking about homes. I felt so comfortable in the coffeehouse with him, and for a crazy fleeting moment I longed to stay there forever.

"Sometimes life can feel more like things happen *to* us instead of us choosing them." The words were careful, as if Oliver was feeling me out. Then his expression brightened into a wicked grin. "I call that my 'shit happens' theory."

We shared a laugh, but then I grew serious again. "Do you really think it's all random, the stuff that happens to us?" I sounded plaintive, but I couldn't help it. For months now I'd been grappling with wonder, trying to discern whether what had occurred in nursing school was a freak accident or something I had brought upon myself. At first the thought that it might have been outside my control was a comfort, but then it made me feel so vulnerable. If life was a string of chance occurrences, how could I ever make something meaningful of it?

I must have looked as disturbed as I felt because Oliver reached over and laid his hand on mine. The humor was gone from his face, replaced with a sober thoughtfulness. "I don't know." He looked pained at the admission. "I go back and forth between wanting to believe there's a rhyme and reason to it all, then thinking that all that does is make me crazy. Sometimes it seems like other people have some magic formula, some way of knowing what they want and making it happen. But that's never been true for me." He shrugged, and I could tell he was revisiting some past disappointment. "There have been things I've wanted, things I've thought I needed to be happy, that haven't turned out the way I thought they would. When that happens, if you don't make some kind of peace with them, those things eat you up."

Oliver and I looked and looked at each other across the table. Tears welled in my eyes, not from sadness but from relief. Mary Grace had been a good friend, but even her patience at my lack of initiative had been wearing thin before I decided to move. Oliver didn't pretend to ignore my crying. He reached one finger out and caught a teardrop as it spilled over and rolled down my cheek. I gave an embarrassed laugh and he smiled, and I saw he was in it with me; he understood and wasn't going to look away. We sat there awhile longer and when I finally dropped my gaze to search out a Kleenex in my purse, he lightened the conversation.

"You work as a midwife, right?"

I shook my head no. Most people had no idea what a doula did, so I had a spiel down from lots of practice giving it. "Basically, I act as a mother to the mother. To the entire family, actually. I offer emotional support. I take care of them."

Oliver's blank look told me he'd never attended a birth and had no clue about what went on at one.

"I teach the dad comfort measures—how to give massage and apply counterpressure to the mother's back when she's having contractions. Or if the dad can't be there for some reason, I do them myself. I also help expectant parents get information about the choices they might have to make at the birth for things like inducing labor, epidurals and C-sections." Oliver looked taken aback at the terms that had become so familiar to me, and I giggled.

"So you get to be there to see the baby the second it arrives, huh? Did you always know this was what you wanted to do?" Oliver sounded impressed, and I thought that surely his authentic interest in others had helped him make a sale on more than one house.

"First I followed in my mother's footsteps and went to nursing school." I nearly stopped there but Oliver leaned in closer as if he wanted to hear more. "I lasted until nearly the end of my second year but nursing seemed less about caring for patients than filling in endless medication logs and insurance forms. So I dropped out." That wasn't the truth, but despite his obvious warmth and depth I wasn't ready to tell Oliver about what had happened. Instead I avoided his inquiring eyes, looked around the coffeehouse. I was searching for the woman who'd gone into the bathroom. I'd developed a kind of radar that tuned into pregnant women around me, but I must have been so engrossed in talking to Oliver that she'd walked past again without my noticing.

I returned to our conversation. "You could call me something of a late bloomer." I mimicked the shrug I'd seen Oliver give when he was talking about his travels and what had brought him back to Milwaukee. "The last two years really have been crazy. Once I gave up on nursing school I got stuck in this weird limbo. I wasn't sure what to do next." Just speaking about it brought back the pain of feeling caught in a protracted adolescence. "I spent all last summer sitting on the pier at our cottage in Michigan trying to figure out who I was, who I wanted to be. I wanted to help people, so I became a birth coach." I thought of Ruby and our chat about working as a doula. I kept the things she had given me, the healer statue and the Queen of Pentacles card, in my birth bag now. I liked feeling that they kept Ruby near to me while I was helping at a birth.

"Anyway, I've been talking a mile a minute about me." I didn't want Oliver to think I was self-centered. He was so easy to talk to that I'd gone on and on. "I can't believe we've both known MG so long and we've never met before. Were you at her wedding? I was maid of honor so I was kind of busy most of the night." If Oliver had been there, I hoped he wasn't insulted that I didn't remember.

A shadow passed over Oliver's face. It was similar to the expression I'd noticed when I had asked what had brought him back to Milwaukee, but this one was more pronounced. It was only there a moment, replaced the next with that same even look he'd given when MG had announced she wasn't coming with us.

"I couldn't make it." He didn't offer a reason but I knew that there was one and that he didn't want to share it. He picked the blue binder up from the table. He flipped it open and was about to draw my attention to the houses we were going to see when someone else diverted me not only from asking more about his personal life but away from Oliver entirely. I hadn't missed the pregnant woman who'd gone to use the bathroom. She'd been in there all this time.

Ten

Now she was standing just outside it, looking around wild-eyed. Below the bulge of her belly her dress was soaked through. Our brains are wired to make associations between events, perhaps to aid us in understanding what's happening. My eyes registered the drenched fabric clinging to the woman's thighs and my mind jumped to the hem of Momma's white nightgown, crimson seeping through gauzy cotton. But I didn't have time to revisit that right now. This woman wasn't bleeding. Nor had she wet her pants. Her water had broken.

She was carrying really low. In utero, where babies sit is measured on a scale from -2, high under their mother's ribs, to +2 when the head is crowning. 0 is at mom's navel. I estimated this baby's "station" at +1. When the baby moves down the birth canal to +2, it's time to push.

I guessed that the pressure of the baby's head had burst the amniotic sac when the woman squatted to use the toilet. If it hasn't already begun, a broken bag usually means labor is imminent. With a first-time mom that's not necessarily cause to get too excited; it can be hours, sometimes even days, before things progress and the baby is born. But given the gargantuan size of this woman's belly and the position of the baby, I feared she was going to give birth right there in Steam. She winced. My own body twinged in sympathy as she struggled toward the nearest chair, clutched its back with both hands and waited for the contraction to subside.

"Take a look—"

I held up a hand, interrupting Oliver as he tried to show me the binder he'd brought. "Be right back." I crossed the few feet between me and the woman, leaned in close to her from one side. "How many contractions have you had since you went into the bathroom?" I adopted my professional persona, keeping my voice low, calm.

She looked up at me, gratitude shining in her eyes along with tears. "A few," she murmured. "But they're coming faster now. I didn't get a break at all between the last two—" She leaned forward as another one hit, letting the chair take most of her weight.

"My name is Caro and I'm a birth coach." I used the more modern term so I didn't have to waste time explaining if she didn't know what a doula was. I looked around the café but no one other than Oliver, who was still seated at our table, mouth agape, seemed to be paying us attention. "Is someone here with you?"

"No, no." A little gasp escaped her lips and she held up a finger, gesturing for me to wait a moment. When she could speak again she said, "My husband took our son to his soccer game this morning. They're supposed to meet me here for lunch. We thought we'd sneak in some family time before the baby came. But we didn't think it was going to come *today*. I'm not due for another two weeks."

"Well, like most of them, this one's on its own schedule." I hoped the joke might help her feel less anxious. She smiled but it turned to a grimace as another pain hit. I did a quick calculation in my mind. We'd only been talking a couple of minutes and she'd already had four contractions. "I think we should get you to the hospital." I spoke as neutrally as I could. "It doesn't seem wise to wait for your husband any longer."

Her eyes widened. "Do you think something's wrong?" Her voice pitched a notch higher and I hastened to assure her everything was probably fine but her labor seemed to be moving along rapidly.

"Oh yes," she agreed. "I think it's definitely my birth time. But I want to go to the birth center, not to a hospital." She sounded adamant.

"Right," I said, regretting my assumption. I'd only assisted at hospital births; Chicago didn't have any freestanding birth centers. Obviously things were different here in Milwaukee. "My friend can drive you." I pointed at Oliver. "Can you walk out to the car if I help?"

The woman nodded and I took her arm, let her use me as a replacement for the chair as we shuffled toward the exit. Without anything more than a nod of my head, Oliver caught on to what was happening. He shot up out of his seat and swept the binder into his briefcase. "I'll pull up out front," he muttered as he passed by.

By the time we made it outside Oliver was waiting, the back door of his Mercedes wide open. An old blanket was spread out over the backseat. He was so fastidious that it must have been killing him to think his leather seats might get stained with bodily fluids, and I silently thanked him for not pitching a fit about it. I helped the woman, whose name I still didn't know, climb in. Then I went around to the other side and got in next to her, leaving Oliver to play impromptu chauffeur to two women he'd never met before that day, one of whom was in active labor.

Eleven

B esides an ambulance driver, if there's anyone you want driving to the place you're going to give birth, it's a Realtor. From his years of taking clients to view houses, Oliver knew all the streets and neighborhoods of Milwaukee well, even those in the suburbs. He got us to BirthRight Family Birth Center with just the address alone, despite the fact that the place was down an unmarked farm-to-market dirt road.

After alerting her husband to meet us at the center, I tried to help my spur-of-the-moment client manage her contractions. In the brief moments between them, I asked how her first labor had gone.

"Geoffrey came early, too. There was a full moon and I guess that old wives' tale about the tides pulling on women's bodies is true. I was so excited that I didn't have to wait until my due date, or after." She smiled at the recollection. Then she looked over at me. "I'm Lana." She introduced herself as if she had just remembered we were strangers. "Lana Reed. I'm really sorry to interrupt your coffee."

I caught the laugh before it escaped my mouth but had to stifle another one when I saw Oliver's disbelief in the rearview mirror. Women in labor could be really funny. During contractions they drew deep inside themselves, engrossed in the process of moving the baby down and out. But sometimes they'd get a break and their personalities would surface again. Then they'd make small talk, as if they didn't want to seem impolite or appear to be ignoring their hostess duties.

I assured Lana that she had in no way ruined plans that couldn't be rescheduled. We chatted for a few more minutes, and I began to wonder whether her labor was stalling. But as we pulled into a driveway marked by a large wooden sign announcing that we'd reached the birth center, the contractions picked up again. We rode during the last little bit of the trip in silence as she concentrated and I rubbed her neck and shoulders.

I had the car door open before Oliver came to a complete stop. I was helping Lana negotiate her way through the white picket fence and up to the porch of a cheery yellow Victorian house when the front door opened. The black woman who stepped out was easily six foot two, not fat but muscled, sturdy, with shoulders meant for a linebacker. Her gray and black cornrowed hair was pulled back into a ponytail that fell between her shoulder blades. As we approached I saw she had a hair band in her hand, along with a brush. I had called the birth center en route and its owner, midwife Deirdre Moore, was ready and waiting.

We paused on the wide verandah to let another contraction pass. Afterward, Deirdre stepped behind Lana and gently pulled the hair back from her face. "There now, love, that's the first thing we can do to make you a bit more comfortable," she soothed. "Your little one's decided today's the day, eh? Well then, we'd best get on with it." I looked up in surprise at the Irish brogue that tinged her words, dulled a little by the flat tones of the Midwest but still strong.

Deirdre walked around to the side opposite from where I was still offering Lana support to stay upright. We helped her into the waiting area, then up a long flight of stairs, stopping twice for contractions. Deirdre guided us into the first of three bedrooms, each appointed with beautiful antique furniture. I spied enormous four-poster beds through the open doorways, along with ornate armoires, rocking chairs, fireplaces. Pleasant and inviting, the center felt more like a country inn than a place to have a baby. Deirdre told Lana she would give her a moment to change out of her wet dress and into the maternity sweats and T-shirt arranged on the bed, then came back out to where I was standing in the hallway and shut the door. She looked at me expectantly.

"Carolyn Connors." I held out my hand and she clasped it in both of hers, which were as large as a man's. "I'm a doula. I just happened to be in the coffee shop when Lana's water broke. I'm visiting from Chicago." The words spilled out of me. I didn't want this formidable woman to think I'd intentionally treaded on her territory. Deirdre arched an eyebrow.

I continued, unnerved. "Your patient's definitely in active labor. She's been contracting every few minutes since we left the coffee place, which was twenty, maybe thirty minutes ago now." I was speaking too fast but I hoped that if I sounded like I knew what I was talking about Deirdre would stop inspecting me with that dubious raised brow.

She seemed to make up her mind about something. "Perhaps you could use her first name instead of referring to my client as a 'patient.'" Heat filled my cheeks even though her tone hadn't been unfriendly. Deirdre walked over to a large cabinet on the other side of the hall, started gathering linens from it. She brought a pile of folded towels to me, plopped them into my arms and started to turn away again, then stopped. Her expression softened.

"Look around you, love." She swept an arm out wide. "What do you see? Hospital beds, IV poles, noisy monitors?" She shook her head. "Here we have a different approach. I like to call it a 'womb with a view.'" Impish delight lit Deirdre's eyes, matching the wide grin on her lips.

"Words are as important as environment," she explained. " 'Patient,' for example." She shook her head again, exasperated. "It has a terrible connotation. The woman's not sick, for God's sake, she's going to have a baby! And she's strong enough to do it, especially if we encourage her with words that help her believe in herself."

I bowed my head, feeling chastened but not berated. When I looked up again Deirdre's expression had turned thoughtful. "How long have you been serving at births?"

I'd never heard my job described as service but I liked the way it sounded. "Only about a year, but I've done—er, *served* at nine so far." I tried to sound confident yet appropriately humble, since

I was in the company of someone who had obviously been doing this a lot longer.

Deirdre sighed. "And you've never served one outside of a hospital, have you?" The words weren't so much a challenge as a resigned declaration. "Right then." She pursed her lips, heaped more towels onto the pile in my arms. "Come on, this might as well be your first introduction to the way it's been done for thousands of years. My assistant Jane is on her way but Lord knows if she'll get here in time. You can put yourself to good use tending to Mom while I coax the wee one out." She knocked sharply on the bedroom door, then opened it and went in to see to Lana.

I quickly made my way downstairs and filled Oliver in. "I'm going to stay and help. I'll call you later when I'm finished. And thanks so much for driving," I added.

He nodded. "I'll go into the office and see about rescheduling our appointments for tomorrow." I had forgotten all about our plans to tour houses. I must have looked alarmed, because Oliver laid a hand on my arm. "It's fine," he assured me. "You go do your job and I'll do mine. Yours can't wait."

Twelve

With the exception of the scrubs Deirdre wore, the birth center bore little resemblance to the hospitals where I'd attended births in the past. Instead of harsh fluorescent overhead lights, Lana's birthing room had a dimmer switch, which cast a soft glow over the room. It also had windows, so I could track the time as afternoon faded into dusk. I remembered Deirdre's remark about a womb with a view and chuckled. She had certainly created a lovely space. A large portable tub took up one corner of the room. Deirdre was filling it with warm water via a hose hooked up to the bathroom sink. When I caught sight of it, the tub took me back to the bathroom at the lake and I held my breath, fearful that another image would inform me of something awful about to happen. But the memory faded and I exhaled, grateful at its passage.

"I'm so glad you're still here." Lana smiled up at me from where she was sitting on a birth ball near the fireplace, tired but in good spirits. A shy look crossed her features. "I feel like you're some kind of guardian angel or something. What are the odds I'd find a doula in a coffee shop?" Then her expression grew worried. "Please don't leave. I think you're supposed to be here for the whole thing. Do you mind?"

I was glad she wanted me there, and I promised I'd stay until the baby came. That reassurance, along with the arrival of her husband, Jack, seemed to settle her. She quickly progressed. The pressure waves grew even stronger. Deirdre's assistant arrived and I watched as Jane encouraged Lana to make good use of her uterus's efforts by squatting down and grabbing hold of one of the posts of the giant bed. Squatting shortens the cervix by as much as a third, and in that position pressure from the baby's head can dilate it faster. The giant four-poster bed served as more than just pretty décor; the idea of gripping the bedpost was ingenious because Lana didn't have to hold her own weight.

It was nearing eight o'clock when Lana looked up at Deirdre and said, "I'm not sure I can take any more." Her excited chatter between contractions had turned to moans and sighs, occasionally even screams as the sensations built inside her. She refused to eat any more of the protein bars and melon cubes Deirdre had me offer her and took only small sips of apple juice and water to keep her strength up. She vomited a couple of times as her body tried to empty itself of everything, especially the baby. Jack and I encouraged her, telling her what a wonderful job she was doing and that the baby would soon be here.

Her eyes sought Jack's. He moved his tall, slim frame in to give her a quick hug, whispered in her ear. Deirdre offered to do a pelvic exam and check her. She had only done one since we arrived because the broken bag of waters meant a higher risk of infection. Lana had been dilated to six that first check. I was fairly certain from how she was acting that by now she was well past seven, which marks transition, the last few centimeters of dilation required before pushing.

I helped Lana onto her back on the bed. Deirdre inserted two gloved fingers into Lana's vagina, staring up at the ceiling as if the information she sought was written there instead of inside Lana's womb. "I can feel the baby's head," Deirdre reported. "And I'd say that you're between a seven and an eight, love. Good girl. Just a little bit more and you'll be ready to push."

Lana looked more discouraged than heartened by Deirdre's report. It was progress, but hard-won. And slow. She had already endured eight hours of intense contractions with little amniotic fluid to cushion the pain ripping through her. She had to dilate to ten centimeters before she could start pushing. That might happen in as little as thirty minutes. But it could also take hours. She looked so tired. "I'm afraid I'll be too exhausted to push the baby out," she whimpered.

I remembered a trick another doula had taught me to help

dilation. It seemed like the perfect time to try it, before Lana got too caught up in feeling defeated. I explained what I wanted to do. Lana had her eyes closed but she nodded and rolled off the bed to stand.

"Jack, you stand behind and wait for the next pressure wave," I said.

"Here it comes," Lana moaned.

I moved nearer to the couple, placing Jack's hands around the enormous bowl of Lana's belly. "Lift up and in," I told him. "You won't hurt the baby," I said in response to his questioning look. "You're just helping the head put pressure on the cervix more effectively."

"Ahhhhh." Lana let out a huge sigh as Jack lifted. The pressure wave subsided. She turned and laid her head on Jack's shoulder. "Christ. That hurt like hell. But Little One moved down. I felt it." She ran a hand over her belly. "Let's do it again with the next one." Jack nodded and stroked his goatee, looking pleased to be of some help. Then he stepped behind Lana again. They did four more contractions using the method I had shown them. After the last one, Lana lifted her head up and looked at me. All the fear was gone from her eyes, transformed into the kind of fierce determination that gets a woman through. "I can do this. I'm going to have this baby. Now."

"Then let's get you into the tub, shall we?" Deirdre said. "A bit of warm water might just take the edge off enough for your body to relax and open up." Deirdre topped off the tub with more hot water before helping Lana into it. For a moment I yearned to be pregnant myself, to have Deirdre's competent wisdom guide me through that rite of passage so essential to understanding what it meant to be a mother.

Thirty minutes later, Deirdre plunged an arm into the depths of the tub and felt for the baby's position again. When she pulled her dripping hand back out, she looked at Lana. The room was quiet, anticipation pulsing around us.

"Love, your babe is ready now. The head's already out," the

midwife said. Then Deirdre did something astonishing. Instead of reaching back down and bringing the baby up, Deirdre encouraged Lana to do it herself. "Why don't you just put your hands below and draw your wee bairn to you?" Deirdre's words were husky with emotion.

Lana's eyes filled. She blinked to clear them, gave a little sob as she looked down into the water, saw the thick hair covering the back of her child's head. Then she did as Deirdre had suggested and hooked her index fingers under the baby's armpits, slowly lifting her out and up.

In one fluid motion Sadie Reed moved from the waters of her mother's womb to those in the tub. Triumphant contentment radiated from Lana as she drew Sadie up onto her chest, where the tiny girl nestled and rooted for her first taste of mother's milk. In most hospitals, after a brief snuggle in their mothers' arms babies are whisked over to a warming table to be examined, weighed and measured. I keenly felt my clients' pangs of separation in those moments when their babies were newly out and away from them but had resisted my instinct to speak up against hospital policies. Instead I encouraged the fathers to go place a finger in their newborns' fists so at least they would sense one parent nearby while the OB delivered the placenta and cleaned up. But this approach of immediate skin-to-skin contact between mother and child felt so much more humane.

"We'll just wait until the cord stops pulsing before we cut. That way we're sure this little missy's gotten all her nutrients," Deirdre explained. Jane was busy at the armoire, which contained all the supplies necessary for cutting the umbilical cord and other aftercare. She handed Deirdre a clamp and a pair of surgical scissors.

"Dad, you want to do the honors, don't you?" Deirdre guided Jack on where to cut, then tied off the end of the cord. After Lana expelled the placenta Deirdre inspected it to make sure it was intact, then excused herself to dispose of it.

"We hadn't decided on a middle name." Lana looked shy as I poured warm water down the baby's wrinkly pink back and Lana's deflated stomach. "Is it okay if we give her yours?" She looked up at me with such gratitude that my throat tightened around tears.

"We can't thank you enough," Jack added. "I don't even want to think of what might have happened if you hadn't noticed Lana at Steam. We appreciate all your help." He grabbed me in a gruff bear hug that took my feet right off the floor and we all laughed, slightly hysterical at the close call and how well it had turned out. Then I stepped out of the suite to give them some time alone with their new daughter and went in search of Deirdre.

I found her downstairs in the kitchen, putting soiled linens into a washing machine housed in the walk-in pantry. Something was baking in the oven. It smelled delicious. "You have an incredible place here," I said as I moved into the kitchen. The Reeds had been happy I was there but I had no idea how their midwife felt about my presence.

Deirdre had changed from her scrubs into a flowing white linen tunic and pants that heightened her striking appearance and highlighted the deep tones of her chocolate skin. She was barefoot. She moved competently around the countertop, readying a breakfast tray with a teapot and two cups, two plates, flatware and napkins. "I do." The words weren't arrogant, just matter-of-fact. "It's been a long time in the making." There was a small hint of pride in her voice now.

But I appreciated what a feat BirthRight was. "We don't have anything like this in Chicago. I think there's one midwifery practice that will do home births but no one has a dedicated space like this. You've thought of everything." I had walked through the other two birthing rooms upstairs, both of which had the same tools and supplies as Lana's room. One room even had a hammock in it, although I couldn't imagine anyone in labor wanting to get in it.

"I didn't have to think about it, I just paid attention." Deirdre set me straight as she moved to the oven and removed a pan of steaming egg strata. "Womb service," she quipped, that impish smile brightening her face again.

But then she grew serious. "How many hospitals do you know of that provide mothers with a home-cooked meal after they've birthed? That's what they need then: nutrients to replace all the energy they expended. Just like they need something more than ice chips to keep them going during." Deirdre's words carried an undertone of reproach. She deftly slid a knife through the casserole, used a spatula to place some of it on each of the plates.

Birthing is a topic on which people tend to have very strong opinions. I believed every woman had the right to support for birthing in whatever way she felt was best. From what I had just observed upstairs, I liked and admired Deirdre Moore. But I'd met doulas who refused to work with clients who weren't completely committed to natural childbirth, like those who felt okay about medically inducing if they hadn't gone into labor by the time they reached their due date or who didn't mind having an epidural or a Caesarean section. I wondered about Deirdre's views. I had thought that the center's name stood for every woman's right to choose to birth her child in the way and place she felt best. But perhaps it was meant to imply that birthing anywhere other than there was *wrong*.

Deirdre answered my unspoken musings. "I've been tending to mothers and their little ones since I can remember." She had stopped putting items on the tray and was looking at me. "Way back in Lisdoonvarna, before you were even a twinkle in your father's eye, I daresay. My mother had four while I was still in my teens, so of course I did my part with those. Then the neighborhood midwife needed some help and she taught me what another wisdom-keeper had taught her. That's how I learned. Not in some sterile building run by men, or nowadays women who act like men but don't have the first clue about how to guide a woman through the fiercest rite of passage she'll likely ever encounter." Defiance sparked in her eyes, earned by years of fighting the system.

"Most women in their childbearing time, they don't need much more than someone who's been through it before to tell them everything's okay, encourage them to let their bodies do exactly what they know how to do. The ones who are afraid to feel, who don't really want to experience their power, well, they should be in the hospital. But I want to make sure those who understand that along with their babes they get born in a whole new way themselves have a place for that to happen without someone mucking it up."

I thought about what Deirdre had just shared, her respect for the mystical nature of childbirth. "What if something happens though?" I asked softly.

"It does sometimes." I had expected her to scoff at my concern but she was quick to acknowledge the truth. "I'm careful about the clients I accept here. They have to be low-risk. Even then, sometimes we have to do a transfer. But only three times in twelve years." She sounded proud of her record. "It's good to have OBs who can do emergency C-sections. Thank God for them. But what I can't stand is that most of them have no idea how to let a woman be without meddling. And that's what leads to the majority of those so-called medically necessary procedures. Don't even get me started on the 'mommy makeovers.'"

I cocked my head quizzically.

"Elective Caesarean followed by a tummy tuck." Deirdre's arched brow spoke volumes more than her explanation. She shook her head. "It gets my blood pressure up just thinking about it." She picked up a small pitcher of milk and a pot of honey, added them to the tray. Then she looked at me expectantly, as if waiting for me to ask something else.

I didn't need to know anything more. Deirdre was an extraordinary midwife, a gift to the women she served. Something she had said earlier kept tugging at me. She had helped at her younger siblings' births when she was just a teenager. This reminded me of my own youth, my first experience of the losses particular to womanhood. Standing in the warmth of the birth center's kitchen, I drew upon this connection to Deirdre. I felt so at home. I wanted to move into BirthRight. I couldn't do that, but I could spend more time there. I didn't even have to be pregnant to do so. I just had to garner the courage to ask.

"I came to Milwaukee to look at houses." I forced myself to look at Deirdre. "I'm going to move here. I'd like to work with you. I'd like you to teach me everything you know about taking care of women and their families." Conviction steadied the part of me that was afraid to ask for what I wanted.

Deirdre nodded as if she'd just been waiting for me to ask. "I could use you," she said. "Jane's fabulous, but we've too much to do just tending to the birthing to offer the mothers the kind of comfort you give. And you have the gift."

I frowned, unsure of what she meant.

"You feel as keenly as the mothers do and you aren't afraid to be in it with them. There can be a great cost to that. But the beauty of it is worth any price. You already know that."

She was right. Serving at a birth had the most fulfilling payoff.

"Get yourself moved here and we'll work out the details of when you'll come on with us."

I didn't yet have a place to live in Milwaukee, but I had a job waiting for me. Deirdre reached out and gripped her capable hands around mine with a firm shake that sealed my future.

Thirteen

Jane gave me a ride from the birth center to Mary Grace's around ten that night. Mary Grace had left me a note on the front door saying she was going to bed and that I should make myself at home. I made a cup of tea in the kitchen, then tip-toed through the cavernous house, looking around.

I was seeking more clues about who my friend was these days. It seemed she had a new life as well as a new house. I walked into the formal living room. It was sumptuous but I felt more like I was standing in the Sistine Chapel than in someone's home. I picked up one of the picture frames from an end table. MG and Brad were dressed in formal wear, posed in front of a sunset so flawless I guessed it was painted on a screen. MG wore a sequined gown, her sculpted cleavage front and center. I was studying the picture, trying to make out whether or not MG looked happy in it, when the hair on the back of my neck bristled. I lifted my eyes from the photo. MG's husband was standing alongside the fire-place. He'd entered so quietly that I hadn't heard him, only felt his presence. I nearly dropped the frame as I fumbled to put it back where I'd found it. I felt oddly caught.

"Hello!" I managed to say, my voice as perky as MG's en-hanced breasts.

"Brad Schaeffer," he replied evenly. This threw me off guard. I'd been in his wedding, for God's sake, and here he was, acting like he'd never laid eyes on me before. Completely out of my ele-ment now, I felt the wet of the tea stain on my top; I'd sloshed it on myself walking around. I was wearing a baseball hat, my curly hair sticking out every which way from under it. I looked a mess after the day I'd had. I wanted to hide but there was nowhere to go. Besides, that would have made me look like a total freak.

I had disliked Brad Schaeffer from the first time MG introduced us at their rehearsal dinner. I felt bad about this; I wanted to appreciate some good qualities in the guy with whom I had to share my best friend. But Brad came across as self-absorbed, interested mostly in business opportunities that would make him a lot of money and acquiring things like sports cars and big homes.

I'd been thinking the animosity I felt toward Brad was some character flaw in me. Jealousy, perhaps. But I saw now that my repugnance went beyond simple envy. Brad carried himself with an air of entitlement and power that extended past self-confidence into full-blown arrogance. His eyes were piggish, set deep into the sockets. The brows over them were knit into a permanent disbelieving frown. He was only in his thirties but he already sported the matched set of jowls and beer gut middle-aged men of wealth acquired. I looked everywhere but at his face, refusing to acknowledge his frank stare. My eyes settled on his hands. He'd curled one into a fist, wrapped the other around it. He had ugly fingers. They were stubby, thicker than they were long. Distaste rose from my gut. I shifted my gaze once more, searching for a spot above his head to focus on.

"You a Cubs fan?" The question sounded like an accusation. I must have looked blank, because Brad touched two fingers to his forehead. Right. My cap.

"Born and bred, although my maternal grandmother was always trying to convert me over to the White Sox. She'd probably roll over in her grave if she could see me wearing this hat." My laugh came out more like the bray of a donkey. Brad squinted his tiny eyes even smaller in distaste.

"The Brewers are gonna wipe the field with those FIBs this season." Brad trained his eyes on me, waiting to see what I'd say to that. "FIBs" was short for "Fucking Illinois Bastards," Wisconsinites' nickname for tourists from the neighboring state who came up and wreaked havoc with booze cruises on the lakes and rivers most weekends. Those of us from Illinois had a nickname for Wisconsin natives too, though I didn't think it nearly so offensive: "Cheeseheads."

Brad's stare unnerved me. I was afraid that if I opened my mouth, disgust would make me say something I'd regret. And I was already in a precarious position with MG from the boob comment earlier.

"Well, I had some unexpected excitement today and MG's already in bed, so I think I'll turn in too. Nice to see you again." I felt idiotic talking so formally to my best friend's husband but he had made no effort to put me at ease. I beat a hasty retreat down the hall toward the guest wing, suddenly grateful for the large amount of space separating my quarters from the master bedroom.

A hot shower washed away not only the grime of the day but also the feeling that I'd been slimed by my encounter with Brad. I didn't like him but I was going to have to get along with the guy since I would be helping with MG's birth. I wasn't so sure how long I'd be able to stand living in his house, though. I just hoped that tomorrow Oliver would live up to MG's promise and find me a place I could call my own.

"Quite the excitement yesterday, huh?" Oliver grinned as I got into his car. He had thoughtfully scheduled all our appointments for after noon so I'd been able to sleep in. The blanket was gone from the rear seat. I grinned back. "Did you toss that blanket in the wash when you got home?"

"Wash?" He made a face. "No way, lady. It went right in the trash."

I laughed, then remembered there was something I wanted to share with him. "I've been thinking about what happened in Steam and our conversation about whether or not things happen for a reason. Incidents like that seem too perfect to be mere coincidence." I shot Oliver a look to see if he was going to disagree, then went on before he could. "Maybe that's all they are, but I've decided to look at meeting Lana as the universe's way of dangling a carrot before me, the 'reward,' so to speak, that tells me moving here is the right choice." As I spoke the notion sounded naïve but it was too late to take it back. Besides, it felt true to me. But if Oliver scoffed, I'd be a little hurt.

"Hmmm." He was thinking over what I'd said. "I see what you mean. I'm not sure I buy it . . . I'm kind of a cynic by nature. But if it works for you, run with it. I did manage to get us into all the properties we had scheduled, which can be considered a minor miracle, so maybe that's another sign that you're headed in the right direction."

I flashed him a grateful smile. "You're really earning your commission on this one, aren't you?" I teased.

"I might have to charge you double," he shot back.

Whatever the formula behind his approach, Oliver found me the perfect place. It was the second one we toured. My soon-to-be new home was on the upper floor of a two-story building. I'd have three neighbors around me. Oliver had done some investigating and learned they were all female and mostly around my age.

We stepped into an entryway made bright by the sunlight coming in the living room windows. The unit was spacious, airy. Hardwood floors made it seem bigger than it was. We moved through the kitchen and dining room, Oliver noting aloud quaint features like the original butler's pantry and the vintage glass doorknobs.

When we stepped into the bathroom he pointed out the Jacuzzi.

"I can't stand taking baths." The words were out before I could stop them.

We were standing alongside one another and Oliver caught my eye in the mirror's reflection. "How do you feel about showers?" He gestured toward the spigot above the gleaming tub, watching me.

"Fine," I replied, feeling flustered. "They're fine."

"Good thing. Then it's not a deal breaker."

I was so relieved when he didn't press me for an explanation about my odd comment that I nodded brusquely, then pushed my way past him back out of the bathroom, eager to leave it behind us.

The bedroom had a sliding glass door that opened onto a porch, with stairs leading down into the backyard. I had decided the place was perfect until I stopped in the entryway to the bedroom, saw the door at the far end of the room leading outside.

"Here," Oliver boomed as if he were showing me the pièce de résistance, "is the bedroom porch with access to the garden!" He was trying his best to act as though I should be thrilled but I felt his hesitation as he awaited my reaction.

I stepped toward the door and he slid it open, gesturing for me to walk outside and see the view. It wasn't much of a garden as far as I could tell—just a pile of dried-up tiger lilies wilting along the back fence and a dirty scruff of grass that the listing sheet had optimistically referred to as a "manicured lawn." I looked up at Oliver, who appeared to be holding his breath. I'd told him about my safety issues, how I was used to having lots of people around and that the idea of living alone scared me.

"Oh, Oliver, I don't know . . ." I hated to make a big deal out of one thing but the rear entry door *was* a big deal to me. I stepped back inside and turned around. From the center of the bedroom I could see through the eating area all the way to where the pretty afternoon light streamed in through the front window. The unit was drenched with enough light that right then I couldn't imagine ever feeling afraid there, not even in the middle of the night. But when I turned toward Oliver there was that door, with stairs running from the ground floor to my bedroom. How could I create that sense of refuge Oliver had made seem so possible over the phone?

Oliver's features sagged. He was sweating. He pulled a handkerchief out of his khakis pocket and blotted his forehead. His body had a softness about it that might have made him pudgy if he were any shorter. He wore baggy clothing, as if fearful he might wake up one day having gained fifteen extra pounds. He'd confessed over coffee yesterday that he'd been chubby as a kid and even though he ran several times a week he was self-conscious about his weight. But his form gave off a masculine yet welcoming energy, so inviting I found myself fighting off the urge to ask him for a cuddle.

Oliver looked out the back door again as if hoping that the answer to my housing dilemma might be out there among the wilted lilies. "I know this is the place, Caro, I just know it. The feng shui in here is great. I'm telling you, this is the place. *Your* place."

I looked around the room once more, then decided to trust Oliver's expertise. "Okay," I announced. "I'm sold. When can I move in?" Giddy, I kicked off my shoes and twirled around a few times on my tippy toes like I used to do as a child, the room spinning around me, the walls coming close, then falling away.

" 'Dance, when you're broken open, dance, if you've torn the bandage off . . . ' " Oliver recited as I collapsed into a giggling pile on the floor.

"Rumi!" I trilled, surprised that he knew the mystic Sufi poet well enough to quote him.

Oliver stood above me, arms outstretched. "*The Essential Rumi,*" he corrected me, referring to the title of the popular translation. He reached down and grabbed my hands, helped me to my feet. "Dance naked, if you want to . . ."

He winked and I stumbled, wanting to believe he was still kidding around. But I detected an invitation in his words that lingered in my thoughts long after I closed on the condo and officially moved to Milwaukee to start my life anew.

Fourteen

Less than a month after I went house-hunting I was officially a resident of Milwaukee. Gradually and almost without recognizing it, I eased into a new tranquility and came to believe it had indeed been good fortune to relocate. I left my hometown with five boxes and a kitchen table and chairs that had survived my childhood almost better than I had.

Those early days in Milwaukee I grew lulled into thinking that I had successfully stepped beyond my past. The first week I called Momma daily to reassure her that I was doing fine, but by the end of the third weekend I had only spoken with her once in two weeks. Starting over in a strange city was intense, but I found myself riding waves of disorientation more exhilarating than nerve-wracking. This was something I'd picked up from my doula training, a skill I encouraged my clients to practice. Fear was just a surplus of emotions, an interpretation of energy growing inside you. You could let it wash you away or you could breathe and feel, allow it to build into a thrill that could get you through. That was how I'd come to view labor: as an energy storm. What mattered most for a positive outcome was where in your mind you took shelter.

Yet despite all the good things that had come about with my move persistent tugs from my past, memories of growing up with Momma and the ABCs in a family that had always felt knit together a little too tight, kept pulling at me. In Milwaukee those reminiscences moved through me like contractions, growing stronger despite my best efforts to deny them.

One Saturday shortly after I moved in, someone knocked on my door. "Hi there. I'm your neighbor Helen Palaggi." A petite woman offered me her hand. It was as warm as the look in her eyes. "Welcome to the 'hood." She smiled, and although she had woken me up I couldn't help but return her grin. "I've got bagels and coffee. Want to venture across the hall for some breakfast?"

I had to be at Mary Grace's in an hour and a half. That left me time for a quick bite. "Yes, thanks," I said to Helen. "But do you mind if we make it a pajama party?" I gestured at the robe I had just thrown on over my nightclothes, even though it was after ten. I'd helped Deirdre with another birth yesterday and had slept in this morning.

Helen let us into her place and motioned for me to have a seat in the living room. Something near the front door caught my attention. "You've got a thing for red shoes, huh?" I pointed toward the shoe rack by the entrance. It held several pairs of footwear in styles from loafers to running shoes, all in shades of red.

"They're kind of my trademark. It's a Dorothy thing. Remember *The Wizard of Oz*? I figure if I'm ever in a jam, I can try clicking my heels three times and see if it gets me home." Helen wiggled one foot clad in a red patent Doc Marten. Her hair was short as a boy's, dyed an auburn that reminded me of autumn leaves.

Red was definitely her color, imbued with all the power and creativity Helen exuded. I sensed immediately that Helen took her rightful place in the world. I admired this about her. It reminded me of what I appreciated in Mary Grace. I often felt like a chameleon, changing personas at the whim of those around me. Although I guessed that she was probably the younger of the two of us, I wished I had half as strong a sense of myself as Helen.

I watched as she tore off a piece of bagel, smeared it with cream cheese and popped it in her mouth. "Every once in a while I let myself splurge and eat one of these." She looked like she thought she owed me an explanation. "I work over at Medical City, and every day it's like walking through a field of land mines."

I sipped my coffee, waiting for her to explain.

"Doctors and nurses are some of the unhealthiest people I've ever met. You'd think we would know better." She shrugged, pursed her lips.

"You're a doctor? What kind?"

"No." Helen snorted. "I actually wanted to get to know my patients, so I went the other route. I'm a neonatal intensive care nurse." My regard for my ebullient neighbor grew tenfold. The NICU was a stressful environment with preemies and sick infants, and families worried to death about them. "Yeah, I fell in love with the munchkins when I did my pediatrics rotation in school, so when I graduated I took a job at Children's in Seattle, which is where I'm from. Then this unit director position came open last year, so I moved." Helen seemed so capable and competent it didn't surprise me that she was a manager.

I took another look at my across-the-hall neighbor. I might have shared that I'd gone to nursing school briefly too but decided against it. I didn't feel like getting into what had happened. "I work with families, too," I said. "I'm a doula."

"Wow, that's great! If I didn't work in the NICU, I'd want to be in labor and delivery." Helen's admiration was obvious.

A small burst of pride made me stand a little taller. I was pleased that we had this mutual love of our work in common.

A pretty locket sat framed in the V-neck of Helen's angora sweater. It was a puffy silver heart, with *Hell'n* inscribed across it.

"That's an interesting way to spell your name."

She smiled broadly. "It's my dad's nickname for me. He gave me this." She leaned forward and unlatched the locket's door so I could see the photo of a dark-haired man with a mustache and the same smile Helen wore. "He always says that for me, he'd be willing to go to hell 'n' back.

"And more than one person thinks the spelling fits my personality." She gave a half shrug, a playful glint in her eye. "I drive a Corvette, I have a tattoo, and I like to rock-climb and bungee-jump. I guess they're right." The self-assessment was frank, devoid of apology.

"Do you miss him?" I was thinking of my own father, how far away he seemed since I'd moved. He wasn't much for talking on the phone; if he answered when I called home he'd ask how I was doing, then hand it off to my mother. That's the way it had been in our family as long as I could remember: Momma at the center of everything, binding us all together whether we wanted it that way or not.

Helen's cheery demeanor dimmed. "Every day. My parents were older when they had me, so he's in his eighties already. And he has Alzheimer's. I had to put him in a nursing home. Then I had to take the job here to pay for it." She winced. "It was the hardest thing I've ever done. I hate being so far away from home. But we had some pretty close calls. He wandered away twice. The second time it took the police nearly twenty-four hours to find him. It's an excruciating thing to realize you've reached the point where you have to take care of those who once took care of you." The words rang with a resigned wisdom I sensed Helen was still grappling to accept.

"That's a truth I've been trying to get my head around for years," I said. "My mom and I have kind of a complicated relationship."

Helen looked appreciative and brightened again. She leapt up from the couch and disappeared into her bedroom. I knew we were already friends when she returned a moment later with a small blue pillow in her hands.

"Here. You can take this with you if you want. It says it all."

I looked down at the embroidered fabric. Gold needlepoint letters read, *If it's not one thing, it's your mother.*

Fifteen

I left Helen's and went home to dress for my meeting with MG and Brad. By implicit understanding, neither MG nor I had brought up my role at her birth while I was staying at their house. I'd discovered that most people have very particular preferences about having and raising children. At one time I might have guessed that MG and I would feel similarly about these issues, but after our unexpected tiff over her breast enhancement I was careful to avoid any topics that might turn confrontational. After I moved, I was torn between approaching her and waiting for her to contact me about being their doula. She saved me the worry by calling one day and asking for an appointment for the three of us to discuss their birth plan.

When I arrived, Brad answered the door and motioned for me to follow him to the living room. In the couple weeks I'd stayed with them, he had traveled frequently for work. Mary Grace and I mostly had the place to ourselves. The few nights Brad was home he had been civil to me but never what I'd call friendly. I treated him in a similar manner. More than once I'd caught Mary Grace looking pained as we struggled to make conversation over a meal. Brad usually ate quickly then left to go watch sports on the gigantic TV that dominated the great room.

MG entered the living room carrying a sterling silver tray with three crystal goblets of water. "Caro, Brad is so excited about this baby and about participating in the birth. Isn't that right, honey?" I sensed MG was used to mediating between her husband and other people. Her empathy made MG a phenomenal counselor, but it must have been exhausting to continually run interference in her personal life. A pang of remorse shot through me. It was obvious that MG wanted Brad and me to get along.

"That's terrific." I forced a smile as we all sat down. It was an attempt at a truce. I hadn't ratted on him for acting as if he'd never met me before the day he'd come upon me in his living room a few weeks back. But if Brad noticed my loyalty he didn't let on. Despite his lack of appreciation I gave myself a talking-to. I was there in my professional capacity in addition to as MG's best friend. I had to set aside my emotions and locate the neutral stance I took with my clients when educating them on their birth choices.

"Let's start with what will happen around your due date." I held my checklist and pen in hand, adopting my expert demeanor. "First babies often come late, so you'll need to ask your doctor how far past your date he'll let you go. But in the event he wants to induce you, do you have concerns about that?"

I looked from MG to Brad so he would feel included in the process, but I needn't have worried. He was accustomed to being in charge. Before MG could answer he leaned forward and laid a hand on my thigh, as if staying a pet. "We've hired the best baby doc in the city. We'll follow Stryker's advice." He seemed to believe that if he glared hard enough I would roll over and play dead. "On everything," he added as I started to ask another question.

At a loss, I looked to MG. She had always known what she wanted, what was best for her. It was disconcerting to see her demurring to a man. Before that day, I would have bet MG wanted to have the baby naturally. But that was based on what I knew about the MG I'd grown up with, not this person who, when she was around her husband, seemed more an uncertain girl playing house than a mature woman preparing for motherhood. Did MG truly want this child? Or was it just the next accoutrement on the list, a required collectible to go along with the husband, the house, the lifestyle? I pushed the ugly thought aside.

"What about the delivery? Were you thinking a vaginal birth or a Caesarean section?" I was careful not to make it sound as if I judged one as better than the other.

Brad answered again. "The usual 'out the chute.' But if they need to do a C-section, Stryker's got the plastic surgeon lined up." He turned and stroked MG's cheek. "No scars for this beauty."

Repugnance swept through me. What seemed to concern Brad most was that his "playground" remain intact. "I'm feeling like Brad's the one who is pregnant here." Taking my cue from his casual language, I tried to damp down my revulsion, couch my concerns in a joke.

"Well he is the father, and he wants to be very involved." MG sounded defensive.

"That's great. My job isn't to replace Brad," I backtracked. "I'll be there to coach him about how to help you have an easier time. But ultimately, you're the one who has to get the baby out." I tried to keep my tone light. But I saw the I-told-you-so look Brad gave MG, as if I had just said I'd be the one calling the shots at her birth.

MG frowned at her husband. I feigned ignorance of the building tension. Brad didn't want me at their baby's birth. With any other couple I would have voiced my perception. But when MG wanted to, she had no trouble speaking her mind.

"Honestly, right now it's still hard to imagine what it will be like to be in labor," she said, hedging.

I softened, remembering that there was still a lot of time for her to get her head around the fact that regardless of who was there to help, she was the only one who would give birth to her child. I looked down at the list on my clipboard. "Let's talk about pain relief."

MG's eyes darted to Brad. She seemed to pull into herself, and I realized that she was taking stock, weighing something in her mind. She must have found it necessary to do this often in her marriage, to decide if and how she could bear the cost of accommodating Brad's demands.

Then for the first time since we'd sat down, the MG I knew and loved emerged. She shifted away from Brad and, without waiting for him to give his opinion first, jumped right in. "I'm having the baby naturally. It's okay if it hurts. I know I can have Bean without any drugs." She patted her belly. "I can do it." Her voice carried the conviction that had been missing earlier, the kind a woman in labor needs to make it through natural childbirth.

Brad's perpetual scowl deepened. "I don't want to see you in pain."

I resisted pointing out a second time that since MG was the one who had to endure labor, her needs might be of more concern than his.

"I'm clear about this." MG sounded firm. I looked from her to Brad. There was an opportunity here: If I wanted to get on his good side I'd be smart to tell MG she could always keep the epidural as an option. But after all her deferring to Brad's wishes for everything else, her insistence made it seem even more important that she have the baby naturally. The dread that had surfaced when she called to tell me she was pregnant rose again. I fought it off, finished the interview.

Afterward MG walked me out to my car. We stood on the driveway. She looked as awkward as I felt about what had just taken place. Uncertainty played over her normally serene features, and I resisted the urge to reach out and smooth the furrows from her forehead.

"I know what you're thinking, Caro." When she finally spoke her words were resigned but certain. "But Brad's got a good heart. He really does. He loves me and he's so excited about this baby." She watched me, looking for some sign of judgment, I guessed. "And for someone who grew up without a dad around much, well, it's nice to have a man who provides for me and who will take care of this little one."

I recalled MG as the fierce and fiery young girl she had been near the end of childhood. With her father gone most of the time she had tended to her mother as much as Marilyn did her. I knew all too well the cost to a child charged with raising a parent. Sympathy for the girl MG had been, and in some ways still was, washed through me.

"I need both of you there with me. I don't want you to miss it."

The bald admission, along with the tears dotting her eyes, told me my friend hadn't completely lost herself in her new lifestyle.

I should have felt that our friendship had been redeemed, celebratory over MG's good fortune and pleased to be a part of it. Instead my uneasiness about MG's birth lingered long after we said good-bye. I hugged her hard until we were laughing and crying, Bean enveloped in our embrace. Then I left, hoping we could cradle that baby safely into being on its own in the world.

Sixteen

As fall went on, my life grew into a cornucopia of goodness. Helen's impromptu breakfast invitation turned into a weekly ritual. She introduced me to several women who were labor and delivery nurses and thanks to their referrals I had already served at two births at Medical City, in addition to helping out at Deirdre's.

Oliver and I were also becoming friends. We shared a mutual love for cycling and we met two or three times a week to marvel at the beauty of the rolling autumn countryside, where maple and oak leaves raged in urgent blazes of gold, orange and red before falling away.

One October evening he suggested a route along the lake. Milwaukee was experiencing an Indian summer. Oliver and I rode along for about an hour, hugging the curve of the lakeshore. The temperature was in the mid-eighties, the air thick with humidity. The sunset should have been a beautiful sight, but I was in a melancholy mood. The lake reminded me of Paulie and that awful fall following his death.

Oliver signaled for me to pull over in a small grassy park. He got off his bike and unlatched the clasps on its panniers. We had packed a light picnic dinner. We laid out the blanket and set up the food in silence. Oliver opened two single-serving bottles of chardonnay, then held one out to me.

"Remember wine coolers?" He smirked after taking a swig. "That's what these midget bottles remind me of sometimes."

"All too well." I winced. "MG and I spent more than one weekend hungover from those Blue Hawaiians and Orange Sunsets. We used to sneak them from the coolers the grown-ups brought out on the pontoon boat up at my family's cottage. They had what they called 'booze cruises.'"

"I'm sure you two were quite the pair." Oliver stretched onto his belly and looked out at the lake. He swiped at the sweat on his forehead and temples. "Man, it's hot. I'm tempted to go jump in the lake and cool off but wet spandex is gonna feel gross." He plucked at the edge of his bike shorts, snapped it against his thigh and grimaced. "Of course, I could go in my birthday suit . . ." He turned a wicked grin on me. "Did you guys skinny-dip those summers of sin?"

"Ollie!" I had adopted MG's nickname for him, doing my best to sound offended. Most of the time Oliver came off as a serious sort of person. But every once in a while the rebellious teenager who wanted to see how badly he could shock took over. It was arresting but funny and usually involved some gross sexual reference. I hadn't decided whether it was his way of flirting or just prurient fun.

"Don't tell me you've never skinny-dipped." Oliver pushed himself up onto his elbows and peered at me. "Aw, then we've got to initiate you."

I shook my head. "I don't swim." I looked out at the lake that had forever changed my life. I hadn't been in it since the day my brother drowned.

Ollie scooted nearer to me on the blanket. I was sitting cross-legged and he reached over and lightly tapped me on the knee with his knuckles. "What happened, champ, did your dad scar you for life by throwing you into the deep end?"

"My brother drowned in the lake when he was nine. I was supposed to be keeping an eye on him and he drowned." I brought my hands up, cupped them over my face. I hadn't spoken of Paulie in so long. My parents didn't talk about him and I never wanted to be the one to bring the painful topic up.

"Caro, I'm so sorry." Oliver crawled over and wrapped his arms around me. The intuition I'd had about what it would be like to hug him had been accurate. His arms were warm, his chest solid, his heartbeat a steady reassurance that despite all I had lost, I was still alive and worthy of care.

"You remind me of him in a lot of ways." I hadn't known this before I said it, but it was true. "Paulie was funny and wise. He was an old soul in a little kid's body. It's been twenty years and I still miss him so much." Oliver held me for a while. He stroked my hair and told me again how sorry he was.

"Is that why you can't stand taking baths, because you're afraid you're going to drown?"

I collected myself again and moved back out of Oliver's arms. "No." I barked out a sardonic laugh. "*That* would be related to yet another family tragedy. But one is enough to get into right now."

Oliver looked thoughtful. "I can respect that. But you could have relocated to the mountains or the desert. Yet here you are, still near the lake, even if you won't go in it. Maybe it's time for you to reframe what it means to you. Water doesn't just cause harm. It keeps us alive too."

We'd been sitting there so long the light was beginning to leave the sky. We would have to use our headlights for the ride home. But I could still make out Oliver's features well enough to see he wasn't just suggesting that after so many years I should get over my grief. "Ollie, how do you know so much about loss?"

"I had what I call an upheaval a couple years ago." A haunted look filled his eyes but was gone before I could see what it held. "I kind of jumped the gun a little on the proverbial midlife crisis." He turned and looked out over the water.

"When people leave, you have to find a way to deal with the hole that's left behind. You have to grieve, but then you've got to find some way to turn your attention elsewhere, find something you still care enough about to keep you going." Oliver's eyes were dark pools that didn't reveal his own sorrows but instead reflected my own broken self back at me. "You don't have to spend the rest of your life in misery to make up for what was an accident."

"Thank you," I whispered. He had answered a question I'd been carrying inside for years, too afraid to give it voice. We sat together in silence, the night deepening around us, neither ready to go. The stars above reflected in the water, its surface so tranquil it was difficult to believe an urgent current ran below.

In addition to my time with Helen and Oliver, I got to spend more time with MG. She started calling more often, as if now that we had the professional bit out of the way we could enjoy our friendship again. We met at least once a week for coffee or lunch. It went without saying that Brad and I probably weren't ever going to be buddies, and I was grateful MG seemed to understand it was better not to invite me out with the two of them. Once or twice I suggested asking Oliver to join us. But she brushed off the idea, saying that three was a crowd.

The Sunday after Thanksgiving she surprised me, knocking on my door with two cups of coffee and Amtrak tickets for the ten fifteen to Chicago, saying, "Let's celebrate your birthday a couple weeks early." She handed me a sheet of paper. It was a reservation for a special exhibit at the Art Institute. "I know how crazy you are about all those haystacks and water lilies." MG wasn't much into museums, so I appreciated the thoughtfulness she'd put into finding me a gift I'd really like, even if she didn't have a clue that it was a Caillebotte exhibit, not Monet.

We were, giddy as kids on a field trip as we rode the train from Milwaukee toward our hometown. As we sped along I realized this was the first Sunday ever that I'd be in Chicago and not have dinner with my family. I enjoyed the exhibit with a sense of reckless daring. I hadn't called home to say I was in town. Nor would I tell Momma I'd been there the next time I talked to her. The guilt would have canceled out all the fun.

I had always liked Caillebotte's work. In his most famous piece, *Paris Street; Rainy Day,* he had ingeniously re-created a wet street from just the right perspective to make a viewer feel as if she were strolling along it with all the figures in the frame. But this time it was a different sort of painting that captivated me. Called *Nude on a Couch,* the image was rendered in soft pastels. The model reclined on a divan, shoes kicked off onto the floor below. She was Rubenesque, with pale, fleshy thighs; generous hips that had surely borne children; a blossoming abdomen and a pair of equally lush breasts that lolled to either side, her breastbone a dry riverbed between them. Her dress lay draped over a cushion of the couch behind her head, discarded and forgotten.

Standing before the painting I gasped with recognition. She might have been just a woman napping, except for the placement of her left arm. Caillebotte had painted it cradling her head, flung across her brow. It cast an impression of weary melancholy. The look on the woman's face called to mind photos of Momma taken when I was little, her face wan and angular, weary. Caillebotte had captured perfectly the expression I had often seen on my mother's face, the way I also felt myself at times—in need of respite. It was as if he was paying homage to the courage it took just to keep going some days. The image was a balm; I found it difficult to draw my eyes from it.

After we viewed the rest of the paintings MG and I had tea in the small café attached to the gift shop. We sat in a window seat, watching storm clouds gather in a reflection of Caillebotte's rainy-day portrait. MG raised her teacup. "Happy birthday, Caro. I'm so glad we're friends." Genuine appreciation filled her eyes and I savored the sweetness of her toast.

Passing through the gift shop on the way out, I bought my first piece of artwork for my condo. It was a print of the nude. Looking at the model, I felt a sharp rush of understanding and compassion. The bareness of the woman, her naked essence captured by the artist, soothed me. It made me feel as if I had permission to rest, to slide under the cool sheets and down comforter on my bed and shut my eyes without worry.

Mary Grace was quiet on the train ride back to Milwaukee. The long day had left her tired. She napped while I stared out the window, content to watch the scenery go by as the last of the light dimmed from the horizon. I thought about how full my life was these days, how much more joy and peace I felt doing a job I loved, enjoying my friends and the fun of exploring a new city. I was settling into a new, bigger life. There was just one more thing I wanted. But I was doing my best to focus on what I had instead of what was missing.

As if she had picked up on my silent musing, MG opened one eye and looked at me. She closed it again. "Have you been on any dates since you moved?"

I made a noise that was more discontented muttering than answer. MG knew my history with men: short and insignificant. MG had been the one with all the guys after her. Throughout high school I'd gone out with her boyfriends' buddies just so we could double-date. At least I had my first kiss before I left my teenage years behind.

Once MG left for college, I was in charge of my own social calendar. In my early twenties I dated a boy I'd known in grade school, Jamie Kincaid. He had cinnamon hair and freckles, and he liked baseball as much as I did. We spent a summer eating hot dogs and drinking beer in the bleachers at Wrigley Field, and I lost my virginity to him on the pier at the lake. I had hoped that Jamie and I might be the real thing, the kind of love that led to forever. But he'd gone back to college in Minnesota, where he was double-majoring in philosophy and biology. By Christmas break, he'd written to tell me he'd fallen in love with a girl in his human sexuality class. I spent the holidays in bed, recuperating from a broken heart.

After I recovered from getting dumped by Jamie, being employed in a funeral home didn't offer much opportunity to date people I met at work, especially since apart from Daddy and me, the only employee was Mrs. Grimm, the housekeeper. She had a son, Charlie, who was a few years younger than me. Sometimes he came to pick her up from work in his late-model blue Camaro with an eagle painted on the hood.

"Hi, Caro." He'd leer up at me from beneath a shaggy fringe of hair that hung over his reddened eyes. I was never sure if Charlie was a little slow mentally or just perpetually high on marijuana,

but he gave me the creeps. More than once I mentioned a ficti-
tious love interest in front of Mrs. Grimm so she'd know there
was no hope for Charlie and me.

Then came nursing school. It was still mainly a woman's world,
and I was busy studying. A few girls set me up with a brother or
a cousin, but there were no sparks with any of them. It had been
years since I'd felt passionate about someone the way I had about
Jamie. I'd hoped that moving to Milwaukee might change things,
but so far no luck.

MG shifted around on her seat, opened both eyes this time.

"I haven't had the time to meet anybody."

MG shot me a look that said she wasn't buying it.

"My neighbor said she knew a cute male nurse, but it turns out
he's just started dating someone." I shrugged, not letting on that
I'd been disappointed when Helen gave me the news.

"Well, we've got to find you someone," MG declared. "Maybe
one of Brad's fraternity brothers. They still all hang out a lot. Most
are married, but there's a few left who would be gaga over you."

I must have looked doubtful, because MG sighed. "C'mon,
Caro," she said, sizing me up. "You've got a cute figure, especially
when you wear something other than scrubs. Those jeans you're
wearing today look great on you. So do the shoes."

"Thanks." I nodded, pleased that she had noticed the red Mary
Janes with the wedge heel I'd borrowed from Helen to match my
sweater.

"If you'd let me take you to Enzo for a cut he could give you
layers to frame your face, play up your dreamy brown eyes and
those cheekbones I'd trade my right arm for." MG held out her
arm with a swooning expression and I laughed.

She went on. "The right haircut and you'd have guys fighting
over you, I promise. I'm not entirely objective because I'm your
friend, but you're a catch, Caro. You're sweet and caring, you do
something cool for a living and you take really good care of the
people you love. On top of that, you're beautiful on the outside,
too. Any man in his right mind would see on the first date that

he'd better not let you out of his sight." MG finished with a flourish, nodding her head vigorously to make her point.

I blushed at her assessment. I was glad to know glamorous MG thought I was attractive. "Oliver and I did some bike-riding before the weather got too cold. And we e-mail once a week or so." I hadn't told MG about our outings before. Somehow that felt deliberate, though I hadn't been conscious of it until then. But now I hoped she'd tell me that he had mentioned them, and maybe something about me, to her.

"Really?" MG placed her hands on the shelf of her belly, rubbing up and down as if to soothe the little one inside. "So you guys hit it off? I thought he was dating another Realtor from his office."

If MG was hiding something behind her offhand tone I missed it. I was too caught up in the sudden disappointment that flared at her announcement about Oliver's colleague. Our bike trips had never included anything more than friendly goofing around. But in the couple of weeks since the weather turned, I had missed Oliver. Several times when my phone rang I found myself hoping it was him. I wasn't about to make the first move and call him to suggest a replacement activity for biking. But despite the fact that he hadn't shown any romantic interest in me, it was disheartening to discover Oliver wasn't available.

"Ollie's a good egg," MG said slowly, as if I had offered some evidence to the contrary. "But I don't think he's the kind to settle down, if you know what I mean." Her estimation only made me more disappointed. It confused me, too, because Oliver had always seemed so genuine. He didn't come across as the type to play games. But MG surely knew him better than I did. A handful of bike rides didn't make me an expert on his character. I decided to take the information MG had given me about Oliver as a blessing. Now I could stop daydreaming about him and get on with my life. If I wanted it to include a boyfriend, I'd have to look elsewhere.

Seventeen

Lots of people meet their significant other at work. But one hazard of working as a doula is that with the exception of some of the delivering OBs, the only men I encounter on the job are usually the fathers of my clients' children. I was intimidated by the idea of Internet dating and wasn't about to go to a bar alone to try to meet someone. Then the holidays approached, and as if some Secret Santa had heard my wish for a lover, one arrived like an unexpected Christmas present.

On December 20 I was waiting for one more client to go into labor before I took a break over the holidays. My bags were already packed. After Cassandra Pappas delivered I would load up the car and drive home. I hadn't been back in nearly four months, long enough to dim my memory of the family dynamics that had sent me off and heighten the thing I missed most about being with them—how I felt known there in a way I'd never be anywhere else.

I'd been looking forward to Cassie's birth since she'd inquired about my services. Cassie wasn't having the baby at a hospital or BirthRight. Instead she was birthing where she'd conceived—in her own bed. Hers would be my first home birth, and I could hardly wait to get the call that she was in labor.

Cassie worked at Steam, which had become one of my favorite hangouts. In her late twenties, she was going to be a single mother. When the guy who had fathered her child learned of her pregnancy, he'd left town, vaguely promising that maybe after a few months in the Montana wilderness he'd be ready to settle down. Cassie was youthfully idealistic, but she wasn't an idiot and held no expectation of his further involvement. Instead she had sought out a "village" of people willing to support her and help her care for the baby.

Cassie had moved into a community on the far outskirts of town known as the Enclave. A run-down but neat ring of wood-frame cottages set on thirty acres, the place was a throwback to the hippie era. It had been around that long, although its residents changed over the years as people came and went. But two of the founding members, a midwife and her husband who were now in their seventies, were still there. With her white hair piled atop her head in a neat bun, Agnes "Pixie" Perkins resembled a miniature angel. When we met I had to resist the urge to peek around and look for wings on her back. Her appearance, coupled with the gleam that seemed to perpetually shine in her eyes, had earned her the apt nickname. She reminded me of Ruby, and I fell in love with her the minute we met.

Local lore had it that back in the late sixties Pixie and her husband, Bert, had caravanned from California around the country with eight other young couples in a dilapidated school bus. The bus broke down on one of the prairies outside Milwaukee. The old farmer who owned the field was ready to sell, so the group scraped together the money to buy the land and started the community.

At the height of its popularity the Enclave had been home to over forty adults and nearly twice as many children. It was a self-sufficient entity, and the Enclave's members lived close to the land long before "organic" and "locally grown" were common household words. The men farmed the surrounding land while the women sold eggs, honey, jams, baked goods and produce in season.

According to Cassie, who always spoke of Pixie in hushed awe, the diminutive woman had been the visionary behind the collective, the one who kept things running smoothly. A glorified den mother to a group of hapless wanderers, Pixie pulled them together into a makeshift family. She had studied midwifery in California, so when women in the first group of people at the Enclave became pregnant they were able to receive prenatal care on-site. In keeping with the group's commitment to self-sufficiency, the majority of babies born to parents at the Enclave arrived on its grounds. In over thirty years only six women had been transferred to a local hospital to give birth.

By the time Cassie introduced me to the Enclave and its infamous crone, the community was internationally known as an alternative model for birthing. Ten years ago the Enclave had opened its doors and arms to the public, offering its services to any woman or couple who wanted to make their birthing time a ceremony rather than a medical event. It had become *the* place to give birth naturally with assistance but without interference.

As with most choices associated with pregnancy, when mention of the Enclave came up in mixed company, the name met with one of two reactions: people either loved the idea of what it offered, how it empowered women to be in charge of their births, or they saw it as a group of tree-huggers thumbing their noses at authority, putting infants' and mothers' lives at unnecessary risk.

I was thinking about how environment impacts outcome when I walked into the pleasant-looking cottage Cassie had spent weeks decorating in anticipation of her child's arrival. My doula training had been in an urban hospital setting and was aimed at helping women birth there. My experiences with Deirdre at BirthRight had opened my eyes to the critical importance of setting as well as quality medical care. An inviting space wasn't just a nice touch; it helped mothers relax and feel safe enough to birth.

"The hospital's for people who are sick. Notice how you feel the next time you attend a birth in one," Deirdre had told me when I'd commented on how feminine and nurturing her center was. "Most of us, we walk through those double doors onto the unit and immediately feel like there's something wrong with us. Put a laboring woman in that atmosphere and watch . . . every intervention they do seems to lead to more." She had shaken her head, resigned to what she knew all too well from experience.

Deirdre's comment had reminded me of one of the first births I had served at in Chicago. My client had wanted to do a vaginal birth after Caesarean, a VBAC. Her OB was willing to let her try, since the Caesarean had occurred when her body only dilated to six centimeters after two days of labor, instead of because of some imminent danger to mother or baby. We all hoped that this time things would progress as planned and she could experience the kind of birth she wanted.

The mind is a powerful thing. My client had called me from her home, where she'd been having strong and steady contractions for several hours. When they intensified, I met her at the hospital. She had a few more good strong waves on the way from the car to the L & D ward, but once she was admitted and hooked up to the fetal monitor, her contractions subsided. When they didn't pick up after an hour the OB sent her home again to wait until she was closer to complete and ready to push. Being in the hospital had reminded my client of the Caesarean she'd had there last time and had stalled her labor.

Cassie's rough-hewn cottage was tiny, only four rooms including the bathroom, but infused now with an air of lively anticipation that filled me as soon as I walked in. I marveled again at the vast difference between the fluorescent lights, artificial air and beeping monitors in even the most family-friendly hospital birthing suites and the setting at the Enclave. A live fir took up one corner, adorned with handmade ornaments, twinkly lights, the quaint touch of cranberry and popcorn garlands. I breathed in a whiff of fresh pine, savoring images of my own Christmases past that the aroma conjured.

The scent shifted when I entered the kitchen. Pixie was seated at the table making notes in a file. Tricia, one of the midwives-in-training, was stirring something on the stove. Hints of cinnamon and cloves wafted from the pot.

"Mulled cider?" Tricia offered me a mug of steaming liquid, which I accepted gratefully. The cutting winter wind had chilled me in the brief walk from my car to the house.

"Dear heart is four centimeters, eighty percent and as excited as a kid on Christmas Eve." Pixie treated me as graciously as if I was a member of the community. When Cassie had told me that she would give birth at the Enclave, I thought Pixie and her staff might not be happy about working with an independent doula. But Pixie had insisted I come for one of Cassie's prenatal checkups, and since that first visit she'd taken me in as if I was a daughter. I wondered whether there was anyone Pixie didn't automatically treat with love and respect. She simply expected people to live up to their best potential and refused to see them as anything less, despite behavior to the contrary. I admired her perspective, since my first inclination was to look for what was wrong.

I nodded appreciatively to Pixie for filling me in, then went to say hello to Cassie. She had transformed her bedroom into a giant cocoon. While the rest of the house felt cheery and bright, this room was dimly lit, infused with an expectant hush. Luminarias with hole-punched Christmas trees lined the windowsills. The votive candles inside them cast a reassuring light. The bed was a nest of quilts and pillows where Cassie dozed, curled into herself like the child inside her. Instrumental carols played on a portable stereo, "Silent Night" evoking the mystical wonder of another amazing birth long ago. I looked out the window. A moon round as a woman great with child hung high above. I grinned at the sight of it. I'd had a feeling the full moon would bring Cassie's baby before her Christmas Eve due date.

Headlights swung into the yard, illuminating snowflakes as they dotted the evening darkness. They drifted down into a blanket that added to the hushed, contained feeling in the house.

"Goody, you're here." Cassie rose up, her voice soft but strong. She looked toward the window at the lights. "That must be my cousin. I'm so glad you two made it before the snow got too deep." A satisfied smile lit her face. "The baby will be here by morning." Her calm certainty filled me with a surge of joy. Cassie had let her intuition guide her, from choosing to keep the baby when she'd learned she was unexpectedly pregnant to deliberately planning where and how to bring her child into the world. That intuition had led her to hire me, even though I knew that with Pixie and her staff in attendance I would likely be superfluous.

Cassie had also wanted one more person at her birth: her cousin. "I have a feeling I'm carrying a boy," she had confided to me earlier. Like most of the women who birthed at the Enclave, Cassie had opted to keep the baby's sex a surprise until it arrived. "Now that Johnny's out of the picture, it feels really important to have some positive male energy at Quinn's birth. My cousin Michael's only a couple years older than me. We grew up together. We're both only children so we're more like brother and sister than cousins. He's really cool and creative. He's an architect and a professor at the U."

Her expression had turned shy. "I hope you don't think it's weird that I want to have him there. He's going to be Quinn's godfather and he's almost more excited than I am about this little one's arrival." It was an unusual scenario but I admired Cassie's ingenuity at offering her child some kind of substitute for a father.

I was helping Cassie to her feet so she could use the bathroom when a knock sounded on the bedroom door. "C'mon in, the party's definitely in here," she joked, perking up at her cousin's arrival.

The door swung open. A man filled the doorway. He was well over six feet tall and slender. Green eyes gleamed in the candlelit glow, made my breath catch in my throat. It wasn't just the beauty of his face, though it was arresting. It was the totality of him—the wavy brown hair, the broad shoulders, narrow hips. Most attractive of all was the way he stood there waiting to hug Cassie, delight shining from him as if he understood this was the very best way anyone could ever hope to spend a holiday night.

Eighteen

When a newborn's head crowns, the world shrinks. Everything outside the birthing room falls away as everyone present focuses on drawing the baby forth. As Cassie had predicted, Quinn Michael Rogers arrived at 3:47 A.M., well before dawn's first light. Her labor was slow and steady, the best kind. Cassie moved with the rhythms of her body as it opened to allow the baby passage into the world. She was her own best support during her birth time, the rest of us witnesses to the wonder.

Deirdre was a great midwife but her no-nonsense attitude sometimes felt cold to me. Pixie's approach was more maternal. She cared deeply about the families she worked with and wasn't afraid to show it. Now she coaxed Cassie along, reassuring her that she was already taking such good care of her baby.

Cassie's cousin, overwhelmed I think by the reality of an empowered woman in labor, hung back and took it all in, occasionally calling out, "Good job, Cass!" I had to bite my lip at his earnestness. Yet I couldn't keep myself from looking over at him, stealing glances delicious as nibbles of a Christmas cookie. It had been several years since I'd been with a man. Suddenly I was ravenous for affection and touch.

When the time came for her to push, Cassie was on the bed, propped up by a pile of pillows. Michael stepped forward and moved alongside his cousin. We were directly across from each other, flanking Cassie on either side. Pixie sat on a small stool between Cassie's legs.

The baby arrived in just four pushes. Pixie massaged Cassie's perineum liberally with olive oil to keep the tissue from tearing. Cassie had been quieter than most women birthing naturally, pulling her awareness deeper inside herself to tap into her strength.

She gave a strong grunt with the last push, though, and at the sound Michael looked up. His eyes found mine. We looked at one another, the acknowledgment passing between us that we were together in something of such import neither of us would ever forget it. Although I hated to break our connection I nodded down toward the baby. I didn't want Michael to miss what we had all gathered to see.

Quinn was born with the amniotic sac attached to his face. I had never seen this before but knew it held great meaning to certain cultures, who believed a caul signaled that the child possessed extraordinary powers. Pixie clucked as she tenderly picked pieces of it from the infant's head. "This one's marked with a big life, there's no doubt." I watched in fascination as she crooned at the child. She cradled the tiny boy's head in one palm, his body extending up her forearm. Quinn was wide-eyed, alert yet quiet, taking in his surroundings. Already he looked wise as a sage. With her other hand Pixie made circular motions, first over the top of Quinn's head, then at several other spots down his body, as if sweeping something away.

I didn't understand what she was doing but as Pixie's hands swept the air above the baby he quivered, then let loose with not a cry but a gulping chortle that sent an appreciative thrill through me. Pixie laid the baby down on Cassie's stomach, set both her palms against the soles of his feet and sighed. I shivered at her movements. I wanted to know what they meant and made a note to ask her later.

More than any other birth, Cassie's affirmed the amazement I experienced whenever I served at one. In the exquisite atmosphere created by his mother, during that already special time of year, Quinn's arrival proclaimed the wonder of birth. Michael's presence there heightened it.

Normally I leave a new family shortly after the baby arrives. Adrenaline fuels me through whatever number of hours it takes for the birth, but I come down, wiped out, soon afterward. Plus parents and baby need time to savor each other before the rush of other family members ensues. But that morning I wasn't inclined to go anywhere anytime soon.

While Pixie and Tricia made Cassie comfortable I went out to the kitchen. Michael was there, talking on his cell phone. "Yeah, Ma, yeah, she had him. Yeah, it's a boy." Michael was as excited as a new father. "Cass is fine, and so is he. His middle name's Michael." Pride filled his words. "I was here for the whole thing. I saw him come into the world. It was awesome. Just awesome."

I waited for him to finish, suppressing a smile at his ebullience. "You acted like a natural in there," I said when he hung up. "I know some men who would love to have you with them at their wives' deliveries. You should consider becoming a dads' doula." I was only half teasing. Michael's patience and quiet demeanor had added to the morning's good outcome in more ways than just providing me with great "scenery."

"Wow, thanks." He offered me a bashful grin. "That was . . . extraordinary." He shook his head, reliving what we had just seen. "Seriously, I don't know what I was expecting it to be like, but that, well, that blew me away."

"Yep," I said, "there's nothing else quite like it."

"So you get to do this all the time?"

"Whenever I'm lucky enough to be asked."

"And here I've been thinking teaching college kids was the coolest job. You've got me beat."

"Believe me, I wouldn't trade places with you for the world."

Michael laughed at my admission. Pixie stepped into the kitchen, took one look at us, winked and ducked back out. I poured two mugs of steaming tea, then sat down at the kitchen table, where I remained while the next several hours flew by, chatting with Michael until well past sunrise.

Nineteen

It was nearly nine by the time I left Cassie's that morning. I'd been awake for well over twenty-four hours but despite the lack of sleep I left reluctantly. It wasn't until I was driving back toward town and my bed that the adrenaline, which had been keeping me going along with Pixie's strong tea, drained out of me. I was a mile from home when I grew so exhausted I couldn't see straight. My weary brain maneuvered my Honda on autopilot. It was a crisp, bright morning but my vision clouded over. The last thing I should have been doing in my condition was operating heavy machinery. I was in an altered state, jittery, off-kilter. I rolled down my window, hoping the blast of frigid air would jar my mind into alertness. Only a few more lights and I would be home.

Then I heard the squeal of tires. The sound jolted me out of my fog but I was already traveling forward through the intersection crosswalk when I realized the traffic light had turned red. I hadn't seen it flash yellow. I was about to T-bone a silver Mercedes station wagon, but stopping felt beyond my abilities. I felt separate from my body, as if I were a bystander observing instead of driving my Civic. Somehow my right foot found the brake and slammed the pedal to the floor. My right hand grasped the clutch, downshifted. I strained against the safety belt, then shot back into the seat as the car screeched to a halt. I steered my car off the road, then lifted my left hand off the steering wheel. It shook as I held it in midair.

The woman swung the Mercedes off onto the shoulder then jumped out and strode toward me, her black coat fanning behind her like a witch's cape. "Look what you did!" She jutted her head in my open window, so close I caught the flash of silver fillings in two molars. I recoiled from the charge but my seat belt was still fastened. There was nowhere to go.

"My babies," the woman yelled, wild-eyed terror fueling her fury. "You nearly killed my babies." She waved a hand in the direction of her car.

I looked toward where she was pointing. In the back was a car seat with an infant. Beside the baby sat a little girl, maybe six or seven years old. She had wide, slanted eyes and was staring at me in blatant reproach. Down syndrome. I looked back to the woman by my side. "I'm so sorry." The words were inadequate but I hoped she caught the sincerity in them. Her life couldn't be easy on a good day and I had just added to its struggles.

The woman covered her face with both hands. When she looked up again tears spilled from her eyes. Her fear and anger were gone, replaced by the raw recognition of everything she would have lost had I not come to in time to keep from ramming her. She let me see this, and I apologized a second time, hoping my words gave her some solace. Wordlessly she turned and went back to her car, where she gave each of the children a fierce squeeze before driving away.

The rosary Ruby had given me long ago hung around my rearview mirror, the same place she'd kept it in her red pickup. I reached out, rubbed the metal cross hanging off the end between my finger and my thumb as a gesture of gratitude to whatever unseen forces governed fate. A shiver passed through me. The day wasn't even half-over and already I'd been part of two miracles.

I shifted into first and pulled into the parking lot of a gas station. A car swung in behind mine and as the driver got out and walked toward me, my gratitude burst into first a thrill, then mortification. Michael.

I rolled down the window, chagrin burning my cheeks. I was so exhausted I hadn't even been aware that he'd been driving behind me.

"This career of yours can be high-risk, huh? How about we leave your car here and you let me drive you home?"

"It's only six more blocks, but if you don't mind . . ." I let the words trail off, relieved I wouldn't have to decide between staying at the wheel and walking in the bracing cold. Michael held out his hand, helped me from my car and led me to his. If he noticed I was shaking he didn't ask whether it was from the chill or the ordeal. He drove me the rest of the way home, then walked me to my door.

"Thanks so much," I said, then stopped, unable to continue without breaking into tears.

"No problem," he replied quietly. I couldn't detect any re-crimination in his words. "I know you need to sleep, but what do you say I come back tonight and take you to get some dinner? You've got to be as starving as you are tired after what you did at Cassie's."

"I'd love that." I was so grateful for Michael's thoughtfulness I could barely get the words out. But even the anticipation of a date with him couldn't keep me awake any longer. I fell into bed and a dark, dreamless sleep so heavy I didn't surface until Michael gave me a wake-up call at nearly six to say he was on his way back to me.

Michael took me out to what he promised was one of Milwaukee's "hidden gems." He was right about the restaurant. My instincts had been right, too; I fell for Michael that first date, tumbling into lust and longing that had been dormant so long I'd begun to won-der whether I was still capable of feeling that way.

Ganesha Gardens was more than an Indian restaurant. It served up love on a plate. Operated by a Hare Krishna commu-nity, the café was housed in a temple not far from the university. The neighborhood had a run-down but inviting air, especially the homes surrounding the temple, where Caucasian parents and children who looked as if they were playing dress-up cloaked in *salwar kameez* and saris waved from the front porches as we drove past.

"This way." Michael stepped aside to let me go first down the narrow hall past the gift shop and into the café. Incense filled the air. We chose a table in the enclosed courtyard. Sitar music accompanied the lyrical fountain in the center of the space, water crooning as it splashed down into a pond where gold, orange and white koi swam.

"This is amazing," I whispered, not wanting to disturb the tranquility.

"Wait until you try the food." Michael looked pleased with himself for being the first person to bring me there.

Maybe I was caught up in the magic of the ambience, the string of tiny white lights that sparkled like stars against the dark sky, the candle flickering on the table between us, but I swear affection spiced every luscious mouthful of *palak paneer* and the samosas stuffed with potato and peas.

"Try a bite of this. It's killer." Michael held out a forkful of chickpeas in red gravy.

"Mmmm." It was all I could get out as I savored the tangy tomato sauce. Nutmeg lingered on my tongue. "What *is* that?"

Michael grinned, looking happy to discover I was a fellow foodie. "*Chana masala.* The best you'll find this side of Mumbai."

"Have you been?" By unspoken agreement that the food deserved our undivided attention, we'd eaten most of our meal in companionable silence. But now we chatted while we awaited rice pudding and blueberry halva for dessert.

"Not yet. Maybe next summer when I'm up for a sabbatical." The waitress, a stunning black-haired girl clad in a gold and teal sari, flirted with Michael. She gave a sheepish nod toward me as if to say she couldn't help herself. I didn't blame her. When he returned from the bathroom I watched as people at the surrounding tables looked up, appreciatively taking note of him as he moved past. I was happy to be seated across from him, where I could enjoy the light and shadows playing over his features, the way his hair fell across his forehead.

We spent the better part of the evening getting to know one another. Like my neighbor Helen, Michael was easy in his own skin.

"We're living in Generica," he pronounced when I asked how he felt about the architecture in Milwaukee. "It's not just the

Midwest. Travel to any city in the good ole U.S. of A and I guarantee you'll find strip malls filled with the Gap, Starbucks, McDonald's, and a 7-Eleven. That's why I patronize places like this. I don't want all the great mom-and-pop joints to go out of business.

"It's all about safety and comfort, which I can understand," he conceded. "People don't want to be disappointed. Folks know that when they order a Big Mac at the Golden Arches, wherever they are they're gonna get the same two all-beef patties, special sauce, et cetera, et cetera they'd get at their local outlet back home."

Michael blinked. "I'll get off my soapbox now." He shook his head, did a funny little half bow. "But one more thing, while we're on the topic." He held up a finger, eyes gleaming. As if he couldn't help himself, he was revving up again. "The chain stores are bad but worse are the housing developments. Every fifth house is the same, like cutouts. There's no originality, no innovation. Just a lot of ostentatious frills, like those god-awful turrets that are so popular right now with the McMansion crowd." He made a face.

Inwardly I sighed, thinking of MG and how she seemed trapped in the big castle her "prince" had given her. I agreed with Michael, at least in part, but hiring a doula took funds. I made my living mostly off people who owned McMansions. It seemed bad karma to bite the proverbial hand that fed me. Still, I knew what Michael meant about the trend toward uniformity and blending in. Most people took comfort in being part of the crowd. Demonstrating one's individuality might lead to celebrity but could just as easily signal exclusion. It seemed to me that most of us secretly hoped never to be singled out for what we believed. I admired Michael's courage to voice his convictions.

"I don't mean to bitch and moan," Michael explained. "'Bland land' has inspired me. I'm designing a series of houses and commercial buildings where the space becomes part of the experience and positively affects the people who live or work there."

"Really? You should meet my friend Oliver. He's a Realtor and he feels the same way about living spaces." I was excited to say I knew someone here who might be interested in networking with him. "And I'd love to see some of your work someday." I wasn't just feigning interest out of politeness.

Michael grinned. "You're sitting in it right now."

I looked around the serene courtyard again, taking it in with a new appreciation. "You did this? It's incredible. I'd move in if they took boarders," I joked.

"Thanks." Michael seemed pleased, and I recalled the way he'd looked telling his mother about Quinn's birth, his excitement bringing forth a boyishness that was as attractive as his vision for changing the way people lived.

From that day we met, whenever I thought of Michael I saw him standing at the edge of the planet, arms flung wide to take in whatever wanted to come his way, as if he felt inherently worthy of every good thing life had to offer. Eager for a place where I could take refuge, I stepped into his open arms, never once wondering whether they would cradle me while I grew into myself or squeeze the life out of me so I could fit into his.

Twenty

Hypervigilance, willful ignorance's sibling, was a second coping mechanism I had learned to cultivate early on. Another of the hallmarks of magical thinking, it lent a false sense of security: if I kept close watch for danger drawing near, I might somehow avert it. I'd spent most of my life waiting for the proverbial "other shoe" to fall. In my family's line of work, it always did. Death creates drama fit for a soap opera. Despite her fragility, my mother thrived on all the ups and downs, grew lost in the rare moments no one was dying or in need of her care. The thrill of the rush made her an excellent trauma nurse. That way of meeting life's challenges wore at me, but for as long as I could remember I had lived perpetually on edge, awaiting whatever calamity instinct insisted would cause my downfall.

Despite the near-accident coming home from Cassie's birth, as the holidays gave way to the new year I practiced a determined resolution: I gave up anticipating future peril. Instead I savored the joy of unexpected romance, along with all the other goodness coloring my days.

Looking forward to another opportunity for a fresh start, I even threw a New Year's Eve party. I'd wanted to introduce Michael and Oliver ever since I discovered their mutual interest in aesthetic architecture. And I really wanted Mary Grace to meet my new boyfriend. Michael and I had only been dating a little while, but the holidays are such a wonderful time to be in a new relationship and that made us close quickly. He had even come to Chicago for a few days after Christmas. With his winning grin and his easy manner, he'd charmed not just my mother but the rest of my family, too. At dinner one night Samantha had made eyes at me from behind his back, mouthing the words, "He's yummy!" as she mock-swooned. Since we had come back from Chicago, I'd spent the last three nights at his place. I was dizzy with passion from our lively lovemaking, our craving to discover one another inside and out.

I invited Helen to the party, too. Michael's lighthearted yet ardent affection was so refreshing I was glad that Oliver hadn't pursued me after all. I thought Helen might give Oliver a run for his money with her rebel-girl attitude, something MG and I could delight in giving him a hard time about.

Michael liked to cook, so we prepared a gourmet meal of beef Wellington that even Brad, who was a food snob, had to grudgingly praise.

"I'd like to make a toast," Michael announced once we all sat down. "To a stunning evening made possible by a stunning woman. I can't wait to see what the next year holds, for her and for us." He looked at me as if we were the only two people in the room while everyone clinked glasses then sipped their wine.

I beamed at Michael and looked around the table. There was my best friend, Mary Grace, and the new life she was bringing into the world. Brad sat alongside her. I vowed to try harder to understand what MG saw in him. Next came my two new friends, Oliver and Helen. Then my gaze landed back on Michael, whose hand was roaming my leg beneath the table. He squeezed my knee, grinned when I squirmed.

We bantered over the main course, steering clear of topics that might darken the merry mood. Brad was an arch-conservative and I knew that just one liberal comment from Michael could well spark a battle that would spoil the evening, but everyone seemed on their best behavior.

After dinner, Helen proposed a game: each of us had to predict where we would be next year at this same time.

"Since you came up with it, you go first." Michael smirked. She had teased him earlier about stealing me away since I hadn't made it to our standing Saturday breakfast last week. Now he was kidding around with her. I was glad to see that he liked my friends.

"Okay, I will." Helen wasn't one to back down from a challenge. "I predict that next New Year's I will be on a yacht in the Riviera, drinking exquisite champagne without a care in the world!" She raised her wineglass triumphantly and saluted, her eyes bright from the alcohol and the fun.

"I think that's a prediction we should all share. We'll just relocate the party from Caro's place to Monte Carlo," Mary Grace declared. Michael nodded his head in vigorous agreement.

"I was thinking the Italian side but I could make do with France," Helen said, conceding playfully.

We went around the table and everyone took a turn. When Oliver was up, he shook his head. "Not me," he said. "Ever hear that old adage about what to do if you want to make the powers that be laugh? Well, I swore off making plans long ago. And I'm sticking to that approach." I noticed Helen watching Oliver thoughtfully. But then Brad made some wisecrack and she turned her attention back to the chatter.

Brad and MG had contributed several bottles of champagne for the evening and we were well into the second one, the mood mellowing as we waited for midnight. I stacked the dinner plates in the dishwasher, then ambled toward the living room. We split off into pairs, but not the romantic couplings I had expected. Instead Brad and Michael were slouched on the futon, deep in discussion about the Green Bay Packers and the upcoming Super Bowl. Mary Grace and Helen were in the living room too, huddled near the window bonding over their mutual shoe obsession. Helen was trying on one of Mary Grace's Louboutins. "We're the same size!" Helen announced like she had just won the lottery.

I wandered back into the dining area, where Oliver was nursing the dregs of his wine. He looked up. "So, you really want to be in Times Square next year?"

"I like New York. It's a great place to visit. Especially at the holidays." I shrugged, a little embarrassed. Michael had offered that as his prediction and I had eagerly seconded it. But Oliver's scrutiny made it seem as if he was disappointed in me. I almost asked why he cared, but I knew he'd give me some answer that would take us into the kind of thoughtful conversation better suited for one of our bike rides. For a second I felt sorry for Oliver. I loved his sensitive nature, the earnest way he approached life. But sometimes it was nice just to relax and have a little fun.

I was still standing there, not wanting Oliver to be all alone, when Michael hollered from the other room. "Hey, babe, c'mon back in here. They're about to drop the ball!"

I looked down at Oliver, inviting him to go with me. "You go ahead," he said evenly. "I'm cool." For a moment I wondered, then decided that he was a big boy and could take care of himself. I had invited Helen to keep him company; if he didn't seek her out that was his fault, not mine.

Twenty-one

Following the first celebration of that new year, I had almost six wonder-filled months. In February the groundhog's shadow failed to appear. As if living up to the prophecy, within a few more weeks the snows melted, giving way to insistent blooms bursting from their bulbs. Tulips, crocuses and paperwhites craned eager heads toward the sun. Oliver and I resumed our bike rides, though now that I was dating Michael my free time was more limited. Oliver teased me sometimes about my lack of availability but I was too happy to care, or to wonder whether it meant more to him than the lack of a cycling pal. We had run into Helen one day in the hall after a bike ride, but although Oliver remembered her from my party and chatted amicably, he never mentioned her afterward. I never asked about, and he never brought up, the other Realtor MG had told me about.

A slew of new babes arrived in a kind of feverish deluge that spring. I spent lots of time working with Deirdre. When I wasn't at BirthRight or with Michael I often went to the Enclave. I told myself I was doing postpartum visits with Cassie and Quinn, but by May Cassie's "fourth trimester" was over. I enjoyed the vibe at the Enclave. The nurturing environment soothed me as much as it did those who lived there.

Although we never spoke of it formally, Pixie had taken me on in a similar capacity to the midwives under her tutelage. I had no interest in "catching" babies, but the way Pixie worked with energy enthralled me. Pixie's birthing mothers were more likely to birth peacefully than painfully. I sat in on classes where she offered moms-to-be hypnosis techniques that replaced in their impressionable minds the cultural norm of childbirth as something to be endured with the suggestion that it could, at times at least, feel good.

Prior to meeting her I'd heard only scant mention of folks like the pioneering French OB Michel Odent, who did groundbreaking work on what he called "orgasmic birth." Until I saw Cassie bring Quinn into the world, I hadn't believed that childbirth could be filled with pleasing sensations.

I asked Cassie about this one day in late May. She was sitting in a wooden rocker in the corner of the living room where her Christmas tree had been. Five-month-old Quinn was nursing, making lusty smacking sounds as he drank.

"Early on the contractions felt painful, but once I used the hypnosis they turned into sensations of pressure. But remember right near the end, when I was standing in the bathroom doorway pushing against the doorjamb with my hands?"

"You let out an enormous sigh while you were standing there."

"Right!" Cassie's eyes shone. "Well, there was all this . . . *power* running through me." She shook her shoulders, scuffed her feet on the floor as if trying to move something out of her way. "I can feel it again now, just telling you about it. It started around my middle and just built and built until I had to push it out. That's why I gripped the door frame so hard. I sent it out my arms, and also down into my legs. I was pushing down so hard I was afraid my feet were going to break through the floorboards! It was so strong but it didn't feel bad. It felt amazing, actually. I felt like I carried so much strength inside of me that I could do anything." Her awe lingered around us. I had felt that surge of energy in Cassie, had watched in fascination as she negotiated her way through the last few centimeters of dilation.

I looked at her; she was beaming, so satisfied now that the arduous task of giving birth was behind her. "I'd do it all over again in a second," she blurted.

I was thrilled for her, and envious. Some gateway had opened before her and Cassie had stepped through it. She was the more expert of us now, initiated in a way I would never be unless I too had a child.

I left Cassie cuddling Quinn and went in search of Pixie to ask for her impressions about Cassie's experience. Halfway to the cottage that housed her office, my phone rang. It was MG, and I was so glad. People have a perverse tendency to share bad outcomes about pregnancy. MG had heard some doozies. "Is it true sometimes they have to break a baby's arm to get it out of the birth canal?" she had asked me not long ago after a therapy client blurted out a birthing horror story. Now I could share Cassie's glowing report, counteract some of the fearmongering.

"What a gorgeous day, huh?" I wanted MG to know the loveliness of this place, to understand that when she gave birth three hundred thousand women the world over would be doing the same, and that like Cassie she too could tap into all that female wisdom and strength.

"You sound like you're over the moon," MG said. "Must be the boyfriend. How is Loverboy these days?"

"Michael's delicious as ever but actually, I'm at the Enclave and it just feels so *good*. I swear there's something special in the air around here."

"Or in the water."

"Okay, okay, joke about it all you want. But I'm telling you, the more I come out here the more special it becomes."

"That's great," she quipped. "Just don't drink the Kool-Aid."

I like to think I'm careful not to impose my own desires on the families I serve. But MG was so much more than a client. I had seen how incredible childbirth could be, and I keenly wanted my best friend to experience all that magic. She didn't know what she was missing. I did, and it felt like my responsibility to make her understand. The disturbing image I'd seen the night she'd told me she was pregnant flashed in my mind, and I thought that maybe this was my chance to change things.

"Seriously, MG, I know you're set to have Bean at Medical City, but you should visit here with me one day, meet Pixie, take a look around. It will blow you away. Maybe there's something you could learn here that would help you even if you do birth in the hospital."

The minute I spoke the words I regretted them. I had overstepped, and like that day I had expressed my incredulity at her breast augmentation, I felt MG withdraw.

"You know, Caro, not everyone wants life to be one big, never-ending 'growth opportunity.' Can't it be enough for the baby to get here safely?" Before I could defend myself or apologize for my overzealousness, she continued. "This is exactly what Brad is concerned about.

"I love you, Caro, and I'm really happy that you've pulled yourself together," MG said, charging on. "But I'm not you. I don't have the kind of faith you do that somehow things will 'magically' turn out. I need Brad."

She added, "And of course I love him," as if I had questioned her devotion. "The last thing I want to do is choose be—"

"You don't have to choose between anyone, MG." I talked over her before she could finish the words that were filling her voice with tears. "Not because of me, at least." I wished we were speaking in person so I could see as well as hear her. The MG I knew used to be incapable of hiding her feelings. Now, though, she'd grown expert at covering them. Out of what necessity had she cultivated that skill?

"The thing is, Caro, I feel like I do need to choose." A weary sigh filled my ear. "This tension between you and Brad has made me a nervous wreck from the beginning. I called to make sure you were on the same page with us about the birth. But from what I'm hearing today I can see that you're not." Now she was speaking in the clinical, removed tone she used with her clients.

Her charge hung between us. More disturbing images flashed in my mind—of bloody sheets, MG writhing and Brad looking furious. I thought I could change the outcome of what I'd seen. But how could I do that if I wasn't at MG's birth?

"What are you saying, MG?" I summoned the courage to ask when I couldn't stand the silence any longer.

"What I'm saying, Caro, is that I need to choose my husband. My family."

Until that day, I had never been fired by a client. But the sting of rejection was soothed somewhat by the balm of relief. This way I wouldn't be there if things went as badly as I'd seen. I'd tried to help MG but if she didn't want me, there wasn't much more I could do. I looked around the Enclave, its grounds still serene despite the grief splintering me.

"Are you there, Caro?" MG's voice sounded small, pained.

"I'm here," I said. "It's not my choice, but if it's what you need I won't be there for your birth. Good luck, MG." I ended the call before she could respond. There was nothing she could say that would soothe the pain tightening around my heart as I loosed the threads of friendship that bound us and let my best friend go.

I tossed my cell phone into my jacket pocket and broke into a run toward Pixie's office. She wasn't there but I spotted her some distance away in the woods that ran along the property's back boundary. Whenever she could make the time, Pixie liked to wander. She said she did her best thinking and meditating on those jaunts. I was interrupting her solitude but I knew bighearted Pixie wouldn't mind. I'd already told her how excited I was to share MG's birth time. If anyone would understand my anguish over our "breakup," it was Pixie.

"What I can't comprehend," I said after filling Pixie in on what had just happened, "is how a woman as headstrong and sure of herself as Mary Grace turns into a doormat who defers to her husband about matters involving her own body." I shook off my jacket and tied it around my waist. I was sweating. Pixie kept up a good pace while she woolgathered.

"Pregnancy," Pixie clucked. She wasn't terse; she just never used more words than necessary.

"Say more." I borrowed Oliver's phrase.

"Women change when they're carrying a baby. On the inside even more so than the outside. They know more, too. People say pregnant women are stupid because all the blood's going to

the baby instead of to their brains. It's true; I've known more
than one pregnant mother who forgot her own name at times.
One even left the car running a whole hour while she was in the
grocery store. But while their minds maybe aren't so sharp, their
intuitive powers make up for it. They *know* things. Not in a way
that makes sense logically but in some other way that matters just
as much. Maybe more."

I'd never heard so much come out of Pixie's mouth at one time.
I stopped. She walked on a few paces ahead, then turned and
faced me full-on. "Trust her." She pointed a gnarled index finger
at me, looking even more cronelike than usual with her white hair
flying around her. "You have no idea what's really going on. It
might be that you'd regret being there. So maybe she's done you
a favor, letting you off the hook." Pixie turned and set off again.

I contemplated Pixie's advice. Then I took off after her, sprint-
ing to catch up as she disappeared around a bend in the long
prairie grasses. "But I want to be there for her." I sounded like
a petulant kid but I didn't care. It was the truth; being at MG's
birth mattered deeply to me. *She* mattered to me. "I just want to
support her."

"You can do that wherever you are," Pixie shot back.

"It would be a lot more effective if I'm right there with her." I
almost mentioned the stillbirth that had flashed in my mind when
MG had told me she was pregnant, but part of me was fearful that
just talking about it might somehow make it happen.

"You saw me running energy over Cassie's babe the night he
came in." Pixie's words were a declaration, not a question. "You
can do the same with Mary Grace. Send her good thoughts and
loving-kindness. That will get through to her no matter where you
are when her little one decides it's time."

I must have looked unconvinced because Pixie stopped. "Listen," she commanded. "You have no idea what her birth time is
meant to bring her." The certainty in her tone brought me up
short. Still I battled against accepting that Mary Grace's choice to
fire me might be the right one.

Pixie must have sensed I needed more encouragement to let it go, because she started talking again. "The body doesn't lie. And new motherhood offers us profound chances to heal. I've had women in labor rediscover long-buried memories of a stepfather or uncle sexually abusing them when they were little girls. And others who have had to come face-to-face with some belief they've held about themselves. Like how they have to be the ones to take care of everyone else around them, for example." Her expression told me that one was directed at me.

"You want to help women have babies? I'll tell you what you do: start asking for the women who will most benefit from your gifts to find their way to you. Don't just take any client because you need the money or because you feel like you should work with them since they've asked for your help. That's giving charity, not empowering them. Your friend wants to birth in a hospital. That's not where your heart is. You can do good there, but if you're with her it means you can't be with some other woman who might actually be willing to work with all that you have to offer. Start calling in the ones who care as much about themselves as you do about them. You start asking and they'll show up. I guarantee that."

With Pixie's words a new vision formed in my mind, as if she had just watered the seeds of a dream that had been lying dormant in my awareness. Now images sprang alive, of a place where I could offer the services I longed to provide. It was similar in spirit to BirthRight and the Enclave but different at the same time, a place born of my own imagination.

"Pay attention and heed what you're seeing." I sensed that somehow Pixie was privy to the pictures appearing in my mind. Her piercing eyes reminded me so much of Ruby's it was eerie.

By the time I made my way back to where my car was parked, I had decided that Pixie was right: I didn't want to birth in hospitals anymore. Maybe, with time, I would come to believe that Mary Grace's phone call was more blessing than curse.

Twenty-two

When you follow your bliss . . . Pixie had written Joseph Campbell's quote on a scrap of paper I taped on my bedroom mirror. I started playing with the techniques Pixie suggested, visualizing myself serving at more and more births outside of hospitals. It grew into a fun game, and it seemed to be working. I was getting just as much business as before, but now the majority of women contacting me were choosing to give birth at home or in places like Deirdre's and Pixie's.

It wasn't just the quantity but the quality, too, of my clients that changed. These women had educated themselves fully about all the choices available and were more inclined to take charge of their births rather than rely on their caregivers to make choices for them. I admired them, preparing for motherhood with dedication and awareness. And I discovered a new, deeper camaraderie with these clients, which eased the ache of missing MG.

Despite my increased client load, I was still very aware of my former best friend's approaching due date. The first half of the year had passed in a blur so fast it frightened me a little. MG's baby was now just a month from being born. I couldn't help but keep track as each day went by. Often MG appeared in my dreams, wandering lost in vast deserts, fields, forests. I wondered whether I would somehow know when she went into labor. I hoped so, since I wanted to send her energy as Pixie had instructed. But despite the erratic flashes of insight I sometimes got when it came to wanting to know something, I wasn't confident in my own intuitive abilities. I spent a few moments every morning sending peace and love MG's way just in case it turned out to be *the* day.

Late one afternoon I was out at BirthRight, working on paperwork in a small room off the kitchen I'd repurposed into an office. Deirdre's brusque invitation to house my business there had touched me deeply. I was still an independent contractor but we both understood that as soon as she could afford to, Deirdre would hire me full-time. This was a huge boon in the industry. One hospital midwifery practice I knew of had two doulas on staff, but most of us spent our entire careers on the periphery of the formal partnerships set up by OBs and midwives, coming in only when hired independently by the birthing parents.

"I just got off the phone with Connie Stetson from Coalition for the Homeless." Deirdre's head popped around the edge of the office doorway. She had all her braids coiled on top of her head, reminding me of a snake poised to strike. "Mary came to her office. It looks like she's ready to go." Deirdre accepted some pro bono cases in her practice. Most of them were referred to her by social workers like Connie, who worked for an organization that ran a soup kitchen, shelter and lifestyle-education services center for people living on the streets.

Mary Smith was a fixture in the neighborhoods near the university where she wandered aimlessly most days. Although she wasn't much older than most of the students, she stood out among the busy coeds in their jeans and chinos. Mary typically wore every piece of clothing she owned, layering several skirts one over another until she resembled a Russian nesting doll. Her face was so grizzled from living out in the harsh elements of the Midwest that I suspected she was younger than she looked, which was around thirty. She'd told Connie she'd become pregnant from a rape.

"Is Connie driving her over?" I had been at Mary's prenatal visit the day Connie and Deirdre had explained to her how important it was that she let Connie know when she felt the first signs of labor.

Deirdre shook her head, a troubled frown pinching her features. "Mary got agitated and left before Connie could get her in the car. I'm going out to take a look for her. Want to come along?" Her tone was even, and I marveled at her calm. I thought for a moment. It was after six. I had dinner plans with Michael and some of his friends from the university in a couple hours.

Mary both disturbed and fascinated me. She had decided to have the baby despite the awful circumstances leading to her pregnancy. She also had a history of mental illness. When she took her medication she was reasonably stable. But she wasn't always consistent with the meds. According to Connie, Mary sometimes vanished for months at a time. But she had shown up for every one of her prenatal visits with Deirdre. I had hoped that I might happen to be at BirthRight when she gave birth. "Is Jane going too?"

Deirdre shook her head a second time. "Can't. Jerry's out of town and her babysitter's sick, so she's got the kiddos tonight."

Nothing about her demeanor suggested that she cared much whether I said yes or no, but I didn't feel right about letting Deirdre go in search of her renegade client alone. I made up my mind. "Let's go." If Deirdre wanted me to stick around for the birth, I could call Michael later and beg off dinner.

Deirdre and I drove around the periphery of campus for the better part of an hour, occasionally stopping passersby to ask if they had seen Mary.

"I just hope she didn't hop on a bus." Deirdre was beginning to look resigned after the last person said the same thing as everyone else: no one had seen a disheveled pregnant woman in the last few hours.

The image of Mary on a Greyhound heading for home popped into my head, though I knew that wasn't remotely what Deirdre meant. "Do you know anything about Mary? Like where she's from, where her parents are?"

Deirdre shrugged, leaned forward and peered out the windshield. "She's a runaway, like most of them out here. They come to towns like this because they're a little safer to live in than the bigger cities like New York and Chicago. Plus I think the transient air around college campuses helps them feel more a part of the mainstream."

"I just wonder if her mother's missing her." I couldn't imagine having a child who one day disappeared, no matter how old he or she was.

"Not every woman who has children wants them or has the resources to raise them." Deidre hadn't spoken harshly but her words cut through my naïveté, reminding me that most of the clients we served were upper-middle-class women who had chosen to become pregnant. Who knew what kind of background Mary came from?

Deirdre turned a corner onto a quieter side street lined with duplexes and small apartment buildings. Sorority and fraternity banners graced many of the balconies, but it was the end of the spring semester and many of the houses looked empty, abandoned for the summer.

"Do you have children?" I felt a little funny asking because Deirdre was so reserved. I'd never asked about her personal life before. She was so dedicated to BirthRight that I couldn't imagine that she might have a life outside of her business.

"No little ones for me."

I looked over at her but couldn't detect any regret from either her expression or her words. "You're so nurturing. You'd have made an amazing mother."

"I don't have the heart for it." Her voice was matter-of-fact, as if she had long ago come to terms with this truth about herself.

We rode along in silence as I tried to make sense of what she'd just said, which had shocked me.

Finally she spoke again. "Mothers die a million deaths. Every time a child reaches a milestone, its mother has to let go a little more. With each passing day her little one is moving out into the world, farther and farther away from her. And the person that child was dies away as he or she develops into the next phase of life. The newborn gives way to the infant, who is no longer completely dependent on its mother for survival, then the infant becomes a walking, talking toddler. Next thing you know, they're teenagers who can't wait to leave home.

"The most mind-boggling part is that this is what happens if you're *lucky;* this is the way life is *supposed* to go. Because the most tragic experience a mother can live through is the death of her child. Over and over again as a child grows, its mother must mourn the loss of who her child was as that little one moves ahead. It's the most bizarre mix of grief and gratitude, all tangled together."

I was absorbing this outburst of wisdom when Deirdre stopped the car. "There she is. I'll be right back." We were at the edge of a heavily wooded park. I looked hard at the thick grove of trees, caught a flash of red and purple. Deirdre had keen sight; had I been alone I would have missed Mary, crouched between two giant oaks.

Deirdre got out, grabbed a bag from the backseat and made her way over to the huddled figure. Soon she guided Mary toward the car, then into the backseat. Mary lay down the length of it, mumbling, while Deirdre performed a pelvic exam.

Deirdre frowned as she straightened up. She motioned for me to get out of the car, then shut the back door before telling me what was going on. "She's in labor all right, but there's a problem." Deirdre's frown deepened. "Her blood pressure is sky-high. And she's kind of in and out of it. I can't tell if she's talking crazy because she hasn't been taking her meds or if she's got preeclampsia. Either way, I can't take her to the birth center. She'll have to deliver at Saint Elizabeth's."

For the first time since we'd left BirthRight I heard a mixture of frustration and defeat in Deirdre's voice. "They won't let me deliver her there. I don't have hospital privileges. I have to turn her over to the care of the midwife on staff. They're great there, but I can't go with her." She waited a moment, and I had the sense she was trying to find a way to ask for what she wanted without letting me know how much it mattered to her. "How do you feel about going in with her as her doula?"

Deirdre's demeanor told me that the choice was mine to make; she'd respect whatever I chose. She knew I had decided against doing hospital births but this was an exceptional situation. I peered in the back window. Mary was curled up in one corner, looking like a feral cat. How would she manage in the hospital?

No matter how well-meaning, the staff there were strangers to her. Of course I would go.

Deirdre dropped us off at Saint Elizabeth's L & D looking loath to leave. I assured her that I'd call with an update soon. I ushered Mary in, stifling indignation at the raised eyebrow of the admitting nurse. Yes, Mary smelled, but she was still entitled to decency and respect.

Deirdre had been right about the hospital midwife, Laurie, though. She exuded the same kind of professional warmth Deirdre did. I wasn't surprised when she told me she had trained with Deirdre and worked at BirthRight for several years before getting pregnant herself. After her baby was born, she had chosen the more predictable hours of hospital birthing instead of returning to Deirdre's.

"Do you happen to know her preferences for this birth?" Laurie and I were chatting in the hall outside Mary's room. At the sight of the clean bed Mary had uttered a small delighted cry, clambered underneath the sheet and promptly fallen asleep. I considered this a blessing since it would make it easier for the nurses to get her IV in and put the fetal monitors on.

"I don't know what she decided but you can call Deirdre," I told Laurie.

"Her blood pressure is on the high side but she's resting comfortably right now and her bag of waters is still intact, so I see no reason to rush things. I'm going to monitor her for the next hour and we'll see how things look then. Meanwhile, I'll catch up with Deirdre." Laurie gave me a smile, then headed off down the hall to make her phone call.

Mention of the phone reminded me that I hadn't called Michael. Now it was after seven, and I felt bad for waiting so long to cancel. He sounded annoyed when I explained where I was.

"I don't know how long I'll be here, but she doesn't have anyone else. There's no father, no family. Nobody." I tried to push away the feeling that I was defending my choice.

"Okay. Call when you're finished, even if it's not until

tomorrow some time," he finally said, conceding. "I'll come pick you up if I'm not in class." I felt better after his sweet offer, which I took to mean that he was already getting over the disappointment of being stood up.

Childbirth is one of the few experiences in life that still contains many unknowns. Despite all the science and technology, no one's been able to conclusively determine what triggers labor. For three days I sat beside Mary as we awaited the arrival of her child. Her midwife was as committed to woman-centered birthing as Deirdre and for the first two and a half days did no interventions, only monitored Mary's progress as her body slowly dilated. Mary spent much of that time dozing. While I didn't get anywhere near a full night's sleep, I managed to drift off at intervals in the rocker alongside the bed.

Hospital birthing rooms are often windowless. After a few hours in one it's easy to lose all track of time passing. So when a scream woke me with a jolt, I wasn't sure whether it was daytime or the middle of the night. We'd been there over forty-eight hours, which meant it was just before noon, but the lack of natural light really disoriented me. I stood up from the rocker so quickly it made me dizzy, and I had to sit back down again to keep from falling.

The screams were coming from the bed. After resting peacefully through many hours of early labor Mary was now in the throes of it, and not at all happy about the experience.

"Get out! Fucking get out of me!" She was crouched on the bed, clawing at her hospital gown. She yanked it off, then drummed so hard with closed fists on the mound of her belly that I winced. Then she opened her palms and laid them on top of the sloping ridge, pushing down with all her might. Her face purpled with the effort. "I said, get the fuck out of me!"

I thought at first that she was talking to the baby but then recalled what Pixie had told me about abuse memories triggered by labor. Mary was fighting off her attacker, not her child. Her eyes roved the room as if she was somewhere much more dangerous than the sedate hospital room. Her shrieks grew wilder, more insistent.

I went to her side, reached out a hand to steady her. "Mary, look at me. It's Caro Connors. I'm here with you." I tried speaking the same way I had observed Deirdre interact with her during prenatal visits. But today Mary was much more disturbed than I'd ever seen her at BirthRight.

"It fucking hurts!" She lashed out and her palm caught the side of my face, burning a slap into my cheek. Impulsively I lifted my arm, ready to ward off a second blow. But Mary jumped off the bed, scuttled across the tile floor and rushed into a corner, where she sank to her haunches, wailing and pummeling her stomach. The fetal monitors had come undone when she jumped up, and the IV had ripped from her hand. Multiple alarms were ringing in cacophonous accompaniment to her wails.

A brief knock sounded, then the door flew open before I could get to it. The nurse looked toward the empty bed, then in the direction of the screeching coming from the darkened corner. I had turned the lights off so Mary and I could rest, and the room was like a cave. The nurse flipped the switch and the fluorescent glare momentarily blinded me. The light must have stunned Mary; she went utterly still. But the next moment she started shrieking again, this time louder.

The natural childbirths I had attended had taught me how to bear witness to another's pain, to resist the instinct to alleviate those sensations and instead walk with the laboring mother *through* the feelings. This offered her a profound passageway into a new sense of herself. It was one of the most difficult aspects of my job, but one I had grown convinced was crucial to the task. But watching Mary's face contorted with terror as she endured increasingly stronger contractions, I could see that her struggle was psychic as much as physical. She was battling demons far more disturbing than the tightening in her middle. I tried once more to connect with her, to bring her back into the present. But her eyes remained vacant, her screams growing more and more primal as she pulled deeper within herself to a place I couldn't follow.

We managed to get Mary back onto the bed, where she thrashed until we restrained her. The nurse gave her a sedative. Once it took effect I did what I could, stroking her arm, telling her that she was going to be okay. Laurie returned and did a pelvic exam. Afterward she straightened up, looking resigned as she pulled the gloves from her hands.

"Her cervix is closing," she announced. "She was making good progress and was almost at nine, but now the tissue around the cervix is swelling. It's almost like the reverse of dilating, which isn't the direction we want to see things go. I can give her more time but given the severe response she had to things picking up and the way her body is acting now, a vaginal delivery would likely be traumatic." The midwife glanced at Mary, lowered her voice when she spoke again. "Given her prior history and her actions here, I'm afraid she's experiencing pregnancy psychosis. She might have a complete breakdown if things get more intense. And with the condition of her cervix, they will."

Laurie was not making decisions on Mary's behalf but instead offering me information to share with Mary. I looked down at her. She was quieter now but she kept balling her fists, even though the restraints kept her from hitting her belly. Tears were streaming down her face. I offered a Kleenex, held it while she blew her nose, her breath coming in huffy sobs. Before I could explain what the midwife had said, Mary looked at me, her eyes filled with raw suffering. Mary was a terrified child trapped in a woman's body. Laurie was right. It would be cruel to put her through any more. Labor wouldn't empower her; for Mary it would be like being raped all over again.

The OB who performed Mary's C-section was as compassionate and accommodating as the midwife. He let me accompany Mary into the operating room. It was my first time observing a Caesarean and he treated me like a med student, explaining what he was doing and why with every step of the procedure. Mary lay listless on the operating table, seemingly disinterested, but I kept encouraging her to stay awake. She finally stirred when the baby mewled in protest as the doctor lifted him from his mother's womb.

"There's a baby here." Mary sounded amazed, as if she'd had nothing to do with the child who had appeared. I walked over to the Isolette, where the nurses where recording the infant's Apgar scores. He looked as blissfully unaware of the dubious circumstances of his birth as any newborn, and I found myself praying that now that he was born he might have an easier time of it than he'd had in utero.

A couple of hours later I was still with Mary and the baby in the hospital. I couldn't make myself leave. Mary was seated in the rocker that had been my perch for the last few days. I stood nearby, wanting to give her and her son some time to get to know one another but not yet comfortable about leaving the room altogether. Mary was crooning a disjointed lullaby to the bundle in her arms but every so often she swept her eyes around the room like a trapped animal, her expression as wary and wild as it had been in labor.

Connie Stetson's appearance a little while later shouldn't have surprised me, but it did. She poked just her head in the room, took a long look over at mother and child, then motioned for me to join her in the hall. "How's she doing? I heard it got pretty hairy near the end."

"It did." I spoke quietly. "But she seems better now. She's showing interest in the baby. I think that's a good sign."

"Maybe." Connie's expression belied her agreement.

"Why wouldn't it be?"

"He's going to a foster home." Connie pressed a sheath of papers she was carrying to her chest. "I'm here to take him."

"*What?*" I don't know what I had expected Connie to say, but it wasn't that. I took a step toward the social worker, who looked alarmed at my approach. "This poor girl's been through hell and now you're going to take her child from her?"

"What would you do, Caro? This *poor girl* is mentally ill and lives out on the streets. But she's over the age of majority so I can't force her to get help, or take her meds, or better her life in any way. Believe me, I've tried. The midwife told me that Mary was pounding on her uterus. That's not exactly the way a woman who wants to keep her child acts." Connie glared at me, indignant. "Mary can't take care of her son; she can't even take care of *herself*. This is the only option that offers that kid a chance."

I looked through the glass at Mary, who was kissing the infant on the nose. In this moment she appeared like any doting mother. But Connie was right about Mary's erratic behavior and her instability. It was stupid for me to think the baby would be safe with Mary. As if some door inside of me had just slammed shut, I went numb to all the dismay and anger that had been coursing through me just moments before.

"Does she know?" I murmured.

Connie nodded. "We've talked about it throughout her pregnancy but now, well, obviously the reality is more difficult."

I had assisted many women through labor but Mary's was a different kind of crucible. "I'll stay with her after you take him." It wasn't typically part of a doula's job, but if I left now I'd be abandoning her. I couldn't do that. No matter how awful it was, I would help her through. I refused to look at Connie, fearful that doing so would tear off the fragile scab forming over my emotions and I'd be back to flailing inside in anguish, much like Mary had during labor.

Connie and I went back in. Mary beamed at her social worker, as proud as any mother I'd ever worked with. Her smile never dimmed as she held her cocooned newborn out, offering him up to Connie. Perhaps it was the sedatives that made her so compliant. Or maybe the only coping mechanism Mary possessed was to distance herself from her baby. But there was another possibility: maybe she loved her child so much she was willing to bear even the cost of giving him up if it meant a better life for him. Whatever her motivation, Mary was stoic as Connie accepted the newborn, hugged her good-bye, then slipped from the room with Mary's infant in her arms.

I was the one who fell apart in a maelstrom of sobs. And it was Mary who did the consoling. "Come, come." She beckoned from the rocker where she was still seated. I stepped before her, the harsh world blurred by my tears. Mary reached for my hand, pulled me down until I was sitting on the floor alongside the rocker, my head nestled against her calf.

"Hushabye, little one. There, there." She settled back in the chair a little deeper again, crooning to me as she had to her tiny son while she went on rocking, her arms folded in her lap as if the baby remained cradled there.

Twenty-three

Mary fell asleep and I finally left Saint Elizabeth's. I headed for BirthRight in a cab and strode into the birth center around two o'clock. Deirdre was in the exam room filling out a chart. I didn't explain how things had gone with Mary, didn't even bother to shut the door. I didn't care who heard me. "Why the hell didn't you tell me that baby was going into foster care?"

"You never asked." Instead of dousing it, Deirdre's answer fueled my anger.

"You knew, though. You could have told me. I had a right to know, too." Then something occurred to me. I recalled the conversation Deirdre and I had shared in the car while looking for Mary, about the courage it took to be a mother. I had just learned that sometimes serving a woman in labor required the same fortitude. "Is it true that you couldn't come into Saint Elizabeth's to help Mary, or did you just not have the heart to go there?" I deliberately picked the same phrase she'd used to explain why she didn't have children.

Deirdre's face pinched as she continued filling in data on her chart. But I wasn't going away without an answer. Finally she looked up at me. "You have to learn to wear a thick skin if you want to have any hope of a long-term career in this field, Caro." Louder than any words, her hardened countenance told me she was speaking from experience. "Women miscarry. They give birth to stillborns or babies with profound defects. What happened to Mary is tragic but it could have been worse. If you hadn't been with me then yes, I would have said to hell with the rules and gone into the hospital with her myself. But you *were* there, Caro. You chose to go along with me to look for her. You were the best one to help her."

"Why?" I couldn't understand how Deirdre, whose expertise made mine seem paltry, could possibly believe that.

"Because you haven't learned how to quit feeling. Do this job long enough and sometimes, a lot of the time, it's just that—a job. If you're lucky, every once in a while you do a birth that reminds you why you got into this messy, uncertain business in the first place. But when you do birth after birth, month after month, the mundane inures you to the fact that every single one is a miracle. You're still fresh, Caro; you still care in a way I wish I did."

The balm of Deirdre's confession only lasted a short while. Then something else occurred to me. I was furious with her for keeping me in the dark about Mary, but in truth I had played as big a part in the deception as Deirdre. Like many mothers-to-be do, I had focused most on getting through the birth time. I had never stopped to consider what would happen *after* the baby came. Instead I had practiced my well-honed willful ignorance, as if by overlooking the fact that one day the child would be here, it would all somehow be okay once he arrived.

I was driving home when my phone rang. "Hey, Ol." I didn't bother to cover up my sour mood.

"You picked up." He sounded surprised.

"Why would you call me if you didn't think I would?" I was way too tired for guessing games.

"It's Thursday," he answered. "You didn't call, so I figured you were with Ken."

"Ken" was Oliver's nickname for Michael, after Barbie's boyfriend. "No man should be that good-looking," Oliver had grumbled after my New Year's party. "The average guy can't compete with that. It's a betrayal to our gender."

Michael taught an evening class Thursdays so that was my night to stay home. Most weeks I found myself on the phone with Oliver. We had chats that lasted for hours and went late into the night, covering everything from our childhoods to the things we most wanted to do before we died.

"Right. Sorry. No, I'm not with Michael. I had a birth that broke the record. It was a marathon three days long. I'm on my way home now."

"This isn't the 'high on life' voice you usually have afterward." Ollie sounded cautious.

I told him about Mary's birth and the baby going to foster care. "I thought birthing would be so much easier than the funeral business, Ollie. You know, happy arrivals and all. But between MG blowing me off and now this . . . well, I just don't know if I can take it anymore."

"I want you to remember what I'm about to say," Oliver said. "You really know how to be in it with people, Caro. MG acts like an idiot sometimes. She makes these ass-backward decisions that are against her own best interests. It isn't just you; I've seen it before with her. You've got to let her be.

"But this other thing, this birth with Mary. Not everyone has your courage, lady. It sounds like you were a rock star in there. I know it wasn't all happy happy joy joy, but what was it you told me before? Something about how being at births makes you feel like doing anything else is a waste of time?" Ollie waited until I grudgingly agreed. "Right, then. I rest my case. Go home, get some sleep. Call me tomorrow when you're feeling more like your usual bright self again, sunshine."

When I finally made it home, Michael was seated at my kitchen table. I had called him from the cab on the way to BirthRight, hiccupping over fatigue-fueled sobs that refused to subside long enough for me to talk coherently. He had let himself in with the key I had given him. There was a bowl of cereal for me, set out on a place mat with a pitcher of milk and a spoon alongside it. I collapsed into the chair with a flash of the countless times I'd eaten meals in it as a small child. I felt diminutive now, my inability to accept the difficult realities of the world around me leaving me powerless against them. But I felt a little better after a few spoonfuls of raisin bran and Michael's tender ministrations.

Unlike Oliver, Michael didn't ask for details. Nor did he mention that I'd been gone much longer than I'd said I would. After I finished the last of the milk from the bottom of the bowl he walked me into the bedroom. He pulled back the comforter while I undressed, feeling more than ever like Caillebotte's nude, which I'd hung above the bed. I crawled in and Michael slipped in too, his lithe body spooning tight up against me. I thought of Mary and how alone she must have been feeling. The notion nearly undid me but I willed it away, reminding myself that even with the awful way things turned out, Oliver was right. I was grateful I'd been there for her.

I settled deeper into Michael's strong embrace. He nuzzled my neck, his breath hot against my earlobe as he moved his mouth nearer to my ear. "I'm so proud of you," he whispered. "I love you, Caro."

It was the first time either of us had said the words. I wanted to repeat them back to Michael but exhaustion had already dragged me too far under, and I slipped away into sleep's oblivion before I could tell him that the feeling was overwhelmingly mutual.

PART III

Death

Twenty-four

When you come from a family of funeral directors, the telephone rings ominously in the middle of the night. For a doula, that same peal resonates with eager anticipation. Either way, it always means lives are about to change. It was early evening and still so bright outside it seemed the daylight would never fade away. But for me it *was* the middle of the night; whoever was calling had woken me from the kind of sleep that approximated how I guessed it might feel to be dead. Michael reached over to silence the buzzing but I waved his hand away and picked up the phone, ignoring his grumbled protestations.

"Hello?" The greeting came out in a whisper. I was still too befuddled to speak up.

"Caro? It's me. Do you have a minute?"

The last time Mary Grace had asked me that question my best friend had followed it with big news. I shook the fog from my head.

"I'm at the mall," she said. "I was picking out some last-minute things for the layette. And I needed to pee—of course I needed to pee, right? So I went to use the ladies' room and—"

"What is it?" I interrupted her nervous rambling. Mary Grace hadn't called to chat about what she'd purchased, not after three months of silence between us.

"Blood." She spit the word out like a curse.

"Brownish?" Brown would mean the baby was probably fine, and a call to the OB would lay our worries to rest.

"Red. Bright. About the size of a quarter." MG sounded terrified.

I pictured my best friend on the other end of the phone, jaw tight, as if by clamping down on it she might contain the fright coursing through her. She knew a mother's emotions could affect a growing fetus. She had been doing prenatal yoga and meditation daily in an effort to provide the baby with a serene environment.

"Where are you now?"

"Outside Saks." She sounded plaintive, and I guessed that she hoped I would tell her what to do next.

"Sit tight. I'll be there as soon as I can. Meanwhile, call your OB. Let him know what's going on."

Michael had propped himself up on one elbow and was studying me as I pulled on the same pair of jeans and blouse I'd worn to BirthRight before Mary's birth time. The outfit was going on four days ripe but I was too scared and tired to waste precious minutes searching for clean clothes.

"Let me guess." Michael picked up my purse from the floor, where I'd dropped it before falling into bed, and held it out to me. "One of your clients needs you."

I was about to tell Michael who it was but he went on before I had the chance. "Caro, you've barely slept in days. You're in no condition to do another birth. Call your backup. Let her go." He reached out and grabbed my wrist with his hand, pulled me toward him. His lips met mine in a hungry invitation. "Baby, I promise I'll make staying here as worth it as any birth," he growled seductively.

Had it been any other client I might have called Sylvie Cavanaugh, another doula I had met through BirthRight. She and I had agreed to help each other out in the event that we couldn't be at a birth. But this wasn't *any* client.

"I have to go, Michael. It's Mary Grace. She's bleeding." I walked out, calling back at him over my shoulder, "Stay as long as you want. If she's not in labor I'll be home soon." Then I flew downstairs and out to my car, praying this was a false alarm and that I would be back in my bed making love with Michael before nightfall.

* * *

I spotted Mary Grace as soon as I pulled into the parking lot outside Saks Fifth Avenue. She was seated on a bench, looking wan but not panicked. "MG, you're going to kill yourself in those shoes," I admonished while holding the passenger-side door open for her. She was wearing high heels. I was frightened about the blood she'd found on her panties, so I tried to distract us from it by yelling at her about something we could change. She got in and I took off for Medical City.

"I'll stay off the stilettos," she moaned after I lectured her about her shifting center of gravity. As pregnant as Mary Grace was, her balance was precarious barefooted, never mind on four-inch spikes. She gave a long sigh at yet another of the sacrifices pregnancy demanded. "But I will *never* be one of those women who trade down to flip-flops.

"It's bad enough they call me an elderly mother." Mary Grace had been put out at the medical establishment's term for anyone over thirty and pregnant. "I won't add 'dowdy' to the picture," she huffed. "I'll get myself into L & D in my lucky sling-backs even if I have to squeeze my feet into them *and* make Brad carry me." She waggled a foot clad in the very shoes she was talking about and looked at me hard, daring me to talk her out of it. We giggled in unison at the thought of Brad staggering into the hospital, Mary Grace spilling over his arms like an overgrown baby herself. And just like that, all the tension between us broke.

Mary Grace laid a hand lightly on my arm. "Thanks for coming. I mean it. Brad and I had a huge fight this morning and I don't feel like dealing with him unless I'm really in labor. And if it's time for this one to arrive, I really want you to be there.

"If you're okay with that," she added quickly. "You're still going to be this little one's godmother, despite our recent hiatus."

I shifted my gaze from the road to her face. The tears shining in her eyes started mine going too. I hoped that this scare was just meant to mend things between us.

* * *

Fifteen minutes later we were in Medical City's L & D. Mary Grace lay on her side on the exam table, hooked up to the fetal monitor, which showed the baby's heart galloping along reassuringly. We were waiting for the doctor to do a sonogram. The nurse who'd started the monitor thought that everything looked fine and that Ava Jane wasn't in any immediate danger, but the sonogram would tell us more definitively.

I was sitting in a chair alongside Mary Grace, holding one of her hands. My other hand rested on the bump that was her baby. Mary Grace had her eyes closed. She looked peaked and drawn. I was feeling the effects of sleep deprivation myself and had just drifted into a light doze when MG spoke.

"Is there such a thing as doula-client confidentiality?"

I looked closely at her. She hadn't shifted position or even opened her eyes. But she seemed weighted down with a load heavier than the baby she was carrying. "You mean like therapist-client privilege?"

MG nodded, eyes still shut.

"I don't know that anyone's ever explained it that way, but I guess if a client asked me to keep something in confidence I'd honor her request." A few more minutes ticked by. Mary Grace remained still, mulling something over. "But you know, MG, there's the privilege of best friends . . . that trumps even the professional guidelines, so you can swear me to secrecy about anything anytime you want."

The doctor came in to do the sonogram and a pelvic exam. Mary Grace turned onto her back. As the nurse set her feet in the stirrups, MG giggled. She pointed to the ceiling. The words "I hate this" were printed and taped overhead. I laughed too, and then the doctor joined in. "We do what we can to make this fun," he joked as he donned a glove to check her cervix.

The baby seemed fine but Mary Grace was still bleeding. She'd begun cramping, too. Stryker wasn't taking any chances. He decided to admit her and monitor the contractions, try to prevent her from going into premature labor.

We moved from the examination bay into a birthing suite. After MG got settled she called Brad. "Caro's with me," she told him in a small, falsely cheerful voice. "I called her. She picked me up from the mall . . .

"Well, you were working and I didn't want to worry you." She put her head down, perhaps embarrassed that I was overhearing the conversation. I motioned toward the door, mimicked leaving to give her privacy, but she shook her head. "No, don't rush. It's not like I'm about to have the baby or anything." She looked over at me, perhaps wanting to see if I would contradict her.

Once she got off the phone I looked at her a moment, debating. "What did you want to tell me before the doctor came in?" I finally asked.

MG closed her eyes, her hands resting on the shelf of her belly, fingers tapping on it as if she were conveying a message to the baby in Morse code. "I slept with someone.

"Not Brad," she said, clarifying, although that was obvious. "It was a mistake. Brad and I hadn't been getting along so well, and then he went out of town. I worked late on a Friday night . . ." She winced. I guessed that she'd probably heard myriad versions of this well-worn story over the years from clients with marital troubles. Mary Grace raised her hands from her belly, covered her face with them. "After work I had some drinks at a bar near my office and I slept with someone."

"It wasn't a client, was it?" I was stunned, trying to mask my surprise and fill in the gaps in what she'd told me so far.

She shook her head. "I'm not *that* stupid," she muttered from behind her hands.

"Then who?" She'd confided to me on our trip to the Art Institute that her marriage had brought a number of challenges. Brad liked things a certain way and wasn't one to make concessions. But despite his obnoxious behavior, he adored her. Mary Grace was everything to Brad; even I could see that. "You didn't pick up a total stranger?"

She shook her head again, rubbed her fingertips along her

temples. "A friend," she said vaguely. She looked over at me and I made a face to let her know I wasn't going to be put off that easily. The news of her infidelity shocked me, but what hurt worse was that she hadn't confided in me when it happened. I thought we told each other everything. If it had been me, I would have told her right away.

"I'd rather keep him out of it. It was a mistake. A one-night thingy. Not some great love affair." Then her tone turned to disgust. "I slept with someone and I'm too big a coward to tell my husband because I'm afraid that if I do he'll leave me and this one." She pointed a finger toward her belly. "And I want to stay married and have this baby. At least I think I want to stay married. I thought I could keep the slip to myself and everything could go back to being okay between me and Brad . . ." Her words trailed off. "But now, with the blood . . ." She made a vague gesture with one hand as she went on. "If something were to, you know, happen, well, it seems important that someone know. Even if that someone never told anyone else." She looked at me meaningfully.

I thought about what she was asking of me, considered saying that I found her decision to tell me about the encounter now selfish. But pregnancy made women vulnerable, and I couldn't blame Mary Grace for her worry. I looked over at her. My usually composed and confident friend looked worn to exhaustion.

"Look," I said, making up my mind. "Your secret's safe with me."

A bit of the heaviness around her lifted and I was glad I hadn't given her grief. It wasn't my place to tell Brad about MG's indiscretion. But just as I was about to reassure my friend that I wouldn't tell, something else occurred to me.

"MG?" I reached out and for the second time laid my hand on her belly, as if I could shield the baby inside from hearing us. "When?"

She knew what I was asking. The trembling in her hands as she placed them over mine told me as much. She lowered her head, looked down at her belly. "A few weeks before—"

Just then, her husband came in.

* * *

By the time it grew dark it was clear that despite medication to stop the contractions, the baby was coming into the world. It was summer solstice, the longest day of the year. When Brad arrived I gathered my things to leave, even though MG had said earlier that she wanted me to be there for the birth. She looked up, alarmed. "Stay," she mouthed over Brad's shoulder as he hugged her.

Brad didn't say anything when I set my keys and purse back down again. I wanted to get out of there, go home and get back to catching up on the sleep my throbbing head and aching body needed. But the thought of getting a good night's rest was a joke. I had so many questions for MG. If I left now, I'd lie in bed driving myself nuts trying to come up with answers I could only guess at. Here I might get the rest of the story.

Four hours later, I knew nothing more. Brad was growing antsy. I suggested he go down to the cafeteria and get both of us coffee but he scowled as if he sensed I had an ulterior motive.

"Are you sure everything's okay?" he asked Nicole, the nurse, every time she came in to check vitals, until she reassured him the doctor on call was on her way. As is typical in hospital-based OB practices Stryker had gone home, leaving MG in the care of his on-call colleague overnight.

Brad seemed surprised about this. "Get Stryker in here," he insisted.

Apparently he didn't have the kind of pull he thought, because despite his strident demands Nicole refused to page Stryker. When Brad whipped out his cell phone and angrily punched the numbers for Stryker's answering service, he was told by the operator that Stryker wouldn't be available until the next morning. No, he didn't want to speak to the physician on call, he spat into the phone before snapping it shut. I winced in sympathy for the operator and wondered whether Brad's performance was an indication of how he would behave the rest of the birth.

A few minutes later I groaned inwardly when Dr. Leslie Mark entered the room. I'd heard from Sylvie Cavanaugh that she wasn't fond of doulas, thought we meddled more than helped. A doula made it possible for the OB to focus more on the delivery, less on his or her bedside manner. But I had encountered more than one physician whose ego bristled when I appeared in the delivery room.

"The baby seems to be doing well." Dr. Mark filled Mary Grace and Brad in after introducing herself and studying the fetal monitor strips. "But you are officially in labor. You're dilated to three, eighty-five percent effaced. This baby is coming." She paused and looked down at her watch, then back up toward the Schaeffers. "Sometime tonight maybe, but more likely in the morning."

As if her body was taking issue with the doctor's self-assured tone, Mary Grace's water chose that moment to break. A loud pop filled the room, like a gunshot signaling the beginning of a race. I pushed my growing impatience for answers aside. Once the amniotic sac breaks, it's only a matter of time before the baby arrives. The question was, were we running a marathon or a sprint?

Twenty-five

The moment a baby crowns is always a thrill. Ava Jane Schaeffer's head peeked out after thirteen hours of labor. Mary Grace had labored without any pain medication. She looked worn out but determined to finish. I turned to Nicole, who was charting at the counter. "She's complete," I said.

Nicole reached for the phone to page the doctor. "Dr. Mark's on her way." She turned back to Mary Grace. "Just a few pushes from now, you'll be holding your little one in your arms." The pert young nurse smiled a wide grin at Mary Grace, trying to ease her discomfort. But the grin turned to a frown a moment later. Nicole had directed Mary Grace to push again, probably thinking it would take a few more contractions before the baby arrived. But Ava Jane was ready now.

"I can see almost her whole head," I told Mary Grace. That seemed to encourage her and she brightened a little.

"I need to talk to you. In the hall." Brad's curt demand startled me. He had moved alongside me and whispered it under his breath. Despite his efforts to control things during MG's pregnancy, since he'd arrived in the L & D suite he'd kept his distance, standing for most of the night at the opposite end of the room from where his wife labored.

I nodded at him, then told MG I'd be right back and moved toward the door.

"Mary Grace is bleeding," Brad said once we were out of the room.

"Yes . . ." I didn't understand what he was getting at but was relieved that it had nothing to do with the baby's parentage. "There's usually a lot of fluid. She might poop, too, when she pushes the baby out." I figured I'd better prepare him since he seemed clueless. "It can get a bit messy."

"But blood? Blood is normal?" Brad looked as if he wanted to believe me but wasn't convinced. His eyes roamed the hall. Finally he looked straight at me. "I can't lose Mary Grace. She's my world." The hard edge to his features melted and his face sagged. "You have to help her through this."

I'd found Brad controlling and hadn't liked him for it, but with his plea I saw the tremendous fear beneath his arrogance. Right now he looked more like an overwhelmed teenager than a confident businessman.

"I'll do everything I can," I promised.

He laid a hand on my shoulder as he walked past me back into the room. He knew that while we didn't see eye to eye we both adored MG. He believed I would keep her safe.

When I returned to Mary Grace, she was breathing faster, her chest heaving toward her chin with every inhale. Breath wracked her body like sobs. When I'm with a laboring mother I audibly inhale through my nose and exhale through my mouth in a big lazy sigh, loud enough for my client to hear and mimic. It helps a birthing woman hold on to the breath through labor. But I was tired from the day's relentless tension and frazzled by Mary Grace's secret. I broke my rule of setting the pace. I started panting like her—in sharp, shallow breaths that inflated my chest but never made it any lower. My breath grew thinner and thinner until I was hardly filling my lungs at all.

"My bottom. It's burning." Mary Grace moaned. She reached a hand down and clutched at her buttocks. Then she looked up at me wide-eyed as her fingers roamed forward, grazed the top of the baby's head.

Nicole put a hand down between Mary Grace's legs. "No, Mary Grace, don't push yet!" she admonished.

I looked up, as confused as MG.

"What's the matter? What's wrong with my baby?" Mary Grace asked in that panicky voice adrenaline provokes in laboring women near the end. The pushing is the most strenuous part of labor. It's poor design that the hardest phase comes at the end, but that's the way it is.

"Why can't I push?" MG's voice held a tinge of near-hysteria that signaled she was almost out of resources. Brad was sitting on the couch back in the corner, his hands gripping his knees so hard his knuckles were white. Every few moments he looked over at me. We communicated wordlessly while I tended to Mary Grace. She lifted her head off the pillow. A lather of sweat shone on her forehead. It had been a long, hard night of slow laboring and riding out the pains, a night of no sleep and back-to-back contractions. Now the end was here, but the nurse was commanding her to hold off.

"You need to wait for Dr. Mark to deliver the baby." Nicole made a "tsk" sound with her tongue, as if Mary Grace should have known better than to think that she was capable of birthing her baby without a doctor's help.

I looked at Mary Grace. Her nostrils flared and her eyes rolled back in her head at Nicole's instruction to wait. She was barely holding on. Before Nicole's rebuke I had pulled MG's left leg up in the optimal position for pushing, with her knee near her shoulder, heel braced in my armpit. Now I placed MG's foot in the footrest and peeked around her leg. The top of Ava Jane's head was sticking out between her mother's thighs. I could see not just the crown but nearly the whole head. If I'd knelt down underneath Mary Grace, I could have looked her daughter in the eyes.

Mary Grace moaned and writhed as another contraction built. Along with the baby's head there was more blood coming now. Brad fixed his eyes on me, silently reminding me of my promise to keep MG safe. And I, mother to the mother, the one who was supposed to be advocate and voice for the family, I could only look on the child as she hung suspended between the womb and the world.

How awful it must have felt to be stuck in that in-between place, how badly the baby must have wanted to emerge and utter her first cry. An insistent voice, hers mingled with mine, rose from my belly. I wanted to yell at the nurse that it was not okay to leave the baby waiting. But my throat clamped tight around the head of a scream, and like the child in front of me it remained lodged in my throat, strangling there while only the faintest whimper escaped my lips. I put my hands around my throat. The muscles were knotty, constricted. My teeth clenched so tightly it hurt to pry them apart again.

The child's head turned a sickly gray that reminded me too much of that stillborn I'd seen in the funeral home, the one that had appeared in my vision. That baby's skin had been covered with downy fuzz, his eyelids pulled down tight as if he'd never wanted to let in the light of the outside world. What I had seen when MG told me she was pregnant was coming true. Ava Jane was turning the same awful color as that baby corpse.

I lunged forward, fueled by panic and guilt, into the wide chasm of Mary Grace's legs, knocking one out of the stirrups in my haste. Mary Grace looked up, saw the terror I couldn't hide, and started screaming. She screamed and screamed, as any mother should when her child is in danger. Brad jumped up but then stood frozen, watching the turmoil unfolding as he had feared it would. I reached down and hooked the tip of my index finger around the blood-slick pulsing cord cutting off Ava Jane's oxygen supply, pulled it back from her neck to give the air safe passage.

"Get out of the way." Dr. Mark arrived, shoving me aside as she donned her gloves, then maneuvered her fingers under the cord just as I'd been doing. In a matter of seconds her hands were covered in blood. "Mary Grace, stop pushing. Stop pushing or you'll make things worse!"

Mary Grace craned her neck to look down between her legs, desperate to see what was wrong.

"Call Anesthesia, Peeds and the backup OB," Dr. Mark barked at Nicole as she moved the thick cord away from Ava Jane's neck, then coaxed one of the baby's shoulders out of the womb. In another few seconds both arms and the torso were free. The legs followed. So did another crimson rush of fluid. A pall hung in the air. "C'mon, baby girl, c'mon." Dr. Mark held the baby upside down by her ankles and slapped her bottom, lightly at first, then harder when she got no response.

The door swung open. A swarm of doctors and nurses burst into the room. Helen was one of them. Dr. Mark swung around. "Somebody take her!" She held the baby aloft.

Helen plucked Ava Jane from Dr. Mark's hands and whisked her over to the warming table at the far end of the suite, where she shook her like a rag doll, then whacked her once, twice, three times on the back. A few of the other nurses watched, urging Ava Jane to breathe with the fervent reverence of a prayer group holding a vigil. I had backed into a corner, where I stood watching.

"What's going on?" Brad demanded, keeping his distance from the ministrations.

Dr. Mark turned her attention back to Mary Grace's raging uterus. "The baby wasn't getting enough oxygen," she explained as she probed between MG's legs.

In the next breath she muttered, "Nicole, get me more towels. And where are the damned sutures?

"The pediatric team is reviving your daughter now," Dr. Mark said to Brad distractedly as she applied pressure to Mary Grace's perineum with the wad of towels Nicole handed her. "She's having trouble breathing on her own and needs to be in the NICU."

Mary Grace's eyes searched out Brad. "Go with her." He looked reluctant to leave but she insisted. "She needs you now."

Brad moved across the room toward the doctors and nurses crowded around the Isolette. Helen had started CPR. Her fist covered the baby's chest entirely as she pumped down. She placed her mouth over Ava Jane's nostrils and mouth and exhaled in an effort to blow life back into the tiny body. Brad stepped alongside Helen, punching his closed fist into his opposite hand over and over. His recriminating eyes found mine once more. "You promised," he hissed as he followed Helen and the Isolette from the labor and delivery room.

While Brad did as Mary Grace asked, I stayed behind, gripping her hand as Dr. Mark worked frantically to staunch the blood pouring from her vagina. In the moments right before Ava Jane arrived I'd had the sense that Mary Grace was no longer there. Her body was on the bed, but when she spoke her voice sounded far away. Perhaps this was what it took to bring a child into the world. Two entities can't physically occupy the same space simultaneously, so maybe mothers make room for their little ones to come through, then find their way back into their bodies afterward.

I gripped Mary Grace's hand and tugged, hoping I might be able to move energy the way I'd seen Pixie work it over little Quinn, help MG come back down into herself. *I'm so sorry,* I repeated silently in my mind. *I saw this coming from the beginning. I should have told you, should have found some way to help you earlier.* As if she heard me, MG offered a small smile. For a second I thought she'd returned. But then she uttered a long sigh. Her hand loosened in mine; the light in her eyes dimmed. As that summer solstice night brightened into dawn after Ava Jane emerged from womb to world, her mother slipped off like the moon making way for the sun's first light. And I was finally forced to acknowledge that for years I'd been suffocating on all the dark things I'd witnessed in my life.

Twenty-six

Monday morning. Three days had passed. I'd spent seventy-two hours in bed, grateful for the precious oblivion of sleep that came between fractured dreams in which I lost Mary Grace over and over again. In one, we were rock-climbing and I let go of the rope that kept her on the rock's face, watching as she tumbled past me. Next we were in the car. I was driving and when I made a sharp turn Mary Grace's door popped open and she sailed out and rolled down the street. Despite the varied circumstances, the scene that inevitably startled me fully awake was an all-too-vivid reenactment of what I had just lived through: watching helplessly while a raging red river bore the infant along out of my best friend, taking every ounce of Mary Grace's life with it.

After a birth I'm always a little surprised to see people going about the tasks of ordinary life with no inkling of the miracle I've just seen. For certain life events time seems suspended. Perhaps it's the environments in which they happen: labor and delivery suites, funeral homes and courtrooms share a surreal air. Life hangs in the balance in these locales; experiences there become markers for a lifetime. Afterward it's unsettling to reenter the world, similar to what I imagine a newborn feels: regret that it's no longer inside but also relief that it's finally free.

After the unfathomable happens, it can feel like an insult for life to continue. But between the handful of moments that ultimately define us come wide stretches of ordinary time spent awaiting the next epiphany. The simple distractions of the mundane offer a kind of refuge. But today would not provide any such respite. Today I would attend my best friend's funeral. I was well acquainted with the rites and rituals of dying. I had chosen to work at the opposite end of the spectrum, hoping that birthing would bring the optimism of new beginnings to my life. But Ava Jane Schaeffer's birth would be forever intertwined with her mother's death.

The realization brought a sorrow so visceral I doubled over, crossing my arms around my body as if I could protect myself from it. The anguish of losing MG stabbed at me. A part of me had died along with my best friend. The pain was familiar from when I'd lost Paulie but it felt sharper, the additional years I'd had with MG a longer dagger goring the soft underbelly of my body and soul, scarred over from the childhood grief. With swift slashes this new loss slit open all the others again.

The last funeral I had attended was Ruby's. Now the ghosts of the ABCs hovered as I dressed for Mary Grace's. I donned panties and bra, stockings and a modest black dress. I paused a moment before my open closet, as if Aunt A might appear in the dim space and hand me one of the hats she and her sisters had always worn without fail.

Childhood offers such a limited perspective. We think the circumstances we're raised in are typical until we grow up and our experience of the world broadens. I had lived out my youth under the illusion that everyone went to funerals on a regular basis. I was in my twenties before I realized that few people outside my family considered them a spectator sport.

Every evening I can recall, B stepped out her door and around the corner of Halsted Street to the funeral home, pausing on the front stoop to bend over and pick up the *Sun-Times* and the *Tribune*. She'd sit in the overstuffed chair by the kitchen window in our apartment over the funeral home with a cup of black coffee, the front section of first one newspaper and then the other spread wide in her arms as she proclaimed the day's obituaries. Aunt C would make a list of people they knew who had, as B so delicately put it, "bought the farm."

A second list was begun on the next page of the notepad, of rival funeral homes in the area, with an asterisk placed next to each establishment for each client they had. From her perch in the window B would occasionally lift her head over the top of the paper and crow, "Beginski's got one—some old Pole from Thirty-Second and Aberdeen.

"Does 'Banakevich' ring a bell to you?" she'd ask her sisters. This continued until B reached the bottom of the entries.

This was how the ABCs set their calendar. The funeral industry is unpredictable. Social engagements were subject to cancellation in the event of a death within the city limits. During one fruitful season, the ABCs averaged three to four funerals a week. Winters tended to be busier than the summer months. A lot of folks got worn down by the rigors of holiday shopping and revelry.

The doorbell rang, delivering me back to the present. I hurried my feet into black patent pumps, plucked the only dark clutch I owned (maroon suede, all wrong for the occasion) out of the dresser drawer where I kept things I almost never used and hurriedly stuffed it with toilet paper since I couldn't locate the Kleenex. I shut the clasp on the purse and rushed to the front door, which I flung open. I was prepared to dismiss whoever was on the other side with a curt explanation that I was running late. But when I saw who it was, I came to a dead halt.

At first I mistook Momma for B. She was wearing one of my grandmother's hats and so resembled her that I thought Momma was a ghost called up by my reminiscences. For a moment it was like déjà vu as I recalled opening our front door as a girl and the ABCs charging in full blast to take over for my dispirited mother. But then I realized my error.

"You're here," I blurted in disbelief.

"Of course I am." The curtness was her way of pretending I'd never left. As if we were back home instead of in what I knew she considered the foreign territory of my condo. "I left at seven thirty to make sure I'd have enough time. Plus, traffic was light." Her mouth tightened as she peered at me. "When did you sleep last? You look like a raccoon, the circles under your eyes are so dark." Momma had a second black hat in her hand, one of Aunt A's, with feathers and a short black veil. "This will hide them." She reached out and set the hat on my head, fussing with the veil, arranging it just so. Then she nodded her approval. She leaned down and gripped the handle of the suitcase waiting beside her, slid it past me through the doorway into the condo, pulled the door shut. Then she turned and walked toward the front entrance of my building, expecting me to follow without further discussion, which is what I did.

As long as they didn't involve her personally, Momma lived for times of crisis. I think she welcomed distraction from her own troubles. I shouldn't have been so surprised by her appearance. She had walked me through my nursing school debacle, reminding me time and again that I would survive it. Never once in that awful time did I see her lose her composure. She had learned that even unfathomable loss didn't kill you; as the years passed somehow the grief grew manageable, made room for glints of joy to shine in even the most devastated of hearts.

Momma also knew better than anyone what Mary Grace had meant to me. When we were growing up she used to say that Mary Grace and I were the kind of friends who would be there for each other until the end. Which, unthinkably, was where we were now.

Twenty-seven

Momma and I rode to the church in silence. Grief left me too exhausted to talk, and for the moment she seemed content to let me be. Michael was waiting when I pulled into Our Lady of the Lake Catholic Church's parking lot. I parked alongside his familiar green Volkswagen. He looked puzzled when he saw I had a passenger. The expression turned to astonishment, and when I caught his eye over the top of my car I shook my head in warning to prevent him from asking what Momma was doing there. Momma was sensitive; she'd take his inquiry as an insult.

"Hi, Mrs. Connors." He managed to keep the surprise out of his voice as he held the passenger door open for her.

"Nice to see you again, Michael." She smiled prettily. Momma had beamed every time he walked into the room last Christmas. I knew without her saying so that she was thrilled I'd met someone so "normal." He leaned in and placed a perfunctory kiss on her cheek. The undertone of a giggle escaped before Momma could stifle it. I looked away from their exchange, focused on getting inside before the pallbearers brought Mary Grace's coffin out of the hearse, which was pulled up at the curb outside the church's behemoth doors. An usher handed me a square Day-Glo orange FUNERAL sticker to place on my windshield for the procession to the interment.

Momma proceeded up the aisle as if she attended Mass at this parish every Sunday. That's one consolation of tradition, the familiar sense that you know exactly where you are and what's going to happen any time you enter a church regardless of where it's located. It's like going home to family, in a way. Momma would have marched all the way up the aisle to the row right behind where Brad Schaeffer was seated with his parents and Mary Grace's mother, Marilyn Hanover, had I not tugged hard at the fringe of her black shawl just a few rows from the back. I moved into the pew, Momma and Michael following, although Momma shot me a questioning look. Maybe I was a coward, but I didn't think that I could make it through the service if I had to witness the family's mourning from such close proximity. I pulled at the kneeler, knelt on the padded board and shut my eyes. I wished I had thought to grab Ruby's rosary when I got out of the car. I offered up a quick Hail Mary to my friend's namesake instead.

Organ music filled the church but I stayed where I was, kneeling for a little while longer. When I finally opened my eyes the church around me was filled with people. Some I knew, but many were strangers. An unsettling thought filled me: we live so much of our lives in isolated parts, each one a mystery to the others, divided into time with family, friends, work colleagues. I wondered whether Brad was feeling the same. Or did he know most of these people who'd felt close enough to Mary Grace to attend her funeral?

The pallbearers rolled the casket up the aisle toward the front of the church. Out of the six I recognized only Mary Grace's little brother, Jacob, and Oliver. I watched Brad as he turned in the pew to track the casket making its slow way to the altar. His jaw was set hard, resolute. Most of the pallbearers' faces mimicked Brad's, as if they were taking their cue from him. Jacob seemed stricken, lost. Mary Grace had been as much a second mother as a big sister to him. Although he had moved to California several years ago, the bond between them had remained strong. Oliver looked as if he had aged years. His cheeks were gaunt, his profile sharp. Grief had carved away the few extra pounds that used to soften his features.

I knew my best friend was in that casket, yet I couldn't quite believe it. As kids, Mary Grace and I sometimes snuck into the showroom at the funeral home. The caskets were displayed in rows, like cars in an auto dealership. We'd run our fingers along the satin linings inside them and wonder how it would feel to be buried in one of those boxes.

Always the braver of the two of us, Mary Grace had once scrambled up into one and insisted I shut the lid. I had been the one panting with fear for the short time she was in there. When I lifted up the lid again she had grinned and said she kind of liked the peace and quiet of it. Now the recollection of our antics turned my stomach.

Where did we go after we died?

I had asked my father once not long after we lost Paulie, but he'd only looked pained and muttered something about my guess being as good as his. Coming from a family of funeral directors didn't offer any insider information on what happened after we put a body in the ground.

Mary Grace hadn't been sick or preparing for her death in any way; she'd planned to be around for a long while yet. I couldn't imagine any mother willingly leaving her child, especially a newborn. I willed myself to feel for her presence, to see if she was there with us still. I looked up toward Brad, squinting to make out some shimmering image of my friend hovering near him. But if she was somehow able to stay close, wouldn't she be with her daughter now?

The thought of Mary Grace's spirit lingering near Ava Jane in the NICU felt so right that the grief knotted tighter around my heart and I gasped, loud enough that Momma shot me a sharp look. She dug around in her purse and came up with a handkerchief Aunt C had embroidered with tiny violets and roses decades ago. The lace around the border had faded and was now more cream than white. The sight of that delicate square of fabric broke me further, and I sobbed into it for all the people I dearly missed—my brother, Ruby, the ABCs—until I had no more tears left to shed.

As the priest gave his homily about how many people had loved her, my mind went to MG's affair. I wondered what else I hadn't known about my best friend. In an effort to ignore my grief I had almost convinced myself to let MG's secret lie along with her. But the truth has an insistent way of surfacing. Then something occurred to me: what if her lover was here now? Of course he would be, wouldn't he? Or would he have chosen to mourn his loss in private? Did he even know she was gone?

There were several good-looking men in the church, but then most men look good in a suit. I never did find a man that felt like the *one*. But I got distracted after searching through just one side of the aisle, because sitting in the pew behind Brad was someone I did know. Someone I hadn't expected to see at the service. It was my next-door neighbor, Helen.

She was dressed to kill, as the saying goes. If anything, in her tailored black suit and stilettos, Helen looked the part of a grieving widow. I put a hand to the hat on my head. It was more suitable for Helen's chic look. I spent the rest of Mass fretting that I'd made a gaffe. I was Mary Grace's best friend and here I was, sitting in the back of the church. Seeing Helen so close to Mary Grace's family sent a stab of misgiving through me.

Choking on sorrow that was rising again, I watched my best friend's casket come back down the aisle, followed by her family, who walked behind it clutching on to one another. Even in grief the mourners clung to the comfort that orderliness seemed to bring as people filed out pew by pew, emptying the church.

The last notes of "I Will Raise You Up" lingered around me as I stepped from the dim entryway out into the shining brilliance of a faultless summer day. Much of the crowd was making their way toward their cars to queue up for the procession to the cemetery. A police car stood sentry in front of the hearse. Brad and his family were gathered at the bottom of the steps. People stopped to offer their condolences as they passed by on the way to the parking lot. Marilyn was standing next to Brad's mother. Her eyes were dry and she seemed stoic. Part of me yearned to go to her for a soothing hug but I stopped, feeling guilty for the childish urge to seek comfort from her when I ought to be offering it instead. Momma moved toward Marilyn. I whispered to Michael that we were going to speak with the family.

"I'll go pull your car into the procession line." Michael seemed relieved to have a reason to escape.

While Momma and Marilyn embraced as if they were old friends instead of neighbors who rarely socialized, I moved toward Brad. He looked stunned as he watched the pallbearers transfer the coffin into the hearse.

"Brad, I'm so sorry." The words were inadequate but none could describe the grief we were struggling to make sense of that day. Brad startled. Then his jaw tightened harder, setting against more than just anguish now. He stepped nearer, trampling my foot with the hard sole of his dress shoe as he grabbed my arm.

"You're sorry," he parroted. "*You* promised you'd keep her safe. We trusted you. But you killed her." He hissed the words, his face jutting into my own. The accusation stunned me. I tried to draw back, put some space between us, but he held fast to my arm. Just as I thought I might lose what little composure I had managed to summon, a hand settled lightly between my shoulder blades.

"We're all in a lot of pain, Brad." I heard Oliver's voice behind me, turned and looked gratefully at my rescuer as he removed the white cotton pallbearer's gloves from his hands.

Brad turned on Oliver. "Don't compare your feelings to mine. I was her *husband,* not her drinking buddy."

I looked at Oliver. Anger flashed in his dark eyes but he held his tongue. Brad was glaring at Oliver, waiting for some kind of response, but he'd struck both of us mute. He gave a shake of his head as if we disgusted him, then stalked off, making his way toward the cop standing at the curb alongside the squad car.

I thought Brad was satisfied he'd had his say, that his outburst was over and he was signaling the officer to lead the motorcade out into traffic toward the cemetery. I turned and was about to ask Oliver if he wanted to leave his car there and ride with us when his expression turned wary. He was looking at something over my shoulder. I turned back around again. The policeman was standing there.

"Mr. Schaeffer directed me to tell you that you aren't welcome at the cemetery, ma'am." The words were ominously formal but the cop's face remained impassive, as if he was issuing me a traffic ticket. He tipped two fingers to his hat in a self-conscious salute, then abruptly departed. Delivering the message was just a distasteful part of the job for him. For me, an already awful day had just exploded all to hell.

Twenty-eight

I turned to Oliver to make sense of what was incomprehensible to me. He looked as incredulous as I felt, so I made my way over to the car. Michael was opening the door for Momma.

"Caro?" Michael started to ask me something, then stopped. Momma turned. They both looked at me quizzically. I forced myself to appear as collected as I could under the circumstances, although inside I was coming undone.

"Um, the thing is, I can't go to the cemetery." My voice cracked and I gulped in a breath, searching for something to counter the overwhelming emotion rising in me.

"What?" Michael asked, bewildered. "Babe, I know it's tough but you have to go. She's your best friend. We'll be right there with you." My boyfriend looked to my mother for support. She stared at me hard but didn't say a word.

I shook my head, incredulity turning me petulant. "I didn't say I didn't want to go, Michael. I said I *can't*. As in Brad won't *allow* me there."

That announcement earned matching stunned expressions from Michael and Momma. I went on, the words breathy and thin as they escaped my lips. "He told the cop over there to let me know I wasn't welcome at the graveside. Maybe you two can go for me and I'll just . . . I guess I'll head on home." I faltered, completely at a loss now about what I was supposed to do next.

Oliver stepped up beside me. "If you two can pay Caro's respects for her, I know a place where we as her best friends can give Mary Grace the kind of send-off she deserves," he said.

He looked to Michael as if asking his permission to take me away. Michael nodded toward Momma. "Yes, of course," Momma said. "If Michael will drive me, I'll give your condolences to

Marilyn and Jacob." I knew she had intentionally left Brad out of her promise.

"I know a place more to MG's taste, anyway." Oliver's voice trembled, with anger or sorrow; I wasn't sure. Probably measures of both. I appreciated how he included himself in my plight. He grabbed hold of my elbow and I let him steer me across the parking lot to his Mercedes. As I got in, reminiscences of our trip to BirthRight with Lana reminded me how much Oliver and I had shared between us in the short time we'd been friends.

I relaxed a little as he drove. I felt oddly relieved to be with him right then instead of with Michael and Momma. My shoulders ached and I moved them a little side to side, easing them. I let out a breath I hadn't known I was holding, then studied Oliver surreptitiously. I had come to appreciate his steadiness, his ability to listen without trying to make things different or better. I leaned my head back against the headrest and closed my eyes. Oliver was so different from Michael. Michael could be cynical at times, but his was a cynicism born of optimism, his wish for the world to be a perfect place. Easygoing and cheerful, he was a lofty dreamer, blessed with an ability to enjoy what I thought of as life on the surface. He expected things to work out for the best. It was one of the qualities I liked most about him.

It had felt good to be around Michael from the very start. I had slipped right into his life, formed my own around him. Living in a new city away from my family for the first time, I found that a huge comfort. But was that comfort a kind of cheat? Was I damping down the itchiness I often experienced inside, the sense that there was something more I wanted? Michael had once told me that someday he wanted a family. I thought I wanted the same thing but when I imagined myself with a husband and kids I saw not myself but Momma, overburdened and defeated by the time she was my age. When had I so closely identified with her that I believed myself doomed to repeat her experience?

Oliver was more complicated than Michael. There was a turbulence about him that both enticed and unsettled me. While

Michael liked to reassure me that everything was going to turn out okay, Oliver knew the underbelly of the good life. He understood there was a very real possibility nothing would ever be okay again.

"We're here."

I opened my eyes at Oliver's quiet pronouncement and looked around. We were parked beneath a giant oak tree in front of a dilapidated yet appealing wood-frame drive-up restaurant painted a fading yellow. Dozens of miniature bulbs lit an electric sign that screamed 1960s. It blinked PARKY'S—CONCRETE YOU CAN EAT.

I got out of Oliver's car and looked around. The street was a busy thoroughfare, jammed with retail stores and other fast-food restaurants. We weren't that far from downtown but I didn't recognize Rosewood Avenue; I hadn't driven down it before.

The drive-in took up two full lots and had obviously preceded many of the businesses around it. Picnic tables peppered its yard, and lunchtime customers dressed in suits and ties were wolfing down hot dogs and French fries, briefcases temporarily abandoned at their feet. For most, today was a normal workday. Judging by the throng exiting the Sears across the street, retail therapy was alive and well. I longed to be one of the women who blinked as they emerged into the bright day, burdened with nothing so grave that a few purchases couldn't soothe it away.

"We're *where*?" I asked Oliver.

"Sweet-tooth mecca." He guided me toward the remaining empty picnic table. "Our diva had a dirty little secret." Oliver winked and for a moment I froze, thinking he was referring to MG's affair. "She had a thing for concretes. That's what we call frozen custard mixed with candy, fruit or nuts here in the dairy land, although 'cholesterol in a cup' would be the more accurate description.

"The mall is right around the corner." Oliver gestured vaguely. "Whenever MG went shopping she made me meet her here after. Brad called her my drinking buddy, but he's clueless. She was my sugar momma." Oliver's grin was twisted with pain and I suppressed an urge to throw my arms around him.

"Wait here." He walked off toward the walk-up counter. I heard him order a large concrete with Heath Bar crumbles and two spoons.

By the time he returned, I had given up on brushing away the tears streaming down my cheeks.

"Caro?" Oliver's voice was heavy with concern. He set the dessert on the table and moved next to me.

"Oh, Ollie." My head drooped onto his shoulder and I turned into him, never doubting that he would hold me up. He draped an arm around me. "She was always taking care of people," I wailed. "And she always wanted everyone to enjoy life. We used to go to the corner store for Heath ice cream bars—" I stopped short as the tears gathered in my throat. The memory of the two of us as young girls flying along on MG's green Schwinn, me atop the handlebars and her pumping furiously on the rose-printed banana seat, was too much to bear.

Oliver held me while I cried. He seemed perfectly at ease despite the stares and whispers coming from the other diners. I'd spent a lot of time trying to make sense of how I related to men, but it had only resulted in more confusion. My tendency was to think of them in terms of sex and romance, not as confidants I could depend on. Maybe this was what Mary Grace had appreciated in Oliver. He was the kind of person who could hear anything without judgment. I fleetingly wondered whether we might fill in the space left in each other's life by our mutual loss.

I wiped at my eyes, trying to figure out how to ask Oliver if he knew about Mary Grace's affair. A tender look filled his eyes. Was it the benign concern of a friend or was a bigger desire there? If I could melt into Oliver, let him circle his arms around me and rock me into the sweet lull of a dreamless sleep where nothing and no one could hurt me, then maybe I could also let down my guard about what would happen while I rested there. Instead I backed out of his arms, trying to regain a grip on myself.

But Oliver refused to let me run away. He stepped into the small space I'd cleared between us and jutted his head forward, landing a hard, dry kiss on my mouth. My body responded with fervor fueled by anxiety as I fought to ignore my growing sense that more and more of my life was moving beyond my control. I pulled away again. Oliver and I looked and looked at each other, neither of us breathing as we weighed the aftermath of that kiss. Then all the tension growing between us erupted, and we giggled with the giddy laughter of children who have just gotten away with a major act of misbehaving.

Twenty-nine

G iven the circumstances, the kiss I shared with Oliver might have been excusable had it ended at that. Close proximity to death heightens desire. Maybe sex is the ultimate act of defiance, reassurance that we're still alive and well. After a few too many Manhattans my father once disclosed he'd long ago stopped counting the number of couples he'd interrupted getting it on in the restrooms during wakes and visitations.

Oliver grabbed my hand and hurried me to the car. We drove in silence. Part of me wanted to blurt out that I needed to go home because Momma would be waiting, but another part burned from the sensation of his tongue slipping between my parted lips. I half hoped and half dreaded that Oliver was headed for his house. The hope outlasted the dread, and when we pulled up in front of a cedar A-frame, tingles ran down my back. It took Oliver five tries to get the key turned in the lock, mostly because he was distracted by the path of kisses my lips trailed down the side of his neck.

Once we were inside, my pumps landed with a thud that echoed reproachfully from the bottom of the stairs as he led me up to his bedroom. It was hard to see at first; the shades were drawn and it took my eyes a moment to adjust to the dim light. Oliver walked over to the windows behind the king bed and yanked the blinds up. Sunshine streamed in through the panes.

"I like the light better." Oliver grinned as he pulled me down onto the bed. "This way I can see all of you." Then he reached over and unzipped my dress, moaning as his lips brushed my bared shoulders.

We got tangled up in each other's arms. I was wearing a lavender lace bra and boy shorts set that Michael had bought me, and now I wondered what I had been thinking when I'd dressed that morning for MG's funeral. Remorse shot through me.

"Ol, I think this is a mis—"

His tongue parted my lips again, cutting off the protest and igniting the same shivers of passion I'd felt at Parky's. Oliver moved on top of me. He parted my legs with his. The weight of him was more substantial than Michael's lean form. It drew all the grief in my body together, pressed it down far into the hollow at the small of my back. I shut my eyes, checked to see if I could still feel it. It was there but easier to bear now. Oliver brushed his hand across my cheek and I opened my eyes again, staring into the dark pools that insisted I look while we did this. Then he was inside me, gauging my body's responses and adjusting his rhythm until he was thrusting in long, deep strokes, his eyes locked with mine.

Our fucking was as concentrated as our conversations. Orgasm was often elusive for me, but now I let myself succumb to the current building within, hardly caring where it might take me. We climaxed simultaneously. Most of the time I blanked out as I came, the physical sensations pulling me away from my partner, making my satisfaction solitary no matter how deep my affection for my lover. But I felt Oliver with me throughout and we burst free of our bodies, spinning so far out along some cosmic pathway that I intuited this was what death might be like, a neverending ecstasy. Our shared orgasms carried with them a kind of childlike wonder that burst out of us in rippling echoes of our earlier laughter. It was far removed from the punishment I'd gone to Oliver's to inflict upon myself for failing MG. But the pleasure bittered almost instantaneously into regret, with an aftertaste sharp as blood.

I sat up in bed, jumbled memory fireworks lighting up the sky of my mind—me and Paulie in the lake, MG and Ava Jane standing on the pier calling to us while the ABCs and Ruby looked on from the front porch of the cottage. I blinked until everyone faded away, leaving only Oliver, lying next to my incriminating imprint in the sheets. It was early evening, and the light coming in the window behind the bed was weak now, washed out by growing shadows.

"Hey, beauty." Oliver rose up on one elbow and kissed me long and slow, another invitation. But an affair with Oliver was the last thing I needed. Momma was waiting for me. And oh God, how was I ever going to tell Michael about what I'd just done?

"I don't know what you're thinking but I sure hope it involves you spending the night and kissing me a whole bunch more." Oliver looked up at me hopefully.

His expression turned my stomach. That was the last thing I wanted to do. "I can't stay. My mother's going to wonder where I've been." I jumped from the bed and grabbed at my hastily abandoned clothing, strewn across the floor. My lower lip trembled. All the guilt I'd held at bay while making love with Oliver now flooded through me, along with a new measure added by my infidelity. What had I done?

Oliver came over and took me in his arms. "Hey," he said softly. "Look at me." He lifted my chin with his index finger, held it there until I looked him in the eye. Through my tears, he was blurry in front of me. He mistook my shudder for a chill. "Grab my robe from the closet. It's on the back of the door. I'll run you a hot shower before you go." His gracious manner of letting me off the hook lifted my spirits a little. He patted my behind gently as I walked off toward his closet. I opened the door and found the hook on the other side, but it was empty.

"Ollie?" I groped along the wall for the light switch. "It's not here on the door."

He couldn't hear me over the rush of water. Before I could call out to him again my fingers stumbled into the toggle. I blinked, waiting for my eyes to grow accustomed to the burst of light from overhead. Dozens of shoe boxes lined a shelf near the ceiling, each box labeled with the color and kind of shoe inside.

Oliver had a lot of clothes, too. The closet bar was jammed full with suits in dry cleaners' plastic. I spied a plaid garment toward the far end of the rod and thought it might be the robe. Just as I reached out for it my foot caught something on the floor, half-hidden beneath a wool winter coat. It sent me sprawling toward the wall and I swore as I reached out and tried to break my fall before I landed with a thud. I'd be mortified if Oliver found me in a disheveled heap in there. The unruly robe landed on my head. I yanked it off, shaking my hair out of my eyes where it clung, staticky from rubbing against the fabric. I reached a hand under Oliver's coats, groped around until I grabbed hold of the offending object that had tripped me up and hauled it out into the light so I could get a better look at it.

It was a shoe, which should have warranted nothing more than replacing it in one of the boxes above. Except this shoe didn't belong to Oliver. With teeth gritted to keep myself from screaming, I pulled the coats aside, looking for its mate. When I had one in each hand I turned them over, searched their soles for the size. *Seven.*

I backed out of the closet, a red sling-back in each hand. The pair Mary Grace had sworn she'd wear into labor. And she had, at least as far as the admitting desk, where she'd unfettered her feet from them with a satisfied curse.

Standing in the dim light of Oliver's bedroom, anguish rose up within me. These shoes should have been with Mary Grace forever. Now I pictured her feet bare in the casket, still swollen from pregnancy, the absence of the shoes I held in my hands incriminating.

"Shower's ready!" Oliver called out from the bathroom. "I'll wash your hair for you if you want. I give a great scalp massage."

A barb of grief and anger caught in my heart, so sharp it made me dizzy. I looked down at my best friend's shoes, taking in the full meaning of finding them in Oliver's closet. Then I saw Mary Grace, as clearly as if she was standing right there in front of me, slipping off these heels, followed by her dress, in much the same way I had shed my own just a few hours ago.

She'd been lonely, she had told me. Had met a friend for drinks and one thing led to another. Brad had referred to Oliver as her drinking buddy. A fleeting vision of Mary Grace and Oliver embracing formed but I shook my head, shattering it to bits and pieces that wouldn't hurt as badly as it would in its entirety.

Recalling Helen's quip about wishing for the ability to click her heels and disappear, before Oliver could come see what was keeping me I dressed and left, Mary Grace's shoes in the middle of the bedroom floor, all the explanation necessary for my abrupt departure.

Thirty

I'd moved to the other side of the lake to make a new start. But my penchant for trouble had delivered me into the thick of it. As punishment for my wicked deeds I decided to walk the mile home. I left Oliver's and marched several blocks fueled by adrenaline and fury before rising blisters reminded me I was wearing dress shoes. Then I remembered that Momma was at my house, which brought a pain sharper than the blisters. One look at my disheveled state and she'd know I'd been up to no good. Well, too bad. I was a grown woman, not a teenager sneaking around behind her parents' backs. I could damn well do whatever I wanted.

I stopped at a crosswalk and took off my shoes while I waited for the light to change. I wished so badly that Mary Grace was still alive. But my best friend was dead, and I'd just slept with the one other good friend I had left in Milwaukee, who'd also slept with our mutual friend *and* was very possibly the father of her child. A child who certainly would be emotionally damaged forever.

Since Mary Grace's nightmarish labor, I'd agonized over whether my actions had been heroic or had instead interrupted some celestial grand plan, some intentional dictate of fate. Now my best friend's daughter was going to grow up without the single most important person in a child's life: her mother.

I knew all too well what abandonment did to a child. I could never compensate Ava Jane, lying in an incubator in the NICU, still making up her mind whether she wanted to stay in the world. As the one who had saved her I now bore a duty to make up for Mary Grace's absence in any way I could. It was an endless debt, one I could never discharge.

I started walking again. As I made my way toward Momma my

unruly mind churned, dredging up more events I hadn't thought of in years. As a very young child, I'd believed myself as mature as any adult. Fueling my naïve conviction was a deep-seated wisdom I relied upon without question. But I had learned to override that intuition to meet the demands of those around me. Even in utero, babies pick up on their mother's emotional states and respond to them. It was that summer I turned twelve, with Momma's miscarriage and all that followed, that our roles reversed. When the events of that season threatened to carry her away from me, I had grasped on to Momma with a fierce love that came to overshadow everything else in my life, even my own instincts.

What I was discovering as I got older was that in the same way age made bones brittle, the psyche grew more fragile too, less able to withstand life's rigors. Walking home toward Momma triggered the memory of moving along that straight and narrow yellow line back to the cottage after Paulie drowned. Only now Daddy wasn't behind me. Panic swelled inside, making me light-headed. My heart pounded. The symptoms were like contractions, building to a peak and then subsiding again, over and over. I shook my head as I pushed onward, trying to clear the dizziness. But now I couldn't get a deep breath. Wave after wave of fear and the compulsion to move faster washed over me. A sob caught in my throat. I repeated one silent word over and over as a prayer: *please.*

I stopped in a gas station bathroom on the next block, feeling so afraid as I rinsed my face with icy water from the faucet. If I passed out it might be hours before someone found me. I pictured myself free-floating, my dead brother grabbing for my hand. I imagined I could look down and see my body lying on the dirty tile floor like a crumpled paper towel.

I couldn't stay in the bathroom any longer. I slipped back out into the neon-bright night like a ghost, hoping that I had left my crazy self behind in the ladies' room. I checked my watch. Just after eight. It felt like three in the morning. I wanted to curl up in someone's arms and sleep like a swaddled baby. I considered going back to Oliver's but the thought made the panic bigger. I timed the next several rushes of panic—six in less than ten minutes. They were coming closer together and growing stronger in intensity. I have my doula clients rate their contraction pain on a scale from one to ten, with ten being unbearable. The sensations running through me were an eleven.

Somehow I managed to get home. Yet after racing to get there I pulled myself up short in the parking lot, trying to control my emotions before I went in to face Momma. The last thing I wanted was for her to see me coming apart. A light shone in my living room window and I strained for a glimpse of my mother. I thought of that long-ago time when I had filled her shoes. Despite their overbearing presence in my childhood, now I longed for the ABCs in a way that made me feel homesick for something that went far beyond being around family. Some part of me wanted to go back in time to when we were all together, but another part knew that the reality had never measured up to how I now hoped it might have been.

A car engine started. Helen's yellow Corvette glided out into traffic. At first I wished I had seen her before she'd driven away; I could have asked how things had gone at the cemetery. But then I was grateful I'd missed her. It was too late that night for any more turmoil. And I still had to face my moment of reckoning with Momma.

She was waiting for me at the kitchen table, the one we'd eaten on for so many years when I was a kid. There was a knowing look in Momma's eyes as she watched me come in. It told me I had just confirmed I was as bad as she'd always suspected. I wondered whether she thought she was here now to take me back to Chicago. The notion both lured and offended me.

"Oliver took me to the cemetery late this afternoon, after the service was over. I didn't call because I didn't think you'd answer my phone." A rush of emotion like those I had suffered on the

way home rose again. To my own ears I sounded like the desperate liar I was becoming.

But Momma didn't challenge me. Instead she picked a large
envelope up from the table. I hadn't noticed it sitting there until
she held it out. She watched closely as I took it from her and
opened it, removed the thick sheaf of papers inside.

It was a legal complaint, accompanied by a subpoena.

"Oh, Christ." I glanced at Momma, who usually acted insulted
when I cussed. "Brad's filed a lawsuit."

I read the subpoena, which told me I had to appear in court.
"I have to testify about what happened at Ava Jane's birth," I
told Momma. "I wonder if he's suing the nurses along with the
doctors." I flipped through the inches-thick document. I was concerned for Helen. She had been in the delivery room but I hoped
Brad had spared her since she hadn't been involved with the delivery itself. There were a lot of names listed under "Defendants"
on the front of the complaint. I recognized Dr. Mark's, then a
Nicole whose last name I didn't know but who I guessed was the
labor and delivery nurse. Helen's wasn't there. But the relief I felt
for my neighbor vanished as I caught sight of one all-too-familiar
name: my own.

"He's suing *me*? But I'm, I *was*, her best friend." I tried reading further but the complaint was so filled with legalese I could
barely understand it. The words kept swimming, no matter how
hard I willed myself to focus on them. The document named
more than ten defendants, but two entire counts referred just to
me. They claimed I had practiced medicine without a license, re-
sulting in Mary Grace's wrongful death as well as alleged harm to
Ava Jane. My eyes skipped over phrases like "irreparable injury,"
"hypoxia," and "brain damage."

Other than our altercation at the church that morning, the
lawsuit was the only communication I'd had from Brad since Ava
Jane's birth. I had called and left several messages telling him
how sorry I was about what had happened and asking him to let
me know how the baby was doing, but he hadn't returned my

calls. He and MG had fought the day she went into labor, and I wondered whether the lawsuit was his way of getting back at me for being her confidante. I looked to my mother again, suddenly grateful that she was there. I hadn't called her, but she had come anyway, as if she had known even before I did that I needed her now in a way I hadn't needed her in years.

I started sleeping with my mother again. After I had gotten Momma settled out on the futon, I lay in my bedroom, obsessing over the events of the night. First I thought about Michael, how guilty I felt for cheating on him. But I couldn't deny that my remorse was mingled with satisfaction at the amazing sex I'd shared with Oliver. Which led to a replay of that awful moment when I found MG's shoe. Then I made the mistake of reading the summons and complaint again before I shut off the light and tried to sleep. My heart throbbed as panic set in again. It began as a tiny droplet, then worked its way into a swelling crest of fear. I breathed in raspy shallow gasps, certain I would pass out and never regain consciousness. My arms and legs trembled. I got out of bed and paced, once, twice, so many times I finally lost count.

Momma must have heard me from the living room because she eventually padded into my room, led me back to bed and gently tucked me in. "Have you been crying?" she asked.

Don't make me tell, I thought. But the wave knocked me down again. I was drowning in a sea of fear and a new accompanying sadness that bubbled ferociously. I choked back a sob.

"Caro." Momma's voice rang out sharply. "What's the matter? Is your heart pounding?" she demanded.

"How did you know that?" I looked up at her, feeling like a small child again.

"Are you dizzy too?"

"Yeah . . . and it hurts to breathe," I admitted.

"You're having a panic attack." Momma identified what I had known but refused to acknowledge, put a label on the terrors and the trembling and named me as her heir. She went into her purse, plucked out a pill bottle. This was the price one paid for magical thinking.

"It's all in your head." Momma repeated what I'd heard the ABCs tell her for years. It rang like a death sentence. "Take a Xanax. It will help you relax." She shook a tiny orange pill into my hand. "Now go to sleep. Believe me, honey, it's not the end of the world."

But that's what it felt like to me. I hated the thought of needing medication to function. I slipped the Xanax into my mouth, purposefully tasting its lingering bitterness as it slid down my throat. *Let this be something else,* I entreated as I shut my eyes and willed my body and mind to quiet down. Anything but what I was afraid it was: the same plague of fear that had driven Momma to her bed when life grew too big for her to handle. Momma's presence split me open, allowed me to finally disassemble the brave façade I'd been struggling to keep in place most of my life. She sat on my bed that night in the dark and rocked me, gently stroking my hair while I cried for what I'd lost—my friendship with MG, my confidence in myself as a doula and also my childhood.

When my sobs quieted to shudders Momma lay down with her back to mine. I turned so I was facing her spine, tucked my knees into the hollows of hers. Eventually I fell into a half sleep, dreamed of being a small girl again in the bathroom at the cottage. Ava Jane floated lifeless in the tub while I stood over her, my legs scrabbling against the smooth porcelain sides. I was unable to get a foothold and climb out but it felt like a matter of life and death to avoid letting the corpse touch my ankles or feet. I leaned down to pull her up from the water but she slipped away from me and swirled down the drain, where I could see my dead brother's face smiling up at me. I pulled my little-girl hands up from below the surface. They were empty, dripping blood instead of water.

I jerked awake from the nightmare, grappled to orient myself. I wasn't in the cottage. I was home in my own bed, with my mother beside me. I slowed my breath until it matched the easy rhythm of hers. I closed my eyes and thought about that string of nights I'd spent with her when I was young. It had seemed as if they would go on forever. I wondered how I had gotten here, to this place where Momma was finally mothering me the way I'd needed her to then. I felt little again now, so fragile that when she rolled over in her sleep and wrapped an arm around me I let her hold me tight. I lay as close to her as I could. Throughout my life I'd never been able to make out where she ended and I began.

Thirty-one

As a kid I believed shutting my eyes made me invisible. When I thought about the legal charges I was facing, I wanted to disappear like that. But since I hadn't yet learned how to time-travel, I settled for hiring someone who might be able to win my case. Two days after MG's funeral, I met with Annabelle Armstrong. Oliver had left a sober message on my voice mail, sounding bewildered but chastened at my abrupt departure after our lovemaking. He didn't mention MG's shoes. I didn't want to talk to him, so I e-mailed a brief message about the lawsuit. He immediately responded with contact information for Annabelle, another former client of his who specialized in medical malpractice litigation.

As I stood in the bathroom applying some much-needed makeup prior to the meeting, I replayed my last conversation with Mary Grace. Something had occurred to me, born of a survival instinct. I could air my best friend's secret and contest Ava Jane's paternity. It felt ugly, but if Brad wasn't the baby's father, maybe he couldn't sue me. Self-preservation insisted it was the right thing to do, loyalty to my dead friend be damned. But what if the baby was Oliver's? Would he take on the lawsuit against me? Although I had just slept with the man I couldn't say what he might do if I brought the truth to light.

Momma slipped into my bedroom, sat on my bed. She picked up the lawsuit. "You can get through this, Caro. You're just like your father, so strong." Her eager expression told me she meant the words as encouragement but I bristled, taking them as her way of denying that I, like her, might need some help at times.

I *was* more like Daddy than Momma, in temperament as well as looks. But I was so damn tired of her characterizing me as able to withstand anything. That self-serving impulse, the same one that was pushing me to spill the beans about Mary Grace, *that* was a trait I'd inherited from my mother. I wished that she would bring up the past—her miscarriage, Paulie's death, nursing school. I needed to talk about these things, to tell Momma what they had cost me. But the little girl in me clamped my mouth shut tight every time I tried to speak up. She'd lost her mother years ago. Now that Momma was here, my younger self wasn't about to let me say anything that might send her running away.

The law offices of Armstrong and Young occupied two floors of a skyscraper downtown. While it wasn't Chicago's Loop with its jeweled skyline and the flourish of Buckingham Fountain, I liked Milwaukee's business area. You could walk from one end to the other in a matter of minutes. Just beyond it lay the lake, creating the same familiar border at the edge of the world that I had known back home. With the lake I could look out over the wide expanse of sparkling waters and get my bearings.

The first thing I noticed about my attorney was the huge purple stone hanging around her neck. A cross-section like a cut from a tree trunk, concentric circles emanated from its center. I couldn't take my eyes off the talisman suspended from a thick silver braided cord. My hand automatically went to the base of my throat, the same spot where the necklace rested on Annabelle.

Whenever one of us was sick as a kid, Ruby gave us amulets to ward off evil spirits. She'd creep to our bedsides in the middle of the night and set the artifacts in place. I'd often awaken in the morning with a relic under my pillow or in my hand. When I returned them to her Ruby would whisper that they were the bones of Saint Francis, a lock of hair from Mother Cabrini or splinters of the holy cross. I suspected that the same piece changed identities since the bones all looked alike, but Ruby always claimed they came from different saints. Annabelle's jewelry reminded me of Ruby. I hoped it was a sign that my attorney was as enchanting and wise as my great-aunt.

Annabelle walked toward me from behind her desk. Her smile was open and friendly, her green eyes clear. My lawyer was dressed to the nines, as the ABCs would say. Her tailored suit accentuated her pretty curves without appearing suggestive or unprofessional. Whether deserved or not, I had been carrying a load of guilt around since I found out I was being sued. But when I met Annabelle relief flooded through me. I might be good at denying trouble when it's plain as day, but I know when I believe in someone, and I believed in Annabelle Armstrong's ability to help me.

With the exception of a stack of accordion files on her desk, Annabelle's office was pristine. The top file caught my eye. It had my name typed neatly across the outside. A large spiral binder of medical records sat inside it. Above Annabelle's desk hung a print of workers laboring in a rice paddy somewhere in Asia. Thailand, maybe. *Peace Corps—Good Works for Good Causes,* read the title below the photo.

"Were you in the Peace Corps?" I asked.

She shook her head. "Not yet, but someday. When I retire from law and want to save the world in a different way." Annabelle had a charming manner of cocking her head to one side as she grinned at me, as if she'd just shared a secret. My gaze wandered down to her left hand. The ring on her third finger was a modest sapphire solitaire set in platinum. A matching wedding band was studded in small diamonds.

"Do you have children?" I found myself asking before I could stifle the question. Silently I chastised myself for the kind of nosy inquiry I would have been furious at Momma for had she been the one to make it. Annabelle might have been perfectly content and fulfilled with her career.

A slight pause followed, and in that moment I knew that she was having difficulty getting pregnant.

"Not yet. Maybe someday." She answered with the same non-committal words she'd used when I asked about the Peace Corps.

"Too busy with work right now." She grinned at me carefully, an expression meant to mask a less positive emotion.

She gestured toward the file with my name on it. "Let me explain how I suggest we approach your defense." She waited a beat. "Because we're not settling a case you shouldn't have been named in to begin with."

She must have seen the doubt on my face. "Let that sink in until you believe it. I'll go get you some coffee."

As I watched her stride from her office I caught a glimpse of how well prepared and credible she would appear in the courtroom. I might have been feeling guilty for having been named in the lawsuit, but I'd believe a woman like Annabelle Armstrong if she argued that I had been wrongly accused.

While Annabelle was gone I snuck a look at the photos on the credenza under the windows. In one shot she was running a race. Her legs were long and toned in her shorts. She looked younger with her hair swept up into a ponytail under a baseball cap. Her photos exuded the same confidence she possessed in person. A brief pang of resentment at my lack of that same faith in myself shot through me, then quickly waned. I liked Annabelle too much to be jealous of her.

One wall of the office housed a bookshelf, full of the expected legal treatises and texts. But on the uppermost shelf sat a collection of poetry and prose. Books by Robert Frost, David Whyte, Maya Angelou. Kahlil Gibran's *The Prophet* rubbed shoulders with Ram Dass's *Be Here Now*. Next came Gandhi's autobiography, alongside two works by a Buddhist nun. I pulled down the next book in line, a volume by Eudora Welty. It fell open to a passage underlined in red:

The memory is a living thing—it too is in transit. But during its moment, all that is remembered joins, and lives—the old and the young, the past and the present, the living and the dead.

"Okay, let's get to it." Annabelle swept back into the room. I jumped at her voice. "Oh, I'm sorry I startled you!" She gave an apologetic laugh, looked down at the open book in my hands. "Oh, I love that one," she said, pointing to the verse I'd been reading. "She's an amazing writer, isn't she?

"What people remember can make or break a lawsuit," she added meaningfully. "So let's go over *your* story." She gestured toward the lavender suede couch and the glass-and-chrome coffee table at the other end of the room, then reached over to her desk for a yellow legal pad and a pen.

After I filled Annabelle in on what had happened, she told me how she would approach my case. "Things go wrong at births all the time, which is what I'll tell the jury in my opening argument," she began. "And in the course of their careers nurses and doctors get sued. Sometimes it's clear that they've injured a patient, usually by accident. That's what we call negligence. In cases like that, we do our best to settle with the plaintiffs out of court.

"But there's a fundamental difference in your situation." Her eyes lit up. I almost told her to breathe; in her excitement she reminded me of one of my laboring moms. "You're not a doctor *or* a nurse. You're not involved in the medical aspects of a birth; you're there for emotional support. It's a role that's separate and distinct from the medical staff.

"In fact," she said, "yours is the first case in which a plaintiff has sued a non–health care provider for professional negligence at a birth. *Ever.*"

Leave it to me to be the first in my profession to get sued.

"Nowhere in Wisconsin, nowhere in the entire country," Annabelle went on, "has a plaintiff ever sued a doula before. And I'm going to make damned sure the jury knows it first thing." She paused, eyes gleaming with satisfaction. But I didn't understand why it was so important. "I like a challenge, especially when it's an opportunity to create new law," Annabelle explained. "The plaintiffs are claiming you practiced medicine without a license. I think we can beat the claim *and* set a nationwide precedent against suing doulas for malpractice."

Bolstered by Annabelle's confidence at the unusual twist in my situation, we spent the next four hours rehearsing what I would say at my deposition and when I took the stand at trial. Because the case had been filed on behalf of a minor, Wisconsin law dictated it had to be tried in an expedited manner. In some ways this was a good thing; it meant I wouldn't spend months or years tied up in the limbo of litigation. But the flip side was that the case took on a turbocharged pace. We had just two months to prepare. Annabelle had already spoken at length with Brad Schaeffer's lawyer. She peppered me with questions similar to those he would ask, occasionally tossing in a particularly incriminating insinuation. When the attorney tried that in court I was supposed to keep my mouth shut and let Annabelle object, then wait for the judge to rule on whether or not I had to answer.

Once she was satisfied that I'd learned to listen carefully to each question and to answer in ways that would help my defense, Annabelle put down her pad and pen and took both of my hands in hers. "This isn't going to be easy, Caro, but you can get through it. And once it's over you can get on with your life." She offered me a smile.

I nodded, tears forming as I contemplated the enormity of the cost I might pay for participating in Ava Jane's birth. Pixie had been right; Mary Grace hadn't done me any favor when she'd asked me to stay for her labor and delivery. I had already lost my best friend. Now I might lose more that I held dear.

Annabelle interrupted my pity party. "We need to compile a list of character witnesses, people willing to testify on your behalf." She held her pen over her notepad and nodded at me to start giving her names.

"First off, there's Mary Gra—" Realization stunned me into silence before I got the rest of her name out. I covered my face with my hands, ashamed to let Annabelle see the cascade of tears I couldn't hold back anymore. Annabelle gave me time, remaining quiet until my heaving cries subsided.

"You've been through a lot this year. A move, new job, a romance, the death of your best friend." Annabelle ticked them off on her fingers. "Four of the five most stressful life events." She looked rueful. "If it's any consolation, that alone might earn you some sympathy from the jury. Now, who else can tell them how wonderful you are?"

I gave a weak smile in return. "Well, there's Michael. He's my boyfriend. And Oliver. He's a friend of mine through Mary Grace." I hesitated, recalling our tryst and how I'd run out afterward. "He helped me with a birth once." Annabelle took notes while I explained about Oliver driving Lana and me to Birth-Right.

"We probably won't use Michael because he's not an objective party. But since Oliver's seen you in action he might be a good choice. What we really need are some of your colleagues who can talk about working with you." Annabelle looked up at me expectantly.

"I can think of three people. My neighbor Helen's a nurse at Medical City. She was called to the birth, actually. But she's not named in the lawsuit. I'm guessing it's because she's an NICU nurse, not L & D."

Annabelle leafed through the complaint, then picked up another piece of paper. "Helen Palaggi? Here she is. She's not a defendant but the plaintiff's named her on his initial witness list." She looked back up from the page. "So we'll hear from her, one way or another. You think she's sympathetic to you?"

I hesitated. "We're friends as well as neighbors. She came to MG's funeral." I recalled my surprise at Helen's presence there.

"We'll find out where she stands at her deposition," Annabelle said when I mentioned my concern. "Meantime it's probably best if you don't have contact with her. Who else?"

"Number two is Deirdre Moore, the owner-midwife of Birth-Right, the birthing center I work at a lot." I paused, wincing inside as I recalled that the last time I'd spoken with Deirdre was when I'd walked out of her office in a huff after Mary's difficult

birth. It seemed like lately I had developed a pattern of being am-
bushed by unexpected surprises that forced me to flee.

"Tell me about Deirdre," Annabelle said. "How many years'
birthing experience does she have? And how conservative or liberal is she about medicine?"

I gave Annabelle the lowdown on Deirdre. Annabelle jotted
notes. "It's not optimal that she doesn't practice in hospitals but
beyond that, she sounds like a great character witness. Does she
know about your lawsuit yet?"

I shook my head. After MG's death I had called and told Deirdre I needed to take some time off but hadn't mentioned anything
but the most basic details. Milwaukee's birthing community was
small and I knew it would be impossible to keep word of the lawsuit from getting out, but I didn't have to be the one to start the
rumor mill going.

"You have two choices," Annabelle said. "I can send her a subpoena and you can sit tight and wait for her to respond. But since
you work with her, it might be better to go have a talk with her
and let her know you'd like her to testify. Ask her permission, so
to speak. It softens the blow a little that way."

I nodded my assent but inside I dreaded making that visit to
Deirdre's. Asking her to stand up for me in court felt like grovel-
ing. But then indignation sparked in me. I'd gone with Mary to
Saint Elizabeth's. Deirdre owed me one.

"Who's your third witness?" Annabelle asked.

"Pixie Perkins." This time my smile bloomed genuine and full.

"*Pixie?*" Annabelle grimaced.

"Her real name's Agnes but she goes by her nickname." I filled
Annabelle in on the Enclave and its infamous crone. "She'd go
bonkers for your amulet." I nodded toward Annabelle's amethyst.

She lifted a hand, brushed her fingers across the stone. "That's
great," she said dryly. "But despite her impressive birthing cre-
dentials, how do you think your typical suburban housewife or
blue-collar worker is going to perceive Pixie?" She didn't wait
for an answer. "Frankly, I think they're going to see her as an

off-the-grid witch. And I can just see opposing counsel having a field day with her, making all sorts of insinuations about the antics of the hippie freaks. *Not* the kind of company we want to portray you as keeping. No offense to Pixie."

Although Pixie would sing my praises, I could see why Annabelle thought it was too risky to put her up on the stand.

"So it will be up to Deirdre to champion your cause," Annabelle said decisively. "And you, too, of course," she added. "Whether or not we beat the charges will depend in large part on how credible you come off to the jury. Your testimony will carry the most impact and weight. I'll do my best to defend you, but you have to appear as if you believe unwaveringly in what you did there in that birthing room."

"I grew up Catholic," I retorted grimly. "We're raised to believe that we're guilty for everything, basically."

My attorney pursed her lips. Then she walked over and pulled a couple books off the bookshelf. "Read these." She handed me the two volumes by Pema Chödrön, the Buddhist nun. They were titled *When Things Fall Apart* and *The Places That Scare You.* "Maybe they'll help you get clear about what your truth is."

Thirty-two

I'd made up my mind to drive straight to BirthRight from Annabelle's to get the asking over with, but as I was leaving the parking garage Michael called.

"How'd it go with the lawyer? If you want a second opinion, I'm sure my dad could recommend someone."

Michael's voice was warm and deep. I savored the tone resonating in my ear and suddenly missed him like crazy. But I didn't tell him that. His thoughtful offer made me feel worse for cheating on him. "Thanks, but I really liked her. She's all excited to make legal history with my case." I told him about the lack of precedent.

"I've got the rest of the day off. Want to come with me to Home Depot? We could pick out that paint you've been wanting for your bedroom."

I knew I should stick to my plan and go talk to Deirdre about testifying. But I'd been avoiding Michael since my tryst with Oliver. Sooner or later I'd have to see him. Running an errand offered a distraction. I promised myself I'd go see Deirdre first thing in the morning.

Fifteen minutes later Michael picked me up at home.

"Quick poll," he quipped. "How many of your clients go back to work after they pop the weasel?"

I rolled my eyes at his crude idiom for giving birth. In other circumstances I would have been offended, but I knew he was trying to distract me, so I accepted Michael's attempt at diversion gratefully. "I'd say eighty percent or more, just off the top of my head."

"And who's taking care of the kid? An immigrant nanny." Michael threw his hands up in indignation as he answered his own question. "I'd even buy into the argument that the haves are supporting the have-nots by providing employment opportunities.

But babysitting, cleaning toilets and cutting lawns for ten bucks an hour hardly allows for living above the poverty level.

"I've been thinking," Michael said, switching topics. "Someday I want to build us a house. On plenty of land so nature can have its naturally wild way." He swung into a parking space at Home Depot, turned off the car and turned toward me. So much for keeping the conversation light. We lingered for a moment. I looked out the windshield; Michael looked at me. We'd been dating exclusively for six months but we'd never discussed living together. Michael got out, came around and opened my door. He crouched alongside me, tilted my chin so he could look me in the eye. "I meant what I said the other night, Caro. I'm in love with you."

"Me too," I squeaked out, wanting it to be true. But I didn't trust that my feelings for him were coming entirely from my own heart. I'd grown too skillful at reading what other people wanted and giving myself away.

"You love you too? That's good." Michael looked self-assured, as if something had just been solved between us. He grabbed my hand and we walked toward the store entrance.

Funny how a store devoted to making a house cozy can feel so cavernous. As Michael led me toward the paint aisle near the back of the store I stopped, inundated by the thumping bass coming over the sound system, the scent of fresh lumber, an endless horizon of aisles filled with lighting fixtures, plumbing supplies, even full-size garages. All the promises of domestic bliss surrounded me. Why couldn't the happiness—or comfort, at least—that places like this promised be purchased as easily as patio furniture and appliances? Despite memories of my parents' tumultuous marriage, since meeting Michael I'd wanted to believe that it could.

"What do you think about this?" Michael held a strip of paint samples out to me, his index finger pointing to a cheery lemon-yellow shade.

"It's great but I told you I wanted something tranquil, like the sage Oliver recommended." I was careful to keep my expression placid but an aftershock of pleasure reverberated through my body just from saying Oliver's name. Remorse quickly followed though, my emotions as unpredictable as a thrill ride these days.

Michael made a face. Once I had thought the two of them would hit it off, but he and Oliver hadn't become friends. That *would have made for a really huge mess,* I thought sardonically. As if I wasn't already in one now.

"It's not for your bedroom." Michael was looking at me as if weighing whether or not to say something. "I was thinking more for a nurser—"

"Team member needed in aisle eight with a dolly!" The words cut Michael off, bouncing in echoes off the corrugated roof as if issued by God's own voice.

But Michael's expression told me I'd heard him correctly. And that I hadn't managed to hide my shock. He shook his head, frowned the way he did when things weren't going his way. "Caro, you love kids."

But the last one I birthed nearly died. And her mother did. That thought took me back to the delivery room, where Ava Jane's head was crowning. A fine layer of hair light as a halo covered her skull. The baby's head blanched from the vibrant red of a healthy child to the bluish-gray pallor of a corpse.

Michael watched, perplexed, as I relived that moment, my hands again moving automatically toward the little girl stuck between her mother's legs as if they were there in the aisle with us. I blinked hard several times, trying to clear the specters of that awful night. The air-conditioning raised goose bumps on my arms and legs.

"I love kids. So?" I demanded.

"So . . ." Michael drew out the word. "Even though you come home glowing after you've been at a birth, I've never once heard you say that you wanted a baby of your own." He peered down at me.

I blew out the breath I'd been holding. "Michael, I can't have this conversation today." An elderly man in denim overalls and yellow galoshes leaning on a cedar cane glanced at us as he walked past. I wrapped my arms across my chest, hugged myself tight. I took a step back from Michael and looked down the aisle, avoiding my boyfriend's questioning stare. A few feet away a toddler perched in the seat of a cart, banging a play hammer on the handle. To my left an infant reached his arms up from his stroller as he cried for his father to hold him. I wanted to walk over and scoop the baby up in my arms, hold him close and reassure him that this Home Depot in the heartland was a wonderful place. But along with my own childhood, Ava Jane's catastrophic birth made this a lie. There was no certain safety—not here, not anywhere.

I recalled Deirdre's confession that her heart wasn't strong enough to withstand motherhood. All the anger I'd felt toward her since Mary's birth disappeared. I understood all too well now what she meant about the high price one might be asked to pay to bring life into the world.

"Excuse me, dear." A woman with a face as weathered as a Wisconsin barn spoke to me. She wore a long denim skirt and galoshes identical to those of the man who'd tottered past us earlier. Her voice shook along with her hand but the strength of her grip surprised me when she grabbed my wrist. "I'm looking for my husband. He's gotten away from me and I can't find the section where they keep the bits and pieces for fixing leaky pipes." Her eyes were rheumy but still sharp. She went on. "I get so lost in these big stores!" There was a hint of fright in her voice. I knew exactly how she felt. Two aisles over, we found Norbert hunched over a bin full of washers. Would anyone care whether I got confused in Home Depot, or would I wander through my old age barren, without the comfort of progeny?

I closed my eyes, seeking a vision of Michael and me in our later years on the porch of his dream house. It felt so idyllic, so perfect. But that wasn't the way things went in real life. If I had a child of my own, how would I ever keep it safe?

When I opened my eyes again, Michael was there next to me. He reached over and brushed a stray tear off my cheek, cupped my chin in his hand.

"Caro." He dropped his voice to just above a whisper. "I've

been trying to tell you something all day, and goddamn I am screwing it up big-time but I hope you'll understand. The timing is awful but what happened to MG makes what matters so clear." In his eyes I saw the eager little boy he had once been, the one who believed all the goodness his small world held would remain forever. "I want us to get married. Not right away, but soon. I want a mess of kids and a big kitchen where I can feed them and you and whoever else we love enough to invite over for Sunday night suppers. I want to see you big as a house." Michael aped a sweeping bowl of a belly out in front of his slender form. It would have been funny under other circumstances.

The din of shoppers rolling carts and cashiers ringing up sales was sharp in my ears, signaling the beginning of a throbbing headache. Michael's desire pulled at my heart and I had to bite down hard on my lower lip, fend off the urge to say yes right there on the spot just to make him happy. But he was right; his timing couldn't have been worse. I looked into his guileless face, just waiting for a nod from me to burst into a satisfied grin. Affection rushed through me. Michael was loving, attentive, handsome. He was a catch. But why couldn't I stop aching to feel Oliver's hands and lips roaming my body? Why had I slept with him in the first place and jeopardized the kind of commitment Michael was ready to offer me?

An answer rose in me sharp and clear: I didn't deserve Michael.

"I've been thinking about this for months." Michael faltered. He must have sensed the doom I was feeling. His eyes held mine until finally I had to turn and walk away. I hastened toward the front of the store, Michael following behind. He had helped me make a life in Milwaukee. What would it look like without him? Michael reached out from behind and grabbed my elbow, pulling me to a stop. He walked around in front of me, read all the questions in my eyes. I didn't try to hide them. I watched as he struggled to push away the hurt rising off him.

"I choose you, Caro." Michael's expectant optimism had faded to an expression of bewildered longing that told me how much he thought he loved me, thought we were right for each other. He leaned in, dropped the blessing of a kiss on my forehead. "I'm ready. And I can wait. But not forever, baby." His eyes lingered on mine, letting me know he meant what he said. Then he turned and headed for the exit.

I stood there, stunned. At last I flew out of Home Depot into the bright day, feeling that same otherworldly disorientation I did after a birth. I wished I didn't feel so relieved when I saw Michael's car pulled up right out front, waiting for me as if we belonged to each other.

It was that relief that made me tell him. If Michael was going to leave me it was better to know now. I needed to discover whether I had it in me to create a life here on my own or if I would go home with Momma and seek refuge in the familiar confines of family.

"I fucked someone the other night." I blurted the confession before I could swallow it down. The crass term made me wince but I owed him the truth, not a euphemism like "slept with someone," which would have softened the blow.

Michael and I were still in the car, parked in my parking lot now. We'd driven back from Home Depot in an uncharacteristic silence. At my admission, the distance his proposal had put between us broadened into a wide chasm. I wanted to shout assurances across that vast canyon, let the words "I'm sorry," "It meant nothing" and "Yes, I want to marry you, too" resound around us in hope-filled echoes. But when I opened my mouth to speak, every one of those desultory half-truths refused to come forth. My act of betrayal had hurt me, too. I wanted so badly to believe in love, in its power to heal and redeem. I was disappointed in myself for not taking better care to keep it intact between me and Michael.

"I've never thought of you as the cheating kind," Michael said, sounding nonplussed. I had readied myself for an angry outburst, but he seemed perplexed rather than mad. "I would have thought that if one of us was going to have an affair, it would have been me." His words were tinged with irony. Michael fiddled with the key chain dangling from the ignition while he mulled things over.

"Anyone I know?" he eventually asked.

"Oliver."

Michael gave a wry grunt. "When?"

"After MG's funeral. It wasn't something we planned, it just—"

Michael held up a hand. "That's enough details for me. I don't need a blow-by-blow of your escapades over on the dark side." I winced. Michael thought Oliver was so moody he called him Darth Vader.

"You know what I think?" Michael finally looked back up at me. "I think you're scared. You're a scared little girl, and you're in over your head. Good thing your mother's come to hold your hand."

He continued. "But here's the thing." His face wore the expression of fervor I had relished during Cassie's labor. "You need someone on your other side, too.

"I'm not thrilled about what you did. But I meant it when I said that I loved you. I still do. You might have thought that fucking some other guy would get rid of me, but I'm not as wimpy as that." I could sense him thinking, choosing each word carefully. "It's a risk to trust you again. But I think you're worth it. I'm still here, Caro. And I'm gonna be here, until you tell me loud and clear to go away."

I took in what Michael had said. I *had* expected him to break up with me when I told him about what I'd done. So maybe he was right. Maybe sleeping with Oliver was an act of self-sabotage I'd committed to drive Michael away. I knew all too well how to face things on my own, how to seek shelter inside myself. What I didn't know how to do was accept help, to trust that it would be there when I needed it.

Michael kissed my forehead again then encouraged me to get some sleep. He said he'd check in with me later, and I had no doubt he would. I dragged my weary body upstairs. I told myself I'd take a nap and then go to Deirdre's, but instead I spent the rest of the day in bed.

* * *

Momma brought in a tray with some soup and a grilled cheese sandwich. By then it was after seven and unless a client was birthing, the center would be closed. For three more days I found reasons to put off the visit. The longer I waited, the more impossible it felt to go confront Deirdre.

Something woke me in the middle of the third night. This time it wasn't a rush of the panic I'd almost grown accustomed to lately; instead it was my cell phone vibrating on the nightstand. *Jessica Kennedy* flashed across the screen. Jessica was a client from BirthRight. I squinted at the tiny date emblazoned in the upper right-hand corner. Her due date had been two days ago. I had completely forgotten about it.

"Caro, I think it's time." Jessica was a first-time mom, and her excitement bubbled over the phone even though it was two in the morning. "I've been having contractions all night. They've been every three to four minutes for over an hour now. *And* lasting for at least a minute each time." She crowed with satisfaction as she reported on the "411" formula moms in labor use to determine when it's time to go to the hospital or birth center.

"Well then, I guess that means it's time to go have a baby!" I forced myself to match Jessica's thrilled tone. I dressed, willing my mind to focus on nothing but the task at hand. If I allowed it to speculate on whether or not Deirdre had received the subpoena yet I wouldn't leave the house.

When I stepped onto the porch at BirthRight Deirdre's assistant opened the front door before I could reach for the handle. "Deirdre's with Jessica and Scott." Jane shut the door, then turned toward me. "She got the news about your trial today," she told me. "She says that since Jessica called, you should come up and attend, but that you're not to mention one word about what's going on."

I searched Jane's words for a sign as to how Deirdre had taken the subpoena, but they betrayed no emotion.

I walked upstairs. When she saw me, Deirdre gave a curt nod of her head, then bent back to her task of encouraging Jessica to breathe deep with every contraction. I hung back in the doorway. Although the birthing suite in no way resembled the hospital room where MG had died, I relived that last birth in vivid detail as Jessica's progressed. MG had moaned about the burning in her bottom when Ava Jane's head crowned. Jessica's guttural cries sounded eerily identical. They made me skittish, and I had to continually remind myself that pain in labor didn't mean anything was wrong with mother or baby.

Jessica's birth time went quickly and easily, but the few hours it took seemed like days. Deirdre and I worked well together as always, meeting each other seamlessly as we tended to our client. But every time her eyes met mine reproach blazed in them. As soon as Deirdre was satisfied that the baby was latched on for his first feeding, she gestured to me to follow her from the room. She walked downstairs and straight out the front door onto the porch. I followed penitently. It was five thirty in the morning and still dark, but the temperature was already on the rise, the air heavy with humidity and obligation.

"Well?" Deirdre stepped into the golden circle pooling below the porch light, hands clasped in front of her. She reminded me of the principal at my grade school, a formidable nun who had done the same thing with her hands whenever I went before her for misbehaving in class.

"Deirdre, I had every intention of coming over to let you know about the lawsuit but I just couldn't. This is all so overwhelming and I hate having to ask you to stand up for me, but you're the best person in Milwaukee to tell the jury about my doula skills. I'm sorry you have to be a part of it but you see why it's so crucial that you testify, don't you?" I wheedled.

"Christ and all his kin, Caro, the whole thing is feckin' tragic." Anguish replaced the earlier rebuke in Deirdre's eyes. But the consolation that she was sympathetic to my troubles didn't last. Deirdre pressed her palms tight together. I got the sense she was searching for the right words. Or maybe she was praying. Finally she lifted her eyes to mine. "You're a fine doula, girl. You have courage, fortitude and faith. And as I told you the first time you came in here, you have the gift of being able to be in it with the new mothers. If I was having one of my own, I'd want you tending to me." The bite of her brogue sharpened, adding a gruff burr to the admission. I took it for the tremendous compliment it was.

"The phrase 'black Irish' doesn't mean folks like me. It refers to the ones with dark hair and olive skin, courtesy of the Spanish invaders. Ours was the only black family in our entire county." Deirdre wiped a hand across her brow. "Sometimes I thought we were the only ones in the whole country. So I'm accustomed to scrutiny. I've no problem standing out, or standing up for what's right." Pride blazed in her eyes. She had navigated difficult lessons, all of which had helped make her into the strong woman standing before me.

"But what do you think it took for a black Irish midwife to be accepted here in the Midwest?" One eyebrow arched, the way it always did when Deirdre was worked up about something. "It took me *years* to get this place operating successfully, Caro. Now you're asking me to put everything I do here, this place and my practice, at risk. Do you see that, love? The minute I get on that witness stand people will associate BirthRight with you. We're already under constant scrutiny. Certain members of the medical community are just waiting for a reason to shut me down. That's not a sacrifice I can make.

"I can't even afford the risk of keeping you on here." To her credit, Deirdre looked straight in my eyes as she banished me.

I did the same, meeting her stare as the enormity of my situation passed between us. Deirdre was right. The lawsuit had nothing to do with her or BirthRight. I'd be selfish to insist that she jeopardize its reputation. Enough had been lost already; I couldn't bear to see this place shut down, too. I would tell Annabelle not to call Deirdre to testify. I thought then of the witness list my lawyer had made in her office. It had shrunk to just one person: me.

Thirty-three

"Promise me you won't bring up the subject of us getting married with my mother." I was setting Michael's table for dinner a week later, coupling forks and knives on napkins, when I blurted out my request. True to what he'd said in the car, Michael hadn't broken up with me. He never asked if I was going to see Oliver again, but after we made slow, tentative make-up love one afternoon, we seemed to share an implicit agreement that we were still a couple.

Now we were cautiously navigating our way through the summer. My trial was scheduled to begin the day after Labor Day, so Momma decided to stay in Milwaukee until then. She was coming over to Michael's in a little while, along with Michael's parents. With the impromptu gathering of members from both families I had a sudden panicked intuition that Michael might be planning a surprise to force the issue, even though he'd promised me time to think over his proposal.

Momma had been on me to marry since practically my dress-up days. Even more so since I'd met Michael. The pressure I felt was not entirely her fault. I did this thing that was odd for someone trying to cut the proverbial umbilical cord. During our phone calls, despite my intention to give a wide berth to my unmarried and childless status, if Momma didn't bring the topic up I found myself concocting some story sure to open the door to the very discussion I'd said I didn't want to have. I might mention that Michael and I had attended a wedding that weekend or that I'd babysat a client's children. I slipped these bits into our chats offhandedly, as if I were making casual conversation to fill her in. But we both knew it was my way of opening the door for her to step into my love life.

What normally followed from Momma was a flurry of questions: How could I possibly watch all those babies being born to other

women and not want one of my own? What was I waiting for? She
always ended with her favorites, the ones I could count on hearing
at the close of almost every conversation, so that they had become
a mantra of sorts: Don't you know that the longer you wait, the
harder it can be? And if you wait long enough, it will be *too* long?

The last sentence always rang through the phone line with a
heavy foreboding, carrying the underlying though unspoken *And
then you'll be sorry*. While she wasn't cruel enough to say that
aloud I could hear her thinking it. We'd hang up the phone, both
frustrated. But by the next conversation we were ready to go at
it again, in our own kind of dysfunctional relationship. Now that
Momma was staying with me, I made a gargantuan effort to bite
my tongue whenever I felt like picking a fight with her. I didn't
want to get her started because with her here I couldn't hang up
on her.

Despite Michael's committed resolve, a new tension filled the
space between us, a kind of urgent waiting swollen to near bursting. I don't know how MG handled the stress of staying married
after her infidelity. Michael had agreed to give me some time but
he had his pride. If I didn't respond to his proposal reasonably
soon he'd take my indecision as a definitive answer.

Michael hadn't responded to my request. He was pulling salad
greens and carrots out of the refrigerator. He drew his head from
the fridge and closed the door. His hand lingered on the handle.
A tingle ran up my body from the sudden intruding memory of
a different set of fingers—Oliver's—dancing in circles up and
down my spine. If I wanted to work things out with Michael, why
couldn't I get Oliver out of my mind?

I pushed the reminiscence aside, willed myself to focus on the
man standing before me. Michael could be surprisingly vulnerable
for someone so confident. I took in his striking features, his capable hands that so deftly chopped and diced and minced, the wide
expanse of his chest, where I liked to rest my head while we slept.
He had a sensitive streak, which he struggled with from time to
time, his brow furrowed in confusion as he tried to understand

his feelings. Usually that part of him showed up when we were in bed, long after he thought I was asleep. He'd lie there propped up on two pillows, running his hand across my hair and the side of my face that wasn't pressed up against his chest while I dozed, lulled by the steady thump of his heart. The reassuring echo of his heartbeat made me feel I could relax my vigilance, let him take the watch for a while.

"You know, Caro," Michael said now, measuring the words out slowly, as if an angry phrase or a thoughtless frustration might ruin us beyond saving. "I'm not siding with your mother, you know that." Michael knew my relationship with Momma was complicated. "But I just don't get it. Your family is terrific. They're a little wacky, but in a good way." He caught himself so he wouldn't sound impolite. "They seem like a nice enough bunch of people to grow up with. From what you told me you had a good life.

"You had a cool place to go in summer, and yes, your brother died, but you had your other siblings and cousins so you couldn't have been bored or lonely much." Michael was an only child who'd spent a lot of time alone while his parents traveled.

He shook his head. "Whenever I think of the way you grew up, I see the Waltons." Michael looked as if he was a little sad to have missed out on my so-called idyllic upbringing.

I stood before the table biting my lip, not wanting to ruin his boyish dream of my life. I wouldn't admit it but my heart ached at what he'd described. Hadn't I, too, wanted so badly to believe that we were just that, the kind of perfect family we had watched on TV? Samantha and Chris, both married with kids, had bought into the belief that we'd had a childhood worth repeating. Some days I felt that there must be something wrong with me, something defective that kept me from settling down and appreciating the steady hum of sameness that people like my brother and sister had in their lives. And sometimes when I was at a birth, pangs of misgiving ran through my belly like the foreboding cramps of a miscarriage. Why was it taking me so long to figure out my life?

The inquiry led to additional ominous questions. Where did the shadows that haunted me fit into a life like the ones my siblings had made for themselves? When we talked about memories from when we were kids, we disagreed, sometimes violently, about certain events and details. Each of us was convinced that we had it right and the others were wrong. But memory is a murky thing. I'd tried to splice mine and ignore those that threatened my hard-won independence, but now the recollections were haunting me, rising to the surface with a vengeance that my body and mind refused to ignore any longer.

"Michael." I interrupted his inventory of all the ways my childhood must have been wonderful. But I stopped at his name. I didn't know what to say next. The trouble, I realized, was that there was so much I'd kept from him. Michael knew about Ava Jane's birth, but I'd said nothing about Mary Grace's secret or the disquieting memories of Momma's miscarriage and my childhood that were coming up now that Momma was there. He believed it was the stress of the lawsuit that was making me act so strangely.

From the beginning, I had adapted what I told Michael about myself to reveal what I thought he would find acceptable. Now I felt as if he barely knew me. But that wasn't Michael's fault. He just liked things neat and easy. That's exactly what I'd shown him, but I was a complicated mess.

What was even odder was that I hadn't been lonely with Michael. I'd felt warm and safe and comfortable, at ease in a way I enjoyed when I was with him. I stood there puzzling over why I didn't feel misunderstood when I hadn't let him really get to know me. But I hadn't needed Michael to know the murky parts of me because all along I'd been sharing those with someone else. Someone who understood what lay beneath life's surface. Oliver. His face flashed so clear and sharp that I had to shut my eyes. After a moment I opened them again and looked hard at Michael. He was waving a hand in front of my face.

"Are you in there, Caro?" Concern tinged with irritation played across his face.

"What do you want from me, Michael?" He was backing me into defending myself, but against what accusations, I wasn't sure. I jerked my head up to flip a stray bit of hair out of my eyes, avoided his scrutiny.

"We know what *I* want, Caro, that's not the question." Michael walked over until we were standing nose to nose, staring at each other. "The question is, what does *Caro* want?" He dropped his voice so the last bit sounded illicit. He looked straight at me without blinking as he searched my face, looking and looking for an answer he could comprehend.

But I'd withdrawn. Whatever Michael was able to glimpse in my eyes was only a reflection of what he wanted to see there, because I was off somewhere inside myself, searching for answers to my past that would let me create a future worth living.

Why does disagreement make me want to throw up? People argue. It's a healthy part of relationships. It's inconceivable to live with another human being longer than a few days without *some* fodder for fighting, or at least strenuous discussion. And yet, when pressed for an answer—when asked to make a choice, especially by a man with whom I'm romantically involved—I might know exactly what I want, I might, in fact, have a very definite preference, but I find myself saying, "It doesn't matter to me," or "What do *you* want to do?" in the same tone that I've used to say those words all my life, in a voice that automatically comes through me but isn't really mine, as if I am a dummy and Momma, the ventriloquist, is pulling the strings, the two of us behaving like the good girl she raised me to be.

"Look," Michael sighed, breaking our standoff. "I know you moved here to get away from your family and live on your own. You're doing that. You've proven yourself. I know you need a lot of time alone, a lot of privacy. And that's okay by me." He'd started stomping around the kitchen. Michael's cats, Squeak and Meowser, were wolfing down dinner from their bowls on the kitchen floor. They scampered out from under his indiscriminate feet.

"Look," Michael said again. "We can work this out so that we'll both be happy. Land's cheap up here, outside the city. We'll buy a few acres and we'll build three houses, with plenty of space in between them. I'll live in one house, you can have the second and we'll put the kids in their own quarters out back. Maybe Cassie and Quinn will want to move in there, too." Michael worked himself into an animated frenzy. He waved his arms around, gesturing as if drawing for me the structures he was building in his mind.

"It'll be great," he promised. "Every night you and the kids can come over for dinner and on weekends we can invite our friends. At the end of the night when we want some peace and quiet we can say to the kids, 'Go to your house!'" Michael flung his arm out, index finger pointed toward the front door as if the spirits of our future children were hovering around us.

Leave it to the solution-minded optimist to come up with an alternate living arrangement to the conventional suburban model we both loathed. Michael stood there with his arm outstretched, face flushed, hair disheveled. I wanted so badly to laugh, to melt into the hilarity of the moment he'd created out of his love and his desire for a life full of kids and chaos, a life that felt impossibly unreal to me. I wanted to want the life he described, and not just want it but to believe it was possible for me to have it, to take his dreams into my heart and call them my own. But inside me a girlish voice whispered, *Not yet*.

I cared deeply for Michael. But I couldn't deny that I also had feelings for Oliver. I hadn't returned his phone calls but he kept leaving messages. I thought about my condo too, that space of my own I didn't have to share with anyone else. It was my refuge, my place to examine what I'd grown up believing in and how it might shape the rest of my life. I wanted time and space to go deep inside, to discover how I could not only survive but unfurl my wings and soar into a life of my own making. I wanted this more than I wanted anything Michael, or any man, could promise.

Thirty-four

The doorbell rang, calling a temporary truce between Michael and me. I went to the front door, composing myself along the way before putting on a happy face and greeting his parents as if everything was fine. My skirt swished and swirled, keeping time with the beat of my footfalls. My sandals were chunky and tall. I liked the way it felt to sway side to side as I sashayed into the living room. Momma arrived and I made introductions. A glass of wine eased some of my tension. Michael served grilled halibut with steamed vegetables and saffron-infused basmati rice. Simple but sophisticated. We drank a couple bottles of merlot. Michael's parents, Mike Sr. especially, liked to drink, and even Momma indulged. I had a third glass for dessert, two beyond my usual limit, but I figured I deserved a night of letting loose a bit.

We spent a lot of time with Michael's parents. His father was in construction and well regarded in the business community; his mother taught preschool. "My son sure hit the jackpot when he met you," Michael's dad had told me once. "He's lucky that I'm his old man and not the competition!" He'd said it in a way that felt complimentary, not creepy. The two of us had developed a mutual adoration society. It was nice to introduce Momma to such an upstanding family. A small part of me wanted her to see how well I could do away from her.

I stood up from the dining room table and cleared away the coffee cups and dessert plates. Tonight Mike Sr. seemed less animated than usual, but I didn't dwell on it. Gathering a stack of dishes, I started through the doorway toward the kitchen. Michael and his mother walked a few feet ahead of me. The trill of Susan's voice filled the air like birdsong as she told Michael a story about his uncle, Cassie's father. Momma and Mike Sr. remained behind at the table. Mike Sr. was telling Momma he could see where I'd inherited my good looks from.

As I made my way toward the kitchen I swung my hips lightly from side to side, enjoying the dizzy exhilaration brought on by the wine and the walking. For a blessed few minutes I lost track of my uncertain circumstances, caught up in the moment.

"I meant what I said to your mother. You're a beautiful woman." Startled, I swung my head around so fast that my hair hit Mike Sr.'s face. He came up from behind and pulled me close, one beefy arm around my shoulders drawing me next to him. My hip collided with the side of his leg. He was three inches taller than me even in my heels, and although he had thickened around the middle with age, he was still solid.

"Thank you," I murmured.

"You'd have no problem convincing an old dog like Harlan J. Black to let you off easy."

I froze. Harlan J. Black was Brad Schaeffer's attorney. Mike Sr. pulled back, appraising me. I had a strong urge to pull my hair across my face like a curtain. But Mike Sr. reached out two meaty fingers and drew back the few strands shielding me from his imposing stare.

"You know, kiddo, you're the one who made the mistake." Mike Sr.'s casual tone felt deliberate, calculated. I said nothing, caught in a dizzying whirl of surprise and shock. Guffaws drifted from the kitchen, where Michael and his mother joked, oblivious to what was happening. I looked back over the shoulder that wasn't tucked into Mike Sr.'s armpit. Where was Momma?

"There's no reason for Medical City to be involved in your troubles, Caro," Mike Sr. purred. "I'm chairman of the board over there. I've spoken to the other trustees and we're in agreement. If this thing goes to trial, our attorneys will deny all liability. It will come down on you anyway, so why not save yourself the unpleasant experience of digging up every questionable bit of your past and parading it around for all the town to see?"

He continued. "I know Black pretty well. Hunting trips, poker nights, golf outings. You might say we do business together regularly."

My dismay deepened.

"I also know that the only thing Black appreciates better than winning a trial is a settlement before he's spent a bunch of time and money. You're gonna get burned, kiddo. Make it easy on yourself."

Suddenly I felt naked in front of Michael's father. I tossed my head back and looked up into the moonlike orb of the hallway light shining down. Way too much light for me to make myself invisible.

"Caro?" Momma sounded tentative as she came upon us standing there in the hallway.

"Think it over. Make the right choice," Mike Sr. whispered before he dropped his arm from around my shoulder. He walked over to meet Susan as she came out of the kitchen. Susan wore a version of the uncertain smile I'd often seen on Momma's face, that placating look I knew all too well from women of their generation. It was an expression that betrayed every compromise they'd made to keep their husbands happy, their marriages intact. Their collusion allowed men like Michael's father to believe they could push women into whatever role best served their purposes. Mike Sr. was counting on me to keep my mouth shut about his so-called "advice" the same way the generation before me would have.

Mike Sr. and Susan exchanged terse good-byes with my mother, then they all filed out of Michael's house. I was so shaken that I wanted to go home with Momma. But earlier I had promised Michael I would spend the night, and now I was too stunned to come up with a plausible excuse for changing my mind. Michael said I was looking a little pale. He suggested I go lie down while he took care of the last bits of cleanup. I sought refuge in the bedroom, the alcohol-induced dizziness exacerbated by a round of panic attacks. Michael came in a little while later. I heard him looking for me, but before I could tell him where I was, he flung open the closet door and flipped on the light.

"Jesus, Caro! What's going on?" The light flashed on me curled up on the closet floor.

"Can you hold me?" I tried to keep the desperation out of my voice as I stumbled out from the closet. I didn't want Michael to know that if he refused I might go wander the streets all night like Mary Smith. The image of myself looking like that poor crazy girl, hair unwashed for weeks, wearing three layers of smelly, torn clothes and grinning maniacally as if possessed by demons, nearly undid me. But I steadied myself and wondered what had happened to Mary in the days since she gave birth. I hoped she was faring better than me.

The worried look that passed over Michael's face calmed me. I moved away a bit, switching into the competent persona I had picked up from Daddy. "I'm fine," I demurred, hiding behind my hair. "I just . . . too much wine."

I stepped in again and pressed my body against his before he could say anything else. The heat and aliveness of him coursed into me as he raised a hand and cupped one of my breasts. Something leapt in me, a survival instinct, perhaps. I didn't want to think right now. I wanted nothing more than to feel, not sadness or despair or fright but the soothing sensations of being held, caressed, *contained*.

Michael pulled me straight toward the bed as if he had read my mind. I pushed him onto it, made him watch as I stripped down wordlessly, pushing away the memory of having done the same thing at Oliver's. *He* wasn't welcome here. I put my hands on my hips and flounced around the bedroom in my lingerie, showing a little cheek as a tease.

"You're the wildest woman I've ever been to bed with." Michael's voice was thick with delighted anticipation.

I grinned, but the compliment agitated me.

Michael was leering. Just for an instant I could see him as an old man—his cheeks drooping into jowls, his forehead and neck rutted like tree bark, the line of his nose no longer classically aquiline so much as a stark slope pitching in sharp relief against the hollows of his cheeks. Would I know him when he looked like that? That thought distracted me from the shivery whisper of his lips tracing the lacy outline of my bra straps across my shoulders.

My mind skipped to Mary Grace telling me about her affair. Why hadn't she said it had been with Oliver? She had deceived me. And what about Oliver? Why had he thought he could treat me like that? What else were the people in my life up to that I didn't know about?

Michael's mouth explored along my clavicle. Rage built along with desire from Michael's touch. What if I married Michael and he cheated on me? As he entered me, I squeezed my thighs around him so hard that he looked down at me, surprised.

"That hurt!" he yelped. His expression switched from astonishment to mischief. He thought I was trying to spice things up. "Let's see how *you* like it rough and tumble, lady," he said, baiting me. He reached around and smacked my butt, hard enough to sting. Then he looked at me expectantly, a wide grin spreading across his face. Excitement quickened inside me, fueled by anger. I slapped him across the face hard as I could, even though he wasn't the reason for my anger.

"Goddamn it, Caro!" A red blush of shock crawled up Michael's cheeks. The old man I'd seen moments ago morphed into a little boy betrayed, wide-eyed with disbelief. My eyes widened too. I reached up to rub away the crimson print of my hand but he grabbed my wrist, thinking I was about to hit him again.

"Quit it!" he yelled, so loud Meowser slunk out from under the bed, meowing plaintively at all the commotion. Michael looked at me a long moment as if calculating what to do next. The look aroused me even more. I grabbed him with my hand, shoved him deep inside of me where I was already so wet. I put my hands on his hips and made him penetrate me so hard I cried out. We looked and looked deep into each other until his eyes involuntarily closed as he climaxed. When he opened them again, I was still watching. He stayed on top of me, his weight pressing me down, making it hard for me to breathe. A puzzled expression crossed his face.

"Sometimes," he said with a hint of wonder as he stroked his thumb along my jawline, "sometimes right after, I can see you as a girl. There's a tiny little Caro looking back at me and she looks so damn vulnerable that all I want to do is take care of her forever . . ." He let the words trail off, leaving me space to respond. But I didn't want him seeing the child in me just now. She didn't need Michael to take care of her. After the ways I had betrayed him, she needed to know I could fend for myself if he left.

Michael got up and left the bedroom. I heard various drawers and cabinets opening and shutting in the kitchen. He brought me half a peanut butter and jelly sandwich along with a glass of milk. "This should help with the bed spins, if you didn't work them all out of your system just now," he joked. But his searching look unnerved me. "This lawsuit really has you jumpy, huh?" He pulled the bedspread back for me.

"I guess." I was unsure where he was going with the question. "Michael—" I struggled to find words for what I needed to ask. "Your father . . ." I stopped there, waited to see if he'd offer an explanation for Mike Sr.'s awful behavior. But he only gave me a puzzled look. "You didn't tell me he was chairman of the board at Medical City."

A frown crossed his normally smooth features as he held the blanket up so I could slide in underneath it. "Yeah, he is." His face held a shadow of disappointment, as if I'd mentioned something inappropriate. "But, Caro, he's got to answer for the people employed by the hospital. I'm not comfortable asking him to get involved for you too. It's a conflict of interest."

"You're absolutely right." My voice rose, along with indignation and disbelief that he could think I would ask his father to help get me out of the lawsuit. I sat up, paced in front of the bed. "*If* I asked your father to rescue me, that would be inappropriate. Just as inappropriate as your father insinuating I should admit I hurt the baby so the case will go away. Which is exactly what he asked—no, he didn't *ask,*" I corrected myself, then mimicked Mike Sr.'s booming tenor. "He *strongly suggested* that I settle before trial."

Michael and I stared at one another, suspended in the astonishment of what his father had done.

"Whatever he said, he couldn't have meant what you think you heard." Michael was trying to reconcile the gulf between what I was telling him and the man he wanted his father to be. His refusal to believe what I'd told him felt as much like unfaithfulness as if he had slept with someone else.

I stopped pacing, turned on Michael with all the fury that had been building in me since Mike Sr. had cornered me. "Sure, Michael, you're right. Your father didn't ask me to take all the blame for what happened. And I'm sure that in the *unlikely* event that he did, you're going to tell me now that your dad's looking out for my best interests, too, right? That the best choice is to settle and put it all behind me, right?"

I didn't give him room to answer, went on spewing all the hurt, frustration and fear pent up inside. "How convenient would that be for your father and his cronies, Michael, to have me offer myself up? Just what do you think I would move on *to,* if I sell out like your father is suggesting? Your plan to become one big happy family? Is that what you and your dad are thinking, Michael?" I was seething and still so dizzy. Michael looked stunned, said nothing. The adrenaline from our fight ebbed and exhaustion took over. I closed my eyes, slumped against the wall.

"Yes, I would like to think that *we* could move on once this is over." Michael's unflagging optimism hovered between us but I couldn't allow it in. "But, Caro, you've got to believe in yourself. And stand up for what you believe in. I didn't have any idea my dad was going to pull that stunt tonight." Michael's dismay told me he was telling the truth. "Do you really think I'd tell you to go against yourself and lie?" Michael's anguish and bewilderment told me I'd made a huge mistake. I'd assumed he'd take his family's side against me. Now he was insulted. "I don't know what kind of a person you think I am but I want to support you through this. No matter what my father thinks." He moved toward me, and gathered me in his arms. But instead of taking comfort in his embrace, I stiffened. My mind raced, dwelling on visions of terror and destruction that made Mary's life on the streets look idyllic.

There were some demons I had to face alone. Michael didn't get up and come after me, even when I passed through the bedroom door and out of his line of sight. I didn't turn around to try to make things right between us. Wordlessly I let myself out of Michael's house, wondering for a fleeting moment if I might ever make my way back into the shelter I had just left behind.

PART IV

Life, After

Thirty-five

While most Midwesterners savor summertime outdoors, I spent the two months before trial in a self-imposed isolation more suited to the dead of winter. I hadn't taken any doula clients since Jessica Kennedy, hadn't been out to BirthRight at all. I saw Michael occasionally but the tension between us strained our attempts at even the most casual of interactions. I continued to avoid Oliver. Most of that time I burrowed in bed like a fugitive in hiding.

There was one place I sought refuge. Feeling almost as furtive as I had crossing the lawn to Marilyn Hanover's as a child, I muttered to Momma about vague errands I needed to run, then left her to her own devices and fled to the Enclave. Pixie's enterprise was so fringe my presence there would do it no harm. And little Quinn's delight whenever I arrived was a balm to my battered spirit.

The first time I went after that awful dinner at Michael's, Cassie was quick to assure me where her loyalties stood. "Put me on the stand. I'll let them all have it," she'd declared vehemently. "I'll tell them how indispensable you are, how I never could have had Quinn without you." She was as fierce as a mother bear defending her young, but although a client's testimony would be helpful, the jury would consider Cassie as much of an aberration as Pixie. Plus I wasn't about to ask her to jeopardize her relationships with Michael and his parents.

While my time with Cassie and Quinn soothed me, it was the pint-sized midwife whose guidance nurtured me through my exile. Pixie and I walked endless hours in the forest, blazing new trails in our conversations as well as through the woods. One day I finally asked her about the motions she'd made on and around Quinn at his birth. "I was helping his spirit come more fully into his body." She grinned. "That one's a lot like you; he's going to need to be very grounded in the here and now for the big life he's got ahead of him."

"How do you know that?" I ignored her comparison, which I knew was meant to get me to talk about my predicament. I didn't want to get into it that day. But I was fascinated by her occasional pronouncements, which rang with such certainty.

Pixie shrugged. We cut through a stand of oak trees and stepped out into a wide meadow. "Sometimes I just know things. I trust those gut instincts. When I pay them no mind I usually wind up regretting it." Pixie stopped walking and stared at me meaningfully. "Which is why I need to tell *you* something I know for certain, dear one: no matter how this mess you're in turns out, you're a blessing in this world."

Pixie's benediction barely penetrated the doubts plaguing me. My trial was just a week away, and between prepping with Annabelle during the day and nightmares all night long, I relived the events of MG's last hours almost continually. "Pixie, any day now I have to stand up and tell a jury what a great job I did in there that night. I've got to say it like I believe it. But if it was the truth Mary Grace would be here, Ava Jane wouldn't be facing potential brain damage and I wouldn't be on trial." I was weeping before I finished getting the words out.

"When was the last time someone called you God?" Pixie stepped in front of me, grabbing on to my elbow as if she feared I would bolt from the meadow. I looked at her quizzically. "Exactly." She nodded. "Most of life is like birth; we think we get to control it but much of what happens takes us by surprise. The grace is in learning to let whatever comes shape you, not break you."

"But what if I did the wrong thing? What if I hurt that little girl?" Asking the awful questions aloud brought me to my knees in the bright, sun-drenched meadow. From the tightness gathering around my heart I uttered a wounded cry.

Pixie crouched down. "Tell me, Caro. Tell me what you saw."

"Not what I saw, what I *did*. MG wanted to push but the nurse said she had to stop and wait for the doctor to come deliver." I related those harrowing moments to Pixie, laboring through the admission with heaving breaths. Sometime during the telling Pixie sat down in the meadow grass and gathered me up in her lap.

"Dear heart," she crooned, rocking me. "Life is a crucible. I've delivered two stillbirths and a little one so premature she died at two days old." Grief passed across Pixie's face. "Not a day goes by that I still don't wonder if only . . . If only I'd paid more attention for signs during the pregnancies, if only I'd sent the mother to the hospital . . . In hindsight, you can second-guess yourself until you're too terrified to ever attend another birth.

"Sometimes no matter what we do there are complications that can't be foreseen or avoided. It's a hard truth parents learn as their little ones grow up. You'll get through this. Take your time afterward, but go back to work. Mothers and babies need you. Just think of how it might have turned out if you hadn't been there at all." Pixie stroked my cheek. "Yes, your friend died, but you brought her little girl through it safely. And any mother would tell you she'd gladly give up her own life for her child's if that must be the price."

"But now she's got to grow up without a mother," I wailed. I was Ava Jane's godmother. Didn't that imply I was supposed to step in when something happened to her mother? I was struggling just to fashion a decent life for myself; even if Brad ever agreed to let me be in Ava Jane's life, how would I help care for her?

"Oh God, Pixie, I don't know what to think. You just said that we're not in charge of what happens. So what if I interfered with the way her birth was supposed to go?" I finally said it, acknowledged that perhaps I had overstepped a line more crucial than that between birth coach and midwife. Maybe I was more like the medical professionals than I liked to believe; maybe I had willfully stepped into divine shoes. How could I ever make my peace with that, regardless of how a jury voted?

"The Chinese say that when you save a person's life you must take care of them forever." Pixie stood, brushed errant grass blades from her slacks and tears from her cheeks. She reached her arms out and pulled me up alongside her. I towered over her yet still felt like a child hiding behind her mother's skirts. "So I think the question you ought to concern yourself with is, how are you going to continue to look after that little one who needs you more than ever now?"

Thirty-six

Oliver's car was sitting in front of my building when I got home. I contemplated driving right on past but he looked up and spied me. I pulled into the lot, parked, got out of the car and stood there waiting as he approached. He leaned in to kiss me but must have felt me stiffen, because he pulled back and offered me a hand to shake in a gesture so awkward I barked out an astonished laugh.

"Caro, I—" I waved a hand to stop him before he could continue with some lame justification. "Why'd you leave?" He asked the question as if it had been burning in him all this time, and I heard the hurt that fueled the inquiry.

"I think I left all the explanation necessary lying on your floor," I said pointedly. "Or doesn't the phrase 'smoking gun' mean anything to you?"

Oliver had the decency to blush, which softened my anger toward him. "Can we go talk somewhere?" he asked.

The anger that had dimmed a moment ago flared brighter again at his request. "You mean somewhere like your house, maybe?" The barb must have stung because Oliver winced. But I wasn't satisfied yet. "Oh, wait, you've already had me there. And oh yeah, you had Mary Grace there too!" I clapped a hand to my forehead in mock surprise. "What the hell, you're here, why don't you just come up to my place." A couple of people were walking through the parking lot but I didn't bother to lower my voice. I was tired of keeping my mouth shut, tired of guessing at who was for or against me. "Where would you like to fuck with me next, Oliver?"

Oliver looked like he was calculating the best response to my outburst. Then he shrugged, as if he had nothing to lose. "I was thinking we'd go to the cemetery," he proposed.

Fifteen minutes later we were making our way through Grace-land Cemetery in search of Mary Grace's grave. Oliver's unex-pected request felt so weirdly right I'd agreed to go with him. We drove over in silence, as if we didn't want to continue the conver-sation outside our mutual friend's presence. I'd been wanting to visit since Mary Grace's funeral but was too apprehensive to go. Oliver and I stopped at the tombstone that marked our friend's grave. The sight of her name and the dates of her lifetime etched on a marker rolled away the stone I'd pushed over my heart, bared the grief housed within.

No matter her age when it happened, a girl was lost once her mother was gone. Momma and I had a complicated relationship but whenever I tried to visualize her dying I couldn't fathom it. Maybe it was better to lose one's mother before knowing her than to have her taken from you later, after you'd come to rely upon her constant presence in your life. Would Ava Jane ever truly under-stand what she'd lost since she wouldn't know life any other way? In my grief I turned into the comfort of Oliver's arms again.

He held me while I cried out some of the pent-up emotions I'd been carrying around all summer. When my shudders subsided he sat beside Mary Grace's grave, looking incongruous squatting there in his suit and tie. I tugged off my clogs and lay down on my back, the solidity of the ground beneath me and the wide sky above as sweet a relief as Pixie's forest.

I had just closed my eyes when Oliver spoke. "I'm guilty," he said. "I stole her shoes when I went over to talk to Brad about putting the house on the market."

"Brad's selling the house?" I sat up and looked at Oliver, in-credulous.

"He listed it right after the funeral. Apparently it was the second thing on his to-do list, after finding the slimiest lawyer in town to sue everybody he could." There was anger in his tone as he added, "She was hardly in the ground and he'd already packed up most of her clothing and things."

"People are funny about death," I said. I wasn't defending

Brad's behavior; grief birthed strange actions. "Maybe it was just too painful for him to be surrounded by all those things that would remind him—"

"I told him I needed to take a look around." As if he didn't want to hear it, Oliver interrupted my quasi-justification of Brad's behavior. "While he reviewed the listing agreement I went upstairs and looked for something I could take. A keepsake.

"She had those shoes on the day we—" His voice broke on the last word and tears collected in his eyes, then spilled down his cheeks. Oliver didn't bother to wipe at them, and I refrained from reaching over. Better to let him have his moment as graciously as he had just let me have mine. Afterward I'd throttle him for seducing Mary Grace. And me.

"She wanted to be cremated, you know." Regret turned his words bitter.

I *hadn't* known. A momentary jealousy swept through me but I shook my head to let Oliver know it was news to me.

"After my mother passed away, Mary Grace and I were talking about dying and what we wanted when the time came. She wanted her ashes scattered over the lake. She hated the thought of becoming a feast for worms and maggots, said she'd rather be fish food any day." Oliver flashed a weak grin. I could almost hear the wry, pragmatic words coming from Mary Grace's mouth.

"I hadn't realized you two were so . . . close." I wanted to get back to the subject that had brought us there, but it felt crass to accuse Oliver directly.

Oliver shrugged. He slipped off his suit coat, then lay back, taking my hand and pulling me down again too. Maybe it was easier to come clean lying beside me, looking up into the wide expanse of dusky gray twilight rather than into my eyes.

"I've been in love with her for a very long time." The words were matter-of-fact, and I guessed it had been long enough for him to have somehow made his peace with it. But whatever emotions she'd felt for Oliver, Mary Grace had married Brad.

"She told me she'd slept with someone . . ." I paused in an

effort to choose the least hurtful words. I thought back to Mary Grace's confession. *It was a mistake. A one-night thingy. Not some great love affair,* she had insistented. "But she didn't tell me it was you." I couldn't bring myself to share what Mary Grace had said—how she had dismissed the tryst as a mistake—no matter how pissed I was at Oliver. "You guys met in college, right?" If I could get him talking it would keep him from asking for more details about what Mary Grace had confided.

"First day of freshman year," he said. "I was in love with her by fall break."

I tried to remember back to our college years, which now seemed like they belonged to some other life. I'd visited MG once or twice at the university but it was too hard to try to fit in with her friends and life there since I didn't share it. I'd stopped going up, preferring to wait for her to come home to Chicago on holidays, when I could have her mostly to myself. I couldn't remember meeting Oliver on any of the few visits I'd made, though. It wasn't until I decided to move to Milwaukee and she introduced me to him that Mary Grace had mentioned Oliver as someone she had gone to school with at the U. I had assumed he was a casual acquaintance. Had they been more than that at some point during school?

Oliver continued. "We used to talk about chucking it all, dropping out together and traveling. We'd drive out to the West Coast, then get a round-the-world ticket and hit it—Asia first, Europe later, the whole shebang." Oliver arced an arm across the sky, tracing a globe.

I kept my surprise to myself. Mary Grace had never mentioned such plans to me. As far as I knew, she'd planned to major in psychology and become a counselor since forever.

"What happened?" I kept my voice carefully devoid of my growing shock and dismay as Oliver told me more things I hadn't known about my best friend.

Oliver rolled onto his right side, away from me. "Nothing." He snorted. I had to lean in to hear over his back. "Absolutely nothing. At least not between us. After a couple of years of talking about it, I called her bluff. My mom died junior year and I inherited some money. When school ended for the summer, I dropped out. Made that drive out west and bought the plane ticket to everywhere. School had never really been my thing. I was there more just for somewhere to be, not because I had some passion for economics or engineering."

Oliver continued dryly. "Needless to say, MG declined the invitation to join me. I guess the offer of a free plane ticket to unbridled adventure was a little too out-there for her. It was one thing to talk about it with me when she wanted to bitch about her catty sorority sisters, but she felt safer playing the pretty little campus coed. She knew who she was there." Oliver rolled back over suddenly, knocking me onto my back. He was practically on top of me.

"Me, I never fit in. Maybe that's what made it easier for me to go." He looked at me hard, as if he wanted me to tell him I understood. I did understand. I knew what he meant about the easy way Mary Grace had moved through her life as if she belonged to it. Oliver and I were a different sort of creature, though. Misfits, always on the fringe no matter the crowd. Maybe her ease was what had drawn both of us to Mary Grace. Maybe that was what we had sought. We couldn't achieve it ourselves, so we had settled for being near to one who had it. But now that she was gone, how could we sustain the tranquility Mary Grace had offered us through her friendship? Was that what had drawn Oliver to me in Mary Grace's absence, the need to re-create how he felt around her?

I thought of Michael then. He was like Mary Grace in the way he moved so effortlessly through life's changes. I hadn't recognized it earlier, but now I saw that I had replicated my friendship with Mary Grace in my relationship with Michael. I'd given him the responsibility for defining us, slipped into his life without bothering to question the cost to my own.

I glanced over at the headstone rising beyond Oliver's back.

Mary Grace was right there with us. The weirdness of our love triangle struck me then, and the undeniable realization of my own complacency infuriated me. In Chicago I'd been engulfed by Momma and the ABCs. Milwaukee was supposed to offer me the freedom to discover myself. Instead I'd let myself get swallowed up in Mary Grace's and Michael's lives. When would I learn to define myself separate and apart from the people around me?

My anger was mostly at myself but I took it out on Oliver. I got to my feet. "So, what, you got your one night with MG. Then she left all of us." I gestured toward the headstone. "What am I supposed to be, a replacement? Your way of keeping her alive?" The words were scathing but I didn't care. It felt good to speak the hurt I'd felt so deeply when I came across Mary Grace's shoes in Oliver's closet.

Oliver flipped onto his stomach. He propped his head in both hands and looked off in the distance. The lake lay beyond the far fence of the cemetery. If I squinted I could just see the shimmer of the water as the waves rolled in toward the shore. "You remember her," Oliver said. "And you loved her as well as I did. We have that in common. Lots of people spend their lives together with less between them than that. Why shouldn't it be reason enough?"

I recoiled at the suggestion. "In that case logic would dictate I ought to marry Brad."

Oliver grimaced at the idea. "*Nobody* should have married Brad." There was sadness under the strident assertion.

"What about Ava Jane?" We hadn't yet gotten to the timing of his night with Mary Grace and her pregnancy. But it must have occurred to Oliver that the baby might be his.

"What about her?" he asked. He wasn't going to make it easy on me. If I wanted the truth I was going to have to ask for it.

"What if she's not Brad's?" I paused, collecting the courage to continue. I was so tired of conjecture and speculation. "What if she's yours?"

A long silence followed. Oliver stood up, walked over to the

The Doula

grave marker and ran a hand across it. I saw him brushing a
strand of Mary Grace's hair out of her face in the same way,
fought to shut out the intimacy of the gesture.

"She's not. I asked MG. She said she knew she was pregnant
before we . . ." He let the words trail off.

That might have been what Mary Grace had told Oliver, but I
had no need to buy it as quickly as he had. "What if Ava Jane is
yours?" I demanded again.

"She can't be," Oliver insisted. "It was the thing that always
kept MG and me apart. She wanted kids, a family. I didn't. I still
don't." His voice held a barely veiled plea for me to stop challenging him. Oliver took a step away from Mary Grace and toward
me. "I'm smart enough to know I'd make a shitty father. Even
worse than my own." For a moment he looked haunted and I
wondered just what his childhood had been like.

"But I promise you one thing." He took another step toward
me, his eyes holding mine as he reached a hand out to me. He'd
swept his troubling memories beneath the surface again and his
expression had returned to one of certainty. "For the right kind of
woman, I'd make a terrific husband."

Thirty-seven

Despite the late hour, sometime after our trip to the cemetery Oliver arranged for a floral delivery. He sent a dozen pink roses, poised in a smoky gray glass vase. I got the subtle message they conveyed. Neither white for friendship nor red for passion, their color sat smack between the two, a good likeness of our current relationship. I put the flowers on my dresser, taking care to tuck the card into a drawer. Momma would believe they were from Michael.

Then I put all of the men in my life on trial. I sat in bed, making a list of suspects on the legal pad Annabelle had given me for taking notes. I thought if I imagined those who were giving me trouble up on the witness stand I could cross-examine each one and maybe discover the best way to handle them all. Michael and Oliver went at the top, followed by Brad. Then came Mike Sr. I paused before adding one last name. But to round things out Daddy needed to be there too.

When Daddy came home from the funeral home at night, I'd step barefoot on his dress shoes, shrieking with abandon while we waltzed on the cracked linoleum floor in the kitchen. Each night after he made himself a Manhattan I hung around his recliner and waited for what seemed like forever while he sipped his drink and read the *Tribune*. When the pretty amber liquid was gone and just the maraschino cherry rested on the pile of ice, he'd reach into the glass, pluck the bourbon-plump fruit out by its stem and hand it to me. I'd twirl the cherry above my mouth, then drop it in between my lips. The cherry burst open when my teeth bit into it, sweet juice burning a fiery path from my throat down to my belly. For the next several breaths I felt that rush of whiskey when I inhaled, until it slowly faded into a warm glow that left me feeling pleasantly numb, if a little dizzy.

These were the kinds of memories I had of my father, brief snippets of time when he had a spare moment or two for me. Daddy had asked me to fill Momma's shoes when she took to her bed but I'd never thought to blame him for it. He'd been a supporting actor most of my life, the one I relied on to manage Momma and keep her happy.

I looked once more at Daddy's name on my notepad, then put a line through it. Despite what it had cost me, I still believed he had done the best he could once Momma took to her bed and went missing from our lives. I set the notepad down on the floor, shut off the bedroom light and lay faceup on the bed, wide-awake despite the late hour.

In my head I made another list, this one a litany of what I wanted: I wanted it all to be over. I wanted the lawsuit to take its place alongside the other unsavory memories of my past, whatever the outcome. I wanted Momma to return to Chicago and I wanted to pick up and go myself, move somewhere I had no history. Maybe I needed to get out of the Midwest altogether. Surely the temperate climes of places like California or Florida lent a warmth, a sympathetic nature, to the people who populated their cities and towns. Maybe I could take refuge among them eventually. But I couldn't go anywhere until after the trial. And when I remembered that I'd come to Milwaukee because of that same need to flee, I despaired of ever finding a place I could feel at home.

I thought back to what Michael had said to me before his parents and Momma arrived for dinner: *We know what I want, Caro, that's not the question. The question is, what does Caro want?* His impassioned description of the houses in the woods and the cozy hearth with kids and friends gathered 'round was so appealing. Michael had a good heart. Despite myself I could appreciate that he was caught in a tough dilemma too.

I had received two proposals. Throughout that night until the sun started to rise, I considered both of them. Two very different men. Two very different lives. Neither one felt like mine. I imagined reading a verdict to Michael and Oliver as if they were defendants in the witness box. But impressions from much further back kept intruding, insisting I pay them attention. I shut my eyes, hoping for a brief respite from the unsettling flashes of my imagination. But closing my eyes had been a mistake. Doing so only flung open the long-shut entryway to my awareness as if it were a screen door blown off its hinges by a livid and unsettling wind.

It's funny how memory warps time. Whenever I thought of the bad times when Momma stayed in her nightgown all day, it felt as if they had lasted for years. But now I wondered how long that period after the miscarriage and Paulie's drowning had really been. Regardless of its duration Momma had shut her eyes against all the world, me included. From then on, that had colored everything. It felt to me that for years we drifted through the days, pretending that everything was all right as long as no one mentioned what was wrong, until we'd come to believe we had forgotten the tragedies that had quieted us in the first place. But now, with memories rising, the silence was turning into a roar inside me.

As the first rays of morning peeked into my bedroom, I finally had to admit to myself that in my mind time and time again the person up there on the stand wasn't a man. The guilty party was always the one who hadn't kept me from harm. *Momma*.

Thirty-eight

Labor Day weekend dragged on endlessly. I watched Momma, hoping that she would make some mention of that horrible holiday we'd lost Paulie, but if it was on her mind she never mentioned it. Then suddenly the weekend was over, and the first day of the trial was upon me. I got up after a sleepless night despite the aid of a sedative and donned the navy slacks and burgundy blouse Annabelle had preapproved. She'd rejected the brown suit that I'd bought thinking it would make me look professional. "Too cold and clinical," she'd said. "I want the jury to see you as nurturing as well as competent." So the suit remained in the closet, tags still on it. I typically wore scrubs and clogs to births but what I was wearing now approximated the outfits I interviewed prospective clients in, so it didn't feel too much like a costume deliberately chosen for effect.

I could find no similar comforts in the courtroom. Despite the carefully selected clothing I fought the sense that I was naked in public for all the world to see. The feeling persisted through jury selection and opening arguments. I wished I had thought to ask Momma for a Xanax to bring along in my purse but then thought better of it. If the jury caught me popping pills it probably wouldn't be so good for the pristine image Annabelle crafted of me in her opening.

The other side got to present their case first. As the judge directed Harlan J. Black to call his witnesses, I snuck a sideways look at Brad, seated at a table across the aisle. I hadn't seen him since MG's funeral. He looked lost. Haggard and bloated, too. MG had told me he drank too much when stressed, and I wondered whether he'd been taking refuge in a bottle.

Despite my dislike for him, pity coursed through me. For as much as I'd lost with Mary Grace's death, Brad's would always be the larger tragedy. The baby could be a solace for him. But that comfort might be based on a falsehood. Was it better to let the consolation of Ava Jane make up in some way for Mary Grace's absence, even if the child wasn't Brad's? Although disclosing it might have kept me from reaching this day, with Mary Grace gone, hers might be a secret better taken to the grave.

But keeping my mouth shut had felt much more feasible before I'd discovered the identity of the other potential father. I swiveled slightly in my seat. As if thinking about him had made him materialize, I caught sight of Oliver behind and to the right of me, seated alongside Momma. Michael flanked Momma on the other side. I gripped the table with one hand. Annabelle raised her head from the legal pad she'd been making notes on and looked at me, silently conveying a question. I nodded that I was okay, then turned to face the judge at the front of the room just as Harlan J. Black called his first witness.

So much of a trial happens in the days leading up to it that the actual rendering often seems easy to forecast long before it happens. Discovery removes most of the suspense, reins the loose cannons into a tight production staged as deftly as a Broadway play. But as with birthing, there's always room for the unexpected. It amazes me how people can participate in the same event yet come up with such different accounts of what happened, depending on what they stand to gain or lose. In my mind I had done what was necessary to save Ava Jane. But over the next few days I endured multiple recountings of Ava Jane's birth, with various witnesses offering a very different interpretation.

Brad's attorney resembled a striking young Abraham Lincoln. Well over six feet tall and rangy, his long arms ended in hands the size of baseball mitts, with nails buffed to a high shine. His right pinky finger boasted a sapphire set in a large gold band.

I've always suspected men with manicured hands and jewelry of hiding something. Harlan J. Black's demeanor confirmed my suspicion. His face was as lean as the rest of him, with high cheekbones portending a gauntness to come in his later years. Silver streaks danced through the thicket of his hair. His good looks were carefully groomed for maximum effect on the jury.

The smooth lawyer treaded carefully through a minefield of inquiry about Mary Grace's pregnancy, establishing that it had been uneventful until the end. Mary Grace had hemorrhaged to death after delivering Ava Jane. Hospital counsel had felt that trying the wrongful death count would result in a disastrous—and expensive—verdict, so they offered Brad a settlement on that count of the complaint. The hospital apparently believed they could point all liability concerning the baby toward me since Black had included the claim that I had practiced medicine without a license. As a condition of the settlement, the allegations presented at trial were limited to the damage done to the baby, not Mary Grace. The plaintiff still had to convince the jury there was a high likelihood Ava Jane would suffer long-term consequences from her oxygen deprivation; it would be their experts against ours speculating about the probability of developmental delays and learning disabilities.

Black led first the attending obstetrician, then the other doctors and nurses through their renditions of what had happened at the delivery. Perhaps out of gratitude for the settlement, the hospital staff sounded as if they had collectively scripted their stories to exonerate themselves and lay as much of the blame as possible at my feet. I was the outsider; it was easy enough for them to look my way when it came to meting out responsibility. One by one all the physicians and nurses willingly took Black's bait and testified that they believed I had unlawfully practiced medicine without a license.

Except for Helen. "Ms. Palaggi, describe what you saw when you entered the labor and delivery room the night Mary Grace Schaeffer, a young and previously healthy woman, expired," Black said once Helen was seated in the witness box. The jury collectively grimaced at his description of Mary Grace. Black was well-versed in raising emotions to his favor.

"I saw Dr. Mark attending to the mother and child." Helen looked Black straight in the eyes as she answered.

"You also observed the defendant, Carolyn Connors, in the room at the time you entered, isn't that right?" Black asked.

"It is."

"We know from the testimony provided by your fellow colleagues today that Ms. Connors was seen physically attending the infant during delivery. Did you read that in the chart, Ms. Palaggi?"

"I did."

"As an employee of Medical City, and particularly in your role as supervisor of the NICU, you are well versed in the policies and procedures concerning the care provided to newborns." Black charged on without pausing for Helen to confirm this. "Ms. Connors's actions defied hospital policies and procedures concerning who was and wasn't cleared to deliver a baby on hospital premises, didn't they?"

"I work in the NICU," Helen demurred. "I'm not that familiar with the Labor and Delivery protocols."

Black was ready. He grabbed a page off the table behind him and handed it to Helen. "Please read the highlighted policy, Ms. Palaggi."

Helen read the section he had indicated and nodded. The jury looked mildly interested as they waited. "According to this, only physicians currently licensed to practice medicine can deliver at Medical City," Helen conceded.

"Thank you, Ms. Palaggi." Black turned to the jury, looking triumphant.

"But in this case, the baby was coming, and the doctor wasn't there yet. Wouldn't that be considered one of those one-in-a-million exceptions to the policies and procedures?" Helen rushed the question out before Black could stop her. "What was she supposed to do, let the newborn fall out onto the floor?" Helen feigned innocence while the jury snickered but I knew she was deliberately helping me out.

Black scowled but excused Helen without countering her last comment. Maybe he hoped if he paid it no attention the jury would forget it. When she stepped down from the witness stand

Helen stopped alongside me and laid her hand over mine. Her loyalty might cost her dearly at work. I appreciated it so much I had to choke back tears.

"You can return to your seat now, Ms. Palaggi." Black was well aware that the jury was taking in her commiserating gesture.

Despite Pixie's pep talk, which I kept going back to like a touchstone, by the time Brad Schaeffer got up to testify the other witnesses' reports had me second-guessing my actions at Ava Jane's birth again. After the judge called everyone to order, Black stepped in front of the jury and, in a voice meant to convey both sympathy and remorse for having to do so, called his client to the stand.

As he had with the other witnesses, Black took Brad through a summary of his background—his education, where he lived and what he did for work. After this brief recitation Black's demeanor visibly changed. "Now, Mr. Schaeffer, sir, I'm sorry to bring up matters I'm sure you're more than ready to lay to rest." I winced at the words I was convinced the attorney had chosen to raise the ghost of Mary Grace before the jurors, to get them to identify with Brad's plight. It was working; not only were several of the jurors' eyes shiny, tears had sprung into my own. Regardless of how the blame was apportioned, tragedy had struck. No verdict was ever going to compensate for the losses we'd all be forced to live with long after the ruling was handed down.

In the cut-and-dried world of all things legal it might seem an easy thing to divide a catastrophe into bits, allocate blame for wrongs in pieces. But humans are rarely able to compartmentalize emotions from such tragedies so neatly. After nearly forty years in practice Harlan J. Black was skilled in the art of finessing a claim to his client's best advantage. Had Brad followed his attorney's lead he might have come off as the perfect plaintiff, a stricken husband and father seeking only the restitution due him. But as the two primary players in this courtroom drama, Brad and I had

something in common. He might not have been suffering from
panic attacks like I was, but the emotions that had been gathering
within him all summer were roiling as he sat before the jury now,
threatening to rise up into a tidal wave of unfettered rage and despair. And I was sitting directly in its path.

Much as I disliked him, Black made an admirable attempt
to focus Brad on the baby's plight. He led his client through
the hours of labor, then the delivery itself and the subsequent
months in which Ava Jane had remained in the NICU, her future
health and abilities uncertain but most likely compromised. Brad
answered his lawyer's questions mechanically. Once or twice he
tried to get in a detail about Mary Grace but Black reined him in
before he could say anything that might violate the dictates of the
settlement.

Then Black turned to the topic of my role at the birth. When
his attorney asked about their decision to use a doula Brad's grief
darkened into a scowl. "I left it up to my wife," he said. "We
didn't need anyone else there—we had a doctor, the *best* doctor."
His eyes roamed the audience in front of him, looking everywhere
but at me. "We had nurses. And she had me there to coach her."
He didn't bother to mask his resentment.

When Black asked about the additional component to my relationship with Mary Grace—that I had been her friend as well as
her professional support—Brad's agitation swelled higher, crash-
ing over the restraint he had exercised so as not to jeopardize the
settlement.

"They were friends." He spat the last word as if it was a curse,
flipping a hand in the air to make the relationship appear casual.

I wanted to object and correct him, enlighten the jury that
Mary Grace and I had been *best* friends since long before she'd
even met Brad. But Annabelle must have sensed my indignation.
She butted her knee against my thigh, the pressure soft but firm
enough to let me know to keep my protestations to myself.

"My wife was adamant about having her there." Brad never
once looked my way, even though he was talking about me.

"Describe your impressions of the relationship between your wife and the defendant," Black said.

"I couldn't understand it if I tried." Brad shot out a sharp laugh. "It seemed like one of those friendships that went on only because they'd known each other so long. My wife had nothing in common with her anymore. But Mary Grace had this soft spot for people who needed her." Brad's tone softened as he depicted MG for the jury. "She needed to feel like she was helping people, making a contribution to the world. She was adamant about that.

"She really wanted to be sure she made a difference." Brad pursed his lips. Everyone in the courtroom could see he was struggling to hold back his emotions. Before Black could ask another question, Brad's expression hardened and he continued.

"Mary Grace, she was the one with the life. She had plans. She married me, she built her practice, she wanted a bunch of kids. What does a woman like that, a woman full of life, have in common with someone so afraid of her own shadow she still lives with her parents at age thirty?"

I felt the jurors' eyes move from Brad to me, the looks in them shifting too, from pity to suspicion. I fought the urge to crawl under the table, away from their probing stares. Brad's description made me sound like an unstable idiot. I tried to tell myself that he had never liked me, was jealous of my closeness with Mary Grace, and that his opinion wasn't accurate. But what if Mary Grace had felt the same way? What if she had stayed friends with me out of pity, not because she valued what I contributed to the friendship?

"Mary Grace felt sorry for her." Brad confirmed my fear. "She'd say, 'Poor Caro, she'll probably never figure out what will make her happy.' My wife felt so blessed at her own good fortune. I think she felt guilty that her life was working out so well and Caro's was such a mess. She tried to share all the good things in her life with Caro." Brad's face contorted. I watched as a wave of emotion built inside him, rising higher until he couldn't contain it any longer. "*She* was jealous of my wife. My gorgeous, smart, shining wife. *She* couldn't stand it that Mary Grace was everything she'd never be."

Brad poured all of his anguish and helplessness into blaming the only person left for the loss of what he had held so dear. As that swell crested and broke inside him it rippled out from where he sat before me on the witness stand and threatened to wash me away. I was being swept by a current so strong I feared I'd never be able to swim against it. Was this was how it had felt for Paulie in the undertow?

The heat of shame rose up within me. There had been times when I'd wondered what was wrong with me, why I hadn't met the right man, found the right career, fashioned the kind of life I could feel good living. And yes, I'd had some pangs of envy for how easy life seemed for Mary Grace. She had represented both a vision of hope for what I might someday become and a painful, glaring reminder of what I hadn't yet discovered—my place in the world.

"I even wonder"—Brad's voice dropped to an ominous growl, drawing my attention back to his words—"I wonder whether she's happy now." For the first time since he'd taken the stand, Brad directed all his attention at me. His eyes held a hard look, pain and sorrow made tolerable only by transmuting them into anger. "Now that Mary Grace is gone, there's no one for Caro to compare herself to. But she'll always come up short to my wife's memory. Caro's jealous. And she doesn't care who she takes down to get what she wants." Brad looked straight into me as he delivered his own verdict. "She killed my wife."

Righteous indignation blazed, overcoming my shame. Brad was making it sound as if I'd murdered my best friend. But I had come to Milwaukee to help Mary Grace. I'd seen the awful events we were judging here now, had done everything I could to keep them from happening. I was the one she'd called, both when she discovered she was pregnant and when she'd started bleeding. Brad might have been jealous of me but in the end, MG had wanted me at Ava Jane's birth. I recalled the last moments of my friend's life. I had been the one to hold her hand, usher her through both Ava Jane's birth and her own death. Brad had no idea what Mary Grace and I meant to each other. I sat a little straighter in my chair, refusing to look away from the reproach in his glare. I hoped the jury was taking note that I wasn't bowing under his awful accusations.

At Annabelle's objection the judge sternly reminded Black of the strictures limiting testimony. But steering Brad back to the subject of Ava Jane in no way lessened his determination to destroy me. His words were a horrible indictment. Something inside of me shrank smaller and smaller, as if the essence of who I was might be protected from the damage of Brad's accusations despite the fact that I couldn't flee the room.

"The baby. Yeah, she was supposedly trying to save the baby." Brad answered his attorney's next query about the birth. "She's not a doctor or a nurse. She had no business touching our baby!" He paused, calculating something. "If she wanted to practice medicine so badly, maybe she should have been more careful in nursing school. She killed that kid in Illinois. How come nobody's asking about *that*?" Brad's eyes shone with reckless abandon. Several of the jurors glanced at one another in surprise, then looked to the judge. Annabelle jumped to her feet and strode toward the judge, shouting her objection as she moved. But Brad refused to be hampered by legalities now.

"How come"—he stabbed a finger in the air, gesturing toward me—"how come a woman who kills a baby in nursing school can have access to another one in a hospital? How many innocent children have to die before someone locks her up?"

Brad's final accusation deflated all my righteousness. Despair filled me. He had just put my past on trial too.

Thirty-nine

The judge called a recess for the day. Annabelle gripped my arm and steered me out of the courthouse toward her office. As we reached the building, my cell phone rang.

"Come up when you're finished," Annabelle said curtly, then continued inside.

"Hello?" I answered tentatively, holding my breath against the possibility of further verbal assault like the kind I'd just endured in the courthouse.

"Caro? It's Sylvie Cavanaugh. Ellen Peet just called me. She's on her way to the hospital but I'm still out of town." I wondered what that had to do with me but Sylvie answered soon enough. "Like I suspected, she's going early. It figures. There's a full moon and all." The pull of the moon tugged on human bodies of water as well as the tides and often sent women into labor. It was always the busiest time of the month in L & D units. "Anyway," Sylvie sighed regretfully, "I won't make it back in time. Can you go?"

Now I recalled that Sylvie had contacted me about backing her up on this birth months ago when she'd taken Ellen on as a client. Sylvie was in Iowa, helping her mom recover from a broken hip. Ellen wasn't due for another few weeks and Sylvie had hoped to be back in time but she'd asked me to be on call just in case. I'd forgotten to call and tell Sylvie to find someone else. I searched for a way to fill her in on what had happened since we'd spoken last. I was about to say there was no way I could go to the birth. But although I'd forgotten my promise to back Sylvie up, there was nowhere else I wanted to be more right now. Despite the outcome last time and Brad's scathing accusation that I didn't have a clue about what I wanted to do with my life, I had been missing the satisfaction I got from attending births, the sense when I was at one that I was exactly where I belonged. I needed to be part of a miracle now more than ever. I checked my watch. Almost five.

"How far along is she?"

"She was already dilated to five and one hundred percent effaced at her last checkup," Sylvie replied. "It's a second baby and she's carrying really low. Baumgarten joked that she'd be lucky if she didn't wind up delivering at home." Sylvie was referring to Ellen's obstetrician.

I quickly did the math in my head. The "average" rate for dilation was about one centimeter per hour. If Ellen was already at five she was halfway there, which theoretically meant she'd be complete by midnight. Factor in another couple hours to push and I'd still have time to go home, shower and change clothes before I had to be back in court at nine tomorrow morning. Sleep was nonexistent for me these days anyway, so it didn't matter that I'd be awake overnight.

"Okay." I shook away a misgiving about how furious Annabelle was going to be when I didn't come upstairs. "But I have something I can't miss in the morning." If Sylvie hadn't heard about my plight through the community grapevine I wasn't going to tell her. "Which hospital?"

"Medical City," she replied guilelessly.

I hesitated a fraction of a second but held steady with my decision. "I'll call you when it's over, let you know how it went." Then I hailed a cab. I waited until we pulled away from the curb and were moving down the street in the flow of traffic before I punched Annabelle's number into my phone. My demise had just been preempted by a birth.

I entered Medical City half expecting to be apprehended and escorted out by a squad of security rent-a-cops. It was long after business hours, and the bustle of staff and patients had quieted to a hush that descended along with the darkness of evening. Labor and Delivery lay at the end of a series of hallways that made me feel like a rat wandering in a maze. I held my breath as an orderly passed, pushing an elderly man in a wheelchair down the corridor that led to the cardiac rehab unit. No one had said that I wasn't supposed to be there but I couldn't help but feel as if I was revisiting the scene of a crime I had committed.

When I arrived at the L & D reception desk my eyes roamed the board behind the receptionist's head. None of the names of the nurses on duty that night looked familiar, which was a small blessing. The last thing I wanted was one of the women who had testified against me causing a scene.

Ellen and her husband were in room twelve. It wasn't the room Mary Grace delivered in but all the suites were identical so it might just as well have been. I shook my head, refusing entry to flashbacks of the last birth I'd done there.

Ellen's look of anxious determination changed to relief when she saw me. Sylvie had called and told them I was on my way.

"We just got here but the contractions are really intense." She gasped as the next one moved through her. Her husband was stroking her hair. I stepped alongside her, let her squeeze my hands to run some of the energy of the contraction growing in her pelvis up and out.

"Did they check you yet?"

Ellen nodded. "Doctor's on her way," she eked out between contractions. "But it feels like this kid is going to drop out of me any second." She grimaced and clutched at the overflowing bowl of her taut belly.

"She's already at nine," her husband said, finishing for her.

A young nurse stepped into the room. Her badge identified her as Renee. "Ellen, we need you on the monitor for a little while, just to get a baseline on how the baby's doing."

Ellen nodded her assent. I led her over to the side of the bed, where she perched while Renee wrapped the pink and blue straps around her protruding middle. Ellen had managed to slip into a hospital gown but it was untied and hanging open, the bulging baby playing peek-a-boo from the center of it. Renee had just gotten the monitor in place when Ellen lurched up off the bed again.

"Here's another one." She winced, rocking back and forth as if the motion might ease some of the intensity. "They're getting harder." Ellen reached for my hands and squeezed, her face clenching along with her fingers.

"Easy now," I soothed, keeping my voice low but clear. "Easy does it." I was talking as much to my skittish self as to Ellen.

"Dr. Baumgarten will be here soon. She called for an update a minute ago," Renee told Ellen before she left the room to check on her other patients.

Ellen nodded, then bent her knees into a half squat. "The baby's really low." She closed her eyes, concentrating on what was happening inside. "It's more intense than last time." Apprehension filled her words. Sylvie had told me that Ellen had delivered her first child naturally, without a doula. The excruciating pain had left her afraid of giving birth a second time. She had decided she wanted someone to be there with her from start to finish for this one. I coached her for a little while, encouraging her to pay close attention to her breath, keep it strong and steady to help the energy move through her uterus. She had a few more contractions in as many minutes. From the changing expressions on her face I could see they were growing more powerful as they started coming nearly on top of one another, with no breaks in between.

"She just moved down lower." Ellen's voice held both awe and worry. "I felt her move. She's about to come out," she insisted. I looked toward the door as if doing so would bring the obstetrician. I'd been reminded in the courtroom that hospital policy dictated that a doctor deliver every baby born there. Given my last experience at Medical City I didn't want to be connected with the physical act of birthing Ellen's child in any way.

"Tell you what." I was careful to mask my worry. "Let's put you on the birth ball for a bit. It should take away some of the pressure you're feeling but you can still move around on it with the contractions. Sound okay?"

Ellen closed her eyes with a grunt, grabbing the bed rail as the next wave of pressure demanded her full attention. I rang the call button but got no response. I had no more than guided Ellen into a seated position, her legs straddling the ball wide, when her body emitted a loud pop, followed by a gush of amniotic fluid as her bag of waters broke. Brownish-green fecal matter floated in the amniotic fluid. *Meconium.* I rushed over to the monitor, jabbed at the call button and told the receptionist we needed a nurse and an OB *now*.

I was torn between the fear of what would happen to me if I delivered this child and another tragic outcome if I didn't. That was what had chased me across the line between doula and midwife at Ava Jane's birth. Ellen gave a shriek that pierced my recollection. She pushed just once. Then out slid her new daughter into my open and waiting hands.

Just then Renee rushed back in. "Thank God you were in here." She plucked the baby from my hands with a look of gratitude that overwhelmed me.

Half an hour later Ellen had changed back into the shift she'd worn to the hospital and was happily cooing over her newborn. In the throes of labor everything but the immediate circumstances around me fall away and I'm completely present to what's happening. Watching mother and child bond, it finally occurred to me to look at the clock. Eight fifteen. It was a new record for me, the fastest—and easiest—birth I'd ever attended. I couldn't help but get caught up in the euphoria that Ellen exuded. I drank in her satisfied joy until I felt steeped in it, high with elation at watching a new life begin. I offered the Peet family my congratulations, then left them engrossed in getting acquainted with the newest member of their family.

"I couldn't have done it without you." Ellen gushed her thanks, hugging me to her hard. "You made all the difference."

Her words were heartfelt. I didn't bother to contradict her by reminding her that sweet Megan had arrived of her own volition.

Contentment coursed through me as I shut the door and walked down the hall toward the hospital exit. When thoughts of the rest of my life intruded again, I took a deep breath and pushed it all away, savored the bliss I'd felt holding Megan Peet. Despite appearances to the contrary, all was surely still right with my world.

Forty

I might have floated right out of the hospital on the high from Megan's successful arrival had it not been for a sign at an intersection in the corridor. It read, NURSERY AND NICU. I shifted course and moved in the direction the arrow pointed toward, where the two units lay around the corner from L & D. Just like in L & D there was a nurse sitting behind a desk in the NICU, charting into a computer. I told her who I was there to see. My voice must have disguised the trepidation I felt because she issued me a visitors' pass and ushered me in without further inquiry.

Ava Jane was wide awake when I approached her Isolette, gurgling to herself and forming little bubbles with her mouth. I pulled the rocking chair from the corner over to the bassinet, then reached in and lifted the baby out, settling the two of us into the chair. Nestled in my lap, she looked up at me with the frank curiosity of tiny children. She was swaddled tight in a receiving blanket but she'd managed to free her hands and they flailed around her head like fledgling birds. I offered her my pinky and she wrapped her miniature fingers around it. I rocked slowly, soothing both of us with shushing noises. I inspected every inch of MG's daughter, from eyes, nose and mouth to the shape of her perfect fingers and toes. I watched the features of her face change with her expressions, seeking similarities that would identify her as belonging to either Brad or Oliver.

But what I saw imbuing her diminutive beauty were remnants of my best friend. Ava Jane was her mother's child, through and through. I held her tight and rocked, wishing I could ease away all the cares and worries, the sorrows and losses. Oliver had said he wasn't father material, but how could he hold this sweet little bundle and not have a change of heart if Ava Jane was his?

Then there was Brad. He'd answered Harlan J. Black's questions about Ava Jane's health and prognosis, but it had been obvious that his grief was for Mary Grace. Fatherhood was so different from motherhood. Mothers-to-be often began bonding with their babies when they felt them move in utero, but it sometimes took new dads up to their progeny's first birthday to feel attached. Once she was able to leave the NICU and go home with him, Brad might fall in love with Ava Jane. But it seemed equally likely that he could resent her as a permanent, living reminder of what he had lost.

I rocked the baby, thinking about what a few courageous women had confided to me: that there was a darker side to having a child. People assume expectant mothers are thrilled with their condition all the time. There's no room for discussion about any feelings less positive than elation. But any new mother willing to be honest requires a confidante, someone with whom she can unburden her heart about the things no one wants to hear at baby showers and sip 'n' sees—the fear that she'll lose her own identity and be nothing more than a parent the rest of her life, or that, God forbid, she'll turn into her own mother.

Just as devastating is the grief she feels at the impending loss of her own maidenhood. Never again will she think of herself first; there will always be another whose needs she'll consider before her own. And while that's what she's truly wanted, since maybe her own childhood even, it's only once she's pregnant that she finally understands the enormity and the permanence of what she's signed on for. From now on, her life is not her own. She might never spend a day at the movies or in a spa again, free from worry about her child's well-being. No matter how badly a woman wants the child she carries, a part of her must die in order for her to be reborn as a mother.

Despite what I'd heard about the sacrifices, suddenly I wanted a baby. I longed for the privilege and opportunity to grow into a mother, to care for and raise a child. A surge of the same sense of responsibility that had led to my intervening at Ava Jane's birth burst in me again. As if by an invisible umbilical cord, this child and I were inexorably bound.

I shifted Ava Jane up onto my chest, held her close to my heart so its steady beat could lull her into the comfort of sleep. I wanted to hold her forever. For the briefest of moments I allowed myself the sliver of hope that if Ava Jane wasn't Brad's and Oliver didn't confess to the possibility that he was the father, I might be able to adopt her. Perhaps in the process of raising her I would mother the parts of myself that had been guarding the wounds of my childhood all these long years. Ava Jane was gently snoring in my ear. I let the tears building inside me flow without reserve. It was a cathartic cry, and it cleansed some of the tension I'd been carrying inside.

I knew what I wanted now, and it had nothing to do with Oliver or Michael. There was someone else who needed me more, and I wanted to be there for her in every way I could. I thought of all the secrets of my own childhood, how the burden of them had kept me from growing up. Above all else, I owed Ava Jane the truth.

I might have rocked the night away there in the NICU with Ava Jane nesting in my arms. But as I settled more deeply into the chair and started to doze off, a hand came down on my shoulder. Startled, I looked up at Helen. She was watching me carefully. She lifted Ava Jane from my arms. I came instantly awake, afraid that she was going to call security. But after she tenderly laid the tiny bundle of baby in the bassinet, Helen took me by the hand and led me into the conference room where the nursing staff took their breaks.

"How is she doing?" I hoped to distract Helen from admonishing me for being there.

"Better," she said. "It's hard to say how she'll progress." Helen paused, choosing her words with care. "But she responds to stimuli, and she coos and smiles when I hold her. No signs of major brain damage so far. She might be able to go home as early as next week. But she'll probably need the breathing monitor for a while after she leaves here.

"How are you holding up?" My neighbor was acting as if it was perfectly normal for me to be there in the NICU. I shrugged, waiting to see what she would do or say next. Maybe security was on its way and she was stalling for time. "I've wanted to knock on your door and tell you how sorry I am that I had to testify against you," she confided. "But they told me not to talk to you until after the trial." Something harsh passed over her normally placid features. "You and I both know that no matter what I said, no matter how hard I might have tried to convince them that there's no good reason to make a woman wait for a physician to deliver her baby, it wouldn't have made any difference."

She sighed in resignation. "I went back over the charts before I testified. I even pulled the records from L & D." She looked around furtively. "I hoped maybe there was a way I could get around it. But the attending L & D nurse charted that you had delivered the baby, even though she wasn't completely out of the birth canal when Dr. Mark came in. So that's that." Helen shrugged in defeat, then gazed at me with a soft, loving look. No judgment, no accusation, just that resplendent warmth she exuded, that loveliness that made her such a great caregiver. "It can help to talk about it, to get it out. Then you can heal." Helen sounded so sure of herself that I wondered how many tragedies she had endured with her small patients and how she had managed to keep her brightness all the years she'd been working around trauma that so often defied reason. "I'm here if there's anything else you need," she said.

I nodded silently, afraid I'd fall apart if I tried to thank her. All the confidence and joy I'd felt helping Ellen Peet had been overpowered again by the dread and regret of Ava Jane's birth. Helen reached out and embraced me, held me in much the same way I had just held Ava Jane. In her indomitable arms, I let myself grieve for Mary Grace and Ava Jane. And for the little girl

I'd stopped being after that day in the cottage when Momma miscarried, my beginning in this role of witness that so often felt like nothing less than my destiny. I cried over the vague but profound dread I proscribed felt whenever I was around small children, over the belief that it was so damn hard to keep safe at any age.

What's a secret worth? What's the cost of keeping a family intact, of protecting a friend's reputation? Since my mother's miscarriage, I'd felt destined for my role of bearing witness. Maybe there's no such thing as an uninvolved bystander; perhaps all onlookers are ultimately called to take action, speak about what they've seen.

As if something that had been building inside of me suddenly burst, I told Helen everything. I confided MG's secret and all about how I'd slept with Oliver, who'd been in love with MG and had slept with her too. I shared my agonizing attempts to determine what was best—to keep the secret to myself or use it to end the lawsuit. Then I confessed the feelings that had bloomed inside of me holding Ava Jane in the rocker, my sense that I owed the child nothing less than all of me, and my desire to adopt her.

Helen nodded and listened, patting my knee or shoulder from time to time. Momma flashed in my thoughts. Once again I was spilling my secrets to another woman. But I was learning that it took more than one person to raise a child, and I reached out and let Helen soothe me in much the same way I had once looked to Marilyn Hanover to tend the hurting places Momma couldn't.

"One thing I know for sure," Helen mused, when I was finished spilling my secrets. "Every child needs a mother.

"This one is special." She gestured toward Ava Jane's bassinet. "Even with all the kiddos I've cared for, there's something about her that's different. She's a spitfire; she's got spunk. You can see it in her eyes. That means that even more than most she's going to need someone to watch over her the way only a mother can." Helen's meaningful stare made me more apprehensive than her words. I stood there nodding until she turned and opened the conference room door.

"She's due for a bottle," she said, grinning. "Want to do my job for me?"

Fifteen minutes later I was back in the rocker feeding Ava Jane when Brad walked in. When he spotted me from the NICU entrance he did a double take, in that way people do when they see someone they know somewhere wildly out of context. It took him a minute to believe that it really was me sitting there, then for the understanding to translate into rage.

"What the hell?" Brad glared at me. All my contentment drained away. He swung around, looking for someone to explain this unthinkable set of circumstances. The other parents in the room looked up in surprise. Helen walked up behind Brad, two cups of tea in hand, and I fleetingly regretted that I couldn't warn her to hide out in the conference room until I managed an escape. The last thing I wanted was for Helen to be incriminated in a persecution of my own making.

"Mr. Schaeffer, please lower your voice." Helen addressed Brad before I could signal her to stay out of it.

Brad's tone rose in defiance of Helen's directive. "What the hell is she doing here with my kid?"

I rose up out of the rocker, still cradling Ava Jane in my arms. I was so scared that I couldn't get a breath. But I walked across the room until I stood face-to-face with Brad, Ava Jane between us like an offering. "Mary Grace would have wanted me here." My voice was quiet and steady despite the way my body was trembling.

"The hell she would," he countered. "You don't belong here. And I'm gonna make sure you never get anywhere near another kid as long as I live." He was snarling, so close to me that I could feel the heat of his breath on my face.

Helen set down the teacups and stepped up to where the two of us faced each other. "Mr. Schaeffer, I'm going to have to call security if you can't control yourself." Helen's professional tone belied the tough resolve behind the threat.

"Fuck security. I'm calling the cops." Brad Schaeffer fumbled his cell phone from his jacket pocket, swore when he couldn't get a signal, then whirled around and stalked back out of the NICU. I was still holding the baby when Brad called to Helen over his shoulder, "Get her away from my kid." It seemed like an afterthought.

Forty-one

H elen ushered me to the hospital's main entrance, where I was about to call a cab when I spied Michael draped over an overstuffed armchair. His clothing was rumpled, his body melded with the cushions as if he'd been there awhile.

"Call if you need anything." Helen gave me a brief hug, then moved away.

"How did you know where I was?" I looked down at Michael's sprawled form.

"Annabelle called me." He pushed himself upright, rubbed his eyes, then blinked several times as if he'd fallen asleep and was still waking up. "She's livid. Seems she couldn't reach you. *And* she had no idea about what happened in nursing school." I flinched but then reconsidered. Too bad if Annabelle was pissed. I'd done the right thing coming here.

I was about to tell Michael about my time with Ava Jane in the NICU and my realization that I wanted the same things he did, marriage and children. I even giddily considered asking him how he felt about adoption when I noticed that he was looking at me strangely.

"What?" I shot out, impatient to tell him my epiphany before I had to go plead my case before my irate attorney.

"Your mother's here, too."

I scowled as I looked around the empty lobby.

"Where?" Just what I needed, Momma in the middle of this mess. Michael stood and moved nearer to me. The gesture, coupled with a look of pity, sent a jolt of alarm through me. I was all too accustomed to this feeling. It was the same one that had accompanied the ringing of the phone in the middle of countless nights, tugging Daddy from bed to prepare a body for its final rest.

"She had a really bad asthma attack. She was admitted about thirty minutes ago."

All of my life I'd feared that if I turned my attention away from her something awful would befall Momma. I'd been perpetually watchful for harbingers of disaster, yet I'd always felt that even my best efforts at vigilance would one day prove futile. I'd certainly been more than a little distracted lately. Now it looked like this was the day I'd long dreaded.

Michael and I rode the elevator to the seventh-floor ICU. We were on our way to my mother's room when we passed the family lounge. I stopped short outside the entrance. My attorney, seated on the couch, stared at me with a long, searching look, as if she could hardly believe the events of the last few hours. That made two of us. I thought she ought to consider herself lucky; she was representing me but at least she didn't have to live the fiasco my life had become. Michael muttered something about going for a walk and took off.

"I tried calling you on your cell but you weren't picking up." Annabelle's words were terse. "So I called your house and talked to your mother. She started having difficulty breathing. Then she dropped the phone, so I called 911." I heard her unspoken implication, that I had been the cause of the trouble that had brought them all there that night.

"I received another witness notice from Harlan J. Black." Annabelle tapped her index finger on her chin, a habit I'd seen her resort to in the courtroom when she was agitated.

"For who?" I had the uncanny sense that I didn't want to know. I ran through the current list in my head. All the hospital personnel had already testified, along with Brad Schaeffer. As far as I could remember, that left only me.

Annabelle wasted no time playing guessing games. "They want to hear from your mother. Any idea why they might want to do that?" My attorney's words were clipped, controlled. "No?" She went on, her voice tight with anger. "Because although I've been over your history with you several times you've never, not once, mentioned to me that you and your mother worked together.

"And now that I've learned *that* juicy tidbit from opposing counsel, along with the fact that you were involved in another incident where a child *died*"—her voice deepened into a near-growl—"I'm sitting here, practically on the eve of you taking the stand, wondering what else you might have neglected to mention."

"I didn't think it mattered," I stalled. "That was back there—"

"You didn't think it mattered." Annabelle mimicked me, cutting me off. "When I asked you why you decided to move away from home you gave me this quaint story about your aunt Ruby and how you always looked up to her, felt inspired by her, et cetera. And I thought, how cool that she's found the courage to emulate the one family member who dared to be different. How great that we have this little vignette from her past that demonstrates Caro Connors is the kind of person who knows what's right and does it, even when doing so is a huge personal risk." Annabelle was so agitated that she stood up and paced the lounge. "I'm thinking I've found a way to take the fact that a physician and two nurses found you with your hands around a partially born infant's head and umbilical cord and convince the jury that you did a good thing, the right thing, the *only* thing you could have done." Her finger jabbed the air in front of her. "Even though you're not licensed to practice medicine." Annabelle blew out a breath.

"Only now I'm discovering that you dropped out of nursing school *not* because you decided you weren't cut out for the job but because you administered the wrong dosage of pain meds while shadowing on the floor. *And* that your mother was the nurse you shadowed. Shit!" The curse exploded in my ear. "Surely that little incident had *nothing* to do with you moving away from Chicago." Annabelle let out an exasperated hiss. "Because we didn't disclose her during discovery, Black's asked to forgo deposing your mother. He wants to put her right on the stand. Tomorrow.

"If you've got a way to keep him from making it look like you lied at your dep when he asked you about nursing school you'd better tell me, because I'm at a loss." Annabelle's voice softened, as if her anger had worn her down.

"But I didn't lie," I protested. "I answered the question he asked, just like you told me to do. I wasn't kicked out of nursing school. I made the choice to leave. That baby died, but not because of the error. It was born with too many problems to survive. The family didn't sue. I wasn't expelled or disciplined." Even to my ears, my answer sounded defensive. What if my own lawyer no longer believed me?

"Well, he asked enough to open the door to question you further on the stand. And to make it look like you've got something to hide." Annabelle sounded defeated. "Right now, I've got a call in to the judge to request a continuance due to what's happened here. If we're lucky, your mother's just bought us a day or two to prepare. But I've got to talk with her as soon as she's awake. If there are any more surprises coming, I want to deal with them before I throw her to the wolves."

Forty-two

I left Annabelle in the family lounge with a promise not to disappear again and went in search of my mother. The door to Momma's room shushed closed behind me. There she was, sleeping. The dim light over the bed illuminated her face. She looked so vulnerable clad in the thin hospital gown. Her clavicle peeked out through a hole where the fabric had worn away. Her skin was pulled taut, translucent over the bone. I wondered if I would have noticed how much she had aged if I saw her every day. Her midsection had thickened but her figure was still shapely for a woman in her sixties. I marveled that I ever fit inside there, fleetingly wished I could crawl back in.

For a moment I regretted the months I'd lived away from her, this woman who had once made a home for me inside her body. Had that been the best time of both our lives, when she was pregnant with me and I lay content within her? Our lives were so entwined. Would I ever find some way of being with Momma without feeling tangled up in her?

It's funny what memory willfully buries so that we might survive, only to dredge it back up when the time is right to heal. Looking down at my mother now, from long ago I heard a voice whispering in my ear. It was Marilyn Hanover's, repeating what she had said to me that night I'd slept in her bed.

"You know, Caro, there's only one person you can be responsible for in your life." Marilyn had confided. "Do what brings you joy, no matter what anyone else wants. Always speak your truth. You can't give up yourself just to please someone else. Not your mother. Not your husband if you get married. Not even your own kids. So don't. Promise me?"

I hadn't understood what Marilyn was trying to tell me then, but I had sensed how hard she was trying to reach me from some wiser vantage. Now I felt the truth of her words, knew too well the cost to one who betrayed herself, even if it was to make some-one else happy.

As if my reminiscences had disturbed her slumber, my mother stirred. She blinked a couple times, touched a finger to the oxygen cannula in her nose, then grimaced. She reached a hand out and I grabbed it. She gave me a weak squeeze, then lowered her arm back onto the bed.

"I came to take care of you and now look what's happened."

It was all the opening I needed. I would have to speak up for myself in court; I might as well practice with my mother. "Momma, we need to talk about that baby."

Momma closed her eyes again. "That dreadful lawyer insists on dragging that into this like it's some sort of soap opera. But it will be fine, honey, you'll see. I'll say the same thing I told the lawyers at Lakeshore."

I had been referring to her miscarriage but Momma thought I meant the child who had died when I was in nursing school. I was tempted to go along with her, but it was time for the truth to surface.

"I'm talking about the other one, Momma." Images of the bathtub at the cottage flickered in my mind.

Momma waited a beat, then offered a resigned admission. "I didn't want another child." I wondered at our ability to com-municate without words. It was as if this topic had been resting between us all these years, waiting for one of us to acknowledge all it meant. "I had my hands full with the four of you and I just couldn't see how I'd be able to handle another . . ." Her voice trailed off as she grew lost in reverie. "When Paulie drowned I thought I was being punished for not wanting that last one. I thought I was going to lose all of you." Momma put a hand to her eyes, shielding herself from my view.

"And I did, in a way. I lost *myself,* left you all to the ABCs." Momma moved her hand from her face and waited for me to pass judgment on her. She had come to be with me as an act of contrition, to rescue the one child she could. Neither of us looked away. Each saw the other for who she was, a sometimes fragile, sometimes fierce woman learning now how to come into her own, how to thrive. We were so much alike, Momma and I. For the first time in my life I was glad of that.

"It's going to be okay, Momma." The truth was such a comfort, and I thought that my mother was ready to face it all now. "Annabelle's here. She wants to go over your testimony. Are you up to it?"

Momma nodded and I went down the hall and got Annabelle. She followed me back to Momma's room and sat down in the chair I had pulled up next to the bed. I drifted back toward the window, where I leaned against the sill, feeling like a rebellious teenager called to task by her parents.

"Mrs. Connors," Annabelle began, "you need to tell me what happened at Lakeshore Memorial."

Momma waved a hand impatiently. "Caro lives a charmed life. It all turned out fine. Everything always works out for her." The envy lurking in her words took me by surprise. "Caro was a nursing student doing her internship at Lakeshore Memorial. She was shadowing me in the neonatal unit on the night shift." Momma spit out the facts as if she'd memorized them from a script. "A baby was born with multiple birth defects. He had trisomy 13 disorder. It's a fatal condition.

"He wasn't going to live." She stressed this. "We were only giving palliative care. When Caro administered the morphine, she gave a dosage double to what the pediatrician had ordered. The baby had a seizure and went into cardiac arrest a few moments later . . ." Momma's voice trailed off. I had tried so hard to leave that awful time behind me when I moved to Milwaukee but now here it was, exploding around me.

"It was an accident but also a blessing," Momma said reflectively. "He might have lived another day or so but the babe was in pain. That's why the parents didn't sue." For the first time since she had started talking Momma looked straight at me. "It was a blessing," she repeated.

I waited for Momma to clarify what had happened at Lake-shore Memorial that day. But she remained quiet. I looked from Momma to Annabelle, hoping that by some keen sense of collective consciousness my lawyer detected the subterfuge in my mother's account. But my attorney's eyes held no doubt. She accepted the story as told because Momma believed it herself, lending it the credence of veracity.

I saw then with a tremendous, heartbreaking clarity how Momma could take any circumstances, no matter how awful, and twist the truth until she could bear them. She might have believed that I led a charmed life but Momma was a true survivor. And I knew with a prescient certainty that regardless of what had really happened, if I asked her straight out whether she'd aborted the baby she'd insist it had been a miscarriage. For Momma, magical thinking kept anguish at bay. She had built both of our lives around a strict adherence to the ideology.

Like the miscarriage, we'd never talked about what had really happened that night at Lakeshore. The more time that passed without her acknowledging it, the farther away from her I needed to go. I'd run to Milwaukee to escape the secrets I carried for Momma, but no matter where I went I remained an accomplice to her falsehoods. And as the one on trial, I was the last person anyone looking for the truth would believe.

Forty-three

Annabelle and I were making our way from the elevator bank toward the hospital's main entrance. Her cell phone rang and she paused to answer it. Anger at my mother coursed through me, along with stunned anguish at her refusal to protect me.

My thoughts moved back to Brad in the NICU. I had been standing right in front of him holding the baby, yet he hadn't taken Ava Jane from me. A mother would have snatched her child right out of the arms of anyone she thought would harm her. She would have fought tooth and nail to defend her young. Had Brad even looked at Ava Jane? I couldn't be certain, but I didn't think that he had. I swelled with my own protective instincts. Brad was more interested in seeing me punished than in doing what was best for Ava Jane. I was tired of playing the scapegoat. I had to challenge paternity. If Brad was Ava Jane's father I'd be able to say good-bye to her knowing that I had helped her as best I could. And if he wasn't, maybe I'd have the good fortune of helping her grow up.

Annabelle was still listening to whoever had called her when two officers stepped up to us.

"Ma'am," the shorter one said, addressing me. "We need you to come with us, please," the officer said.

The request caught Annabelle's attention and she looked up, her mouth agape. "Hold on, just hold on for a minute," Annabelle demanded of the officers. "I'm her attorney and I'll be right with you." She turned her attention back to her phone call. She listened, uttered a couple of terse comments, then hung up and turned toward me. The officers flanked me, as if they thought I would bolt if they didn't keep me in their sights.

Annabelle erupted. "*What* were you thinking? Do you have

any idea how badly you've damaged your image in this case? Brad Schaeffer has Black filing a criminal claim against you with the district attorney's office as we speak. That was Black on the phone, once again filling me in on your whereabouts and activities. After your visit to the NICU, they're calling you a threat to Ava Jane. The judge has given them permission to keep you in a holding cell until trial reconvenes tomorrow. Do you want to lose your reputation and your livelihood? Is that it? Because if you do, you're doing a goddamn good job. And you don't need me to stand in your way by defending you!" Annabelle's anger ricocheted through me. I retreated from her tirade. The officers looked nonplussed.

"It's okay," I told Annabelle, struggling to hold on to the confidence that I had information to turn everything in my favor again. "I know something that will put a halt to everything for a little while."

Without mentioning Oliver's involvement, I filled her in on Mary Grace's secret and my plan to contest paternity and potentially adopt Ava Jane. "So all you have to do is tell the judge there's a good possibility that Brad isn't the baby's father and he'll have to give us time to do the DNA testing." My voice sounded tinny with false cheer despite my efforts to convince myself that the disclosure would save me.

The silence that followed stretched on so long I thought maybe Annabelle hadn't understood. "Annabelle? Are you with me?"

"Oh, I'm with you, Caro. Unfortunately I'm right here in it with you." She sounded defeated. "But what I'm wondering is, where the hell have you been all this time I've spent preparing your defense? Because if you let this bomb drop now you'll probably spend the rest of your life in prison."

She let that sink in before explaining. "Whether or not you meant for things to go the way they did at that birth, if they find out you had a motive to harm Mary Grace there's no way I can save you from a criminal trial." She was careful to avoid blaming me but I heard Annabelle's doubt as clearly as if she was accusing me outright. Hearing her skepticism I felt as I had for most of my childhood: like I was the only one who could come to my own defense and make everything right.

I spent the night downtown in a cell. I had hoped that Annabelle would come by so I could try to patch things up between us but instead she sent Oliver. He was waiting for me when I walked into the small interview room.

"You don't think Annabelle will drop my case, do you?" I asked him.

Oliver didn't immediately reassure me as I had hoped he would. He scrunched up his mouth while he thought. But then he shook his head no.

"She did tell me to give you a message, though." He ran a finger over my hand, which was clenched in a fist on the table between us. I didn't move toward or away from his gesture. Oliver reached into his pocket, pulled out a crumpled scrap of paper.

"She says"—he squinted, muttering something about not being able to make out his own chicken scratch—"you must participate in your own rescue." He looked up from the paper, opened his eyes a little wider. Then he raised his eyebrows and nodded his head in agreement with Annabelle's wisdom.

The line was meant to inspire or admonish, maybe both. It sparked an insistent need in me. I explained to Oliver what had happened at Lakeshore Memorial, confiding something about that event I hadn't shared even with Annabelle: I'd taken the blame but I hadn't been the one who'd made the error. Then I broached the topic of the other secret I was keeping.

"Ollie, there's one way I could help my case." I waited, hoping he would put the pieces together without my having to spell it all out. Finally I blurted, "When MG died she wasn't sure who the father was."

I fought an urge to clap my hand across my mouth, as if the words had escaped without my consent. But I was miserable from keeping so many secrets. It was time for all of us to learn to live with the truth.

Oliver didn't answer. Some dark emotion swept over his features.

"If I contest paternity and Brad isn't the father I don't think he can sue me." I hated the pleading tone in my voice, hated asking Oliver for his blessing to air the most intimate details of his relationship with MG. Even more I hated my eagerness to do whatever it took to keep myself from persecution.

Oliver's face turned stoic. He shrugged his arms into the jacket he'd hung on the back of the chair, waited until he pulled the zipper up before answering me. Finally he faced me, his eyes clear and bright with resolve.

"You're asking me to choose between you and her, Caro. I care for you. And I want to see you beat this thing." He paused, pressed both hands to the top of his head as if trying to contain something—his emotions, perhaps. But tears leaked from his eyes, betraying all he felt. He blinked rapidly to clear them.

"But when it comes down to a competition between you and her"—he wouldn't say MG's name—"she was the one true love of my life. And I have to believe what she told me." He looked regretful but certain as he exited the conference room, leaving me alone with the secrets that despite my speaking them aloud weren't saving but destroying me.

Forty-four

The next day my mother was released from the hospital. Annabelle escorted her to the courthouse. Momma looked especially sympathetic as she rose to take the stand, dressed in the same sober dress she'd worn for Mary Grace's funeral and pulling a wheeled oxygen canister behind her. She recited verbatim the same details she'd given to Annabelle about Lakeshore Memorial. I scanned the jury box, looking for signs of skepticism among the jurors, but found none. Then Harlan J. Black thanked Momma and, acting the part of the gentleman as expertly as Momma had just played the competent nurse, helped her back to her seat behind me.

Then it was my turn.

"The plaintiffs call Carolyn Connors." Black's booming tone summoned me like a child about to be punished. I looked to Annabelle for reassurance. She gave me a half smile, a small gesture that made me feel a little better since it was the first time since we'd left Medical City that she'd offered me any encouragement. But before I could move from the safety of my seat alongside her, something interrupted.

"What the fuck?" Despite the rule against cell phone usage in the courtroom, Brad Schaeffer was yelling into his. His shouting unsettled me. Countless times I had replayed this scenario in my mind. This was the moment when I faced the judge and crowed MG's secret, saved myself from Black's finger-pointing by contesting paternity and Brad's standing to sue. Brad's words were nearly identical to how I'd imagined he'd respond to my disclosure. But although part of me had desperately wanted to, I hadn't spoken up yet. Nevertheless, Brad rose from his seat and glared at me, the phone still pressed to his ear. Then he grabbed Black's sleeve, hissed something in his ear. For the first time since the trial began

Black's perpetually smug grin turned vexed. He too looked over at me, his eyes burning with indictments.

"Your Honor, we need a recess." Black swung around and addressed the judge, who looked as pissed off about the interruption as Black.

"This better be good," the judge warned him. It sounded like whatever it was wouldn't be good enough.

"Oh it is, Your Honor," Black assured, "but in the interests of maintaining the integrity of the trial I think we ought to discuss it in your chambers."

Annabelle's expression as she and I followed Black and Brad toward the judge's chambers told me she was regretting the day she'd agreed to take my case. Black held the chamber door open while we filed in, then shut it behind us. The spacious corner office looked out over the lake. I'd felt constricted in the courtroom but the judge's chambers offered a wide vista, which allowed me to take a much-needed breath. But when Black disclosed the reason for the recess, the air escaped me again in a gasp.

"Your Honor, the child who is the subject of this lawsuit is missing. She was abducted from the NICU at Medical City sometime in the last two hours." Harlan J. Black extended his arms, palms turned faceup as if to say that things were out of his hands.

The judge swore under his breath. Then he looked straight at me. So did Brad, Black and Annabelle. The incredulity on Annabelle's face triggered a tidal wave of shame through me. Everyone in the room watched and waited. Suddenly I was as much on display as if I was on the witness stand.

"I didn't take her." It was the truth but the words rang false, even to my ears. "I couldn't have taken her." I kept my eyes on Annabelle. If I looked at any of the men staring at me accusatorily, I'd break down. "I spent the night in jail. And I've been here ever since. When did I have the time to go over to Medical City and take Ava Jane, and where would I have put her if I did? Do you think I've got her in my purse?" My voice rose, the sheer idiocy of the scenario and my need to prove myself innocent fueling hysteria.

Annabelle gathered her wits about her. "Judge, can I have a moment with my client?"

The judge nodded. "But nobody leaves this room until we've reached a decision on how to proceed," he commanded.

Annabelle led me into a corner at the far side of the room. "What did you do?" Her tone was low so the others wouldn't hear. But unlike when she'd confronted me about Lakeshore, this time she made no effort to conceal her belief that I was lying.

"I didn't take her." I sounded like a petulant child but I didn't care. I was tired of holding everything in, of trying to orchestrate my life so that no one, me included, got hurt.

"Did you have someone kidnap her for you?"

My heart ached at the question. I admired Annabelle and wanted her to like me. But all I saw in her expression was a determination to get through this and away from me as fast as she could. "You really think I'd do that?" I eked the question out. "I love that kid, Annabelle. I feel responsible for her. And yes, I'd like to adopt her." Then something occurred to me. "How do you know Brad didn't arrange her disappearance to make it look like I kidnapped her?"

Annabelle had the decency to consider this before she shook her head. "I don't know anything anymore, Caro." Her disillusionment was apparent. "But look at him, he looks frantic over there."

She was right. Brad looked the way I'd expect a distraught father to look, wild-eyed and agitated as he kept checking his phone for an update from the police. I couldn't help but feel for him much the same way I felt for myself. We had both lost so much that was precious to us.

"Not a day goes by that I don't ask myself whether I could have done something differently, whether I could have saved MG. I wake up every night from nightmares where I'm trying to save her and Ava Jane." I choked the words out. Then I gave in to the waves of feeling cresting inside me, looking out toward that body of water that was so tied to all the major events in my life. Regardless of which shore I stood on, I perpetually found myself in danger of going under.

Annabelle seemed satisfied that I had no more to do with Ava Jane's disappearance than she did. She let me have my cry while she conferred with the judge and Black about what to do next. When she returned to where I was still standing near the window, my tears had ebbed.

Annabelle asked whether I felt up to continuing with my testimony. "It will look best to the jury if you can go back in and take the stand as expected." She gestured toward Harlan J. Black and Brad. "A recess only helps their case, gives the jurors time to speculate over what happened in here." She shrugged. "It's your call, but since you say you weren't involved there's nothing more we can do about Ava Jane until the police locate her." Her tone was even, the accusation I'd detected earlier carefully covered again.

I nodded my assent. Annabelle squeezed my hand. "Brave girl."

Her words called to my mind Daddy's charge to take care of what Momma couldn't, the role I wondered if I was destined to play forever, even now when I was the one in need of help.

Forty-five

As we filed back in I looked around the courtroom, taking inventory. I found Michael in the middle row. Where was Oliver? I scanned the room. Was he missing because our talk last night had driven him to do something unimaginable? He'd told me he never wanted children; had my pressing him to let me share the secret of MG's affair prompted him to take extreme action? These questions flew through my head as I took my seat. Instinct told me that Oliver wasn't the one who'd taken Ava Jane. It didn't, however, tell me who had.

Then something occurred to me: I'd told Momma that Ava Jane was just a few floors down in Medical City. I closed my eyes and concentrated on my breath, a trick I'd learned in my doula training, to help me stay present. I could feel it come up into my rib cage but it stopped long before it filled my chest. It was like birthing: there were all sorts of signs and clues before the head crowned but if you weren't paying attention, you'd find yourself suddenly scrambling to catch the baby. Now, testifying, I had to hold on, keep my wits about me. So when the memory of Momma hacking down her bedroom door surfaced in my mind, I pushed it away. Momma wasn't above taking drastic measures. But I reminded myself that she was ill and on oxygen right now. Besides, where would she hide the baby if she did take her? Even if she somehow had abducted Ava Jane, right now I couldn't afford to contemplate the disastrous consequences that would follow. I would have to deal with that after I testified.

For the next two hours Harlan J. Black interrogated me. He had a timeline set up on an easel, detailing every moment from the time

I met MG at the mall all the way up until I left the hospital the next morning after Ava Jane's birth. "When did you first understand that you were facing a bad baby scenario?" he asked.

I looked over at Annabelle quizzically.

"Objection to the phrase 'bad baby,'" she said.

"Overruled." The judge nodded to Black to continue.

"A child injured during birth is often termed a bad baby," the lawyer explained. "When did you first become aware that Ava Jane Schaeffer was at risk?"

"When the nurse, Nicole, instructed Mary Grace to stop pushing until Dr. Mark arrived." Out of the corner of my eye I saw the myriad attorneys for the hospital and staff straighten up in their chairs. They were paying close attention now that I had mentioned their clients.

"In your experience, is it common practice for a woman to give birth to a child in a hospital without an obstetrician present?" Black asked after I gave my account of what had happened at Ava Jane's birth.

"Typically an OB is there to catch, but it certainly isn't *common practice, in my experience*"—I mimicked his qualifier, sounding more disparaging than I meant to—"to make a woman who has been laboring for well over twelve hours and whose baby is ready to be born wait in order to accommodate the convenience of a physician. In most cases childbirth is a natural occurrence, not a medical event requiring the skills of a doctor." The man evoked a fury in me that I was having more and more difficulty controlling as he peppered me with questions.

Annabelle shot me a look, warning me to keep my answers short and simple. But despite the careful mask I wore for the jury, inside I was seething.

I was so worried about Ava Jane. Who had her now? Where was she? That worry left me angry at the hospital staff and their ridiculous rules, angry at the way children are put at risk by adults, angry at the damage that was so complete and so completely avoidable, if only those in charge were paying closer attention. I shut my eyes, forcing the tears back. Was I thinking of Ava Jane or myself?

Harlan J. Black threw me another question. "As a doula, do you consider yourself qualified to deliver a baby, Ms. Connors?"

"A doula acts as a mother to the mother—and the father," I explained. "My role is to offer emotional support to the family."

"You are not an obstetrician or a midwife."

"That's correct."

"In fact, other than the few months you spent in nursing school you have had no medical education or training for delivering babies."

"I'm a certified *doula,* not a midwife. I completed the Doulas of North America training program, which teaches how to offer comfort and emotional support to women in labor and their partners. But I don't catch."

"Ms. Connors, did you know at the time of Ava Jane Schaeffer's birth that encouraging a laboring woman to push when the umbilical cord is wrapped around the infant's neck could cause severe damage and even death to the infant?"

"I did."

I watched the jurors' reactions as that last bit of information sank in. Brad Schaeffer's attorney stared down his nose at me. "But Ms. Connors, you didn't wait for the doctor to arrive, did you? In fact, you took matters into your own hands, isn't that right?" He left me no time to answer before firing off the next accusation. "You encouraged Mary Grace Schaeffer to keep pushing, didn't you, Ms. Connors?"

"I never told Mary Grace to push." I didn't admit that I had continued holding her leg back so she could bear down when she felt the urge

"You didn't agree with Nurse Rankin that Mrs. Schaeffer had to wait for the doctor." Black posed it as a fact rather than a question.

"Whether or not I agree with a caregiver is not relevant to how I do my job."

Black was irked by my playing smart with him. He paid me back with the next question. "Isn't it correct, Ms. Connors, that Dr. Mark entered the room to find you manipulating the umbilical cord around the child's neck?"

"Objection, hearsay," Annabelle piped up. The judge overruled her with a scowl and motioned for me to answer.

"I looked down and observed that the baby was in distress. I moved the cord to help her breathe."

"Isn't it fair to say, Ms. Connors, that you have a history of . . ." Harlan J. Black paused as he searched for the exact word he wanted. His lips parted and the light glinted off his pristine white teeth. "Well, let's just say that you have a history of disagreeing with established medical practices, and now of engaging in the unlicensed practice of medicine, isn't that right?"

I almost blurted out *objection!* but Annabelle beat me to it.

A wolfish smile spread over Black's face. He looked pleased with himself for flustering me. "You have very definite opinions about the care you give, and you like to take matters into your own hands, don't you?" It was the second time he'd used that phrase, painting me as a rebel against authority.

Annabelle slapped her palms on the table and stood up. Black lifted a hand in the air, cutting her off dismissively. "Judge, I'm entitled to inquire into the defendant's beliefs about her role at a birth. In fact it's my *duty* to find out what she thinks is within the scope of her job." Black was pressing me harder and harder.

"You are not employed by Medical City, nor do you have privileges or affiliation with *any* health care institution, do you, Ms. Connors?"

"I'm hired directly by my clients." I managed to keep my answer to a minimum although I wanted to shout that if I hadn't seen the cord around Ava Jane's neck that morning, chances were good she'd have died before delivery.

"And your role with respect to those clients is to offer comfort and support during the labor process, not to perform medical procedures?"

"My role is to support my clients and to advocate on their behalf. I act as a liaison between them and their care providers, making sure they understand all the options available to them for birthing."

"And you felt that manipulating the cord around Ava Jane's neck fell under the category of advocating for your clients?" Harlan J. Black raised an eyebrow to let me know he was shrewd enough to use anything I said to his advantage.

An expectant silence fell over the room as I waited for Annabelle to come to my rescue. The question was damning. If I said that touching the cord was not typically within the scope of my practice and that any physical contact for medical purposes was prohibited, I'd be admitting that I had overstepped my professional boundaries. But if I said that it was common practice for a doula to physically intervene at a birth, I'd be lying.

Annabelle didn't object.

I panicked. My lawyer wasn't going to protect me. My breath choked off in my throat and I felt myself float out of my body somewhere up near the ceiling of the courtroom. Everyone was waiting for me to answer.

The last of my resolve came unstuck inside me then. Snippets of MG's delivery had been flashing in my mind the whole time I'd been testifying but now they threatened to eclipse my present circumstances altogether. One moment I was on the stand defending my professional actions during a labor and the next I was right back in the worst of it. The color in Ava Jane's face and head had gone from the pink of a healthy newborn to a blue-gray. It wasn't just the crown of the head that I saw, it was the entire skull.

I struggled to stay cognizant of my current surroundings and the hushed, almost reverent quiet as everyone waited for me to answer the last question. I recalled what Pixie had pointed out about what might have happened if I hadn't been there that night.

"Her *whole head* was protruding from the birth canal. And the cord was wrapped tight around her neck. I inserted two fingers between the umbilical cord and the neck in an effort to ease the constriction." My conviction that I had helped Ava Jane survive grew stronger as I recalled that night aloud. I had done everything in my power to help Ava Jane and Mary Grace. In the guise of Harlan J. Black, words I'd held back for too long finally found a defendant to charge full-on.

"Funny things happen at births without prior warning." I sat up taller. "Regardless of my professional role, I had a duty *as a fellow human being* to alleviate any danger or harm I could. When I saw the cord around Ava Jane's neck, time was crucial. I knew that if it wasn't unwound soon the child would die." I jabbed my index finger over and over at the air between me and the menacing attorney. "I'm an excellent doula," I declared. "I didn't do anything wrong." The truth of those words struck me. I looked over at Brad Schaeffer. "It wasn't my fault," I insisted.

Then I turned and found Momma. The little girl inside urged me on. During the night I had spent in the jail cell, I had asked myself why I felt so compelled to protect my mother. The answer, when it arrived, was like finding the missing piece of a puzzle. Despite the fact that Momma had opted to bring on the miscarriage, as a child I had felt responsible for her misery. My guilt had grown larger when Paulie drowned. "You were supposed to keep an eye on the kids," Momma had accused. I had taken the admonishment to heart. The belief that I owed her, that it was my job to keep Momma safe and happy, that was what had led to the choice I'd made at Lakeshore Memorial.

There was another way to help my case without bringing up MG's affair and the question of paternity. It meant the possibility of losing my own mother. But if I didn't take this opportunity to speak up on my own behalf and set the record straight, I'd emerge from the labor of my trial a stillbirth.

Momma had said that I'd given the wrong dosage of morphine to the baby that night I shadowed her. Technically that was the truth. For a nursing student to make such a mistake was serious but not automatic grounds for expulsion. But Momma was a charge nurse. She would have lost her job, and with it, her sense of herself as a person devoted to helping others.

"None of it was my fault," I repeated. "Not at Ava Jane's birth and not at Lakeshore Memorial. My mother was the one who mixed up the dosage for that baby. I gave him the shot, but she filled the syringe."

Amidst expressions of surprise from the jurors the rage emptied out of me, replaced by empathy for the inestimable anguish mothers bear along with their children.

"It wasn't my fault." I repeated the words like an absolution. "I'm an excellent doula, and I didn't do anything wrong."

Forty-six

While the jury deliberated, I followed Annabelle out into the hallway.

"Why didn't you tell me?" she asked, referring to Momma and the syringe.

I shook my head. "She's my mother." As if that explained my self-sacrifice.

"But she let you take the blame—"

"I went along with it," I said, cutting Annabelle off. "It was my responsibility to speak up for myself." The words were a way to cover the fear I felt. After what I'd just done, Momma might never speak to me again.

She was sitting on the empty courthouse steps, her shoulders hunched. I walked down past her then turned around, faced her from two stairs down.

"Momma?" Despite my performance in the courtroom I was a little girl again, penitent and eager to please.

She raised her eyes to meet mine, the truth undeniable now. Momma caught my eye for only an instant before looking beyond me toward the lake. "It was wrong for me to let you take the blame." Her words were whisper-quiet, stoic.

I nodded but didn't say anything more about the incident. "Michael's asked me to marry him," I blurted out instead. *Here I go, trying to make her happy again,* I thought, chastising myself. But it seemed the right time for sharing confidences. She didn't answer right away. Her eyes traveled over me as if seeing me for the first time since she'd arrived in Milwaukee.

"Caro." She reached out a hand and stroked my cheek. "When I think about your father I see a wide blue sky, empty of clouds. Just a bright expanse of open space. So much fresh air that if I lived in that sky, I'd never need an inhaler. I want more than anything for you to have that kind of happiness. We've had rough patches and plenty of times when I was sure we wouldn't make it, but I'm still glad that I married him and had all of you.

"But you're not me, Caro." She smiled sheepishly. "Much as I might want you to move home, much as I might want you to marry Michael and have a family, you're the only one who can tell if your happiness lies with him. Or any man, for that matter. Maybe being single without the responsibility of a husband and kids will save you from the demons I've never had the courage to face."

My eyes widened at Momma's pronouncement.

"Maybe you're the one thing in my life I've done right." Momma's voice held a surge of hope. "Darling, you don't seem to know it, but you're the kind of woman who lights up a room just by walking into it. The kind of woman I was never able to be."

I'd been using my mother as an excuse for not going after the life I wanted. Now I could no longer pretend that she was holding me back. Momma had set me free. There was one more thing I had to ask her about while we were exhuming secrets: Ava Jane.

Despite the fact that the district attorney was still investigating a possible criminal claim against me, Annabelle had received permission from the judge to let me return home until the jury came back from their deliberations. Momma hadn't been too insulted when I asked her if she knew where Ava Jane was. She'd just shrugged as if it wasn't too far out of the realm of possibility, then joked that she wasn't *that* desperate for another grandchild. I was thankful that I believed her. She'd been in the same hospital as the baby but she hadn't plotted anything that jeopardized either of us.

Ava Jane had been missing nearly eight hours when I pulled into a parking spot alongside Helen's yellow Corvette. It seemed like years since I'd seen my neighbor last. I still owed her a thank-you for standing up for me when Brad found me in the NICU. I was changing out of my clothes, thinking I'd go knock on Helen's door and see if she wanted to order takeout for supper, when I stopped in stunned disbelief, the sweatshirt I'd been pulling on still covering my head.

My hands shook as I drew the garment down the rest of the way over my midsection. I picked up my cell phone, dialed Annabelle's number, asked her to come by my house with a police officer. Then I walked across the hall and knocked on Helen's door.

I had to knock a second time before she answered. She was still in her scrubs when she opened the door. "Can I come in?" I asked.

"Sure," she replied. "How's your mother?" She motioned me into the living room. I looked around her condo, feigning interest in her décor while I looked for clues to what I hoped was an erroneous hypothesis manufactured by my overstimulated imagination, despite what I had seen in Helen's car.

"Momma's much better, thanks. Nice coasters." I gestured toward the cork-bottomed squares printed with images of the Italian countryside. "A nod to your heritage?"

She grinned.

I leaned forward, picked one up as if to get a better look at it. But what I was really interested in was the plane ticket and itinerary I'd noticed near the coasters. Helen was booked on the red-eye to Seattle that night. Her flight left in just four hours.

"Going home?" I was careful to keep my tone light as I straightened up again.

Helen paused just long enough for me to know she was deliberating, choosing her response with more care than the seemingly innocuous question required. Her eyes flicked to the travel documents on the coffee table. "Family matters. Something with my dad that came up last-minute. I was going to ask if you'd water my plants, but I figured you were kind of busy."

I nodded, then looked toward Helen's bedroom. She'd closed the door nearly all the way and the room beyond was too dark for me to make out what lay past the entry. But as if confirming my instincts, a familiar beep sounded from the darkness.

Helen froze, then started talking in a rush. "Tell me about the trial. How'd it go today? Did you testify yet?" Perhaps she hoped I hadn't heard the electronic chirp.

"Helen," I said, then hesitated. She had helped me so much. But I couldn't ignore the truth any longer. "I saw the car seat in the back of the 'Vette."

Helen's face contorted into a pained grimace.

"And I know that beeping is the infant apnea machine." I had to continue even though I could see how much it was hurting this well-meaning woman who had given me those precious moments with Ava Jane in the NICU.

"Helen, she might be strong enough to leave the hospital but you can't take her halfway across the country. And you can't take care of her forever. She needs a parent now, not a nurse." I recalled what Helen had said to me in the NICU, that Ava Jane would need a mother. "You aren't her mother, just like I'm not. No matter how hard we try, we'll never be able to fill those shoes."

I started to cry as I realized the truth of what I was saying. Mary Grace was gone and couldn't be brought back. Oliver didn't want to know if Ava Jane was his. But Brad looked ready and willing to be there for her, to call her his daughter regardless of whether or not she shared his genes. I'd seen the worry and fear on his face that day when he discovered the baby was missing. His emotions were genuine.

My neighbor was crying too. "You remember how I got my nickname?" she asked, fidgeting with the locket that sat over her heart.

I recalled her telling me about her father saying he'd go to hell 'n' back for her, and nodded.

"That's how I feel about this baby." She gestured toward the bedroom, openly admitting Ava Jane was in there. "From the moment I wrapped her in that receiving blanket the night she was born I felt differently about her than any other child I've ever cared for. I wanted my dad to meet her. He would have loved meeting her." In her words, appreciative wonder mingled with regret and grief. I nodded in agreement. Helen was right. Ava Jane was an extraordinary miracle.

Forty-seven

After the jury returned a verdict in my favor, Momma threw me a party. She kept tabs on me from the edge of the room as I walked around greeting people. Even Annabelle had come, which made me glad. I snuck a look over at Momma, worried about whether she was having a good time but not wanting to babysit her. *She's an adult,* I reminded myself. And then, more importantly, *Her happiness is not your responsibility.* But old habits die hard.

Someone walked up behind me and wrapped an arm around my shoulders, guiding me toward the couch. It was Michael, hiding something behind his back. He sat me down, swept his hidden arm forward with a flourish and took a low bow. Michael's support throughout my ordeal had taught me a valuable lesson: I didn't give people enough credit. I expected to be let down eventually. Michael proved the opposite could be true, that I could rely upon the people in my life to be there for me.

"A present for the princess." Michael grinned from ear to ear. "Don't go getting all sappy about it 'til after you open it, sweetheart," he mock-warned me. "It might not be to your liking, but I'm betting that it is." He grinned again and winked. I unwound the bow, nervous about what might lie within the wrapping. A small audience gathered around us.

"Oh, Michael." I peeled the pretty gold paper away from his gift. Tears fell, keeping me from finishing the sentence. I held Michael's gift up in front of me, savoring it awhile longer before I turned it around to let the others see it. He had framed two photos of me side by side, one that he had taken on a weekend trip to the beach early that summer and another of me as a young girl that he had asked for shortly after we met because he said it captured me so well. I wore my hair in a ponytail in both shots.

Michael had brought along his digital camera that day at the beach. In the photo I am twirling around in the sand on my bare tiptoes. I'd turned my head over one shoulder when Michael called out to me and he'd snapped the photo before I could protest. There is a flush and a glow on my face that speaks of having a fabulous time, of little to worry about and much to be thankful for.

The older photo is eerily similar. I am standing on the pier at the lake holding a fishing pole, one leg stretched back high into the air as I balance on tiptoe on the other foot. The photographer caught my ponytail and my fishing rod midswing as I cast the line out over the placid water. The little girl who was once me looks like a child, not like the adult I think of myself as even at a young age. Playful joy radiates from the picture.

So much of what I remember of my childhood is traumatic, but there must also have been moments of carefree abandon like the one I was staring at now. I wasn't sure who took that photo. Daddy or Ruby, perhaps. I looked happy. The image of the little girl with the pole didn't make my heart ache. It made me want to sing.

I handed the frame off into Annabelle's outstretched hand. She gave a slight, nearly imperceptible shake of her head that only I caught, acknowledging the value of Michael's gift.

Oliver had come to my celebration too, although he didn't stay long. " 'Dance, when you're broken open, dance, if you've torn the bandage off, dance, when you're perfectly free.' " As he hugged me good-bye he quoted Rumi, just as he had that first time we'd stood together in my condo. He had a present for me too. Wordlessly he handed me a plastic bag, then slipped out the door before I could open it. I stepped down the hall into my bedroom before peering inside. Lying there was the pair of Mary Grace's red sling-backs I'd discovered in Oliver's closet.

Wiping tears from my cheeks, I walked back out into the living room. Momma looked out of her element in the crowd, her mouth pulled into a brave smile that was clearly false. Could anyone else read the unease in her eyes? Familiar shame flitted through me. Momma's arms rested across her chest as if defending her from insult. I knew Momma too well, knew she was still afraid to say the wrong thing, afraid to say anything, afraid to be. *Forever the forlorn waif,* I thought.

A prickle of anger at her for threatening my happy evening stabbed at me. It seemed there wasn't a moment of my life that I wasn't occupied with thoughts of her. Momma fumbled around in her purse for her inhaler, that reminder that at any given moment she might need help just to stay alive. She had uncapped it and was about to take a puff when I walked over to her, Michael's gift in hand. Momma stared wordlessly at the framed photos, then at me and back again. It was hard for me to look at her now without a pang of longing to comfort her, to tell her that I loved her despite what had happened when I was little. The jumble of anger and affection, sorrow and compassion, was so tangled I was afraid I'd never unravel it. Maybe it could be enough to feel it all.

Annabelle sidled up next to me. She raised her champagne flute in a toast. "Let's share," she said, since I didn't have a glass. I took a sip from hers. She was watching me, a tiny grin playing over her face. I swallowed, then looked at her quizzically. Annabelle was drinking sparkling water. She held her tongue, waiting for me to get it.

"Oh!" I sputtered, water bubbling down my chin.

"Yep," she replied with a satisfied smile. She patted her belly, still flat as a pancake. "I'm due in March. And you're invited."

I bit down hard on my lip but that didn't stop my tears.

"I believe in you, Caro, despite the wild ride. I'm so proud of what you said up there on that witness stand." Annabelle looked almost shy as she folded me in her arms. We laughed and cried simultaneously. "Let me hug you now, while I still can." We giggled and she pulled me closer.

Annabelle reminded me of the lake at sunset, when the wind died down and the waves faded into a serene surface where if you leaned over the edge of the pier you could see your own sparkling reflection. Like Ruby, Marilyn Hanover, Pixie and MG, my attorney was the kind of woman I wanted to be. After several long moments I blinked hard, tried to clear my head. When I looked back up at her again Annabelle's eyes were still there, waiting to take me back in.

I looked back and forth from Momma to Annabelle. Two choices, it seemed. But I didn't have to choose between who I was and who I could become. I could trust what had happened to guide me through the rest of my life. I brought Michael's gift before me again and looked at the two photographs in the frame. The evidence was undeniable: the little girl standing on tiptoe had grown into the woman who'd cast her lot in Milwaukee and had begun to create a new life, confident that she could mother herself. Looking down at the images in the frame I understood one more thing: in order to move forward I had to go back—to the cottage at the lake.

Epilogue

There's this trip advertised by the Great Lakes tourism board called the Lake Michigan Circle Tour. You can purchase a map and drive your way around the circumference of the lake in just a week's time. Or you can take the journey a lot slower, like I did. I'd done the first leg when I moved from Chicago to Milwaukee. Now I'd complete the circle by driving from Wisconsin to Michigan, back to the family cottage. The merest smile played over Annabelle's face when I told her where I was going. She was proud of my courage.

"I'd offer to go with you . . . ," she began.

"But you know I need to do this alone." She broke into a laugh as I finished the sentence for her. "Momma wanted to come too, but this is one journey only I can make."

"Do you know how they say 'giving birth' in Spanish?" she asked.

"I know 'pregnant' is *embarazada,* like you've got good reason to be embarrassed," I said with a grin.

"Well the phrase for giving birth is a lot sweeter. It's *dar a luz.* It means 'to bring into the light,'" Annabelle replied meaningfully. "You're going back for all the right reasons," she said, reassuring me. "You can carry your secrets around with you like your mother's done or you can choose to let them offer you a bright new beginning."

My eye caught something sitting on Annabelle's desk. It was a heart-shaped paperweight. Embedded in the glass were bits of silver and gold and swirls of colors. I picked the paperweight up in my hand. Its heaviness felt comforting. I ran my thumb along one curving side, traced a meandering line of red running like blood through a vein to where it disappeared into the center of the heart. Then I set it gently back down on the desk.

"It's possible for hearts to hold a lot," Annabelle said pointedly.

"Lots of different emotions at once. Think of it as birthing your-self. It's hard and painful and scary. There are lots of uncertain-ties. But there's one thing you can count on: at the end something, *someone,* new is going to emerge. Can you think of one mother you've met who would tell you afterward that all the pain wasn't worth it? Treat yourself with the care that you would a mother in labor, Caro. *Dar a luz,*" she repeated thoughtfully.

I met Annabelle's gaze, searched deep in the clear pools of her eyes until I caught a fleeting reflection of the woman she believed I'd become if I continued to trust myself. Annabelle handed me the paperweight from her desk. The heart settled reassuringly in my hands. "You're ready for this now," she said.

There's an expansive freedom that accompanies remembering things from a distance. That's how I felt about Milwaukee—the city tucked among rolling hills and wide fields was like a vast womb where I'd grown from my past in a way I couldn't have done in Chicago. Before I left I went over to the cemetery, where I said a few words to Mary Grace.

"I promise to be there for Ava Jane as much as Brad will let me," I told her. "I promise she'll always know how much you loved and wanted her, that leaving her wasn't your choice." I remembered thinking that perhaps MG's spirit was still near Ava Jane in the NICU; any mother who could do so would remain by her child. I hoped that somehow the two of them still felt one an-other's love and that Ava Jane might feel connected to her mother throughout her life.

Then I walked to the far boundary of the grounds, where the lake butted up against it. Oliver had said she'd wanted to be cremated. I couldn't scatter Mary Grace's ashes but there was an-other way for me to pay her homage. I pulled the red sling-backs from the bag and threw them as far as I could out into the water, watching as they bobbed away from the shore, lured along by the current.

When I reached Michigan I stood by the cottage that held such a large chunk of my childhood. I ran my hands over my womanly form, felt the comforting scratch of my wool sweater, the sturdy denim of my jeans. Everything around me looked so much smaller than it had when I was a girl. It didn't feel like the same place and I realized, standing there in the back forty, as Ruby had always called it, that after more than twenty years it wasn't the same, just as I wasn't that little girl anymore.

It's funny what the body remembers. How smells, tastes and the way an object or a person feels can lodge themselves like slivers of glass in muscles and bones. The ache can be dull enough for the conscious mind to ignore for decades. But over time those sense memories poke hard enough to do damage. And that's when it's time to pluck them out. The only other option is to build up a carapace of scar tissue, staunch the wound with padding and pray it never opens back up. My body felt newer, more alive than I could ever remember it feeling before. I took off my clogs, removed my socks and slipped my toes into the grass, the blades parting as easily as water.

Was this what memory did after years and years, allowed one to sift back through the accumulated shards of a lifetime and restring them in whatever order made some mysterious healing logic? Or did it simply produce a random flash of a gem, like the teasing glint off a nugget of gold gleaming from here and there among the rubble in which it was buried? We all had our secrets, our pains and our longings. And while we had spent so much time together, I marveled now at how each of us in my family had lived so much of our lives on the inside, separate and hidden from the others.

From the cottage I walked the length of the property until I reached the lake. I looked around at the neighbors' houses on either side. They had already pulled out their piers and winterized their cottages. I slipped out of my sweater and jeans. It had been over twenty years since I'd been in the lake. I reconsidered the impulse to enter the water as I shivered nude on the pier, but I needed to feel it washing over me more than I wanted to stay warm.

I recalled Daddy's look of defeat as I'd huddled in the water the day Paulie drowned. I wondered how he might look now if I told him about Momma's wish to be rid of that last baby. Would he be outraged? Or would he set his mouth in the same grim line I'd seen that Labor Day weekend, resigned to the fact that we were all casualties of the lake as much as my brother? It hadn't occurred to me to consider telling Daddy what I remembered. We had become allies after Momma got sick and I was always his big girl, but it was Momma with whom I'd shared all my secrets.

The tide of memory dredged up my childhood, and suddenly I was eager to be free from it. Despite the cold, I slipped into the lake, went completely under with my eyes wide open. The water rushed around me and over my head. When I broke up through the surface again a minute later I felt renewed.

Soon my body went numb to the cold. Goose bumps pricked as I hoisted myself onto the pier and used my sweater as a make-shift towel. While Ruby used relics and magic words to ward off evil, Paulie had become my talisman for the rest of my childhood. I had relied on the brother who lived on in my imagination, seeing him with me whenever I felt frightened or in danger. By watching with quiet terror as the boat searched for him in vain, I'd made an atonement, an act of sacrifice that I'd fervently prayed throughout the remaining years of my girlhood would keep me safe from all the haunting darkness of that summer. I had chanted his name whenever the specters of that time crept into my memories. My night terrors started the following fall, and I'd always believed that it was Paulie who kept me safe as I scurried from my bed-room to Momma's each night.

Back in my jeans and turtleneck, I stood on the pier, closed my eyes and thought about the baby Momma had lost, the infant at Lakeshore and Ava Jane, and how in that first birth and all that came after I had done the best I could. I thought of Momma then, and Ruby and the ABCs, Mary Grace, Deirdre, Pixie and

Annabelle. They had all mothered me, some well, the others the best they could.

Last, I thought of the man who loved me. When I returned to Milwaukee I would give Michael an answer to his proposal, the answer that in my heart was the truth.

I considered my plans for the future as I skipped stones. Tiny ripples skittered out in the pebbles' wake. Ruby had bequeathed me her land, and I had growing in my mind the seeds of an idea for a center, a kind of spiritual airport of sorts. A place where, surrounded by love, people could arrive by being born and depart via dying. It felt like the best way for me to honor where I came from and who I had become, to bring all the parts of me home.

And I still had plenty of time for a baby, one I could rightfully call my own.

Before I turned to drive back to Milwaukee I sent out a siren's song to my long-lost brother. I hoped that wherever he was after all these years he could feel the memories unloosing from around me as surely as the silken weeds had one day let go their grasp on his body, so the two of us could finally float free.

G

The Doula

Bridget Boland

INTRODUCTION

Caroline Connors felt lost in her life until she found her calling as a doula, a birth coach trained to support women through childbirth. When her best friend Mary Grace experiences complications during labor, Caro steps in and saves the baby's life, but when Mary Grace dies in childbirth her husband blames Caro. Charged with a medical malpractice suit, Caro must endure a trial that threatens her professional future, questions her identity as a doula and a friend, and forces her to confront a dark past that she's been hiding from for years.

TOPICS & QUESTIONS FOR DISCUSSION

1. Caro looks up to women like Ruby, Marilyn Hanover, Pixie, Mary Grace and Annabelle as role models. What qualities do these women share that Caro admires? Who are the role models in your life?

2. Discuss the role of mother figures in Caro's life. How does not having a mother who is present for her influence Caro's character? How does she substitute others for this role?

3. Caro describes the tragic summer at the lake as the end of her childhood. In what ways did the circumstances prematurely usher her into adulthood?

4. How does Caro try to protect both Momma and Mary Grace? Why do you think she chose to take on their secrets? Have you ever been placed in a similar position?

5. Did Caro overstep her bounds during Mary Grace's labor? Discuss why or why not.

6. Caro describes a fine line between birth and death. At what points in the narrative is this line especially blurred?

7. Discuss the themes of medical ethics, spirituality and personal morality throughout *The Doula*. How does each theme impact Caro? Are there any other themes that stood out to you?

8. In what way is the lake a source of both refuge and fear for Caro? For the entire Connors family?

9. Do you believe Michael is the best match for Caro? What kind of future do you think they could have together?

10. Caro describes an almost sixth-sense feeling in situations like Paulie's death and Mary Grace's delivery. Were there any instances where she should have paid closer attention to her instincts? How much weight do you put on your own personal instincts? Has there ever been a time where you wished you had followed your gut? Discuss.

11. *The Doula* discusses the many childbirth options available today. Do you feel it was biased toward or against any particular delivery method? In your opinion, should births be treated more as a natural life process or a medical emergency?

12. Do you know anyone that has used either a doula or a midwife? After reading this novel, would you consider having a doula present if you or a spouse/partner were in labor?

13. Caro sees her family as flawed, while outsiders view the Connorses as an ideal family. How are both true?

1. Discuss the different types of birth options available to women today—from an at-home water birth to an elective C-section—and the merits and risks of each. For reference and additional information, read Ina May Gaskin's *Guide to Childbirth,* and visit the official website for Doulas of North America at www.dona.org to learn about the history and roles of doulas.

2. Watch *The Business of Being Born*, a documentary by actress Ricki Lake and filmmaker Abby Epstein, about the maternity care system in America. Compare the opinions in the film with what you read in *The Doula.*

3. Take a yoga or meditation class with your book club. Note any similarities in the breathing techniques with the methods Caro describes as using with her clients. Do you feel more relaxed? To find yoga classes near you, visit www.yogiseeker .com or www.forrestyoga.com.

A Conversation with Bridget Boland

You make clear distinctions between hospital births and "alternative" births throughout *The Doula*. What are your views on the variety of modern childbirth options?

Modern advances in medicine minimize complications and maternal and fetal death rates. But I am concerned about the almost exclusive attention we currently place on the physical act of birthing. Climbing rates of inductions, epidural use, and C-sections alarm me. Yes, birth oftentimes involves pain, and in some cases interventions are warranted, but when we numb an experience as significant as giving birth we mask not only the discomfort but also the incredible sense of accomplishment that accompanies it.

After the myriad births I served at as a doula—in hospitals, birth centers and homes—I chose to birth my son at home with the support of a midwife and a doula. It remains the most empowering experience of my life. But home is not the location in which every woman feels most comfortable delivering. The philosophy I adopt with my clients is that there is no one "right" way to have a baby. I encourage them to view the process as more than a medical event; it's an emotional, mental, spiritual journey, one that requires preparation and attention in each of those realms.

We can make any birth a ceremonial, holistic experience, even a C-section in a hospital operating room. Locale is only one component to mindful birthing. My vision is that we as a society offer women and their families support and resources to create a true rite of passage around giving birth. For more on this topic, visit www.bridgetboland.com.

How did your personal experience of switching careers from a medical malpractice attorney to a yoga teacher, shamanic energetic healer, and doula influence your writing? Was the trial of Mary Grace's death inspired by any real-life events? How much did you draw upon personal experience?

I've always loved mysteries, and I'm fascinated by the greatest mystery of all: Who are we? I'm a "seeker" at heart, and I like the metaphor of life as a journey. I'm constantly evaluating my experiences for what I can learn from them and tracking my own personal evolution. Many of the clients I see in my shamanic energy medicine practice are also looking to awaken to their life's purpose and create it. Writing is another way to explore what it means to be human. I drew upon what I gleaned from my own long and winding path to help me understand and portray Caro's journey.

Mary Grace's death and the trial wasn't so much inspired by real-life events as by me asking the question, "What if . . . ?" The first thing I did after I became a doula was look for malpractice insurance, since the lawyer in me was concerned about the possibility of being sued. I couldn't find coverage of any kind back then, and wondered what would happen if I did find myself in the position of practicing medicine without a license. So perhaps the book started as a kind of defense mechanism, a place to work out my fear about what I would do if faced with that choice in real life.

In terms of the rest of the book, it's a mix of autobiographical material and pure fiction. I won't spoil the fun of speculation by revealing which is which.

Furthermore, what inspired you to make this dramatic professional move from an attorney to a doula?

I like to think it was destiny! I had always been very interested in medicine and helping people. My mother is a nurse, her brothers are funeral directors, and I was premed (very briefly) in college. When I chose law as a profession, I picked medical malpractice as my specialty. But for me, the legal realm was too far removed from the lives of the people involved. I felt as if I was doing damage control after the fact rather than aiding people in a time of need. My father is also an attorney. Ironically, his passion for the law reflected back to me that I didn't feel the same way. So I set out to discover just what it was I did feel passionately about.

Writing was one thing, health and wellness another. So I took an MFA in creative writing, and also attended a yoga teacher–training course with Ana Forrest. I had no idea how I'd make a living after I completed these educational bits, which understandably caused some worry for the folks back home.

Then a cool thing happened. During the yoga teacher–training, we were asked to write down what we wanted to create in our lives. I wrote goals around teaching yoga, finding a boyfriend and writing. Then "midwife" appeared on my page. I stopped short, trying to make sense of where *that* had come from. Then my brain devised the "logical" explanation that writing characters was a kind of midwifery, and I went on about completing the list.

Six months later, a student in my yoga class became pregnant. She asked if I had ever heard of a doula, and told me she'd like me to be hers. I immediately recalled that list I'd made in training and said yes. Then I had to take the doula certification so I could know what to do when her birth time arrived. That string of events taught me an invaluable lesson about trusting my instincts and following them even when I wasn't sure where they would lead.

What kind of research did you do in preparation for the many technical aspects of labor and delivery discussed in *The Doula*? Were you surprised by anything you learned?

Both my legal background and my doula training provided a lot of knowledge about what happens in labor and delivery. I also consulted with an obstetrician, midwives and several doulas, relying on their expertise to enrich my own. I pored over every book and DVD on childbirthing I could get my hands on. I especially appreciated Ina May Gaskin's *Spiritual Midwifery* and the documentary film *The Business of Being Born*.

One thing that really surprised me came from Catherine Taylor's book, *Giving Birth*. In it she lays out the similarities and differences between hospital, birth center and home births. At the time, I was pregnant and thinking that I would do a natural birth with a midwife in a hospital setting. This felt like the best of both worlds; I'd have a nurturing care provider sensitive to the holistic nature of birthing with all the resources of modern medicine available in case we needed it.

I was surprised to learn that because hospital-based midwives must adhere to the same policies as the OBs on staff, such as limits on the length of time women are allowed to labor without intervention, their care options are often constrained to those that follow the dictates of the hospital. The likelihood of interventions such as induction drugs, breaking the bag of waters and C-section is often as high with a hospital midwife delivery as with an OB. And many midwives work in practices similar to doctors' groups, which means the midwife who sees a client for many months of prenatal visits and develops a relationship with her is not necessarily the one who will attend the client at delivery.

As you explain in the book, "doula" is a Greek word meaning "servant." What first drew you to learn this practice and then write a novel about it?

I first heard the term "doula" from my yoga student when she asked me to serve at her birth. I was honored she asked, but then had to rush out and register for DONA's (Doulas of North America) training since I had never even heard of a doula before, let alone knew what one did. I left that first birth experience convinced there was nothing we do as humans that is more important than bringing new life into the world. It's such an act of courage, hope and love.

Since that first birth, I've served women who delivered naturally in hospitals, those who chose epidural or other medications for pain relief, some who had uneventful and beautiful home births, and others who planned for a home or birth center birth but wound up in a hospital, having every possible intervention, including a C-section. What I became aware of was that, regardless of how the birth actually occurred, what seemed to matter most in terms of how the mother felt about the experience afterward was whether or not she perceived the outcome was the result of her own educated choices versus being told what to do by a care provider. I began to see the need for education about all the possibilities childbirth holds, particularly the emotional support doulas provide, and I wanted to offer that in a compelling manner instead of in a textbook.

Finally, I like to think Caro herself had a hand in insisting this book be born. Prior to *The Doula*, I wrote exclusively memoirs. I'd convinced myself I didn't have the imagination to tackle fiction. Then one morning, I woke up to a tentative voice whispering in my head. It said, "Other women have babies. I watch."

That grabbed my attention. I wanted to know who the voice belonged to. I went to my laptop and the opening of the book emerged from that first whispered confidence.

Why do you think the field of doulas is growing so rapidly—from 750 to 5,842 between 1994 and 2005? Why tackle the subject now?

Happily, I think this is the result of a new level of consciousness about the profound nature of childbirth. Trends occur in birthing; home births were the norm until fairly recently. In most cases things went well. But when they didn't, the results could be catastrophic. With the advent of hospital birthing came reliance upon the medical expertise of health-care providers. For a while "twilight sleep" was a popular way to deliver. An era of women birthed essentially unconsciously. Now, as more women realize that birth is not so much a nuisance to be endured as a powerful rite of passage, they're looking for care providers who are trained in accompanying them on that journey. Doulas are uniquely qualified to offer emotional and spiritual support so physicians, midwives and nurses can focus on the physical care of mom and baby.

As a doula, have you ever had to "cross the line" into the medical realm during a birth? What was the outcome?

Thankfully, I've never been faced with the prospect of what Caro had to deal with, although at one birth my client's water broke and the nurse and I had just enough time to move her from the birth ball onto the bed before she delivered. The delivery happened in less than two minutes. The OB didn't make it in time but the nurse took the role of "catching" while I tended to Mom—and Dad, who was too stunned to do anything!

I have, however, been faced with scenarios where I've felt it necessary to respectfully remind caregivers about the benefits of certain comfort measures like perineal massage, which can keep a woman from tearing badly during delivery. Many Western physicians simply aren't trained in these techniques and their benefits. I often walk a fine line between advocating for my clients' best interests and deferring to the medical practitioners' preferred methods of practice. The negotiating skills I learned in my legal career come very much in handy in these cases.

On your website, www.bridgetboland.com, you describe yourself as a "pilgrim at heart." How was Caro's pilgrimage to Milwaukee a turning point for her?

Stephen Cope and Carol Pearson write about the universal archetype of the Wanderer: the heroine hears a mystic call, journeys forth and undergoes great testing in order to reach a goal. The Wanderer intentionally sets out to confront the unknown, taking a journey that marks the beginning of life at a new level. The Wanderer sets off, always alone, on the "road of trials," which is the initiation into heroism. The Wanderer is visited by an intense but unsettlingly vague sense of homesickness. She is not sure where home is, but she knows that she will recognize it when she sees it, and she knows that she must pursue it at all costs.

This is the archetype I wanted to explore through Caro. Her move to Milwaukee marks a new way of engaging with the world. For Caro, the move itself constitutes a heroic act. It's the moment when Caro finally chooses to participate in her own rescue.

As a first-time novelist, what writers inspired you? What did you find most challenging about the process?

I love to read, so the list of writers who inspire me could be pages long. But some of my all-time favorites include Barbara Kingsolver (*The Poisonwood Bible*), Audrey Niffenegger (*The Time Traveler's Wife*), Marisa de los Santos (*Belong to Me*), Isabel Allende (*The House of the Spirits*), Diana Gabaldon (the Outlander series), Wally Lamb (*She's Come Undone*), and Abraham Verghese (*Cutting for Stone*).

The most challenging thing about the process was feeling so new to it. Grappling with the sheer length and amount of material a novel requires felt awkward, like feeling my way in a dark tunnel scene by scene toward the final resolution. For me, finding the plot is challenging. I typically start out with characters who bring me an idea or issue to explore. Then the plot makes itself known as I discover the particulars of how the characters encounter and inter-act with the themes.

What's next for Caro? Do you see a future for her and Michael? Are you working on any new projects?

My hope for Caro is that she continues to discover herself and live courageously. When I think of her after this book ends, I actually see her traipsing around some foreign country, volunteering in orphanages and further expanding her boundaries. Sometimes I get the impression that Oliver joins her on some of her travels as a strictly platonic soul mate. Both Michael and Oliver were instrumental in helping Caro discover herself. Now that she's reconciled her past, she'll have to decide what kind of life she wants to craft for her future.

I always have new projects in the works. I'm currently writing a "domestic" novel about a marriage struggling to survive in the wake of every parent's worst nightmare: the death of their child. The tragedy is deepened when the father is convicted of murdering the little girl. I'm curious to explore how the human spirit endures such incomprehensible loss.

What is your favorite yoga pose?

It's so hard to choose, since every one has its own benefits and gifts. I love backbends like *Urdhva Dhanurasana* (wheel, or upward-facing bow), because they invigorate the central nervous system. And inversions like the handstand are amazing for offering a new perspective on things, since they literally turn the world as we know it upside down.